THE HONG KONG LETTER

by

Michael Burke

ORIGINAL WRITING

978-1-907179-17-4

A cip catalogue for this book is available from the National Library.

Published by Original Writing Ltd., Dublin, 2009.

Printed by Cahills, Dublin.

ACKNOWLEDGMENTS

I would like to thank Aidan Lucid from Lucid Eyes Editing for his work on this book.

I would also like to thank Michael Lydon for the final proofreading. Your hard work was really appreciated.

CHAPTER ONE

The dredger ship sat in calm waters just off the main shipping channel leading to Hong Kong but she had hit a problem. The dredger driver had cut the power to the winch, he shouted for Diver Ho.

Ho had been languishing on a dirty bunk reading the Hong Kong Star and looking at the vacancies section of the paper. Diver Ho wanted a change in life; he was approaching 25 and had been a deckhand-come-diver for more than five years. He was fed up and was getting nowhere, fast. The thought of foreign shores, a different job, and a different life was appealing to him.

Ho jumped off the bunk and went out onto deck. The deck hand glanced up at the wheelhouse, but there was no sign of the captain.

Ling, the dredger driver, leaned out of his cab and shouted down to Diver Ho,

"Very much stuck on bottom, no budgie."

Diver Ho smiled back, as he turned away the smile died and he muttered under his breath,

"Careless idiot to stick muck raker to bottom, no budgie."

"Hi Ho." the captain said.

"Yes boss, I know, no budgie."

The captain, a tall Eurasian with golden hair and sky blue eyes, patted Diver Ho on the back just to show that they were still good friends, especially now that Captain Kirkland wanted help.

"The tide is taking us against the lay of the bucket, I'm afraid we may get stuck further if we don't get the bucket unstuck but soon." The captain used his most diplomatic pleading tone.

"So sorry, boss, must let water clear. No go down until eye can see what got bucket stuck."

I

"Yeah, yeah, shit." Kirkland turned and considered the lie of the dredger ship, her stern was coming round with the tide and pretty soon now, she was going to be bow on into the tide with the bucket line acting like an anchor chain. It was going to make it all the more difficult to dislodge the snag the more they pulled across the line of the snag. He turned back to the wheel house and called to the first mate to start engines and take her ahead, slow over the snag and hold her steady once there.

They were in shallow water, no more than four metres. The main channel was off to port, and he wanted to stay in close to the snag until Diver Ho established just how the bucket was snagged. There was no point in his trying to manoeuvre them off the snag and maybe get caught in the way of a ship out in the main channel. He needed to know what direction he should be going to be able to pull off in one swift move. Captain Kirkland's main concern was to stay out of the channel until necessary and get back into action and get filled up and out to sea to dump.

Kirkland turned his attention back to Diver Ho.

"How does it look now?"

He went to the gunwale and peered over the side.

"Capt'n, not yet fully clear, but will go and feel my way."

"Good man, Ho." Kirkland slapped him on the shoulders.

Diver Ho pulled on his goggles and took the snorkel in hand. He turned, sat on the gunwale and with a push of his feet off the deck he was gone.

As Diver Ho hit the water he had no idea how this day was going to change his fortune forever.

It was around 3 p.m., so the sun was still high and its light easily reached the bottom. He took a few seconds to establish his bearing, sought the bucket line from the ship, found it and swam towards it and down. He immediately saw a portion of the bucket, or rather the iron frame that allows the bucket to tip forwards and back freely. The bucket itself was lost from sight.

Muddy water drifted up like billowing smoke to be caught by the tide and pulled away. Ho swam round to the tide side of the bucket to see what was causing the snag. The bucket itself seemed to be embedded in the mud. Once around in clear water though, he realised that there was something buried beneath the mud and that it was in this that the bucket had become embedded. He wanted to avoid touching the bottom, for he could have quite easily gotten a leg embedded in the thick heavy mud. As he looked around he realised that there was a shape, almost like a ridge, of mud which, of course, was impossible, for this whole area of Macau Bay was just one vast area of shifting mud. Impossible that there should be a ridge ten metres long by about 1 metre high and about the same width, but there it was. The mud drifting up became less and less and as he waited there gently waving his arms and legs to steady himself, he realised that there was a piece of timber jutting out of the bucket. Not just a piece of a tree.

But a piece of cut and shaped timber, a plank, its end jagged and splintered but it had four perfect sides, and in length? Ho pondered. It disappeared into the rising cloud of mud. He didn't quite know what to make of it, he may never have known what to make of it, but he realised that he was standing in the mud. Looking down in disbelief; Ho knew that he was not sinking into it, but just standing there, maybe a half inch into the mud.

He got down on all fours and waved away some more mud. What was exposed was timber. Ho stood up again and looked around the 'ridge' and knew he was standing on the hull of an upturned Lurca or perhaps a sea going junk.

The bucket had become embedded in the keel of a sunken ship.

"Aiyee!" His brain shouted, and his mind began to race; a sunken ship, upturned so that it had never been salvaged, otherwise it would have been righted or on its side. And its old, maybe 100 or even 200 years old, that could mean treasure. There were pirates in these waters, pirate Kings and pirate Princes, and that means bounty, treasure.

Diver Ho felt water suddenly and realised that he had been down for too long, he kicked for the surface. He hit the choppy surface gasping for air, trying to calm himself.

"She was right," he whispered, "mother will be proud."

"What are we stuck on?" Captain Kirkland's voice came across the void and brought him back to reality.

"So sorry, boss." Ho replied trying to think, he daren't say anything about the wreck in case either Captain Kirkland or any of the crew, wanted a share of the treasure or worse, Buddha forbid, salvage the wreck and cut him out of the reward completely. And would not the operators claim the prize for themselves if they knew about it?

Oh no, so sorry, The Kowloon Dredger will not get any of what is rightly mine. Diver Ho thought.

"Big old bugger of tree, boss, I think, will go and have other look when I get honourable wind back."

"Which way do you think we should pull?"

Ho had to think fast now. It was quite possible that if they pulled wrong, that they could dislodge the wreck. If the bucket dislodged from its resting place it might come to the surface with the assistance of the bucket. He kept a picture of the position of the bucket in his mind, and worked out the possibilities fast.

"Come directly here." He worked it out now as he went along. "Over the wr - snag" He gulped down air to cover his fright for his near blunder. "And I will remove pin and pull wire and you can pull straight up."

"Shit!" He heard Captain Kirkland curse knowing that it would not please him as that meant he had to bring the bucket aboard ship to replace the pin.

"Okay, what do you need?"

He relaxed in the water and told the Captain. It took a little time, and had it been any other occasion, Ho would have given up but he persisted with the hammer once he had taken out the retaining clip but he eventually knocked out the pin. On the surface he swam alongside the ship and handed the hammer, pin, clip and vice grips to one of the crew. Once back aboard, he glanced up at Ling in the cab and said a silent prayer to Buddha that the miserable bucket would come cleanly out of his sunken ship.

The diesel motor roared to life on the dredger platform and Ling engaged the lift gear.

The winding mechanism clanked and the wire spat a spray of water. As the line tightened, the heavy steel wire sang and the ship moved forward as the bucket held firm.

Inside, Ho was in turmoil, he prayed that the bucket would free first time. Now he had to visualise the bucket embedded in his ship all over again. He wanted to say cut the miserable pox ridden wire and leave his bucket there. Captain Kirkland stared at him.

"Go about 180 degrees and pull against the tide."

"Ahead one third, bring her about." The mate followed instruction and took her about slowly, all the time the line was taut and Ho watched the line where it entered the water hoping to get some idea as to what was happening below, and he waited. Then almost as if his ship let go, the line went slack, his heart stopped beating and he shot a glance at Ling. Ling engaged the gear and hauled in the line. Ho watched in fear, afraid not to look, but surely his ship wouldn't surface. It seemed like an age but in fact, couldn't have been more than ten seconds when the bucket broke water, dangling useless without the second line. He didn't wait to see the bucket on deck; he raced below and got an underwater torch. While the crew concentrated on readying the bucket he slipped on deck and went quietly over the side back into the water to inspect the prize.

It was a little more difficult to locate the wreck this time without the guidance of the line and now there was no stream of muddy water to indicate the ridge that was the wreck.

It was the hole in the hull and the torn pieces of timber that indicated the place for him. His heart beat faster as he approached the hole that would allow him into the hull. With the beam of light from the torch, he peered into the sunken wreck. A light mist of floating mud hung in the interior; he could make out little detail from here, everything was a dull grey. He went cautiously through the opening, everything was upside down. It took him some moments to adjust to the benches and bunks above him. He could stand with comfort, but carefully as the beams that once supported the deck above, now below, were exposed and he had to tread between them. There was a lot of everyday type junk on the bottom but apart from tools and debris, there was nothing of immense value. His heart began to sink, surely there must be *something*. He made his way forward past the steep stairs that would lead to deck in better days. The door was jammed that led to the forward cabin. Rather than waste energy trying to shove the door, he went back to the storage lockers and got a hammer. The middle door panel went with the first blow and feeling his way inside, he discovered that something had lodged against the lower part of the door. He scanned the cabin with the beam of light.

His heart sank some more. Despite the fact that this was the captain's cabin, there appeared to be nothing that promised any value. Then he realised that there had to be at least a compass and sextant and perhaps a spy glass. Those would surely fetch a few hundred dollars, maybe a thousand or two depending on just how old they were. Perhaps there was a log book which might be of interest. With the beam of light he located the captain's storage locker. With the hammer he broke the rest of the upper section of the door and went cautiously through.

His feet touched something at the base of the door and he swung the beam of light down. He gasped and nearly drew water into his lungs. There was a skeleton there, its skull cracked, black eye sockets staring up at him.

Diver Ho shone the beam at the door again. Was this man killed by a member of the crew? No, the bolt was still on the door. Strange that this man, or could it be a woman, remained in the cabin while the junk sank, but then there was no sign on the hull that she had been holed, so why did she sink?

Diver Ho deduced that it must have overturned then, and sank suddenly without warning, so that the man, or woman, had no time to get to the door, unbolt it and get out. Ho further guessed that it must have been a freak wave because no captain worth his salt would have put to sea during a storm or typhoon, unless he was caught at sea trying to make port. The wreck was but 3 - 4 kilometres from Macau.

"Honourable breath." he muttered and turned his beam and attention back to the storage locker.

One blow of the hammer shattered the rusted lock, but the door did not open easily. He put aside the hammer and propped the torch so that he could use both hands, and even then it took all his strength to pull the door open. Water rushed in, it was air tight! He brought the beam to bear and examined the contents. The first thing that caught his eye was the small strongbox, it was locked. He rummaged through charts and logs but could find no key.

Of course there was no key, very silly to keep key in same place as strongbox, yes? Ho silently thought. Next came the sextant and the spy glass, but no compass.

Never mind, got strongbox. Diver Ho thought. He bundled them together into an oilskin that lay near the captain's table and made for the door. Out in the main cabin he found a light rope that was reasonably intact and carefully tied the oilskin together to form a bundle and got out of the hull as quick as he could. He was rapidly running out of time.

Ho could feel his heartbeat get heavier and more erratic, he had little or no oxygen left in his lungs. The deck hand swam to the surface gasping for air for the second time that day. It felt as if his lungs were on fire or were about to collapse altogether. Once his breathing was under some semblance of control, he looked about for his ship. She was about 100 metres away. He stroked off at an easy pace, all the time watching the deck for anybody looking out for him. But no one appeared to have missed him. Everybody was concentrating on getting the bucket back in the water. He came alongside the rope ladder and climbed quickly.

Of the three men on deck, two had their back to him and one, although turned towards him, was stooped hammering the pin into place on the bucket and was partly obscured by one of the others. He tested the strength of the rope by pulling the oilskin bundle out of the water, it seemed to hold good. He let the bundle gently back into the water, let it down about three feet below the surface, checked the deck again, then the wheelhouse. It was the sight of the captain that had his heart pumping so loud that he felt it would drown out the *thud, thud, thud* of the marine engine holding the ship against the tide. He sprang over the gunwale and strolled along towards the wheelhouse, one hand running along the rail and holding the rope at the same time. Ho could hear the captain and the mate talking directly outside the door to below deck. Upon checking again, Diver Ho saw no one looking. He leaned over the side and hauled the bundle aboard.

Diver Ho quickly ran below and into his cabin. He knew that it was empty because Ching Wong was on deck and Ching Wong was the only other crew member who might be in this, their cabin. The excited Ho untied the bundle and shoved the oilskin and rope under his bunk.

"Now honourable strongbox, what have you for Diver Ho?" He picked up the strongbox and examined it carefully. It was as he thought - an extremely strong box; it was not light, it was quite heavy and when he shook it, something heavy clanked inside. He looked carefully at the keyhole; it did not appear to be the normal type of key. He thought that this was obviously a job for Ho Chan, otherwise known as Locksmith Ho - his father's cousin.

CHAPTER TWO

Scott Dillon read through Sterns G TI report once more as the 747 went through a 180 degree turn to make its final approach to Tia Tek airport.

"Subject: Anglo Asian Bank, Hong Kong.

Requirement: Security Approval investigation," the report began, it continued. "Jeffrey Reginald Bordes-Aitcheson, Chairman and Managing Director of AAB, requested a security clearance to meet International Monetary Fund (IMF) standards and security ratings." He ran his eyes over the standard requirements that were expected of him, his time allotment was as usual - ten working days, two weeks and he was expected back in the New York office together with his completed assignment report. He then brought forward the A4 size sheet that was handwritten by one of Stern's secretaries but not signed or acknowledged as having come from anybody at all in the Organisation.

This sheet gave a breakdown of the major shareholders in the Bank and it was noted and underlined that JR Bordes-Aitcheson held 40% of the Public issued shares in the AAB. There was no other shareholder who owned any more than 10% of the shares. From the list he saw that only one member of the board held 10%. All seven others held less than that, some as low as 3%,

The bank had a staff of 23 and had two branches; the main bank was on Hong Kong Island and a branch in Kowloon. The bank had a pre tax profit last year of $28 million and has a cash reserve of $67 million on hand. The AAB has assets of $298 million, with loans outstanding of $302 of which $278 is secured. Bad debt provision last year was $3.8 million. He got the impression that he was being told a lot more than he should expect by the facts and figures on the single A4 sheet and just in case he couldn't read between the lines, there was a very brief summary at the bottom of the sheet. There were 12 million equal value shares at HK$24.20 each.

Current value of shares as per Hong Kong stock market last Friday $ 22.50 each.

Okay so what was Stern trying to say, that the shares were undervalued? What does he want me to do about it? Why buy some! Scott thought.

"Excuse me, Sir." A dream of an Asian voice dragged him from a bank vault 30,000 feet up into the air and sat him down on a seat aboard a Singapore Airlines 747, complete with a Singapore girl beaming radiance at him.

"Must be impulse." he said as he gloried in her beauty.

"Sorry Sir?"

"It's Okay," he replied, "It's the altitude and the vision of you in a field of daffodils that takes me to such heights. You can tell the pilot to go home now, I don't need him anymore. I can just stay up here looking at you."

She beamed her very best smile back at him.

"I've got a 24 hour stop over in Hong Kong." she said.

"I've got 19 days, how about dinner tonight?"

"Why not, I'm staying at the Singapore Hotel in Hennessey Road in Wanchai, that's on the Island."

"Great, I'm at the Mandarin; can I call for you at eight?"

The airhostess hesitated before answering, all the time retaining her perfect smile, "Okay, at eight. My name is Linn Chun." She gave a polite little bow, as is Chinese custom and continued. When she had gone, he realised that she had forgotten what she came for, to tell him to belt up. He closed his brief case and placed it beneath his seat and fastened his belt.

"Hmm...looks like my stay in Hong Kong is going to be a pleasant one, for tonight anyhow."

"You Scott?" Dillon looked around and then down. There was a little fella' about 5'2" staring up at him, and he was dressed in black cords and T-shirt. He looked like a bad type, except that he smiled a lot.

"You Scott Dirron?" he repeated.

"Ah yes, I'm Scott Dillon."

"Yes I know, I have trouble with some name. My name is Charrie Chan, see?" He beamed a broader smile, and reached for Dillon's suitcase. "Boss man send me pick you up. I from bank, bring car, I your driver, see?" Charlie took off heading towards the main exit. Dillon was slightly amused by the little fella as he made his way through the crowded terminal, pushing people aside in his hurry to get out.

Once outside the real heat hit Dillon, he had been expecting warm weather but this was like being hit in the face by a hot wet towel. He was so intent on looking around that he damn near ran over Charlie. The little fella had stopped suddenly at the kerb.

"You wait, I bring car." Charlie said and then he was gone at a canter across the apron weaving in and out through cars and taxis.

Dillon sat down his briefcase beside the suitcases and loosened his tie.

"Jesus what heat," he muttered and took off his lightweight jacket, feeling the first beads of sweat begin to break through already.

"Don't worry, it gets better." the dream voice said again. She was beside him and the heat was forgotten.

"It's just after the coolness of the aircraft that you notice the heat here. Within 24 hours your body will adjust, take plenty of showers and 'Yum Cha' and you will be fine."

"Twenty four hours, eh?"

"You won't even notice the heat." She smiled, and he could feel his knees weaken.

"But then, darling, you'll be gone and I'll be alone for 13 days."

"Oh but I will be back next Friday, I have two days. Will you still wish to see me, or will you have found some little Asian lady to keep you company?"

What was she going to say, he wondered, *'some little Asian whore maybe?*

"Lady I don't operate that fast, I'm here to work."

"Oh so sorry, but Asian ladies do, ah, work that fast. Such a fine looking man as you will have them beating at your door." He wondered if this lady was mocking him, but he could detect nothing in her eyes, only that smile. *Jesus this one could get inside me very quickly but she was just a beauty on the make, who didn't want to be alone on a Monday night in Hong Kong.* He decided to lay a few compliments back on her. "'Tis you, my lovely flower, that won't be free. Those smiling eyes will bewitch some handsome man." He was tempted to say young man, your own age, but why consign yourself to Happy Valley while you still got some powder in your pouch?

"And he'll sweep you away to some luxurious villa on the Costa Del Paradise, where you'll make him happy for ever and ever."

"Will you not sweep me away?" she replied. He thought he detected a tone of concern in her voice and the smiling eyes lost a little of their sparkle. But before he could reply, there was a scream of tyres behind him. Scott spun around and there was a black car - a Merc' 300D. The door opened and out popped Charlie.

"So sorry, Boss, for wait." Charlie Chan.

Before Dillon could do very much, his case was swept up and thrown in the trunk. Charlie held the back door open for Dillon.

"Coor, - not hot inside boss."

When Dillon finally gathered himself, he turned to Linn.

"Can I drop you at your hotel?"

"So sorry, but made date with friends to go shopping. I will see you tonight." Just then, two other stewardesses came up to her, she turned to them, and then back to Dillon. "So sorry, us ladies got to go do ladies' shopping."

"Okay, see you tonight then."

The three girls went off chatting and giggling.

"Now Boss?" Charlie was still holding the door.

Charlie Chan was around 24 - 25 years of age and built like a lot of Chinese but Dillon had the feeling that this kid was much more powerful than his stature indicated. He had noticed Charlie's muscles as he lifted the cases; not in themselves heavy, but he had gone at them in a way that said, "I'm gonna lift these mothers." In other words, he was prepared to haul weight.

Watching Charlie now as he weaved the Merc' through the traffic, Dillon wondered just where this guy fitted into the personal file of the AAB. Was he a hireling or a member of staff? Dillon had been through Hong Kong in '84 and knew something of the way things operated here. Profit was the goal and anything could be used to make profit. That included the Chinese Mafia, the 'Triads' or 'Tongs' - groups of mercenaries who did anything for money: kidnapping, blackmail, fraud, extortion, theft, and murder, anything that could result in a financial benefit for the cells of 'Triads'. They hired out vicious assassins and the thought crossed his mind that Charlie was a hired out member of just such a group. Could the AAB have hired such a man to drive Dillon and guard him while he was here? Charlie's 'job description' was one of the first things that Dillon was going to raise with Bordes-Aitcheson in the bank.

The Merc' was now speeding through the tunnel that linked Kowloon and Hong Kong Island. This driver showed no respect for anything; it was dangerous to cross the double white in a tunnel, but Charlie did. Dillon decided that there was nothing he could do about Charlie's driving, so he just sat back and thought about what he had to do while he was here.

Since he had been with Orrang and his World Trade Bank organisation he had become well drilled in Security Investigation. The first thing to do on any assignment was to check the building, second meet the boss, third meet the number two man, fourth meet and observe the staff, fifth check the day's returns over a period or one week and multiply by fifty two, then check their accounts for turnover, allowing for increased money circulation and the figures were almost similar. He did a quick mental calculation; the AAB's turnover for last year was $293 million, so the difference he was looking for was $4 million, anything less than that was petty cash, anything over that meant someone was more than likely on the make. He had often done weeks of work only to find that every cent would be accounted for. But that was the percentage figure that the World Trade Bank accept as the 'Cause for Investigation Figure' (CIF).

Dillon didn't act like an accountant but sometimes he wondered just what he was. He didn't really know why he was being sent to Hong Kong, there were two WTB accountants there already in place in the bank; Oliver and Tina Bolger. Perhaps they had uncovered something that required Dillon's expertise. There was a degree of finality about the way the Merc' came to a halt and Dillon looked out.

"This it, Boss." Charlie was out and opened the door for Dillon.

The building was impressive, just like a bank should look: big, old fashioned and trustworthy. Not like the crappy glass structures that you see nowadays in the States.

"This my hotel?" Dillon joked.

"So sorry, Boss, think you want to meet big boss first, come I take you to hotel, not far, five minute, never mind."

The bank's interior was a curious mix of old and new. There were huge high ceilings as one would expect, with lots of ornamentation and arches. Just to contrast that at ground zero the carpenters had been in, a plush new counter together with bullet proof glass for the tellers, seven windows in all, of which, six were open for business and a long queue was formed.

Dillon turned, Charlie was two paces behind, and he stared at Dillon wondering what to do.

"Is there a rear entrance, car park, anything like that?"

"So sorry, Boss."

Dillon turned back and made a mental note to check the neighbour's buildings and also the rear. A man in his fifties with balding grey hair was staring at him from the open top counter section of the foyer, away from the teller area. Dillon ignored him for the moment and first examined the windows onto the main street and then the walls behind the tellers. Two security cameras were suspended from the ceiling looking out towards the foyer. All pretty standard. He approached the balding grey haired man.

"I'm Scott Dillon; take me to your leader."

Honourable Ruxton bowed politely to Dillon and replied,

"We were expecting you, Mister Dillon. Will you step this way?" He motioned to the end of the counter.

Dillon was shown into the Bordes-Aitcheson office that was exactly as he would have expected. It was very colonial; lots of oak panelling, Victorian furniture and the oil paintings looked like they were originals. The modern stuff consisted of the key phone system and IBM desktop. Bordes-Aitcheson got to his feet to greet Dillon.

"Ah, Mister Dillon, I've been looking forward to meeting you." The handshake was warm and firm.

The Managing Director of AAB was in his fifties, a well built man with distinguished looking greying hair, clean cut and with just a modesty of tan.

"Take a seat."

"Thanks, I will." Dillon said and then sat.

"How was your flight?"

"Good, and then it got better."

"I take it then that your arrival was pleasant."

"Well let's put it this way, if this keeps up I could get to like Hong Kong."

"Have you been here before?"

"Yeah back in '84, but I was just passing through. I only had four days here, I'm afraid I spent them doing all the wrong things."

"It's very easy to do the 'wrong' things in Hong Kong, and you can do a lot of 'wrong' in four days."

The grin seemed genuine so Dillon relaxed a little; he was, of course, waiting for Bordes-Aitcheson to get to things in his own good time, he had found in the past that if he forced the client into getting to the point before he was ready than he usually got resentment, and that resulted in lack of co-operation.

"Hong Kong has changed since I was here last. I remember it as being very dirty, but now it seems clean and organised. The tunnel helps to get around."

"Yeah, that was one of our better investments; the AAB was involved in financing the tunnel. One of our best customers now, he wasn't then, was interested in tendering for part of the sub-contract work and he did the usual rounds, calling to the institutions looking for backing. Even though he weren't with us at the time, but we saw it as being a sound investment so we backed him. It has been a financial success and we won his business. The company developed into one of our best clients."

"That's the way you get good clients, by taking risks and backing the right people."

"The trick being, picking the right people" Bordes-Aitcheson smiled broadly.

"Good judgment being a prerequisite for being a good banker." Dillon replied.

"Judge of character etc, and having plenty of security against the loan." They both laughed.

"You may be wondering why I requested a security clearance from the WTB." Bordes-Aitcheson began. "Well, with this uncertainty about the future of Hong Kong, we find ourselves in a tightening market here. There is little or no new investment being undertaken at the moment. We need to expand our base outside Hong Kong. In order for us to do, we need to comply with IMF rules. One part of those rules is that we are a completely above board and security approved organisation. You will probably have received a copy of our last accounts?"

"I saw the balance sheet, it appeared as if you are quite healthy." Dillon acknowledged, Bordes-Aitcheson nodded.

"We made a considerable profit last year - US $28 million or HK$218 million. We are one of the most profitable banks in Hong Kong, but we are selective, we concentrate mainly on business ventures. I can say that we are probably overly dependant on the business sector, but that's where the return is here. We have very little involvement in the personal borrowing area; the returns may be a percent or two down but they are more secured, and you do get a much faster return."

Dillon listened carefully, but he wondered what was behind Bordes-Aitcheson's outpouring, perhaps it was merely a little regretful thinking. He thought it a little unusual that a bank with a true banking character would steer a solely business track, for any good banker worth his salt would tell you that even though the risks with personal borrowers is greater, the returns are higher. It's also widely known that a bank does not widely give out unsecured loans to personal borrowers, without staying right on top of bad debts, if bad debts get out of control it's the fault of bad management. Of course, just that happened in the late '70s in the States, but the short-sightedness of management caused the situation to get out of control and then the problem became public knowledge and a public debate issue. That's when the banks became the butt of many jokes, which made the matter worse. Bank profits fell as a result and more and more people who would be border line cases for recovery, went over the top and it became 'in' to owe the bank money.

But this guy, Bordes-Aitcheson, was in the opposite side of the track, he had a highly profitable business with good cash reserves but with no one to lend it to. Well there were probably plenty of potential borrowers but he didn't want the new business because of the uncertainty of the changeover. It was not Dillon's position to advise this man but to follow his instruction.

"We propose opening offices in Singapore, London, Tokyo and New York." Bordes-Aitcheson paused for Dillon's reaction.

"That would be quite a costly undertaking, in one fell-swoop."

"We plan to phase the opening over a two year period, starting with Singapore and London. The cost would be less than 40 million, ah that's Hong Kong Dollar by the way, about US$5 million US."

"That sounds reasonable." Dillon replied, wondering how Orrang would feel about yet another bank opening in New York and one with a lot of Hong Kong business and venture capital which would move out prior to 1997 and that business would not be up for grabs. Perhaps Orrang already knew this and thus the note from someone in Stern's office referring to the current value of the AAB's shares. It also crossed his mind that the current undervaluing of shares may be as a result of rumours about the banks current predicament via its position as a business lenders' bank.

"You will find that the security of the building itself is quite good, you'll excuse me for being presumptuous but it has been one of my pet concerns. Thankfully we've never been robbed, although there have been several attempts. I can assure you here and now that all my staff was carefully selected and I do not have a high staff turnover. In the past five years, we have only had to employ three new people. You can see all the staff details for yourself. Mister Ruxton also acts as our personal manager."

"I'll start with him then, what time do you think would be appropriate in the morning?"

"Well, he's at his desk at eight, but I suspect that the jet lag will not allow you in quite that early. Shall we say 10.30?"

As they stood and shook hands Dillon asked, "Where might I find Olli and Tina?"

"They spend their time in the computer room." Bordes-Aitcheson replied with a laugh.

"I'll go and see them then."

*

"You've got a date with one of these Singapore Girls?" Olli enquired with a look of disbelief in his eyes. Dillon always amazed him, and he could pull women at the drop of a hat.

"I'm not sure who picked who up, it was just one of those conversations and it came out that way."

"I take it then that you won't be available for comment tonight?"

"Can't see it, Olli, if she can't keep me awake, I'll be asleep. I'm kinda beat, it's been a long flight. I'm still on New York time."

"You don't want to hear about this place then?" Olli seemed disappointed. He had been looking forward to seeing Dillon again; they hadn't seen each other for a while. There was always a bit of craic, as Dillon called fun, when he was around, but there's something wrong here and hopefully Dillon could solve it. Not that there was any heavy stuff going on, but there were mysterious things emerging that they were confused about. When you go into a bank, particularly an old bank, staff gets nervous, anyone that ever 'misplaced' a single cent gets worried. Something had shown up that worried both he and Tina and he wanted it handed over to someone who could handle it.

"Where's Tina Bolger?" Dillon asked.

"She's over at the Kowloon branch checking out some stuff. They've got a whole set of ledgers that we only discovered the other day. Now it may be nothing, but then again..."

"Have we got a problem here, Olli?"

"We got a number of problems; Okay some of them we can handle, but the most worrying is the set of ledgers that Tina discovered. There's a whole series of assets in the ledgers that don't appear in any balance sheet. It may be nothing, they may have been written off years ago and that's what Tina is chasing now. She's gotta go back to the year dot and then come forward and see what happened to the assets in the ledgers."

"Just when were these ledgers dated and where did you find them?"

"She found them in an old safe in a now disused part of the vault in the Kowloon branch."

"Did you mention this to Jeff?"

"Hell no, we've only seen him twice since we got here. He gives us a free hand, anything we want we ask Ruxton."

"Who the hell is this Ruxton anyhow?" Dillon asked.

"He's the assistant manager of this branch; he's the guy that showed you in here. Were you not introduced?"

"No I was not, I spoke to the guy at the counter, and he took me to Jeff's office. I had no idea as to who he was. Gosh, I feel like an idiot now. I should have introduced myself."

"Someone should have introduced you, it's customary and they are big on custom here in Hong Kong."

"Charlie, the little bastard, he brought me into the bank but didn't introduce me to Ruxton."

"That's most unusual, are you sure you didn't upset Charlie?"

"Oh fuck you; let's meet at seven at the Mandarin, that's where you are staying?"

"Yeah, but what about the Singapore Girl?"

"Shit, forgotten already, let's make it six then."

Olli nodded. Dillon rose and headed for the door.

"By the way, you didn't say when the ledgers were dated?"

"They were dated from 1898."

"Jesus that was the year..." Dillon paused.

"The year the treaty of Hong Kong was signed between the British and the Chinese." Olli finished it.

"Is this by any chance part of your problem?"

"Sure as hell is."

"Look my head is not too clear right now, let's talk about this later, this evening at the Mandarin."

"At 6 O' Clock. Got it."

CHAPTER THREE

Tina Bolger was thirty going on fifty, at least that's the way she felt right now. It was 5.30 and she was standing on the platform waiting for a train; she had been in the bank since 7.30 this morning. Bolger had a rule: never spend more than four hours at any one task for the very simple reason that the brain becomes bogged down on trivial issues and becomes stifled of fresh thought. But today she had broken her own rule because she had became so engrossed with the ledgers. These ledgers were a powder keg. Bolger shook her head to bring herself back to the present and they were a powder keg. They showed that Bordes Wanchai Bank, as it was then known, owned virtually every acre of land in the New Territories including a great part of the land that is now Kowloon. At current day prices, the bank had assets of over $3 billion. The title deeds were, according to the ledgers, held by the board of Bordes Wanchai Bank on foot of a loan given to one Jason Kimberley in the year 1898. Her problem was trying to establish whether or not Jason Kimberley ever repaid the loan, and just who was this Jason Kimberley that owned the land? Bolger had spent the day burrowing through the accounts ledgers for 1899 but could find no reference, not only to loan repayments but strangely enough to the assets themselves, which was rather strange since the assets were of huge financial value. While in 1898, they may have been worth approximately 1 million. Following the treaty, they would be worth 10 maybe 20 times that amount to capital developers under British rule. There was no clue to the repayments or to the assets in 1900 either. She decided that she would do a further check tomorrow.

She pushed her way onto the MTR carriage at the Tsim Sha Tsui underground. As usual it was packed to capacity at this time of evening and there was a lot of pushing and shoving until the doors slid closed and the train began to move. In her briefcase she had photocopies of the relevant pages from the ledger to show Olli. She was due to meet both Olli and Dillon at the Mandarin for six. It occurred to her that it would be useful to cross reference any returns that may be lodged in City Hall but the probability of finding any returns was slim, for she didn't know when the Company law was first enforced in Hong Kong.

'Well I can check that with City Hall,' she muttered, and then caught her breath as she realised that she had probably spoken the words. Bolger glanced around nervously but no one seemed to notice, just like New York. Something may also be revealed from any newspapers of the time. Someone had to sell the land to the first settlers, or investors, in the New Territories. Of course one major problem that arose out of all this was what the banks legal position was, if it was found that someone just forgot about Kimberley's title deeds, and would his heirs have any claim for compensation against the bank?

Bolger pondered further on the matter and asked herself,

And what if it was discovered that the bank had sold the property? In order to do that they would have had to enforce a judgment for payment against Kimberley, in which case it would be in court records, and surely such a case would have been public knowledge in Hong Kong at the time. Because of this, it would appear somewhere and must be on file either in City Hall or the Governor's Residence or the Central Library.

The train pulled into Charter Station and everybody surged to get off. Bolger waited until the rush had eased off and then began to move, that's when she noticed the two Chinese trying desperately to appear uninterested in her. She hadn't paid any attention to anybody during the trip through the tunnel across the harbour or during the stops, and she probably wouldn't have noticed these two, were it not for the fact that this was a terminal. Everybody got off but there was something conspicuous about these two men as they stayed on the train. People began to board the train for the return journey back to Kowloon side, Bolger decided to wait and take her chances.

Of course, I could be wrong. It could be perfectly innocent. These two guys might just be there for the ride. But still a feeling of doubt lingered in her mind.

Just then, the whistle blew to warn people to stay clear of the doors. When she heard the faint rush of air to the door operating cylinders, she followed her gut instinct and jumped forward, getting out just as the doors slapped shut behind her. The two Chinese gave chase but they had been further away from the door than she was and they didn't make it. She watched their faces as the train began to move, one man turned away but the other stared at Bolger, a gleam of determination in his eyes. The woman felt a shudder run through her body; it wasn't fear of physical violence, she had faced that before on the street of New York, it was more alarm that she had stumbled onto something. She knew it couldn't be just a case of attempted robbery; they could have done that at any stop, just grabbed her case and fled. She ran now to catch up with the crowds pouring up the stairways to the hustle and bustle of the street above. The thirty-something beauty did not panic and remained surprisingly calm. Bolger slowed her pace to catch her breath. The woman felt safe now that the thugs were gone and that she was within walking distance of the Mandarin.

Within five minutes she was in the safety of the Mandarin and looking at the smiling face of Scott Dillon. The events of a few minutes earlier began to slip into the memory banks, only to be recalled when needed. It was great to see him again, how long had it been? Too long! She liked Dillon, not because he was the tough action man type with a rugged hard face, but because he was actually quite interesting to talk to. She remembered a job they worked on before together about four years earlier in Bahrain. Bolger recalled that his life was in a mess at the time, as he was going through a rather emotional separation from a woman he had married for all the wrong reasons. She recalled that their eyes had held each others for what seemed a long time and totally unashamedly. But she was happily married at the time, and the last thing she needed was an affair with someone like Dillon.

Now was different, now she the one with a lousy marriage. Stuck with Jack Gannon, a workaholic and an alcoholic whose interest in her boiled down to the occasional stressed sex session whenever he felt sober enough to exercise his dick. The thought of those sessions made her stomach turn; she couldn't even stand the thought of him touching her. Jack was a newsman and his sole interest in life was the news. From morning to night, he talked of nothing but news, his boss, about some stupid story, about some poor misfortunate getting raped in the Bronx. This job was the perfect break that she needed to get away from her alcoholic husband and his lurid romps. Bolger had jumped at the chance to go when Stern offered her the shot at it. This was her first time out of New York in over two years. Even though she did not like Stern, very few did, she knew that he had deliberately not posted her out of New York too often because she had little Colm to look after. But they were simply short staffed in the section and she was needed. She took it well when Stern had told her the bad but necessary news. He understood that it would be difficult for her, but the extra allowances would more than make up for the cost of the extra baby-sitting services she would need and the emotional turmoil that she would suffer being away from her baby for over two weeks.

Stern's files must be out of date she told herself afterwards, Colm was in school. And anyhow, she needed the break from the drudgery of 8 to 5 in Manhattan and 6 to 7 in Queens with that asshole, Jack Gannon.

It was only five days since she left New York but it had been real good. The second night in Hong Kong she had met a real nice guy from Australia called Jeff. From the moment they met, she instantly fell for Jeff and went out with him on two 'dates'. It seemed funny calling meeting with some guy a 'date' after all these years. Bolger had been married for six years and never had gone out with a guy in all that time. Now she was a mother of a six year old kid and the wife of a 41 year-old drunk, and she wanted excitement in her life again. Damn it she was only 30 and not in bad shape. The woman knew that she deserved better than Jack Gannon but Jeff turned out not to be the answer, he was bi-sexual.

*

Diver Ho jumped off the ferry at the Macau Ferry Pier and started to jog up towards Connaught Road West, crossed that and continued up to Des Vieux Road West and up again to Wing Lok Street. Up over a duty free shop was Larry Ho-Chan, the locksmith. He was an elderly gentleman of indeterminable age. Diver Ho had heard speculation that Larry Ho Chan was over ninety but no one knew for sure and it would be a great insult to enquire. The shop area was small, three meters by three meters, but behind the curtain, that stretched the entire width of the shop, there was an area three times larger than the shop. Ho Chan was attending to a client but he acknowledged his cousin's presence with a polite nod. Ho sat his carrier bag down by the counter and waited patiently.

The client was satisfied with his new lock and handed over the agreed number of dollars and left. Ho listened for the footsteps to reach the concrete hall below, and then he turned back to his cousin. They both bowed politely to each other, Ho a little lower as was the custom to an elder.

"Are you well, Esteemed Ho Chan?"

"Ah," the old man smiled wearily, "My bones are sore as always, only a little more so at this late hour of the day. But as always, I have many duties so I must keep my humble business open to the late hour."

"Perhaps then my request for your assistance, however humble my requirement, may reward you for your long hours." Ho Chan raised his eyebrows slightly, this was not at all like the young Ho that he knew, and he expected to be asked for a favour without monetary reward. This was a little more interesting. Ho reached down and took the strongbox from the carrier bag and placed the box on the counter.

"Through my own stupidity, I have mislaid the honourable key for this box. It occurred to me that with your experience you would have little difficulty in making a key for this box."

"Ah, perhaps, let me see." Ho Chan drew the box towards him and examined the keyhole with an eye glass. "Ah very old, so sorry not so simple."

"Will this take long?" Ho knew only too well that Locksmith Ho was trying to figure out how much he could ask for the job. It was very important that Ho remained calm and not appear impatient or concerned. *Must not let Locksmith Ho think box valuable.* Diver Ho thought to himself.

"Not take very long, but years of learning go into this expertise; very difficult for tradesman to make true cost of learning reflect in price charge for the job such as this. You understand?"

"Yes understand, very difficult to price. Why do you not charge as if I not cousin then apply very small discount for family."

"Ah, most honourable arrangement. You not my cousin $400, you my cousin $200."

"Most generous discount." Ho was shocked, but he knew he had walked himself into a trap; there was nothing he could do about it now.

"I will have to go to Honourable money lender in wall for cash."

"Ah, that is fine, I will have job done when you return."

As he went down the stairs it dawned on him that the Locksmith Ho could have that box opened in two or three minutes and see the contents for himself. How could Ho be sure that Locksmith Ho had or not taken items form the box, what if there was money in the strong box, Ho Chan could take half or all the money and say nothing because he was not there when the box was opened?

Ho stopped at the doorway at the bottom of the stairs, the bank was a good five minutes away, five minutes to transact with the moneylender in the wall and five back, fifteen minutes in all.

Ho Chan knows how far away the bank is so he too would be able to work out the time. Ho rummaged in his pocket and counted all the money he had on him: $127, not near enough.

Oh Buddha what to do? Say you "forgot your card." Yes of course, no card no money. Most regretful, Honourable cousin.

26

Ho thought while he stood there for about two minutes, then turned and went back up the stairs. Ho Chan was not in shop, alarm bells rang inside Ho's brain, and he glanced at his carrier bag on the floor, untouched. He approached the counter and tried to find a slit in the curtain but there was none large enough for him to see through from here. He went to the end of the counter and went quietly around it. His heart began to pound in his chest again like it does underwater as he reached out for the edge of the curtain. That was when he heard the gasp from the old man. Ho pulled the curtain aside and peered into the semi darkness beyond.

*

The waiter brought the menu away and for a little while all three of them sat in silence, turning over the ideas in their heads. None of them had even thought about the menus or the fact that they had been sitting there deep in conversation for over 20 minutes. Finally the waiter had approached and asked for their order. They all opted for the special. Tina broke the silence.

"If it could be proved that this guy Kimberley, owned the New Territories, well that could change everything." They knew what they were thinking about but none could even begin to put their thoughts into words.

"Yes but which state, England or China?"

"This is a big legal matter it's about ownership not sovereignty."

"I think we should report this to head office." Olli said.

"I'm not so sure about that, we have a code of conduct that directs us in this type of assignment; our first duty is to the client."

"But hell, the client tried to conceal information from us, so our duty is to report back to New York."

"We don't know that, Tina, we've got no proof that they tried to conceal those ledgers. Let's face it, they know that we found them, they must do. But they haven't tried to cover up or take them away; they were still there this morning"

"OK then, what about the two guys on the tube?"

"That could be anything, muggers, anything." But in her soul Bolger knew those two guys were following her, but why.? If someone from the bank wanted to keep an eye on her they knew where they were staying, then she realised the answer. *Yes, they knew where they stayed but not who they were talking to.* Bolger thought. "Okay, so say we found something we were not supposed to find, put yourself in their shoes, what would you do?" Bolger directed this to Olli but looked at Dillon.

"First thing I'd want to know is what you are going to do about it? So I'd want to know where you go and who you talk to."

"See!" Bolger said in a I-told-you-so tone.

"Okay, but where does that leave us, what the hell do we do?" Ollie asked.

"Report to New York." Bolger repeated.

"I don't agree, I think we should tell Bordes-Aitcheson that we know."

"Well guys," Dillon interrupted, "I'm inclined to think that you're right, Tina, but we've gotta give him the chance to explain first. There may be a perfectly reasonable explanation for all this. I mean just who's to say that he doesn't trust us and may have put a few guys on you to see who you would go to, he may have thought that you could want to blackmail him by threatening to discredit the bank" They both thought this over for a moment, and then Olli said.

"I hate like hell to say sloppy things, but I'm sure as hell glad you're here."

Bolger just smiled and glanced at the apparent strength in Dillon's face, she was glad he was here too, he seemed so at ease with himself compared to the last time that they had met. If anything age suited him. She remembered him saying that he had just turned 32 back in Bahrain; that made him 38 now. He was carrying a little more weight now but he could carry it, he was just over six foot. His hair was a little lighter too but there were no apparent balding spots. He was dressed casual enough not in a suit, but in pale pants and light grey jacket with a white shirt, no vest, she could see, and no tie. He was a man at ease with himself. He glanced at her and caught her looking at him. Dillon held her eyes as the waiter arrived with the first course and served it. They broke the stare and both she and Olli started into the food.

"Its fish!" Dillon exclaimed.

"You're in Hong Kong now."

*

Locksmith Ho could hardly believe his eyes. He was looking at a small fortune in gold sovereigns, there were at least 300 gold sovereigns in mint condition. He did a quick mental calculation, at $1,000 a piece, and that came to $300,000. Then he thought of Diver Ho, but wait, does Diver Ho know what was in this strong box.

So if Ho found this then he doesn't know what is in it? the locksmith thought. The excitement mounted as Ho Chan examined the contents of the box. There were several letters in the box. All of them were written in the same hand and all the addresses were in Macau. The ship this box came of was carrying mail to Macau. One letter in particular caught his attention as he leafed through them. It was addressed to someone he had heard of, a crazy man but the name was not quite as he knew it. He flipped over the envelope, embossed in the back was the name Bordes Wanchai bank. He took a knife to slit the envelope, but in his haste he nicked his finger and gasped as a person would think the worst of a cut. But it was not bad, just a nick but to lose blood for a man of his age was not good. The locksmith opened a drawer at his bench and took out the band-aids.

As he straightened he felt a presence behind him, he turned. Diver Ho stared down at him, he managed to suppress his shock at Ho coming up behind him like that, and he smiled at him.

"Ah, back so soon." Ho Chan was relived to find calm in his voice.

"I asked you to open, not to examine contents." There was fury in Diver Ho's eyes.

"An old man with little time left for this world has not time for fears of upsetting people by being a little curious. I wished to look, my friend, that is all."

"You should not have, I trusted you."

"And I betrayed your trust, forgive an old man his foolishness, so sorry. You are young and now you are rich; there are at least $300,000 there for you. But of course, you will only be entitled to reward, for as you know all sunken treasure that is recovered belongs to the Crown. You will have to hand it over and accept the meagre reward."

"Why go to the Crown?" Diver Ho asked suspiciously.

"That is the law, you give Honourable salvage to the Crown and they give reward ten percent."

"Ten percent?" Ho shouted. "That is criminal, they do not own any part of it, why should I give it to them, and they do not know anything about it."

"Who else does know?"

"No one but you."

"Then Diver Ho, I suggest that you tell no one but dispose of the gold sovereigns on the black market. I can get you money within two, maybe three days and a good price but there will be much work and risk involved. If I was caught, I would be the one to go to jail, miserable thought, there is much risk for me, none for you, 60/40."

"Ninety-ten." Ho replied instantly.

"You are much too generous, but I accept." the old man said cunningly with only the hint of devilment on his face.

"Ten percent is your cut, old man, the gold is mine. I found it, and I risked life to bring it up."

They argued back and forth for several minutes and finally Diver Ho lost his patience. Ho stood erect suddenly.

"Fifteen percent is bottom line. There are many people who would do it for less but because we are family, I would like to transact this with people I can trust." There was sarcasm in Divers Ho's voice. The old man ignored it knowing that he had gotten a very good deal, 15% of $300,000 for doing nothing except selling something that would be easy to sell.

"Ah, Honourable Ho you strike a hard bargain, but for you this once for 15 percent."

Both men had successfully saved much face and the agreement was made. Ho Chan could have the sovereigns sold by morning if he wished, but he didn't, life is not for rushing through, but for savouring and enjoying.

"These letters, what of them?"

"They can wait," Ho replied taking them up and stuffing them into his pocket.

"For now I will keep the sovereigns safe, and I will expect to hear from you when you have the deal made."

"Ah, very good, yes."

Ho left then collecting his carrier bag on the way, Ho Chan watched him go, and wanting desperately to get his hands on the letters, for now he remembered the name on the letter. Jason Kimberley.

*

The US Embassy was already in the shadow of the peak as the Merc zoomed up Garden Road. Charlie seemed to be of the impression that Dillon was in a hurry, he was but not to the extent that he wanted to risk life and limb. But he had learnt years ago not to try and slow mad drivers because the other extreme may be the result. He was on his way up to see Bordes-Aitcheson. After much discussion they had decided to lay it on the line. The basic problem was for Bolger to have to go back into the bank in the morning not knowing if the Managing Director still trusted her.

Bordes-Aitcheson position in the matter had to be established before they could continue with their work. And he also had a responsibility to bear; someone in his organization had set those two men on Bolger. Either a person at the Kowloon branch had hired the men or passed on Bolger's discovery to somebody who had then hired the two. Whichever way it was, a member of staff was responsible. Board-Aitcheson sounded puzzled on the phone when Dillon rang to arrange a meeting and Dillon didn't offer an explanation for the meeting.

The house was well up on the peak and suitably lavish for a man in his position. Charlie passed the intercom at the security gate, gave the name of his passenger and the gate swung open. Bordes-Aitcheson met Dillon at the door dressed in a track suit. He had a towel draped around his neck and he mopped his brow as Dillon entered.

"You'll excuse my appearance, I was just working out."

"You can continue while we talk if you wish." Dillon said obligingly.

"No thanks, I pushed myself enough for one day, come on through." He led the way into a Victorian library. "Care for a drink?" he asked, pressing a button on the phone set at the desk.

"Got any Irish whiskey?"

"Sure, which type?"

"Jameson." Dillon replied slightly amazed.

"Ice?"

Dillon nodded. Bordes-Aitcheson picked up the phone and gave instruction to someone. He asked for a beer for himself.

"Got to replace some of that liquid I lost." he explained. Bordes-Aitcheson waved to a chair and they both sat.

"Someone in your organization doesn't appear to trust us." Dillon began; he had decided on the way up not to play footsie with this guy, either he was going to co-operate or they pulled out. He figured that he'd gotten the man's attention and continued. "Tina Bolger discovered a set of ledgers for the year 1898. In itself nothing unusual, there is little of value in the ledgers." Dillon watched Bordes-Aitcheson closely for any reaction but there was none, just the piercing blue eyes staring back at him.

"But what was unusual was that the set of ledgers were not found in the filing office but in a disused vault room" At this point he considered the option of backing off the accusation that they were hidden but thought against it.

"And what is even more disturbing, Tina Bolger was followed this evening when she left the bank, and followed all the way to Charter MTR where she managed to lose the two men involved. This is extremely disturbing and goes against clear expression of goodwill and co-operation we were getting before these ledgers were found."

"This is a bit of a shock," Bordes-Aitcheson replied and swung his chair around so that he could look out the window at the harbour. Dillon took the opportunity to look around. There were several portraits around the walls and one wall was completely lined with books. From where he sat he could make out only a few titles but they appeared to be mainly banking and law books, with a good amount of Asian history.

This would be a good place to chase down the legal position of the title deeds of the New Territories at the time of the treaty. Dillon thought.

"This is an extremely delicate situation." Bordes-Aitcheson said as he swivelled the chair back.

"I would put it a little more strongly than that."

Just then a striking blond woman arrived with the drinks. Dillon couldn't help but watch her as she crossed the room. She had long legs concealed but accentuated by faded blue jeans.

"Oh Scott, I'd like to introduce my good wife, Stephanie. Steff, this is Scott Dillon."

Dillon didn't rise, he wasn't sure of the formalities around here, and anyhow she was close enough to him that he didn't have to get up off the chair to take the hand she extended to him. He wondered about the two names? He took the hand and shuck it gently, just as she had offered it.

"Pleased to meet you, Mister Dillon." The accent was American, and that surprised him. She sounded Texan, defiantly Southern.

"Pleased to meet you. Do I call you Steff or Stephanie?" He returned the pleasant smile, but he couldn't match the wonderful teeth.

"It depends, Mister Dillon," She glanced at her husband, then back to Dillon again.

"On what?" he asked intrigued.

"On whether or not you get along with Jeff."

"Oh I think we'll get along just fine." Dillon replied enjoying this little game she was playing.

"Well then it's Steff." She moved to take her hand away and began a turning motion swivelling her hips slightly. When he didn't let go she turned back with a slight surprise in her eyes.

"And it's Scott" He said to her and he released her hand. She stared at him a second longer then completed the swirl and left the room. He watched her all the way to the door. He knew he had overindulged in watching her ass and Bordes-Aitcheson probably wouldn't like it.

What the hell, it was a nice ass. Dillon mentally remarked. He turned his attention back to Bordes-Aitcheson wondering what to expect. He was actually smiling.

"She has that affect on men, I've gotten used to it"

Dillon just nodded; at least now he had a fair idea where he stood with this guy.

"Where were we?" Dillon asked.

"Delicate Situation." Bordes-Aitcheson prompted and added

"You will appreciate that I will have to investigate this carefully; I don't want to raise any hares"

"I can appreciate that, you know that part of my brief it to chase down any possible security risks, this in itself may not be classified as a security risk, but it certainly is a breach of confidence in that a member of staff did not inform executive officer of convert action that he planned to take"

Bordes-Aitcheson considered this for some time, and then slowly he nodded.

"Discreetly."

"Naturally, I always am."

"Do you think you can find out who the culprit is without him knowing it? I would like the opportunity of confronting him with the information."

"I'll see what I can do. But I can't guarantee anything."

"That's understandable, but I would appreciate it though."

"I'll see what I can do."

"As for the ledgers being in the old vault room, that is something else. I cannot understand how this could have occurred. From what I know of that bank, and this is stuff I learnt from the day books, it was opened in 1912. That particular vault room was closed down in 1936 because of the problem with the dampness, but was opened again in 1940 and a safe put back in there. Documents were stored there and the door sealed. It was only opened again in 1945 after the 'Liberation'. At that stage it was cleared out but the safe remained. It is possible that the ledgers were left in there by accident, but it is highly unlikely. I'm afraid that there is just no explanation for how those ledgers got in that safe. Perhaps a file clerk placed them there for lack of space?"

"What was peculiar about 1898?" Dillon asked casually.

"Eighteen Ninety Eight, the year the treaty of Hong Kong was signed, the year the Colony became a Sovereign part of the United Kingdom. The year there was finally peace between the traders and the Chinese Empire. Well, I think that was the year, or near enough, that my great grandfather took over the chairmanship of the bank, that would be the year, because of the treaty, that banks in Hong Kong came under the new Banking Charter, and thus the laws of the bank of England"

"Would that have caused a change in accounting practices?" Scott deduced from the man's body language that Bordes-Aitcheson did not expect that question.

"Yes, yes it would. Up to that time accounts could be done up to suit the shareholders, there was no such thing as a balance sheet, just as long as the stated assets were greater than the paid up capital, then not a lot else mattered. That was, of course, unless you were broke, in which case you vanished before someone got a noose. Those were pretty wild days."

"Wild enough to have allowed over stated assets to be inserted into a ledger?" Dillon again knew from Bordes-Aitcheson's expression that the question bothered him.

"What are you saying?"

Dillon reached into his inside jacket pocket and withdrew the folded up photocopies of the relevant pages. He handed them across the desk to Bordes-Aitcheson. He unfolded the sheets and scanned them; he didn't have to peer too closely for the ghost was underlined in red. It was a glaring error made by some foolish file clerk, more than likely on the instruction of his great grandfather, the title deeds were held by the bank to the New Territories comprising all lands north of line drawn between Cheung Sha Wan and Razor Hill. The security for a loan of 12,000 Guineas given to one Jason Kimberley. The very nature of the entry in the ledger implied that the title was held by the bank and against assets on the second sheet, the land was valued at 24,000 Guineas. Of course the entry was utter rubbish for the value of the land was grossly understated, but then it was valued and entered before the treaty. The entry created two separate problems, one that the land was grossly undervalued and how to remedy that without making the original entry look stupid, and 2, now that there was a treaty the Colony was a Sovereign part of the British Empire and therefore the bank was obliged to file returns under the new Charter with the Bank of England. It was one of those silly things done in haste that defies logic. It was obvious that a great error of judgment was made at the time, the loan should never have been granted on those conditions. The true ownership of the land could very quickly be sorted out with the governor. But someone had made a misguided decision and to crown it all, the bank could not enforce the judgment against Jason Kimberley for repayment of the loan for they were already paid in kind by virtue of having accepted the title deed as security. Title deeds which became worthless with the signing of the treaty to the bank as Jason Kimberley was the only man who could have pursued the governor for compensation with which the loan could have been repaid. Obviously having stated an asset of 24,000 guineas in the ledgers and then to realise that they couldn't be capitalised, left the accountant of that time in a predicament. The seriousness of the situation would have become obvious within a few months of the signing of the treaty, as the governor would by now be proceeding to sell the lands. No one noticed the error until this outfit arrived.

Bordes-Aitcheson passed the sheets back to Dillon. "That was a long time ago. Who knows how that occurred, it may even have been a mistake or at worst a confident trickster who took a foolish bank manager for a ride. I presume the asset did not appear in subsequent years?"

"No, it doesn't. Bolger went forward to 1906 but no mention"

"This is a skeleton in our cupboard, what can I say. It does not affect the bank as it is today." Little did Bordes-Aitcheson realise that his words would come back to haunt him in just a few days.

"Of course not, its just one of those things that needed to be answered because it could have been the other side of the coin." Dillon dangled that one. Bordes-Aitcheson went for it.

"The other side of the coin?" He seemed genuinely puzzled.

"Yes, it could have been a confident trick all right, but one perpetrated by the board."

Bordes-Aitcheson was staring at Dillon again, this time there was something akin to hatred in his eyes. He shook his head slowly, and when he spoke he left no doubt in Dillon's mind that this suggestion should never again be heard.

"I have very carefully read the minutes of every meeting of the board of this bank, and there was never any hint of under-hand dealing or attempted deception or stock manipulation of any kind at any time in the history of this bank. I trust, Mister Dillon, that that piece of speculation was merely playing the Devil's Advocate, and that it will never be repeated outside of this room"

"You got that right." Dillon knew when to change tack.

"Good. Would you like another drink, perhaps you would care to stay to supper, meet the kids?" Bordes-Aitcheson brightened considerable. But Dillon saw in his face that he was finished with him, the 'meet the kids' was the threat that if he stayed, he would have to meet the kids, and men are not built for meeting someone else's kids. Their own they could just about live with.

Dillon looked at his watch and it was 8.45. He had forgotten about Linn, the Singapore girl.

"Sorry, I completely forgot that I've got a date. Could I use your phone?"

"Sure, have you got the number?"

"No, ah it's the Singapore Hotel."

Bordes-Aitcheson got the directory, found the number, punched it on the key phone and handed it over to Dillon. After much apologizing, he said he'd pick her up. Bordes-Aitcheson said that Charlie would drive him down. Dillon informed Linn that he'd be there in 20 minutes.

*

She was more radiant than he remembered when he saw her at the bar in Singapore Hotel. She was with her two girlfriends from the airport. They were all dressed quite elegantly and ready for a night on the town. She came to him and touching affectionately, she kissed him gently.

"You're just what I need right now," he said. He had only been in Hong Kong for a few hours and he was tired.

"You made binding verbal agreement, sir. You offered to take me out on the town and buy me dinner. My tummy rumbles so much it is highly embarrassing."

"If that was your interpretation of my offer then I will have to abide by that, however, one late clause which I insist must be inserted."

"Oh, ho," she smiled wickedly.

"I do insist that I get nourishing food, not fish, I insist on steak."

"I guess I can live with that late insertion." Again she wore a wicked smile and bid farewell to her companions. Linking arms, Dillon and his date left the hotel.

They found a delightful little restaurant which did both western and eastern food; she ordered for him and then looked the waiter dead in the eye and said,

"Yum Cha and Shiu Mai quickly." The waiter hurried off.

"What did you order?"

"Tea and dim sum, I am starving." She beamed her teeth as if she was going to eat him if nothing came soon.

"I really am very sorry for being late, but I got tied up in a small crisis that just would not keep until morning."

"Never mind, I will eat all the more, enjoy all the more, break wind all the more." He laughed at her. Linn really was a beauty but more than that, she had no inhibition.

"Do they serve beer here?"

"Sure." She stood up and whistled at one of the waiters. One came running over.

"Cold can of beer, imported, for my man here. Very cold, understand?"

He nodded bowed and rushed off.

It occurred to Dillon that this was not her first time here; the waiter seemed to be very tolerant.

"Do your girlfriends have dates tonight?"

"Elizabeth yes, she is the one with the long hair, Mary has not, but she will not be lonely. She is from Hong Kong, her sisters usually visit her when she is in town."

The waiter returned with the beer and pulled the tab for Dillon, setting it down in front of him; he smiled and scurried off again.

"Doesn't she stay with her sisters when she's here?"

"Her sister's bedrooms are far too busy" Linn's wicked smile appeared once more.

"Ah, so." Dillon replied.

Her order arrived. She looked at it longingly.

"Go ahead, don't wait, no formality." Dillon said.

She wired into the Dim Sums, as they'd say back home, she let the lugs back.

Conversation was forgotten about as she delicately picked the meat and vegetable filled pastries and swallowed whole for the first few, then slowed and nibbled and chewed her way through a dozen or so. She washed them down with tea. Her eyes caught his.

"So sorry, the first ones are to sooth the tummy dragon so I can enjoy the rest."

Another can of beer arrived and the waiter brought more dim sum for her.

"Here, try some." She passed over the plate that was loaded with them. They appeared appetizing enough. They were about the size of an egg, either boiled or steam cooked and over the lot had been poured soy sauce. He picked one with a fork, his place being set for European food.

"Hmm, not bad." He ate the first and went for the second.

"Good ha?" she enquired.

"Yeah, very good" He was on his fourth when the steak arrived. It was a miserable looking steak, but it was nicely cooked, and there was also some salad and jacket potatoes.

It was about 10.30 when they left the restaurant, laughing and belching. Without making any plans, they found themselves walking towards the peak and Hong Kong Central. It was a beautiful night, the horizon still red from the sun just gone and stars were being turned on up there in the sky. A cool breeze came in off the sea to help reduce the humidity and seemingly cool everything down. The day had been so hot and sticky that now with the coolness of the evening, more and more people came onto the streets.

It was much easier to move around for the hectic pace of the day had gone and people just lounged around or strolled down to the shore where the air was coolest.

Dillon and Linn found themselves near the Mandarin Hotel so they went in for a drink and also because he wanted to set Bolger's mind at ease about the morning. He phoned her room and gave Bolger a brief outline of his conversation with Bordes-Aitcheson.

"Do you believe him?" she asked.

"Do you want the blunt answer or the diplomatic one?" Dillon replied.

"I'm not sure I want either right now. I'd rather get a night's sleep first. Let's talk in the morning."

"Okay, nite" He hung up. As he walked back to the bar, he thought of Tina Bolger alone in her room upstairs. He wondered if she was still so madly in love with her Jack, as she had called him in Bahrain. That had been some week. The job was simple, there was a thief in the Bank of Bahrain, and the manager wanted the person caught so that his cousins could take care of it. Dillon knew just what that meant; the thief was going to receive the ultimate punishment, a bullet in the back of the head. It didn't bother him because he knew that if they did not do the job, someone else would. And the pay was good; $50,000 for him, $450,000 for the bank back in New York. Thinking back now he wondered if Bolger knew. It was unlikely that she realised that the guy that she was tracking down with her patience and observational power of examining accounts to trace that unusual transaction, the continued use of a single account for depositing money filtered away from client's accounts. She was the bug that would find the thief, he was the watcher, the minder, the guy that made sure that the bug was safe. He often thought about her long after the job was over, he wondering if she knew just what her part was in the operation and if she knew that as a result of her observations, some poor bastard was going to get blown away. He had met her several times at work, just in passing, never socially and never privately. There were a number of times that Dillon thought about calling her just to talk, say how things are, remember the great night we had bullshitting in Bahrain till three in the morning in the Hilton. But he couldn't, she was a married women and he was afraid that he would ask her did she know what happened to the poor slob that they caught for the theft. He didn't want her to have to carry the burden of the knowledge that she had pointed out the guy for a hit, if she did not already know. There was no need to land that on her. Maybe now, all these years later, they could talk about it and he might be able to learn if she knew without having to bring the subject up. It was very difficult to talk to her not knowing if she knew or not. Her voice had sounded real good, she talked kinda low, not deliberately to sound sexy, it was just her voice. And those brown eyes. He used to be a blue eyes man himself, but her eyes were something else. There was a hypnotic tranquillity about them, eyes that said, "talk to me."

"Jesus," he muttered realising that he was standing at the entrance to the bar watching Linn, the Singapore Girl, the most gorgeous looking thing he had seen in a long time and he was thinking about a woman almost as old as himself who was happily married and out of reach. He shrugged his shoulders and went back to join Linn. She was at the bar; one of the waitresses had stopped to talk to her.

"Ah, Clair, this is Scott Dillon" She introduced him to the long raven haired beauty. Clair was Eurasian, tall, dark and handsome with that seemingly endless smile that made Eurasians girls so attractive.

"Honoured to meet you," She bowed politely. He returned with a curt bow and sat beside Linn.

"I ordered you a beer"

"Thanks, I needed that." Dillon said. Clair took her leave saying she would check with them later if they stayed a while.

As with their walk, they just dropped into conversation again about just about everything. She had seen virtually every city in the world during her five years with the airline. She was one of eight children, five girls, and three boys. Her mother had passed away three years earlier and her father was hale and hearty at the age of 72. He was a shoemaker so he was called Shoemaker Chun, as were the habits of Chinese they called a man by his trade or taken name and added on his birth name to the end of it. The system made for some unusual combinations. He remembered the conversation earlier at the restaurant about Mary's sister with the busy beds, obviously prostitutes.

"How about Mary's sisters then? What would they be called?"

"Ha, ha, there are thousands of names for the Ladies of the Pillow world: Yang receivers, Precious Golden Gully." He listened attentively and was both filled with amusement and awe. This one was a mine of information: clean, dirty, exciting, titillating, everything a man could want in a woman. But he wondered how would someone in say, social circles present an outspoken girl like this into polite gathering where appearances and one's P's & Q's were watched very carefully and a fart was cause for hanging. Dillon eventually came to the conclusion that she would probably fit in perfectly and herself end up becoming a celebrity. Clair made sure that the drinks kept coming and he began to wonder, very slowly, if she had struck some sort of deal to ensure that he got plenty of drink. But she was getting drunk herself on gin and late into the night it was she who fell about the place laughing.

CHAPTER FOUR

Thomas Maxwell's phone rang around 7 0' clock. He was just on his way to the kitchen and took the call there.

"Yeah, hallo?"

"Morning Tom, we got trouble."

"Right here in River City." Maxwell sang recognizing Jeff's voice on the other end of the line.

"Those guys found that bloody 1898 ledger and they are asking questions."

"I was afraid of that; I thought though that they'd never find it in the old safe."

"What's done is done, but something more serious has happened. Someone was following Tina Bolger yesterday evening after she left the bank"

"Is this connected to the ledgers?"

"That's what they think."

"Shit, what do you think?"

"If you were asked the question, 'who might fear the discovery of that ledger?' Whose name pops to mind?"

"Archibald is probably the most paranoiac member of the board. I would say he was the one most likely."

"Was he at the bank Monday?"

"Yes, as a matter of fact he was, now that you come to ask, quite late on in the day. He came after doors close. John Sing let him in."

"Was it common knowledge that Bolger had found the ledgers?"

"No, at least I hadn't heard it, but then I've been bogged down with this new computer system. You know we're going to have to get those people back. It's just not doing what it's supposed to do."

"Okay Tom, Okay, but right now our problem is those ledgers, just how much damage could they do us?"

"Well very little really, from an accounting point of view, an error was made, and I think that is all it was, an error. It was a long time ago, and the proper procedures were not followed and particularly the following year, no effort was made to rectify the error. That's the real difficulty. That was where there might have been a case for questions rather that 1898 itself. If they only put in a clarifying statement; but they didn't. Okay, what damage could it do us?" he asked himself.

"Not a lot really from a legal stand-point, I think the damage could be done in the area of public confidence. There we are vulnerable." Maxwell confirmed Bordes-Aitcheson's own thoughts.

"Look Tom, can you meet me at say eight at the bank and we can talk this through?"

"Yours or mine?" The question being which bank, Hong Kong or Kowloon?

"Mine." Bordes-Aitcheson replied and hung up.

Maxwell held the phone in deep thought for a few moments, then he heard footsteps.

"Morning." Clair said as she entered the kitchen.

"Morning." he replied, she came into his arms and they kissed.

She pulled back and stared at him. "You're a little tense for this hour, something wrong? What was that call about?" Clair asked as she filled the water jug.

He headed for the fridge and got some orange juice. "Oh it was Bordes-Aitcheson, those Yanks have discovered a set of old ledgers going back nearly a hundred years, and Jeff's concerned in case they will damage the bank. It's just routine trouble, it'll blow over." Maxwell tried to sound off-handish.

"Is there something wrong with the ledgers?"

"Yeah, they were found."

*

Dillon walked into the dining room at 7.30. Tina and Olli were already there. They greeted each other.

"Well come on, what did Bordes-Aitcheson have to say?" Tina asked.

"The inside of my head feels like an empty brothel." Dillon either didn't hear the question or felt incapable of an answer.

"You out on the town last night?"

"I sure as hell hope so, cause if this is jet lag, I ain't never gonna fly again."

"What about Bordes-Aitcheson?" Tina asked again.

"He didn't seem overly worried about the ledgers themselves; I got the impression that he knew nothing about the two guys following you."

"That's good?" Tina asked.

"That's bad cause now we got a case of there being somebody in that bank who don't trust us or their boss." Dillon replied.

"That's bad." Tina said absently.

"I'm going to have a little snooping after all. This may be dirty, and may ruffle a few feathers."

"What should we do?" Tina asked.

"How close are you two to finishing your report?"

"Well we were already there until those damn ledgers threw us back. The accounts have been perfect, everything has totted up. We were about to give them a clean bill of health."

The breakfast arrived so they waited.

"You were saying last night that you were going to check City Hall for any records of that period." Olli prompted.

"Yeah I was going to spend some time there this morning." Tina replied. Dillon could've sworn that he saw a quick expression of fear on Tina's face when she answered his question but he dismissed it and thought that he was probably imagining things.

"Okay, you follow that up, I've got a meeting with Ruxton at eight to go through the personal files, that should take till ten, then I'll mosey on over to the Kowloon branch and try to track down this mole."

"Ah, I think that should be beaver rather than a mole, a mole burrows underground to hide himself, a beaver builds dams. I think our man has built a dam to stop the flow of information"

They stared at Olli then after a suitable period of consideration.

"Operation Beaver it is then." Bolger said.

They ate in silence now for a while. Dillon obviously having some difficulty, leaving the egg till last, then putting down the fork with determination, or rather resignation and decided to give the egg a miss.

"There is one other little item here that we haven't mentioned yet," Olli said quietly, leaning forward.

"I don't think this is the place." Tina cut across rather fiercely, even if she did speak as low as Olli.

"Perhaps not," Olli looked around, the dining room was crowded. There were too many ears.

Dillon was rather puzzled by all this, they had obviously discussed the matter before, and by the very nature of the way that Olli had begun, it was highly secretive or highly unethical or both.

"Look, I came to Hong Kong for a break. Now if you've gotten involved in some extra-curricular activity I don't want to know about it." He looked at each of them in turn, their faces were like that of school kids who had discovered the art of reproduction. "Or do I?" He gave it a second thought.

"I think you do." Olli replied.

"But not here, later. Let's get this thing sorted out first."

They agreed. Dillon caught the waiter's attention and told him the room number for the charge.

They got to the lobby where Charlie Chan was waiting for them.

"Morning, Boss." He smiled broadly, "Sleep good, Boss?"

"Morning Charlie, and yes I did sleep well, but I think I got a little jet lag"

"Go to the bank now?" the little man suggested.

"Yes, lead the way."

Bolger remained behind to go her own way; once they'd gone she went to the door and examined the street for any signs of watchers. After about ten minutes, she was satisfied that all was clear and she headed out into street.

From across the street an apparent window browser detached himself from whatever had held his attention and walked a parallel course to that taken by Tina Bolger.

*

Hong Kong at eight in the morning was hot and crowded. Most people got around with the least amount of clothes as was decent. The humidity was 80 and getting worse. Thankfully the bank was only a short distance away where they got into the coolness of the air-conditioning. Ruxton was waiting.

"I'm afraid we were not properly introduced yesterday. My name is Scott Dillon."

"Pleased to meet you, Mister Dillon, I'm Dan Ruxton. Among other things, I'm the assistant manager here and I also act as personnel officer and I understand that we're to go through the personal record this morning."

"Correct, lead the way."

Olli left them to it and he went to the file room.

"Would you care for coffee, Mister Dillon?"

"I would indeed, black, no sugar, and please, call me Scott."

"Thank you. You may call me Don"

Dillon realised as he followed that he was going to meet fierce resistance from this man. His head hurt so much that he couldn't care less. He was going to do his 'due diligence' with the records and then go find Tina.

*

Bordes-Aitcheson didn't arrive at the bank until 8.30, a half hour late. Tom Maxwell had been there since around ten to eight and had waited for the chairman in his office. Tom Maxwell was an American, well his parents were. Maxwell's father had arrived in Hong Kong shortly after the war, together with his new wife. Old Maxwell had joined the bank as a 'junior' assistant manager and rapidly rose to position of assistant branch manager in the Kowloon branch. As with all staff Maxwell had invested in bank stock and soon had a sizeable slice of shares.

Tom joined the bank like his father as a junior, but in accounts and filing, with a brief to improve methods and practices. He took to his task with a flourish and soon proved that he had his father's business sense. Old Maxwell retired in '76 and was co-opted onto the board of management. 'Young Tom' as he was called, moved into Kowloon as Branch Manager. He became a personal friend of Bordes-Aitcheson and the friendship was well tested during the disasters that beset banking in Hong Kong from '82 to '83.

That was the time that the British insisted on handling the negotiations with China's Deng Xiaoping as they had handled the Falkland, but strong aggressive posturing did not impress the Chinese and British had to backtrack and negotiate on the Deng's terms. The result was that in September 1983, the Hong Kong dollar collapsed.

Whether it was sheer good judgment or just hedging, Maxwell and Bordes-Aitcheson had moved a considerable amount of the banks deposit reserves into American Dollars and Japanese Yen.

The writing was on the wall for some time and the wise had made the move, but the staunch supporters of Britain's negotiation ability had been badly caught. The collapse was halted by the intervention of the colonial government and the Bank of England, but for many the damage was done. Those who sold in panic when the rot had started got caught. Those who sold earlier and brave enough to buy back in when the dollar was at its lowest, made money.

The AAB had been one of those that read the situation correctly and had come out of it stronger and in a good financial position. The very nature of Hong Kong that thrives and admires success and smart dealing, gave AAB a huge vote of confidence afterwards. Many moved deposits to AAB to such an extent that AAB dropped its rates one and a half points below other Hong Kong institutes and still kept favour with the depositors.

Despite the deposit interest drop, the AAB held its lending rate within a half point of its rivals so the result was larger profit margins and a very good '84. The problem, however, was staying on top. They had been lucky, they had lent to one exploration Venture Company who had struck oil in the Gulf of Tong King. Part of the security arrangement had been the bank taking 25% of the companies at a nominal cost. The oil flowed at a 40,000 barrel a day rate. The find was big, investors clamoured for shares. Bordes-Aitcheson obliged, when his $1 shares hit $48, he offloaded. The result was a $48 million windfall for the bank.

Tom Maxwell stood looking into the face of Sir Anthony Bordes, whose portrait hung in pride over the very first safe the bank owned.

You'd love to have been around here last year, you old bastard. You'd loved to have seen the big money queuing up to buy our $1 shares for $48. he thought to himself. With his mind being on shares, he thought of the bank's own shares right now. He had checked the Hang Seng stock exchange yesterday evening,

We're still at $22.50, and that makes me nervous. We're- Maxwell's thoughts were interrupted by the door. Bordes-Aitcheson walked in rather quicker than usual. His face was a trifle paler than normal and he wore a worried look.

"Morning, again." Tom said.

"Yeah." Bordes-Aitcheson collapsed into his swivel armchair.

"Boy, I don't know what the hell this place is coming to."

Maxwell sat down facing Bordes-Aitcheson across the desk.

"What's the matter?"

"I've just been talking to Allen Lee," Bordes-Aitcheson paused to light a cigarette; Maxwell knew that Bordes-Aitcheson had a rule 'no cigarettes before lunch'. Allen Lee was the Chief Inspector in charge of the fraud squad, and not someone to speak to at eight o clock in the morning if you could at all help it.

"The Oversees Unit Trust Bank is in trouble; Harry Chan may be arrested and charged with fraudulent trading. Allen says they haven't got enough reserves to cover one tenth of their depositor's money"

"Jesus Christ," Maxwell gasped, "One tenth. Christ any fool knows you need a least a quarter on reserve" That meant that if there was a run, they would have to close their door within 2 - 3 hours.

"How the hell did he get into the mess?"

"He's got a more vacant office space around the town than the Chinese will have in 1997 and that 'Chung Buildings' project he undertook, well Jesus it was just crazy." The rumour around town the last few weeks was that Chan had over 70,000 sq feet of vacant office space and at $25 per sq foot per week that adds up to $1.75 million a week income you're not getting. Then there was the 'Chung Building' project undertaken at a cost of $400 million, not yet completed but already the word had it that as a piece of property, it is a gross waste of money. A realistic value might be HK$250 million.

That was the word around town, but Bordes-Aitcheson had information that it might be worth more, for the particular building could be put to another use other than individually let offices.

About one month back, he had got a phone call from Ding Su Jaing, a member of the Chinese Consular delegation in Hong Kong, for the negotiations with the British on the future of the Colony. Jeff had been suspicious of the approach and wondered why Jaing should call him.

He had explained that his bank was considered to have its hands on the pulse of the business community.

"Sure," Jeff replied, "But what's that got to do with information on office buildings?"

Most of this information was readily available at the planning office.

"Paper alone only gives size and shape of building, not what promoter had in mind. Was office space already booked etc?"

"Well what exactly do you want to know?"

"If major office development is being planned, promoter must start by making plan with bank. Next go and pre-sell some office space. What figure necessary to pre-sell?"

"If someone came to me with such a plan, I would like to see at least 33% of the space pre-sold before the foundations were started, presuming that the developer already had purchased the site."

"Would developers go to most banks or stay with own bank?"

"Well it would depend, most of those guys may be with one bank for many years, but they usually do the rounds to get the best deal on interest rates, even if only to put pressure on their own bank manager for a good deal."

"Therefore, you would know of most developments before they begin?"

"Yes, if the guy didn't come to me I would still hear about it through the grapevine."

"This was why I called you; I do not wish it to be public knowledge that we are making the enquiry about office space."

Now he understood, the Chinese were looking for one large building in which to house themselves, rather than being scattered all over Hong Kong. And they want the enquiry to be discreet, otherwise office space rental could rise substantially.

"There must be office space around that you could chase."

"Must be careful not to cause speculation as this would be seen as interfering in the market. This we are very careful about"

"I understand, I see your problem. I'll keep an eye open for you, if you like."

"We would appreciate that. Do you know if any such development is being undertaking at the present?"

That surprised him, for he got the impression that they wanted to move fairly fast. That was when he thought of Harry Chan's white elephant. He knew Chan of course; he had been at this house on several occasions at his wild extravagant parties. But he didn't mix much on a business level with Chan for he did crazy things. But if he could put business Chan's way, then he would.

"So sorry, but Chan not type of Chinese we wished to do business with, very bad person, much bad mouth People's Republic. Also do some very shady deals with Shanghai Merchant, not in interest of People's Republic to deal with such a man."

There the conversation had ended with Jeff promising to let him know if he heard anything.

Tom brought him back to the present.

"What do you think will happen?"

"Allen says that Chan is being watched and if he steps outta line, he will be arrested. Allen says that Chan has stashed millions away in a Swiss account, or at least he thinks he has, that was why he came to me this morning."

"Remember Chan bought HK$10 million worth of that oil deal-"

"Yeah but that was an investment purchase done by the Unit Trust"

"Allen says Chan sold it off again, privately and kept the money. That's the money they think is in a Swiss Bank."

"Why would he do that?"

"Maybe he saw the writing on the wall, maybe he thought the oil shares would fall, then he could just repay the amount he would expect the fallen shares would fetch."

"That's not just fraud, that's downright gambling!"

"With depositor's money."

"That's fraud. Is there a danger to us? That's a foolish question, I know. How much damage can we expect?"

"The biggest danger is the price of the shares."

"They are already dangerously low; $22.50 is much too low.

"It's this damn uncertainty over '97 then, well God only knows what's gonna happen after that. Would you speculate your hard earned money on high priced shares, that in the short term may or may not rise, but in the long term will have to fall as money leaves Hong Kong prior to the Chinese takeover, eh?"

"The great Chinese take away." Maxwell smiled.

"The foals will bolt, even if the old horses don't." Bordes-Aitcheson observed thoughtfully.

"Damage limitation?" Maxwell enquired.

"But how to go about it? We have the cash reserves to ride out a minor run that will happen if the Unit Trust goes under. But I'm afraid this might trigger a major run on all financial institutes and the resulting fall in share prices. That's our danger."

As much as he tried to avoid the subject his thoughts kept coming back to the current share prices. He was in an impossible situation personally. He had over the years added to his fathers 25% of the shares when he could afford it or when he had to. The collapse of '83 had driven down all shares in Hong Kong and he had used his personal savings to buy up shares to prevent a total bottom out of the price, and he also wanted to avoid the risk of unscrupulous raiders buying into his stock. The risk was there in 1983 and it had almost happened in so far as 8% of the stock were bought up by an investment trust owned by God only knows who, that was the danger, and it could raise its ugly head again if prices fell to the low of $14.25 Hong Kong, that they hit in '83.

"In the event of a run on deposits, which will happen and a resulting fall in share value, how much money can we raise personally, you and I?"

"I've got about one million."

"And I've got around three seven." Bordes-Aitcheson did a calculation on a calculator.

"That's two hundred thousand shares we can buy out of a 12 million share issue"

"That's less that two percent of the issued share capital we can buy, hell that's no good. That won't stop a share dive."

"You're going on a purchase price of $22.50 Hong Kong, if the shares fall in value we can buy for less than that."

"Yes, I know but it still doesn't alter the percentage very much. We're still only looking at $4.7 million worth of shares"

"And then there's the eight percent that this Narrow Investment have, if they came on the market as well." Maxwell left that unfinished; he knew that the 8% resting with this mysterious investment trust hurt Bordes-Aitcheson.

"That would be 2.7 million shares on the market that we could not control or $62 million we would need to stop the arse falling out of the price."

"Hell we're assuming the worst here."

"That's how we made our money in '84, by assuming the worst and getting out of Hong Kong Dollar before it dived."

Bordes-Aitcheson smiled at the simple logic that Maxwell came out with.

"As I see it," Maxwell continued reading the smile as a compliment. "If Chan is arrested the Overseas Unit Trust will go, causing a knock on against us. If that happens as much as 15% of our shares could go up for sale. My guess is that if the shares are offered for sale, this mysterious Narrow Investments will buy. They did in '83 I suspect they will again, but after the price has fallen. But we don't want that Okay, so what we do is we do something to hold the price of our stock if not raise it, the question being what?"

"What would cause our stock to rise?" Bordes-Aitcheson threw back and seemed to be enjoying Maxwell's brainstorming session.

"Acquisition, takeovers, buy-outs, rumours, profits, security, being nice guys"

"Security, we're the soundest bank on the Island, but how to tell that to our shareholders without alerting anybody?" They both shook their heads.

"Profit, we've already done that one." Again Bordes-Aitcheson smiled cunningly.

"Rumours, the governor's secretary is a stock holder in AAB."

"That leaves us with 'buy-outs', 'takeovers' and acquisitions, and in that, where the hell do you go to find something worth acquiring in Hong Kong right now?"

They fell onto silence for a moment, but Maxwell was watching Bordes-Aitcheson who was watching back.

"Just suppose we are coming at this from the wrong end," Bordes-Aitcheson said slowly. Maxwell could decipher from the man's expression that he was pondering on something. "We don't take over anything; we let someone take over us." Maxwell was glad that Bordes-Aitcheson broached the subject for it had formed in his mind as they spoke, and it would be the perfect solution.

"Correction, we make someone fight for us, that's not to say that we let them win"

"But who, and how do we go about it?" Maxwell asked but he could see the glint in Jeff's eyes, he was hatching a plan.

CHAPTER FIVE

Dillon arrived at the Kowloon branch shortly after eleven. Charlie had come to a screeching halt just outside the door. He left the black Merc' 300 on a double yellow line as he ushered Dillon into the bank. Nobody seemed to pay them any attention but Charlie caught someone's eye and a young Chinese came to the security door at one end of the counter. Nothing was said until they were inside, and then Charlie introduced John Sing. Dillon shook hands with Sing and felt an undercurrent. The handshake was firm, almost as if Sing hadn't expected him and was unsure what to do. Dillon knew that Ruxton had phoned Sing to let him know that he was on his way over. He ignored the undercurrent for the moment and followed Sing to the Manager's office.

"Ah, Mister Dillon, may I call you Scott, I'm Tom" Maxwell cut quickly through the bullshit.

He waved him to a seat in front of the large oak desk.

The IBM desktop was standard fitting but this office was modern in design compared to the main bank on the Island. The time spent with Don Ruxton earlier had been pleasant if not enlightening. It was as Bordes-Aitcheson had said, there was little or no staff turnover. The most recent signing had been a bank teller and that had been over two years ago. Still he had gone through the motions just in case. But everything was in order even Charlie Chan had been with the bank since 1980. His official classification was that of bank porter. Ruxton explained that he was now a driver or runner, and the Merc' was a company car.

"So what do you think of our little Island?" Maxwell asked.

"I like it. How much are the Chinese looking for it?" Dillon replied.

"They've got no reserve; I understand that they are open to offers"

"But seriously, if you were to put a figure on the net worth of Hong Kong, what sort of figure would we be talking about?"

"I'm not sure the figure has been invented yet, but if zillions represent one billion, billion, then I would say around a few zillion in value."

"What's going to happen to that money in '97?"

"It's gonna scatter to the four winds and unfortunately it will not be as successful, because here it's like, well, like family, just one big family. People here thrive on success and money, the tax rates are probably the lowest in the world, 18% across the board. In most countries if someone makes a million, there's ten people saying, 'I want some of that too' or 'spread the wealth around'. These people succeed because that's all they know about. Failure is a foreign word. Those that fail thank God for the lesson and go and do it all over again. They're born workers. Most millionaires here are Chinese, they come from the mainland where there's nothing but poverty and here they see success and want to try it. It's an infectious disease."

"There must be a lot of fear about what's to come after '97?"

"There is. Let me put it this way, 90 percent of the population of Hong King have already fled the Chinese system once. They are not going to take the chance of being caught in a water trap this time, last time it was a land trap, but they could walk out. If they wait here now and the Chinese break their promise about allowing a pseudo-capitalist system, they have to swim, and they gotta go a long way to get out of Chinese waters." Maxwell smiled knowingly.

"So the people and their money are going to move. Where to?"

"We have a lot of depositors now opening American Dollar accounts, obviously with the intention of moving to America just before the big day comes."

"So you open an American branch."

"That's one way of doing it. Unfortunately, we will lose the deposits because once they get there, they will scatter to the four corners of the States and take their money with them. Unless you could take Hong Kong lock stock and barrel and move it off to California, we couldn't hope to hold those deposits."

"So it would look like the end of the line for AAB?" Dillon asked.

Maxwell looked taken aback, as if not expecting the suggestion. "I don't think it's the end of the line, it may be the end of an era. But when one era ends, another begins. We will have to learn to operate within whatever system is in force."

"But it will affect the value of your assets."

"We will adapt, in business a month is a long time."

"Your not too concerned then about the value of your shares"

Maxwell stared at Dillon for a moment before he spoke again. "You certainly believe in being rather blunt, don't you, Scott?"

"I just wondered how you felt about the shares, they are undervalued at present. Bordes-Aitcheson has $108 million in those shares, that's a lot to risk by holding on here."

"That's why we want to spread our wings."

"I would say 'have to' rather than 'want to.'" Dillon added.

"Bordes-Aitcheson is not a man to panic, he believes in steady growth and expansion. Why I've seen that man hold fast and refuse to be drawn into so called 'Flyer Ventures' just cos it looks good and everybody is doing it. He leads rather than being led."

"So now he holds firm against the 'let's get out' mentality."

"There are going to be people who will stay behind and continue with development. If the other financial institutions pull out there is going to be a lot of businesses here wanting money. Bordes-Aitcheson won't pull up his roots, and he won't keep all his eggs in the one basket, thus the overseas branches, but HQ will be in Hong Kong."

Dillon smiled, he knew that Maxwell was loyal to Bordes-Aitcheson, and there was no risk here. "Okay, did Bordes-Aitcheson tell you about the ledgers Bolger found?"

"Yes he did, he told me this morning"

"What do you think about them?"

"The ledgers?" He seemed to consider the question then continued, "I'm afraid I can't see the importance of them, somebody made a mistake, a bad one, but let's face it, it was over 90 years ago. Even in Hong Kong all public knowledge of them would do is cause a minor scandal and a lot of speculation, but I don't think that their re-evaluation would do us much harm. They're a ghost in the cupboard, that's all."

"Someone thought they were important, important enough to have a couple off guys tail Bolger yesterday."

"From time to time, people become over enthused with their own importance and probably think that they have a responsibility above and beyond what is asked of them. I think that's what happened in this case. We have here in this branch some overly protective staff that, - oh well, shall we say took duties upon themselves that wasn't any of their business."

It was Dillon's turn to be mildly shocked, unless he was reading this wrong, Maxwell knew the culprit and was tempted to give the name to Dillon, or so he felt. He put Dillon in an awkward position now, to ask the man and perhaps put him in a position where he may be in a breach of confidence.

"Do you think that the situation will have changed since last evening?" Dillon asked.

"To be quite frank, I don't think so. Unfortunately one of our board members suffers from paranoia and I suspect that he may be behind all this."

Dillon could scarcely believe his ears and he knew that Maxwell could see the shock in his eyes.

"We would be better off without these people, not I understand that you made an agreement with Bordes-Aitcheson to provide him with the opportunity to confront the culprit. I feel that this should happen as soon as possible." Maxwell said.

"Just as soon as I find him."

"He showed you into this office."

"I thought the guy looked nervous" Dillon replied as quickly as possible to cover his surprise."

"I think the honourable thing for him to do would be to offer his resignation as quickly as possible. It would be unfortunate if he were forced to go"

"Oh, how's that?"

"His appointment was a board recommendation because there were no Chinese in a senior staff position; it was something that George Archibald had pushed for, for some time. And unfortunately it was for the wrong motives, George believed that a Chinese assistant manager would attract more Chinese deposits. How one man could do this is a mystery." He raised his eyebrows to heaven.

"Archibald saw it as a step in the right direction." Maxwell said.

Therein lies the answer to Maxwell co-operation; he was probably upset by Sings appointment. Dillon thought. "What would the position of a board member be if he colluded with Sing?"

"Well, he would be acting without the approval of the board, and taking decisions without reporting to the Chairman, that would be quite serious contravention of the member's charter."

"Could this result in his removal from the board?"

"He could be voted off it. That would depend on the other board members. A meeting of the board would have to be called."

"What about his shares, what does he hold?"

"Around 7% but I doubt if he would sell, not immediately anyway. He is an extremely stubborn man. He built his fortune from nothing and owns Territories Freight. You'd see his containers at the docks, he's in international freight in a big way. He started off with one delivery truck in Kowloon 20 years ago and has grown ever since. Personally he's worth 100 million easy. You don't intimidate a man with that sort of money."

"Seven percent could be used to weaken shares that are already undervalued."

Maxwell stared at Dillon for a moment. "You seem overly concerned about the value of our shares. You've mentioned it three times already now. You come from a different school of thought than us. If you have something to say why not come straight out with it"

"The current value of your shares leaves you wide open for a take over and there would be nothing you could do about it."

"Did you say this to Bordes-Aitcheson?"

"Of course not, I think that man has enough on his hands at the moment."

"What do you suggest we do?" Maxwell enquired.

"Acquire something; push up the value of your shares by buying into someone with a lot of capital assets but not necessarily with the cash to fight off a takeover."

"As we are right now, do you think that we would get trading clearance from the IMF?"

"To be quiet honest, no. From what I've seen, you're a border line business. You have only $298 million assets. Okay you've got cash reserves of $67 million which is over 40% of deposits, but your assets base is way too low. I can understand that as a bank you are financially sound for the position you're in but you are not in a position to go opening four overseas offices and accept deposits while you are solely dependant on a $298 million assets based in Hong Kong. If one major financial institution went belly up tomorrow morning, you may just survive, but if you have four overseas offices, you've spread your source of deposits but also your risk. If a major institution goes belly up when you have four overseas offices, you're gone. You need overseas assets quickly." Dillon observed as Maxwell shifted uneasily in his chair. From the look of realisation on the man's face, Scott instantly knew that Maxwell thought he was right.

"So what the hell do we do, sit back here and wait till '97?"

"No, you either go on the acquisition trail, or you merge."

"Boy, you're a barrel of laughs." Maxwell got up looking at his watch, it was nearly noon.

"You want a cup of coffee, or Yum Cha perhaps?"

"Jet lag hasn't quite worn off yet so coffee please."

Maxwell had his own suite just off the office and he went and put on the percolator.

Dillon took the opportunity to call Linn. He knew she'd be in her room.

"Morning." she greeted him.

"How do you feel?"

"I am getting back to normal, why did you not wake me this morning before you left?"

"Sorry but you looked so sweet and contented that I just didn't have the heart to wake you."

"Very bad, now I do not know how you look in the morning. My mama used always say, you can tell a lot about a man by how he looks and acts in the morning."

"If you had seen me this morning, you'd never want to see me again. If I looked as bad as I felt, I was bad."

"Did we pillow last night?"

"We were in the same bed, and yes, Yang met Yin." He hadn't realised she was that drunk that she couldn't remember. Or did that say something about his performance. He smiled when he remembered how she explained sex and intercourse and Chinese terms associated with such acts.

"I will be back Friday night. Do you want to see me?"

"Of course I do, what time?"

"Twenty hundred."

"Okay, I'll be at the Mandarin."

"See you then, oh, and watch those Hong Kong Ladies offering free Golden Gully." she laughed.

"And no Yang while you gone."

"Of course, may as well continue this week as I started."

"You stay sober the next time and you'll see what a right Yang looks like."

"Not worried about look, only feel." Again she erupted in wicked laughter.

"Bye." They both hung up and his mind shifted to another female, Bolger! He didn't think about her all morning but he had said he'd meet her in the Kowloon branch when she got through in City Hall.

Maxwell came back with the tray and freshly brewed coffee.

"Did you see Tina Bolger this morning?"

"No, I had a meeting with Bordes-Aitcheson this morning and didn't get here 'til 9.30. I just assumed she was already here, she usually gets here around eight. Why?"

"Nothing, I just remembered that we said we'd meet for lunch"

"I'll check." He pushed a button on the phone; his secretary answered.

"Yes sir?" the secretary's voice came across the intercom.

"Did Tina Bolger come in yet?"

"No, sir, I haven't seen her. You do remember that you have a twelve o'clock appointment, and there have been some calls you have to return."

"Okay, is Jack here yet?"

"Not yet but he did say he may be a few minutes late."

"Okay buzz me when she gets here." Maxwell straightened in his chair and sipped his coffee.

"So how do you want to handle Sing?" Dillon asked.

"Bordes-Aitcheson wants to talk to him so I guess he gets invited over to Hong Kong this evening. I'd like to be present."

"I don't see any problem in that." Dillon finished his coffee.

"So you won't be recommending us to the IMF?"

"I didn't say that, you asked me for my opinion and I gave it. As you stand right now you're fine, I would doubt your ability to withstand a run 'after' you open your overseas branches. But what I will report on is what I see now and what I see is a financially sound institution."

"You'll be obliged to put a footnote through."

"Yes I will, and it would be as I've said; unless you build up overseas assets prior to accepting deposits that you would be a high risk bank. That's what the IMF wants to know about because they would have to step in and bail you out. So yes, if you like, on a rating system of 1 to 10 I'd have to give you an eight."

"Would we be accepted on that?"

"I've seen banks accepted on a six, I've seen 'em rejected on a ten so who's to know. They may permit you to take deposits but set the guide-lines so tight that you'd be unable to expand. You may have to hold such high reserves that you would be unable to lend money at a competitive rate. You could be forced into high risk lending, the stuff the other banks turn away. You're really at their mercy."

"How do you read it, personally?"

"I've given you my best personal opinion. It's really up to you how you read it. I'm not the IMF and I really don't know how they make their decisions. But for what it's worth, you have an outside chance, maybe ten to one. But look, I'm only here a day, I may change my mind."

*

Diver Ho was first off the ferry from Macau. The quickest way to Aberdeen was the taxi, at this time of day, just before the lunch hour rush. He got into the nearest cab, the driver gave him a suspicious look and Ho shouted at him.

"Do you want your money now?"

"No, no not at all, honourable sir" And with that the driver shot off away from the pier.

Twenty minutes later Ho handed over the $27 and ran as fast as he could up the street to his house. Thankfully his mother was out shopping, only his seven year old sister was home. She was in bed with a high fever. The room that he shared with his two brothers was empty so he went straight to his bed and pulled out the old box from beneath it. Opening the box, he saw the letters where he had thrown them. Ho felt better straight away, and now he relaxed for the first time since he left Nisa Street in Macau.

He couldn't quite explain it to himself even now, but when he saw the old Locksmith boarding the ferry for Macau this morning his instincts told him to follow the old man.

He saw the Locksmith go into the bakery shop and he thought that his journey was for nothing but then he remembered that the Locksmith had come from Macau originally so he watched for a while. When he saw that the old man had gone through to the back, Ho got curious. He went along the street, until he found an alleyway going to the rear of the shops. Another alley ran along the back of the tiny gardens at the rear of the shops. He went along them until he could smell the bread. That was when he heard the voice of Ho Chan asking a question. Another old mans voice replied and then the second man continued talking, the same name being repeated many times during the conversation, 'Mad Jason' and Jason Kimberley. Then he heard Ho Chan mention the letter, which was when Diver Ho set off home as fast as he could.

Now he was looking at the letter addressed to Jason Kimberley. Diver Ho pondered on what to do. If he opened it, it was of little value.

He decided to steam the letter open like he had seen his honourable grandmother do so many times when she suspected that a letter addressed to her many sons might contain information that might be useful to her.

He returned to his bedroom and barred the door, he went and sat on the bed and withdrew the letter from the envelope. As he unfolded the paper, a stronger slip of paper much smaller that the sheet, fell to the floor. He ignored that for the moment. The sheet of paper had at its head the printed name of Bordes Wanchai Bank and underneath in smaller print, 'founded in the year 1861'. To the right was the bank's address and to the left a circular motto 'In God we place our trust'.

The letter was dated May 28th 1898. It read:

Dear Jason,

I trust that you and your good wife are in good health and that you find Macau to your liking.

I have placed the documents that you entrusted to me for safekeeping in one of our new safety deposit boxes in our bank. I have entrusted the key to the safety-deposit box in the good person of Captain Formidable Wong who has personally delivered this letter.

I must take this occasion to point out to you that these documents will be of no validity unless you speak to the Governor immediately, for a treaty is about to be signed with the Chinese within the month. I understand that the Governor is prepared to recognise Lord Lo Woks Chop on your documents and compensate you for the land.

As a friend I would advise you to accept a small payment and royalties thereafter. For in this way you can receive income from rents paid to the governor. I greatly advise you to seek a meeting with the Governor at his earliest convenience.

Formidable Wong will also have given you the three hundred sovereigns as requested being the first part of the 12,000 Guineas loan which I approve for you.

As you already know, I will be stepping down as Chairman of the board in two months time. Arthur Aitcheson will be the new Chairman of the board and the General Manager. This may come as a surprise to you but the man has the shares and there is nothing anyone can do about it.

You will therefore understand why I impress upon you the importance of you speaking to the Governor and strike a fair deal for royalties. It would be advisable for you to draw down your full loan before I step down from office.

I look forward earnestly to meeting you again.

Yours faithfully,

Geoffrey Bordes.

Ho re-read the letter several times, then he knew what he must do, he must copy the letter and give the copy to Ho Chan. That will satisfy him, but Ho could see little or no value in the contents of the letter, but perhaps others can. Diver Ho folded the letter and left the house to get it photocopied.

*

"Have you seen Bolger?" Dillon asked.

"No, I thought she was over at Kowloon," Olli replied.

They were in the Blue Heaven teahouse on Queens Road for lunch. The place was packed and noisy.

"I don't understand it; she said he'd meet me in Kowloon branch after she got through with City Hall."

Dillon had phoned Olli and asked where they could meet for lunch, Olli, with a better idea of Bolger's habits, had suggested here, for she had a crush on their Dim Sums and had gotten on well with one of the waiters, but the waiter, Johnny, had not seen her either.

"Well, we might as well eat while we're here."

"That's good for me." And they got the end of a table where three young Chinese were eating dim sum, drinking Yum Cha and rabbiting on at a wicked pace.

"You don't think anything has happened to her?" Dillon asked.

"Ah, she's a big girl. She's well able to look after herself. She's probably still stuck in some old books in City Hall."

"We'll go check after we eat." Dillon thought about his conversation this morning with Maxwell and after the food arrived, he related most of the conversation to Olli.

"He gave you Sing; do you think he's really our man, or just the scapegoat?"

"Well we'll know this evening; Sing has been invited to Bordes-Aitcheson office at 4 o'clock."

They ate in silence for a while; something was bothering Dillon all morning ever since breakfast and that was the little exchange between Tina and Olli at the Mandarin. He wanted like hell to bring the subject up with Olli, after all it had been him that began it but Bolger had cut him off. He half suspected that he know what it was, something that stood out like a sore thumb to anybody who had a close look at the bank, Maxwell knew it too. He had done business studies in the states. But none of them were quite prepared to come right out and say it.

But Dillon couldn't hold it back and wait for Olli to get around to it again.

"This bank is ripe for a take over bid."

"I thought you'd notice, and I suspect that was why Stern sent you over here."

"They didn't give me a brief to that objective but I suspect that they knew it."

"The least whiff of scandal and those shares will tumble."

"And Maxwell knows that."

"What do you make of Maxwell?"

"I think, and he thinks, he's wasted here, but he has loyalties. And he is very loyal to Bordes-Aitcheson."

"I think his father has a lot to do with that, he's a member of the board, you know."

"Who's this Archibald dude?"

"Oh he's a bad can of worms that guy, met him once, one of these self made millionaires, and proud of it. He owns a big freight company"

It was reassuring to get confirmation of Maxwell's honesty.

"How about the other board members? Are they actively involved?"

"Not really, well not that I've noticed in the two weeks I've been here, I guess Maxwell and Archibald are the most active. After that there's Sir Dennis White, he's an insurance mogul who owns Pure White Insurances and around 10% of the stock of AAB. Sir Percy Penderville who's retired was once in the Colonial Office, he's a barrister, very English. His father was a Merchant here and very powerful during the '30s until the war. He's 72 now and from what I learn, wants to return to the family ancestral home in Berkshire. He holds 7%. After that we've got Alistair McMorrow with 5%, he's got a steel manufacturing plant. Howard Humphries holds 5%, he's got Humphries Publishing here in Hong Kong. Then there's Alex Sapherio with 5% also, he's got a shipping transport business as one might expect for a Greek.That's the board, the remaining shares are held by the staff and Charlie public.

"AAB could be the target of a takeover battle then, and JR is hardly in a position to fight off an attack of share dumping to force the price down."

"Financially, the man is on the brink personally. From what I can learn he has not got a huge personal fund. While he has a lot of personal stock, he can't convert that to capital without causing exactly the type of thing he needs the money for."

"Catch'a twenty two."

"With the decimal point clearly defined."

"The question we must ask ourselves is, are we interested in this bank?"

"Should we become 'raiders'?" Olli said with a gleam in his eye.

"I think it's time we spoke to Huston Control." Dillon added.

"Let's go and find Bolger first."

*

The story that Bolger had uncovered was quite a tale, most of it had been gleaned from a press cutting dated 1897 from a report on the Crown case against Jason Kimberley for alleged assault and battery against one Cecil Proud, a sergeant in the garrison at Port Stanley on the Island of Hong Kong. One of the Chief witnesses had been one Corporal Carter, and it was this name that sparked Bolger into looking further, and in the library she had found a 1901 edition of a book called, *The Diaries of Sergeant Carter.*

The 'Diary' revealed the immediate history of Hong Kong at the time and some of the more 'colourful' characters that had lived there. There was one chapter that mentioned Jason Kimberley, telling the story of how he had arrived and the impact he made.

What sent Bolger into the library in the first place was the name Carter, for Robert Carter had continued writing books on Hong Kong up until his death in the Great War of 1914 - 1918. Carter himself was quite a colourful character. From going through some of his works, Bolger had learnt that the man had quite a sense of humour and it was this ability to trivialise the most serious situations that had got him a position writing for *Punch Magazine* at the time.

He took life as he saw it and wrote about it in a very light-hearted fashion.

During Bolger's stay in Hong Kong she had browsed through many bookshops looking for old work and she had often seen the name Robert Carter so when she saw the name Corporal Carter, she put one and one together and came up with, 'chance'.

There it was, after much searching she finally found reference to Jason Kimberley.

She had found the missing link, the mystery as to why the bank had given him what was at the time, a huge loan. She had photocopied all the relevant references and the chapter on Jason Kimberley and Bolger was about to leave the library when she saw the one face that he hoped she'd never see again, the Chinese guy from the underground and didn't know how long he was there. The library was almost overcrowded, with students and other people either checking references or taking out books. She was at a loss as to what to do. If she left here now where should she go? To the Mandarin hopefully to meet Dillon who might be having lunch there. Or to the Kowloon branch but that would mean using the underground or the ferry and she did not fancy the idea of being in an enclosed area with this man for any length of time.

The other alternative was to go straight to the bank, it was a ten to fifteen minute walk and the bank would be open now after lunch. After much deliberation, the nervous woman decided that the best course of action was to head for the bank and meet a policeman, so the best she could do was head for the Bank and hope to meet a cop.

Bolger gathered her stuff together and headed towards the exit. She couldn't be sure either way if the tail had realised that he had been spotted, but right now the important thing was to keep with the crowd and not give this guy any opportunity to do anything stupid.

Bolger had never been in a position like this before; she was an accountant, not a tough person who would revel in this type of thing. For someone who had inadvertently become involved in the dangerous situation, she felt proud of the way she composed herself.

Now the tail was out of sight behind her and this was the time that she feared most. She couldn't see the guy, so he could be three feet behind or 30. If 30, she could live with it but if three then the guy could reach out with a knife.

Bolger broke her line and went along the wall of the corridor that led to the big open staircase. When she got to the top of the stairwell she began to move quite rapidly, then she spotted Dillon and Olli heading into the hall of records. She wanted to shout but more than anything else she wanted this guy stopped. Continuing down the stairs at a fast pace and reached the bottom, just as Dillon and Olli entered the hall of records. When the woman reached the entrance, she saw that the two men were ten feet away from her. They were obviously scanning the hall for Bolger.

She came within a few feet of them and said, "Don't look around."

Olli was about to turn around when he recognised Bolger's voice but the words stopped him.

"I'm still being followed. If you stand still, I'll walk ahead. The guy is wearing a black top and trousers, and he's square faced. For Christ sake catch him." Then Bolger moved past them heading into the hall.

Dillon felt exposed where he was out in the middle of the entrance; he touched Olli and motioned him towards the wall. Dillon leaned against the wall and just watched the passing crowd, spotting the guy immediately. He came to a halt opposite them and looked into the hall, for a moment he appeared nervous as he scanned the area but then he appeared to see Bolger and relaxed.

Dillon went straight across to him and hit him once with his knuckles into the side of the neck. The man gasped for air, his knees buckled and he dropped to all fours. What Dillon had done was hit the nerves and blood vessels that supplied the co-ordination and blood to the brain. The guy was effectively paralyzed and for five to ten minutes, he would be unable to walk. Dillon picked him up; Olli joined him after having caught Bolger's attention. Between them they carried the guy out. A few passers-by glanced at them but they had seen and heard of so many undercover police operations, that they paid no attention to them.

Bolger joined them as they reached the street. Dillon nodded right and they went towards the waters edge about 50 yards away. The guy was just about able to move his head, and when they held him over the protective railing he turned to look at Dillon. Olli backed away and together with Bolger, stood looking on.

There were a lot of people around but nobody interfered.

Dillon had his left arm over the guy's throat pushing him backward over the railing. He was completely off balance and held on to the railings with both hands, it was only fifteen foot drop, but a drop onto the rocks at the waters edge.

"Name?" Dillon asked. The Chinese just starred at him. Dillon brought his right fist down in a vicious arc and hit the guy in the stomach.

"Name?"

"Wei-Ming, please why do you do this?"

"Why are you following this girl?" Dillon let him up far enough to see Bolger, and then he pushed him back again.

"No, not follow."

Dillon hit him again. "Why?" Dillon snarled.

"Job, just job, get paid to watch, no more. Very sorry, no do again." There was genuine fear in the man's eyes now.

"Who paid you?"

"No please, I will die."

"That's right, you will die if you don't tell me." Dillon hit him again. "Who paid you?"

"Please, no more, I tell you. Jason Kim."

The shock was so unexpected that Dillon relaxed; the little guy broke free of Dillon's grip and made a run for it. Dillon stared at Olli and Tina.

"Jason Kim he said, did you hear?"

They nodded.

"So what, who's Kim?" Olli asked.

"It was the 'Jason' part." Tina said.

"Jason Kim, short for Kimberley." Dillon suggested.

"Precisely."

CHAPTER SIX

The trio of Dillon, Tina and Olli, were in the disused attic room on the third floor of the bank building. They had come directly here after the incident at City Hall. After some discussion it was decided to do nothing more about Wei-Ming if that was his name, until after the interview with John Sing later this afternoon. Bolger told them what he had learnt about the real Jason Kimberley.

"He had arrived in Hong Kong in 1861 at the age of 23 on board a ship with others who had come for the new life in the New World. Also on board the same ship was a man called Geoffrey Bordes whose father had founded one of the first banks in Hong Kong.

Jason Kimberley was by trade a civil engineer. Although most of his lifetime, he did something completely different. He took a job overseeing a warehouse building project in Canton. Canton was a particularly rough place in those days with just about every nationality under the sun visiting that city as it was the active centre of the world for opium, silk and tea trade. Jason got quite a reputation as a fighter there, and particularly with the off duty British soldiers.

It was during his stay in Canton that he met a Chinese prince, by the name of Lo Wok.

At that time, the Ruler of Canton was the Emperor Lo Wok, a good fighting general in his day but now in his seventies he was grooming his mature son for power. The Prince was 38 years of age and had seven children.

A few years before this the Chinese and Russians engaged in a skirmish on the border and the Russians held an area known as Kuldja. According to the best written report I can find, the Russians were minding this province for the Chinese until such time as the Chinese themselves were able to maintain order. Apparently, an agreement was signed in 1879 and the Russians gave it back for five million roubles. The Chinese got taken every side, and had to pay disturbance when land was given back to them. Emperor Lo-wok thought this downright wrong when he heard about it and set about making sure that if anybody else tried to take any part of China, that at least the rest of China would know about it.

So he sent his number one son off to organise something he had just heard about, the telegraph. Prince Lo-Wok had been watching the foreign devils dealing in Canton for many years and he didn't trust any of them as far as he would throw them. Then, as the Chinese have a way of talking, he heard about this Scottish devil that picked fights with the British soldiers and must have thought that he was the number one man to talk to. He was surprised to find that Jason Kimberley could not only talk Cantonese, the native dialect but also was a Civil Engineer. Kimberley was only too glad to work for Lo-Wok to help usurp the British Dominance.

Kimberly took the task in hand and provided the first telegraph, linking Tientsin and Shanghai. But more importantly, he taught the Chinese labour forces how to continue linking more cities, this was 1881.

After 1882 Kimberley became a thorn in the trader's side by setting up a customs service for Lord Lo-Wok. He harassed them and drove them crazy by excising levies for the unloading of ships and he took a particular dislike to the opium trade. At one stage a price was put on his head by one of the Tia Pan. But he survived. Lord Lo-Wok gave him one of his youngest daughters in marriage and gave him title deeds to the New Territories as payment for services rendered and for stopping the opium trade by means of increasing the levies.

He fell foul of the law in Hong Kong in the early summer of 1898. This was the year of the Treaty. According to the court report, Jason Kimberley had been to the bank, it wasn't stated which bank but because of his friendship with Geoffrey Bordes, one would assume it was the Bordes Wanchai Bank. Bordes would have been chairman of the Bank for some years at this stage.

After he left the bank, he went to a drinking house, where there were some off duty soldiers.

Words were exchanged; references were made to the China Rat and ass-licker and so on. Tempers flared and blows were struck. The fight continued into the street and there a Sergeant Proud happened to come upon the ruckus. Sergeant Proud, no doubt having heard of Jason Kimberley, just battered the Scot, assured that this would be the end of the matter. But Kimberley didn't go down; he cut into Proud with a vengeance. The sergeant was beaten near to death as were the three soldiers from the drinking house. More soldiers arrived and they overwhelmed Kimberley.

He was taken straight before a magistrate and promptly sentenced to one year imprisonment.

On his way to the jailhouse, he broke free and made it to Aberdeen where he hired a boat to take him to Macau. He never again set foot in Hong Kong. One month later the Treaty was signed and the British had the New Territories for 99 years. It was said that Kimberley went mad and eventually died in 1906."

"So that explains the ledger error. I think the loan was approved but never drawn down, because the poor devil couldn't set foot in Hong Kong to pick it up."

"Well the poor bugger." Dillon said.

"That certainly lays that ghost to rest." Olli added.

"He must have had children though."

"What difference does it make now? It would only be raking over old ashes"

"There might still be a glimmer of a hope there." Bolger said.

"How's that?" Olli enquired.

"Well the lands going back to China, the ruler of which made a gift of the new territories to Jason Kimberley. I think they could have a case for owning that land after the lease to Britain expires."

"If Jason Kimberley has direct descendant still alive and those title deeds can be found and prove valid, then his heirs would own the land and they in turn could lease it back to Britain and Hong Kong. We know it could continue to operate just as it has these last one hundred and fifty years."

"Stock would soar, fortunes would be made" Olli pointed out.

"But, how do we know that the Chinese would accept the deeds? They could just say, 'stiff shit we don't recognise them.'"

"This is an area for International Law, and I would think that the first priority is to locate those deeds." Olli said.

"Just hold on a minute now, where does this leave *us*?" Bolger had other ideas.

"Okay say we find those deeds and locate the heirs, and then the case is tested in International Law. Now one of the first things to happen is the stock market will recover and probably gain ground. If the case is proven good then everybody is happy and Hong Kong continues. Bordes-Aitcheson keeps his bank and may or may not open branches overseas, that's the scenario right?"

"That would be my reading of it, yes" Olli agreed.

"Where do we fit into all this, we did uncover this after all? What's in it for us?"

"Ah ha! I see what you mean. What do you suggest?"

"A flutter on the stock market." Dillon prompted.

"And if it doesn't come off, we'd more than likely lose money."

"Not necessarily," Olli thought out loud. "If we buy now, then leak the information stocks sore, then we unload having made a nice profit."

"Would that be legal?"

"Speculation, that's what the stock market is all about."

"Now hold on, we're getting a little side tracked here. Don't forget what we were sent here for. Now if we indulge in a little speculation on the side then that's fine, but let's remember that we came here to do a job, and we do get paid to carry out orders. So can we get back to that?"

"I'm sorry but I don't agree. We may have stumbled onto the greatest opportunity we'll ever get in our lives, and we do owe it to Bordes-Aitcheson. He has, after all, hired the services of WTB and is paying for that service. I'm not suggesting that we go along and lay all this on the table but I do think that it is incumbent on us to pursue the matter further. After all if the deeds do exist and we do nothing about checking them out, then I think we've done a great disservice to the people of Hong Kong.

There are perhaps a million people here who will have to up their homes and move out because they fear the Chinese, and we could have done something to help them, but didn't? We have to look for the deeds and we have to trace Jason Kimberley's ancestors. We have to see if they exist. And, I, for one will not walk away from that. Okay this may sound like shit, but millions of people go through life without making any impression on history and they're forgotten about within a year. This is our chance to leave our mark on history."

"Tina I never knew you felt that way." Olli was not very serious about the tone of voice he used.

"Screw you too but I'm going to chase this."

"Okay, but let's not forget why we're here. Let's get this thing with John Sing over with. See what reaction he has to the name of that dude at City Hall. Then we contact Stern with an interim report and ask for guidance on whether or not to pursue shares in the bank. I suggest we don't mention this Kimberley thing to anybody for the time being. At least until we find those deeds. Okay?"

*

Locksmith Ho Chan tried to concentrate on his work but was unable to get anything done. He wanted to see that letter. He decided to tell Diver Ho what he had learnt in the hope that the young man would understand his need to see the letter. Now sitting down in his back room he told him the tale.

"Tranquillity was something that Jason Kimberley did not achieve. From the time he moved to Macau, things began to go wrong for him. After spending 17 years in China as Lord Lo-Wok's right hand man, he had gotten used to the idea of having menial tasks carried out for him. He never had to worry about having a house for he had lived in the Imperial Palace together with Lord Lo-Wok. Eating and sleeping there meant he never had to worry about money. When he moved to the lands in the New Territories he had begun the foundations for the new house he was going to build. His wife had a dowry for running the home but this was used to buy materials and pay labour. The truth of his situation was beginning to dawn on him when he was asked to go to Macau.

Seeing this as an opportunity to collect some wealth he moved to Macau and set up a customs service. But his fame had preceded him and the Portuguese were far more careful in dealing with him.

Nevertheless, he gathered a sizeable amount of money. In the winter of 1897, a French trader whom he knew quite well, arrived into port; his riggings gone and masts badly damaged. He had sailed out of Haipong, the main port of Hanoi, bound for Shanghai and had got caught in a storm just south of Macau the night before. The Frenchman was an independent, and owner captain and of limited resources. He told Kimberley that he had a return cargo from Shanghai to Macau and expected to be back in a month. His ship was insured but doubted that the money would come through fast enough to get him repaired and under way in time to meet the deadline for delivery to Shanghai. He assured Kimberley that his insurance money would be paid within a month if only he could get repaired immediately. Kimberley believed him and organised the repairs. He was surprised by the amount of money it cost and he had to borrow a further 300 gold sovereigns to complete the deal. He got receipts for all the work carried out and personally sent them to the insurance company in Hong Kong.

Within the week the insurance company wrote back saying as Kimberley was not the recognised ship builder that no monies could be paid until such time as they had heard from the insured. They never did and the Frenchman failed to show in Macau. Kimberley was furious particularly with the insurance company and despite visits to their offices and threats of a court action, they refused to pay.

To make matters worse, the 300 gold sovereigns that Kimberley borrowed, he was unable to repay with great loss of face and personal humiliation. Kimberley tried everywhere to get the 300 gold sovereigns to repay the loan but even the banks turned him down. He tried the Portuguese traders but in a place the size of Macau, word spread fast and he was turned down by those who had profited from his organization. Jason found it impossible to function in the customs service for the traders; even the Chinese traders had lost respect for him. He was finally asked to leave the customs service which he did with regret but also with the great personal anger and resentment.

He died slowly after that, it took eight years, the last two bedridden and raving. Only his beloved Lo Xian and his three children stood by him. She was a good wife to him, at all times supporting his decisions proud of the help he gave to China. She could walk so tall in those days and she accepted the kowtows that she received in admiration of her husband.

When things went wrong for him, she suggested that they move back to Canton, but he couldn't crawl back there humiliated to beg assistance from his former friend's son and her brother.

But now after Kimberley's death things, sadly, were different. She took the three children and went back humbly to her brother in Canton. Politically, Lo Xian couldn't have gone at a worse time. The whole country was in turmoil; the monarchy system of leadership was coming to an end. Her brother could do nothing for her except give her safe passage to Hong Kong and some money to help her out. Lo Xian made the best of what she had and soon discovered that she had an unexpected talent, fluent English. All those years with Kimberley, she never thought twice about learning English but through the years she had picked it up out of habit.

Her children were not marked as Chinese; they had round eyes so she fared better than most in Hong Kong. Lo Xian changed her name to Kim from Kimberley, not as a mark of disrespect to her husband but for the future of her children. So it was that in 1908 at the age of six that Siever Kim enrolled in school in Aberdeen in Hong Kong.

As the young boy grew up, Lo Xian Kim told him about his father and what he had done for China and how the British had cheated him of his land. The boy was eager to learn and he grew strong and red haired like Jason. She had gotten a job with a shipping company as a filing clerk and could afford to send him to college and on to the University of Hong Kong.

Baker Yim explained that he knew this to be true, for one day in 1927, Lo Xian walked into a shop in Macau. Yim was so surprised to see her that he unceremoniously asked her where she had been. She explained that she had a secret love for Yim's bread as Jason would take some home to her after his regular visits.

She spoke openly of their new life for now her pride was rebuilt in the form of her son who had just graduated from University with a business degree. Lo Xian was fifty one years of age at that time though she looked twenty years younger with the pride she wore. That was the last Baker Yim heard of the Kimberley's."

"So now do you see the importance of the contents of the letter and why I would dearly love to read it?"

"Yes Honourable cousin I understand. I will let you see the letter when we have concluded our deal"

The Locksmith cursed under his breath, he had feared this, he feared that Diver Ho would look for payment, damn his greed.

CHAPTER SEVEN

At precisely 4 o'clock John Sing was shown into Bordes-Aitcheson's office. Dillon and Maxwell were already there.

"Ah, John," Bordes-Aitcheson greeted him in a very business-like tone and waved him to a chair.

Sing nodded to Maxwell and Dillon, and then turned to face the chairman.

"I guess this must be important."

"I think it is, John." Bordes-Aitcheson opened a file on his desk and read from it for a moment and Sing looked nervous while Bordes-Aitcheson was reading. Bordes-Aitcheson closed the file and started at Sing.

"We got a problem, John. As you know we've got people in at the moment from WTB. Now apparently, Tina Bolger found some old ledgers which in themselves are not terribly important. But what happened afterwards made the ledgers seem more important than they actually were. Tina Bolger was followed from Kowloon last evening. It could have been a once off incident, a misunderstanding even. But this morning one of the same 'followers' showed up again this time at City Hall where Tina was doing some research. Luckily, Scott here was able to apprehend the culprit and found out his name."

They watched Sing for a reaction but there was none.

"This was instigated by a senior member of my staff and I'm going to have to take action to ensure that it never happens again."

"Perfectly understandable, I agree." Sing replied, his face bearing a look of curiosity..

"I'm going to have to ask for your resignation, John. Have it on my desk by five tomorrow evening." Bordes-Aitcheson said bluntly.

Sing still appeared quite calm and unaffected by all this. "Why should I resign?" He emphasised the "I" to indicate his surprise.

83

"I will not have members of my staff taking this type of action. You should have come to me and reported the matter."
"I know nothing of this." Sing insisted, but still the face showed no real surprise.
"Tom" Bordes-Aitcheson invited Maxwell to do his piece.
"Why did Archibald visit the Kowloon branch Monday evening around 5.30?" he enquired, his voice low and restrained.
"I don't know." Sing replied, now looking at Maxwell.
"You let him in. You should know, you were talking to him"
"He, ah, came over. I, ah, don't know why he came over." Sing seemed a little ruffled now; he stirred uneasily in his chair.
"Come on, John, the guy arrives well after closing time, you let him in, you talked to him and you're trying to tell me you don't know why he came over?" There was restrained anger in Tom's voice.
"Ah, he, I guess he was just passing and dropped in."
"I checked with his secretary, he was in his office all afternoon until 5 o'clock. He leaves his office crosses over to Kowloon in the rush hour, drops into the bank, and comes straight back here for a 6.30 appointment at his office. Now come on, John." Maxwell said.
"I don't know why he came over" Sing insisted.
"What did you talk about?" Maxwell persisted.
"Just general conversation, nothing in particular."
"Did you mention the ledgers?"
"No." But Sing looked hatefully as Maxwell persisted.
"Just general conversation, nothing in particular."
"Did you mention the ledgers?" Maxwell repeated.
Sing looked across the desk to Bordes-Aitcheson, he ignored Maxwell. He came forward in the chair and an expression appeared on his face that said, 'let's talk this out man to man'.
"I didn't know what to do, Jeff, honestly. Yes I told him that Tina Bolger found the ledgers, he said 'don't worry about it, I'll take care of it'. I didn't think he was going to do anything like that, not have Tina Bolger followed. I was going to tell you. I

had only found out a short while earlier. I was waiting until six, I knew you'd be at home then I was going to phone you. You know how I hate that phone system we got, you hit the wrong button and anyone of about ten extensions can listen in on the conversation, but when I mentioned it to him, he said don't worry about it. So I just assumed he would tell you. That's the truth Jeff"

Dillon watched Bordes-Aitcheson for his reaction, it wasn't short in coming.

"I'm sorry, John. I've made my decision, and I never go back on a decision. Have your resignation on my desk at close of business tomorrow evening." Bordes-Aitcheson stood up and waited for Sing to leave.

Sing just sat there open mouthed looking up at Bordes-Aitcheson. He was dumbfounded, he glanced at Maxwell but the man made no effort to help Sing. Slowly he rose, then as much to himself as anyone in the office he said quietly.

"I've given eight years of my life to this bank. I can't believe what you're doing to me! He was a member of the board; I thought I did the right thing. I was sure he had told you." Then Sing turned and walked across the office, opened the door and went out, closing the door quietly after him.

There was total silence; nobody knew what to say so nobody said anything. Bordes-Aitcheson sat down heavily.

"Well that's that then."

Dillon just looked at him for a moment, and then shook his head turned and left the office. Maxwell followed him out.

In the lobby area just outside Bordes-Aitcheson's office, sat his personal secretary, Kay Herbert. She had heard the news from Sing she motioned Maxwell over.

"He's not in a good mood, is he Tom?" Kay Herbert asked.

"I guess not, not just now anyway."

"George Archibald rang. He was fishing but I suspected that he knew that John sing was here. He rang right after four."

"That is a coincidence. Did he say anything in particular, did he want something?"

"He just asked what Jeff's appointments were for the evening. When I told him he just had one at 5 o'clock, he said he might drop by."

"I wouldn't mention that to Jeff. And I would try and prevent Archibald from seeing him."

"I'll see what I can do"

"Will you phone Maylay over at Kowloon and tell her I won't be back this evening and to advise Sing of that."

Maxwell knew he should stay in the bank until Sing left but he couldn't really face him. He had expected Jeff to back down when Sing told him the truth of what happened and he was surprised at the viciousness of the decision. He had never seen Jeff so cold hearted before and it was quite frightening.

From time to time, every member of staff had to make instant decisions on matters that arose in the course of the day and judgments had to be made. You try to make the right decisions obviously, but sometime you will be wrong, but at all times you do what is best at the time. John Sing couldn't really refuse to pass on the ledger information to Archibald because he was a member of the board. But what really bothered Maxwell was that there was a member of staff in his bank who had phoned Archibald and because John Sing had told Archibald about the find instead of the real informant. Sing was asked to resign and the real informant was sitting pretty. Maxwell knew deep down that this was the wrong course of action to take and had a gut feeling that something was afoot. He sought out Ruxton and enquired as to where Dillon went. The important thing now was to find the mole and Dillon could help.

Ruxton was right, he found Dillon in the tea room on the second floor together with Olli and Tina.

"I did a good job on Sing." Maxwell said as he poured himself a coffee. He was aware that a conversation had been in progress when he entered, it had been abandoned now.

"Not your fault, you saw what you saw." Dillon replied, but there was a tone in his voice that implied that Maxwell had made a mistake.

"What really bugs me is that there's somebody over there that must have phoned Archibald and the bastard is still there."

"That's what we were just talking about." Olli said.

"We were trying to figure out who knew Tina had found the ledgers."

"Ling Chi was in the file room when I brought them from the basement. She came over and looked at them and we talked about them. She said she had never seen them before, she always thought they were lost, and she would know because she filed the other ledgers. Now she was surprised to see them and I hadn't noticed the thing about Kimberley, so I didn't know enough about them to have said to her to say nothing, if your follow me."

"So she could have told everybody in the bank."

"Not really. It was after lunch and we had coffee in the file room at 3.30 and I don't think she left the file room all afternoon. Maybe to go to the loo? No, I don't think she told anybody that afternoon. It was the following morning, Jesus that's yesterday, that I got the impression it was public knowledge. But Archibald came that Monday evening."

"So somebody else had to know, and Sing knew Monday evening" Dillon said.

"So if it wasn't Ling…" He thought for a moment. "Did anybody see you taking the ledgers up to the file room?"

"No I'm certain of that. See when I found them in the safe-"

"How did you open it?" Dillon interrupted.

"I got the key from the secretary-" Tina looked at Maxwell, "Maylay - Anyhow I thought I wasn't supposed to have found them so I made sure that nobody saw me"

Tina's voice trailed off and they stared at Maxwell.

"What are you thinking? Maylay? Never. She's been with me for years."

"Hey, now that I come to think of it Maylay brought us up coffee, well me, coffee and she never did that before. I just thought at the time it was a polite way of getting the key back cause I'd forgotten to give it to her."

"My God and I trust that woman with everything"

"You have two people over there this evening that you can't trust right now, Sing and Maylay"

"I'd better get back there" Maxwell got up and hurried out.

Maxwell made a rapid departure and when he was gone, Olli said, "Jesus you've got to feel for the guy. There he was convicting John Sing while the woman he trusted knifed him in the back."

"Let's not convict her yet, she may turn out to be another Sing"

"No, now that I've thought about it, she hung around for quiet a while in the file room talking to me and looking at the ledger. She even asked me when they were for. After she left, Ling Chi even said that she must be fishing to hang around that long, cos Maylay was normally a cold old fish."

Dillon interrupted them, "Did you have any luck tracking down those deeds?"

"No, apparently all pre-war files are kept over in the Kowloon branch, except of course active ones"

"Okay then we check that in the morning." Dillon suggested.

"What are you going to do about reporting to Stern?"

"I'll phone him tonight."

Before anything else could be said, Mister Ruxton arrived.

"Ah, there you are. Mister Bordes-Aitcheson would like to see you in his office" he said to Dillon.

"Okay, I'll be right there." When Ruxton had left Dillon said,

"Will I catch you guys later in the Mandarin?"

"Yeah Okay, around 5.30 we just got some stuff to finish off here and we're through for the day."

*

Diver Ho was extremely pleased with himself, the compass and sextant fetched far more that he thought. He had first brought his treasure to an antiques dealer. Upon examination, he discovered that the sextant was once the property of the great 'Man O' War', the 'Earl of Gloucester' commissioned in 1775. The 'Earl' was sunk in 1810 but the sextant was saved. It was later used by Captain James Blowfield in the merchant ship, 'Emerald' which was scrapped in 1845 in Macau. From then until Diver Ho found it, its whereabouts were unknown. Obviously it had come into the possession of Formidable Wong.

The Antiques dealer had offered Ho $10,000. Ho said he'd think about it and immediately brought it to an Auctioneer who placed a value of $15,000 on it. Ho paid a visit to quite a few antique dealers and took the highest bid which was $14,500. The Marine Compass fetched $5,000, so already before selling the gold sovereigns, Ho had received nearly $20,000.

He also got a few valuations on the gold sovereigns and was somewhat disappointed by what he heard. The best price he was offered for the 1896 gold sovereigns was $950. Somewhat angered by this, he contacted the friend who had told him last evening that they were worth $1,800 each.

The error was in the year of the mint, his friend had heard of someone getting $1,800 for a 1793 sovereign. But obviously the antiquity value was greater, there were fewer 1793's in circulation. So despite his pleasure with the sale of the compass and sextant, he was disappointed with his gold sovereigns.

Nevertheless, he had made an agreement with Ho Chan, so now at 4.30, he climbed the stairs to the Locksmith's shop. Apprentice Chan showed Diver Ho through to the work area at the rear of the shop. They exchanged pleasantries and sat down facing one another.

"Have you made arrangement for the sale of the sovereigns?"

"I have indeed." Ho Chan replied proudly.

"It was with great effort that I found a reputable dealer who will purchase the entire 300 in one lot and promised not to disclose the source from which he purchased. So you need have no concern about enquires tracing back to you."

"And what price might I expect?"

"Unfortunately, the price of gold has fallen somewhat in recent years because of the rise in the value of the accursed American Dollar, so the value of the sovereign has fallen relatively. A miserable $937 each, for a total of $281,000. I must apologise for giving you dishonourable impression that I could get you $1,000 each"

Diver Ho thought this over, it was not as bad as he expected for he knew that if the going rate was a miserable $950 then the dealer must have percentage. But then did he not ask 'how much you pay?' for gold sovereign. Should he not ask 'how much you want?' But how could he, one Chinaman sell 300 gold sovereigns to tourist who would pay top price. How would he find them? He could be months trying to sell all 300.

"Most disappointing, but like life passing by, if I hold them for more money, every dollar more I get, I would lose equal amount if not more in lost income from invisible earning."

"You will make honourable deposit in bank then?"

"Yes, for sometime, until golden gates of opportunity open."

"I feel that I have dishonoured my agreement with you because of the miserable price," Ho Chan wanted to get the conversation around to the letters, but first a little humiliation, "So I would understand if you wished to re-negotiate my commission."

Diver Ho was caught off guard and immediately replied, "You have done as good as was possible, I also checked the prices and find that your price is good" He had no sooner said it when he realised that he could gladly have cut his tongue out for such an opportunity missed.

"Ah honourable cousin, you are truly a civilized person but in all common decency, I have lost much face because of my inability to conclude the best deal as per our agreement. You must allow me to regain face; I humbly insist that we re-negotiate percentage."

Diver Ho could not believe his luck, he expected Ho Chan to include that letter in the re-negotiation and Ho was fully prepared to include it, for he could not see any importance in it. Perhaps Ho Chan had changed his mind also. Perhaps after Diver Ho left his listening post during Ho Chan's and Baker Yim's conversation, they had decided that the contents of the letter were not that important after all.

"Very well, the Elder cousin, we shall negotiate. What do you suggest?" Diver Ho reluctantly agreed.

"Ten percent."

Of course Diver Ho could not argue with whatever was said for Ho Chan was already humbled. He politely bowed his acceptance of the new percentage.

"And the letter?" Locksmith Ho Chan suggested meekly.

"Ah, now we have arrived at the most precious point, the answer to your question is yes. I will sell the letter to the highest bidder."

"Who else could possibly be interested in the letter?" Ho Chan enquired puzzlement on his face.

"Well there is the bank itself, the present chairman is a direct descendant of the man who signed the letter. Then there is Jason Kimberley's children's, children."

"How much do you want for the letter?" There was a look of regret on the old man's face after asking the question.

"Forty thousand dollars." Diver Ho said quickly.

"That is far more than it is worth. Phooey, you will not get that much, so sorry, but if you were to reduce my percentage to nine, then perhaps we could deal."

"Reduce it to three would be better, then you would receive over $8,000 for the sovereign deal, and the letter for free" Ho Chan was thinking it over and Diver Ho became impatient, threatening to leave.

"So sorry, never mind, will see if I can do better else where."

"Please," Ho Chan humbly begged, "Please sit down, I'm sure that you would not deny your family duty by first offering your humble cousin the chance to correct his mistake and offer to accept five percent for sale of sovereign and letter to be thrown in free."

"So sorry, honourable cousin, but 3.5 percent is my limit."

They finally agreed on 4 percent. Ho Chan phoned Antiquity Chang and told him that they had reached agreement and that they would be both over to him at six o' clock. Ho went to retrieve the sovereigns and the letter from their hiding place.

*

Maxwell let himself in with his key rather than ringing the bell which would have informed all the staff that someone was coming. The counter staff was at their desks finishing the day's balance sheets. As he went behind the counter he felt eyes examining him. By now they would have heard of Sing's dismissal, if Sing had returned to the bank. From the cold, angry and fearful looks that he received, he knew Sing had returned.

Harry Lee was the senior teller and he approached. "Is it true about Sing, that he's been dismissed?" There was a look of disbelief on Lee's face.

"He's been asked to resign, yes."

Lee shook his head not understanding. Maxwell realised that he would have to speak to the staff and explain to them what happened, just in case malicious rumours would circulate and bad feelings were created.

"Look, can you tell everybody to keep quite about this until after we have a staff meeting in the morning. I don't want any gossip to start about what's happened. If a wrong story started around town, it could damage the bank."

"Why not do it now, make sure no gossip starts?" Lee countered.

"Is Sing in the building?"

"He came a short while ago but left again, just before you got here."

"Okay, get everyone into the tea room and I'll be up in ten minutes." Maxwell headed for his office.

Maylay was at her desk; she almost jumped when she saw him, and she got to her feet and said,

"Ah, Mister Maxwell, I got a call from Kay saying that you wouldn't be back this evening."

"Can I see you in my office? Please." He waved her in.

Maylay was 47. She was one of those dowager types, probably a pretty woman in her younger days but dedicated herself to work to the detriment of all else. She wore her hair in an unfashionable bun at the back of her head, but the one thing that he had always admired her for was her efficiency. She planned his calendar better than he could do himself and he had long ago reached the stage where he did not have to plan his day. His usual request to her was, 'what do I have to do next'. She set out his free time; she loaded his appointments to suit his schedule without having to ask.

And now he gazed at this woman who treated him like a son and knew he had to fire her because she betrayed him.

"Why the hell didn't you tell me about the ledgers, instead of calling that dickhead, Archibald?" He saw her shoulders slump and knew it was true. Her eyes went from his and she stared at her hands in her lap. Maylay didn't answer.

"Maylay, you've been here longer than I have, and I can tell you that it hurts me,"

He couldn't even begin to string his thoughts together properly, "Jesus Christ, what the hell were you thinking of woman? Who the hell do you think you are that you'd go and phone that, that idiot, that damn fool? Your responsibility is to me, not to Archibald."

She got to her feet, suddenly poised, "I think it would be better if we had this conversation in the morning when you have cooled down."

"My God, woman, you have some nerve!" He felt the chains snap one by one that bound them together and he knew that his hope was forlorn, that somehow she could justify her actions and he wouldn't have to fire her. "You will sit down and explain to me why, why you felt you had to tell Archibald." He stared at her; she stared back but didn't sit.

"If you really must know, then I will tell you. George Archibald is the only member of the board that has the future of this bank close to his heart. He recognises that the way forward it to place more Chinese in position of Senior Management. He fought to get John Sing his position here and you have always resented his appointment. George Archibald should be the chairman of the board and not Jeff. Jeff's grandfather forced his way into this bank and he destroyed a lot of people."

"What the hell are you talking about?" Maxwell couldn't grasp what she was saying; he had never noticed any great affiliation for George in her before.

"I'm talking about Arthur Aitcheson, the lecherous half person who unseated Jeffery Bordes as chairman of this bank in 1898 and reneged on deals written down in those ledgers. He dishonoured commitments entered into by Jeffery Bordes and he set out to destroy Bordes' connection with this bank. He drove Bordes crazy and into an early grave. But luckily Bordes had the foresight to bring his brother out from England to take his place on the board and he fought Aitcheson until Aitcheson finally died. And it's Aitcheson's grandson that runs this bank today. And until such time as that man is unseated from the board this bank will never be right, will never be trustworthy. George Archibald knows that and he will fight to right those wrongs."

Maxwell was taken aback at her angry outburst, but he couldn't for the life of him figure out what the connection was.

"What the hell has this got to do with the ledgers?"

"You still don't understand, although you know what makes those ledgers special-"

"The only thing special about them was a loan that never was." Maxwell interrupted.

"You're wrong, the loan that was stolen, Jeffery Bordes approved a loan for Jason Kimberley and Arthur Aitcheson stole that money, he never gave him the loan, but kept the money for himself and told no one. Jason Kimberley died a madman unable to understand why the money never came"

"That was over 80 years ago, what's that got to do with it now?"

"You really are very foolish Tom Maxwell, the whole thing is very much alive, you see,"

She spat out what her mother swore her never to reveal, "I'm Jason Kimberley's granddaughter, we promised to vindicate our grandfather, my father before me tried and died. Ah," she snapped,

"This is not worth the effort!" She turned on her heel, she had achieved her greatest moment, she strode out of the office.

Maxwell was left staring at the door trying to figure it out, how could Maylay Dulles be Jason Kimberley's granddaughter?

CHAPTER EIGHT

Bordes-Aitcheson looked like a worried man when Dillon went into his office.

"Drink?" Bordes-Aitcheson enquired, he was decidedly edgy and he failed for some time to meet Dillon's eyes.

"Yes I could do with a stiff brandy myself. It's been one hell of an eventful day."

"Of course, you've had your troubles too" Bordes-Aitcheson brought the bottle of brandy to the desk. He poured two stiff measures and gave Dillon his.

"Health."

"And peace of mind." Dillon replied, wondering if he should tell Bordes-Aitcheson about what they had learned of Jason Kimberley.

"You think I was rather harsh with John Sing?" It was more a statement than a question. Dillon decided not to reply. "It was harsh but there's more to this than you know, my decision to dismiss Sing was not just related to the incident of the ledgers" Bordes-Aitcheson sipped his brandy and finally allowed himself to stare at Dillon.

"I understand from Tom Maxwell that you have your doubts about our acceptance by the IMF. I suspected as much myself. It was perhaps a forlorn hope that we would be accepted as we are without having to change the very nature of our direction. However, now I realise that we must change, that we must expand our investment base, that we must go on an acquisition program. For our own safety, we increase our assets to force our share value up to a realistic level" Bordes-Aitcheson said thoughtfully, he continued. "This has been a source of concern to me for some time, but as you know, the acquisition trial is a minefield. One wrong move and bang, we're gone, and therein lies the biggest threat. If our shares drop we are left wide open to a concerted take over bid. I've known for some time that an effort was made to buy out a major stake in our bank. Luckily I had the funds to stem the price drop and bought up as many shares as I could afford. Despite that an outside investment company was able to buy up to eight percent of our stock. The result of that '83 attempt was that I was forced to purchase stock to a total of 40% of all issued shares. I'm in no doubt that it was an unfriendly bid and someone in the guise of an Investment Company, was attempting to purchase a major stake with a view to take over. I've never been able to learn who's behind the other company but I know that whoever it is, is just waiting for another fall in value to make another attempt, and I suspect that George Archibald would not be unsympathetic to such a bid. John Sing is a personal friend of Archibald and his appointment was steamrolled through the board by Archibald. His appointment was undeniably meant to weaken my authority so you must understand that it was not the ledger incident alone that forced me to dismiss Sing. This is my way of reasserting my authority and proving Archibald wrong before the board for all to see."

He finished the contents of the glass and poured some more.

"Nice scenario." Dillon commented, "Does it matter whether he's guilty or innocent?"

"Not really, he was caught in an action likely to bring disrepute to this bank. And for that he has to be punished."

"We suspect that Maylay may have been the source of the original information reaching Archibald. She was the first to know about the discovery." Dillon decided that it was time to throw that in and see how things emerged.

Bordes-Aitcheson's frown deepened as he considered this. Dillon went on to explain Tina's recollection of the events immediately prior and following the discovery.

"I never thought of her being in cahoots with Archibald. Tom will deal with that, although he has great time for her."

"That doesn't change your opinion of John Sing?"

"No, he has to go. My mind's made up on that."

They sipped their brandies and Bordes-Aitcheson refilled. He looked at Dillon as if wondering whether or not he should conclude the discussion or start something else, perhaps something unpalatable. Dillon waited.

"Ah, you've had a fairly good chance by now to look through our books. You know our financial base, and you know my predicament via increasing my personal stake in the bank. You know the danger we face from a takeover bid."

"The thought occurred to me that your organization might want to acquire a stake in a Hong Kong bank, namely ours."

"It's certainly something worth looking into; I'll throw it to my superiors in New York and see what they think."

Dillon watched his eyes closely, but they showed nothing now, he was back in control. He had probably gotten something off his chest that he had been considering for sometime.

"It would depend on what sort of deal was involved of course, what percentage and what price?"

"What I envisage was reducing my personal stake to say 20 % and I feel assured that a further 15 to 20% could be bought at current market value if it was handled properly."

Bordes-Aitcheson watched Dillon carefully, stating every word clearly.

"Or perhaps a little bit less, on the open market, within the next few days"

It was Dillon's turn to frown suspiciously wondering what Bordes-Aitcheson was up to.

"If you can get approval from you superiors and say the use of US$200 million I can get you not just one bank, but two."

"Two hundred million?" Dillon enquired more to keep him talking while he tried to work out what Bordes-Aitcheson was proposing.

"It would be a contingency fund, to be used to by ourselves, I expect there to be a major bank on the market within the next few days, and it would be my intention to acquire that bank for the AAB. Thus your superiors would be buying into a single large bank with assets of over $1.5 billion for a figure of 200 million, and that's tops. You would be able to acquire up to the 40% of the assets for 200 million. But the timing is going to be crucial. It's important that you get the use of the money as quickly as possible."

"And apart from assets what's in it for us?"

"Forty percent of the bank turning in 100 million profits per year at standard rate tax of 18%, that's a net of 72 million a year after tax.

"Impress upon them the urgency of the matter, I could probably handle this myself, but we would be strung out for a couple of years and very vulnerable and that's what I want to avoid and the reason for my offer to you. Naturally anyone with inside knowledge of what was about to happen could purchase some shares and within a few weeks, could perhaps double their money."

The last suggestion had occurred early in the conversation to Dillon, but of course that sort of thing is illegal. In Hong Kong, all deals were conducted with a certain amount of prior 'educated' knowledge.

"Okay, I'll get back to you on this." Dillon said and departed.

Tom Maxwell sat in his office. For the first time in a long time, not knowing what to do next. Normally in situations like this, he would buzz Maylay and ask 'what next'? But she wasn't there now to help guide him. It was like having lost a mother for the second time in his life. He felt strangely awash with self pity and anger too, for someone he had trusted for so long, to turn on him like she did, it came as a total shock.

The phone intercom beeped, he pressed the button, and Harry Lee's voice came on.

"Sorry to bother you, Mister Maxwell, but I have the staff gathered here in the tea room."

"I'll be right there." He had forgotten about that. Now there was a more pressing problem but for the moment, he had to carry on and push Maylay to the back of his mind.

He went to the tea room trying to formulate what he was going to say, the truth, but not mention Maylay until he spoke to Bordes-Aitcheson. Once he had everyone's attention he came straight to the point.

"You've probably heard that John Sing has been dismissed."

There was a rumble of conversation.

"Mister Bordes-Aitcheson has asked for his resignation, that's true but I feel that you should be made aware of the reasons why this came about. As you no doubt have heard, a set of ledgers dated back as far as 1898, were found by the accountant. John Sing failed to report this to me or to the chairman. "

Again a gasp of disbelief went around the room.

"Instead he took action which would place this bank in disrepute. The chairman had no other option and I agreed that John Sing should hand in his resignation. That is the position he has until 5 o'clock tomorrow evening to hand in his resignation. Needless to say, this is deeply regretted by both Mister Bordes-Aitcheson and I. However, we must bear in mind the danger of speculation and the effect that this would have on the depositors and shareholders. "We must place the integrity and reputation of the business first, that is in all our interests, for any breach of trust would cause a run on deposits and we all know the effect that that would have on the security of our jobs here."

Maxwell let that hang for a while; he knew he had their undying loyalty. When jobs are at stake one's loyalty to one's colleagues tends to drift just slightly. He waited a courteous minute for any comments, none were directed at him, and he nodded to Lee who dismissed the staff.

When he was alone, he made his way to the front door and seeing Lee out, locked it. He went back to his office to collect his thoughts and decide what to do. Alone now in the bank with only the occasional whirling noise of the automatic money dispenser being used out on the main street and the clink thud clink of the night safe users depositing the day's takings, he had time to think.

Of course the first thing now was to phone Bordes-Aitcheson and let him know, but how to explain the crazy cocked up situation of discovering after all those years that Jason Kimberley's granddaughter 'had been', working in their bank. And what the hell was the connection to George Archibald? How could these two seemingly completely different people possibly have anything in common? A wild though hit him and he swivelled his chair to the IBM desktop. She was on stand-by.

The computer was not just an in-house system; it also hooked up to the telephone and telex systems and could communicate with other external systems. He keyed into the Prestel service that operated on the Island and New Territories and also to the British Prestel system. He got across to the company's office and requested a menu.

The company register office main menu came up on screen. He moved the cursor down the menu until he got shipping companies. Next he picked overseas registered companies and hit return. The list of companies scrolled up the screen. Within a minute he found Territories Freight & Shipping Company (HK.) Ltd. He hit the return key and a further menu appeared, he moved the cursor until it came to 'Board Members'. He hit return. The names of the board members appeared and their positions. It was like getting a slap on the face, he recoiled in shock momentarily at a loss as to what to do. Maxwell grabbed the phone, punching the speed dial for the Hong Kong branch of the bank. It rang on and on but there was no reply. He looked at his watch and it was 5.35. Of course, Bordes-Aitcheson wouldn't be home because it would take him half an hour to reach his house from work.

Maxwell reached into the bottom drawer and got a floppy disk and wrote an adhesive tab to title the disk. He wrote 'Personal" and placed the tab on the disk, placing the floppy into the disk drive and hit copy. The disk whirled and all the information on TF & S Co was saved to disk. He placed the disk back in its sheath, and typed print. He could hear the printer out in the bank run off a copy of the information. Placing the disk back in the drawer, he cleared the computer memory and switched it off. Out in the bank he folded the print-out and placed it in his jacket pocket.

He left the bank and as the emptiness of the building was about to overcome him, fear gripped the man as he pulled the door closed and locked it.

Inside the bank, the door of the gent's toilets opened slowly and a figure emerged. The door was merely 2 paces from the printer. Maylay Dulles had stayed behind after she left Maxwell's office for by the time she had passed through the doorway she realised just how much damage she had done. She felt utterly stupid for her outburst but the anger that was within her because of the way the arrogant Maxwell spoke to her, was too much to handle. Maylay unleashed her anger with the one weapon she knew would hurt most, and that weapon was the secret. But she knew the time was not yet right to reveal the secret. The family would not like it if the efforts they had made down though the years, were foiled because she had allowed herself one selfish outburst. So she stayed on to keep an eye on Maxwell. But he had gone off to the staff meeting so he was out of the way for a while. She was alone then during the meeting so she had time to go to the file room and remove the relevant page from the ledger.

Maylay knew that Ling Chi would not be returning there after the meeting for she had taken her stuff with her. So Maylay waited here for she could watch the phone lines from here. There were four lines and if any of them were used, a little red light would come on. She wasn't really sure what to do, but she had to do something. The best thing was to wait and see what Maxwell would do. She heard the meeting finish and watched the staff go, and Maxwell go back to his office.

All the time she watched the phone set ready to interrupt any call that went out but as she waited she knew that the time was approaching when it would be too late to call Bordes-Aitcheson for at 5.30 sharp he left his office and went home. When Line 4 lit up she was confused because this line was not the line that's usually used for phone calls. That's the line kept exclusively for the telex and Prestel operations, the computer line.

She ran quietly down to the floor below and switched on the IBM and set to receive the incoming information. She couldn't understand what he was at for a while until the name of George Archibald's company came up on the screen.

Maylay watched with a growing sense of horror as the list of board members appeared on screen.

That was when she realised that all was lost, Maxwell knew everything, and all because of her stupidity, she would have to make amends. Then the number one phone line lit up but she felt reasonably safe now, for Bordes-Aitcheson would be on his way home.

The printer started up behind her and damn near caused a heart attack. She switched off the IBM and ran into the nearest hiding place, the gent's toilet. She prayed that he didn't want to go.

Maylay went to the door now feeling that Maxwell would be away from the bank and going to the underground car park. She felt for the letter opener in her bag, knowing what she had to do. Maylay switched off the alarm momentarily, counted to five and switched it back on again. Now she had ten seconds to get out without setting off the alarm and did so successfully. She pocketed the key.

It was a three minute walk to the car park; she made it in two and a half. Maylay quickly found Maxwell; he was approaching the red Mercedes 300L. He fumbled in his pockets for his keys, he was delayed by the briefcase, and he had to shift it to his other hand to search the other pockets. He had found the keys by the time she reached into her bag for the letter opener.

*

Ho Chan and Diver Ho walked into the main street shop of Antiquity Chang. The shop was aimed mainly at the tourists. All the front part of the shop was taken up with small gold, silver, bronze or brass items. All small and easily portable. Every credit or cash card conceivable was acceptable.

Antiquity Chang lead them through the 'local antiques', the larger pieces and period furniture area and into a tiny office at the rear. In the office, two big men stood watching a briefcase. Diver Ho was slightly shocked at the presence of the two men. After they had performed the introductions and other pleasantries, they conducted business.

"Necessary take precaution, large amount of money." Antiquity Chang explained.

Ho Chan motioned Diver Ho to produce the Sovereigns.

"As promised, we have brought 300 mint condition 1896 gold sovereigns. You may check."

Antiquity Chang examined the coins, they were indeed mint condition.

"Not necessary test, these good coins, price agreed $937 each." Antiquity Chang said.

He got out his calculator as if he hadn't done this before, and he arrived at the total price.

"Two hundred and eighty one thousand, one hundred dollars. You agree?"

Both Ho Chan and Diver Ho had calculated the figure several times so they nodded.

Next came the counting of the dollars bills and it concluded with a single $100 bill. All was done correctly and they agreed. Antiquity Chang formally handed over the money in 25,000 bundles. When it was done, he bowed formally and waving the two security men away, they left Ho Chan and Ho alone to conclude their private transaction.

Ho counted out 11,000 dollar notes then took the remaining $240 from his pocket and handed the total $11,240 Hong Kong over to Ho Chan. The amount was actually worth about $1,440 US, but not a bad sum for such little work.

Next, came the letter. Ho withdrew the original envelope which he had re-sealed with the copy of the letter inside. He passed it over to Ho Chan who took it with care. He had waited so long; he could wait a little longer for he wanted to be back in his own shop before he opened it.

Together they left the shop after being wished many days of wealth and happiness by Antiquity Chang.

It was after they parted company that Ho Chan realised that Ho had said at his shop that the letter was signed by the grand-father of the current chairman. How could he possibly know that unless he had seen the letter? Ho Chan stepped into a doorway and withdrew the letter. With a small pocket knife, he slit the envelope and withdrew the sheet of paper.

He examined the contents reading the letter twice but then he realised that this was not an original, it was one of those photocopy things, he had often seen them but this was good quality, but nevertheless a copy. Diver Ho had duped him. It didn't matter as the contents of the letter were the same. So the bank had given Jason Kimberley the loan, the three hundred gold sovereigns was to have been the first instalment so that he could repay the loan that had lost him so much face in Macau. It was not the bank that let him down, but fate.

He did have the title deeds after all; it was just that Jeffery Bordes advice had not reached him. From the letter it looked as if Bordes had already spoken to the governor and all that was needed was for Kimberley to speak to the governor. And the 'documents' were in a safety deposit box in the bank. All this time and all the trouble that Kimberley and his wife went through and the 'documents' were in the safety deposit box. What irony that the answer to Kimberley's miseries was there all along, dead with the letter at the bottom of the sea. And the man that Kimberley cursed, he cursed in the wrong because he tried to help but then his own circumstances changed.

Without knowing it, standing in the doorway on that street Ho Chan shed a tear for Jason Kimberley, and such a pity that fate had been so cruel to him.

Tom Maxwell's three minute walk from the bank was full of surprises, the first being that he suddenly lost his fear, he was in control. Of himself yes, but also in control of the thorn in Bordes-Aitcheson's side, George Archibald.

Maxwell felt that as well as the information on Jason Kimberley's descendants, they had information on George Archibald that he did not disclose to the board. He was involved in a company, one of whose board members was an avid activist in removing Jeff from the board of the bank. And George Archibald must have known that Maylay Dulles was a member of the Board of TF & S and was also a descendant of Jason Kimberley and whose position as secretary to Maxwell, must have been in conflict with her stated intentions to bring about a change of the chairman of AAB. This was an interest which he failed to disclose to the board, so it would now be possible to force him off the board and also to offer his shares for sale at current market rate. If needs be, a vote could be forced to ask the board to vote him a person unfit to hold shares and although he may refuse to dispose of the shares he could be barred from purchasing any further shares. Maxwell knew that there were several ways to force him off the board now that they had the ammunition.

"Where are those damn keys?" he mumbled.

Something alarmed him; a tingling sensation in the nape of his neck told him someone was behind him. He began to turn as fear grabbed him. Something bright and moving fast came towards him. As he began to bring up his briefcase; something hit him in the chest. He had the brief case up now but it became hot and heavy and he dropped it on the ground. There was a face in front of him, he couldn't make it out, there was a sudden pain in his chest, he glanced down, something sticking out of his chest. Gasping in pain, he couldn't raise his right arm. His left arm came across and touched the protruding object. As he touched the hard steel object, he realised that he had been stabbed.

This sort of thing doesn't happen to people like me. Maxwell thought. His vision was blurred now but he saw blood, then slowly the darkness overcame him. The last sensation he felt was hands going into his pocket and he heard paper being withdrawn.

CHAPTER NINE

Bordes-Aitcheson toyed with the idea he had put to Dillon as he drove his white Mercedes 300DL up Gardener Road, past the American Embassy. He was running a little later than usual because he went to get the evening papers to glance through the business and social columns to see if there was any reference to the OUT bank or Harry Chang. There was not even a mention, let alone any gossip.

So he was still able to proceed with his plan but first a number of pitfalls had to be circumnavigated and the first one was George Archibald. He felt that he had flushed Archibald out into open conflict with him by dismissing John Sing. Surely Archibald couldn't resist the temptation of another opportunity to try and trip him up. He had to confront now, to try and defend his position of support for John Sing and Bordes-Aitcheson hoped it would be sooner rather than later. So it was with joy that he greeted the sight of the Silver Rolls parked in his driveway when he got home.

Bordes-Aitcheson had his plan of attack ready when he entered the hallway to be greeted by Stephanie.

"Hi Jeff" her twanging Texan voice greeted him. It always amused him that after 25 years in Hong Kong, she still kept her accent but then she did have her circle of American friends and she knew everybody at the American Embassy where her father had been Ambassador up until ten years ago.

"George Archibald is in the library, sorry honey, but he insisted on waiting for you."

"That's Okay, Steff, I've been expecting this and I dismissed John Sing this afternoon."

"Was that wise?"

"It had to be done; I'll explain it to you later. Come on."

She went with him into the library. Archibald's greeting was polite, but they both knew that pressure was building up.

"Sorry for coming up here like this, but I felt I'd miss you at the bank."

He glanced at Stephanie.

"Would you like a drink, George?" she enquired.

"Perhaps I may need it. Yes, I'll have a beer."

"Same for me, Steff."

She nodded and left to get the drinks.

George Archibald was younger than Jeff, at 44 years old Archibald was worth perhaps 400 million. But word had it around town that the shipping collapse of the early '80s had greatly reduced George's net worth. At one stage in the '70s, George and his partners controlled 18 super-tankers but with the recession, there had been a considerable drop in the charges for shipping freight and their income fell rapidly.

George was known around town as 'Flash Arch' because when things were going well for him he showed it, the Rolls was just one of four cars that he used, he had a Ferrari, a Range Rover and a Merc' parked outside his mansion on the westerly side of the peak. His wife was part English, first generation, and daughter of an Earl. She threw some of the best 'bashes' in Hong Kong and was the 'Queen Pin' of social life, she knew the governor and was proud to say they were related.

George himself was healthy, fat and proud of it. He wore his clothes slightly tight so he always looked as if he 'had' just eaten well. He was around 5' 6" and was always well dressed.

Over the years Bordes-Aitcheson had learned to tolerate him, but this evening he was ready for confrontation.

"The weather is positively oppressive these last few days." George said.

"It's the time of year for it" Jeff made the standard reply.

"Yes possibly, actually I thought it may be certain development at the bank was causing the heat."

"Oh?" Bordes-Aitcheson enquired.

"I've heard that you've taken exception to John Sing's behaviour. What do you plan to do to discipline him?"

"It's already been done actually" Bordes-Aitcheson was somewhat surprised to learn that George didn't already know.

"Oh, and what action have you taken?"

"I've asked him for his resignation, he cannot stay on now."

Archibald showed his surprise but contained his disbelief. "Resignation, that's a little harsh?"

"Not harsh enough, he failed to report to his immediate superior, he failed to report to the executive officer. Instead of that, he reported to a minority board member, namely you. You took unilateral action by hiring two thugs to follow Tina Bolger without consultation with me, the chairman of the board. And in so doing, you jeopardised this banks chance of being approved a reputable organization to transact business in the overseas market. Your actions are far more reprehensible than John Sing's so I have no option but to ask you for your resignation from the board."

Archibald just sat there looking at Bordes-Aitcheson; he was completely dumb-struck by the request that confronted him. He knew that if this went to a board meeting he did not have enough support to survive a vote. Unless he would talk his way out of this he would loose his place on the board and thus his source of information of what was happening in the financial market and a lot of inside knowledge.

"For Gods sake, Jeff, don't take it so seriously. I was only thinking of the bank. So what if we get turned down by the IMF, it's not the end of the world. We can still continue to trade and grow."

"Growth is not *the* great aim in life George, survival is. And we will not survive unless we open new markets overseas, to open new markets we need the approval of the IMF. To do that, we have to show a structured organization. We can not say that we are above board when a board member who takes actions like you do. We have no choice but to ask for your resignation, if you do not oblige, I will be forced to inform the other board members of your actions. I'll have you voted off the board."

"You wouldn't do that." Archibald's face was riddled with shock.

"If you don't offer your resignation right now, I will bring the matter up at the monthly board meeting tomorrow morning and you know that the board will side with me in which case you will be disgraced before all Hong Kong. You know what will happen to you. If that happens, a lot of business will leave you; it will be in the papers. Your credibility will be doubted, chances are that you will be ruined."

Archibald was in dire trouble and Jeff knew it. Archibald only had 7% and control of a further 8%, that was not enough to take on someone with 40%. Of course Jeff was right if it became a boardroom battle, it would be public knowledge and, undoubtedly, Archibald would loose business that he could ill afford.

"Okay, Jeff, I'll give you what you want, but I'll also give you a warning. You have reached the end of your reign as Chairman and your 40% will not save you for much longer, a big fall is coming maybe much sooner than you think and when that fall comes, you will not have the resources to beat off the challenge that will be mounted for control of AAB. The way forward is into China and you cannot accept that. You will have to stand down, eventually. When you do, I will be waiting in the wings. Our people are ready for 1997 and this bank will lead the way for Hong Kong into the new Middle Kingdom. There's only a year left, count down to the end of your reign."

Archibald stood up satisfied that he had suitably confused Bordes-Aitcheson; he turned on his heels and stomped out.

Stephanie came in with the two beers.

"Join me." Jeff asked, but despite the joy of having shifted George he was physically shaken. The open threat was more than he had anticipated, and what was all that crap about joining the Middle Kingdom.

"That was some little outburst, I heard it as I was coming up. But what did he mean, 'our people will be ready for 1997?" She handed him the beer noticing that his hand trembled slightly.

"Huh, that was a rather peculiar statement and it would seem to confirm that he had ambitions above and beyond that of an ordinary board member. He is actually looking forward to Hong Kong being returned to China, and it just doesn't make sense."

"I got the impression that he was part of an organised plot to bring about the takeover of the bank." she pointed out.

"Makes me wonder if Archibald knows who the people behind Narrow Investment actually are and he is part of it. If that's the case, then they control 15% of the stock already."

The full implication of that thought worried him. Fifteen percent in the bag?

Another five or ten percent here and there to be of 25 or 30% stock revolt. Jesus if they could get that type of voting block together against him then board members he trusted could be swayed. It became even more imperative to tie up those loose ends, in particular Sir Percy Penderville. He wanted to retire to England and his seven percent could be bought out. He was most likely to sell and Archibald knew that and if he was tied up with Narrow Investments, they would know too in which case, now that a die of sorts, was cast, they may go for the shares most likely to move.

"Is there a danger of them owning more than 15% between them?" Steff was obviously thinking along the same lines.

"It's a possibility, I've gotta check the register and see if anything has changed hands lately."

"Just how healthy are we if there's an open share battle?"

"We're very badly fixed, to be quite honest. We'd be fully stretched to buy a further two percent."

"Oh my gosh! That bad? What are you going to do?"

"Well," He decided suddenly to tell her about the offer to the WTB. She listened carefully as he laid out his energetic plans for the takeover of Harry Chan's bank and the sell off of one third of the shares of AAB including 20% of the shares he held.

"Will it work?" she asked the simplistic question that had a thousand 'if's' in the answer but no definite one.

"I'm assuming that Chan's bank will go belly up, and that Narrow Investments don't know about it and that there will be a general stock exchange fall and that Penderville will sell to us and that WTB will go for the idea and that they wont just go for Chan's bank on its own and that I can trust this guy Dillon.

There's a lot of hope involved, this is far more risky than any-thing I've ever done, but that's the way I've gotta do it."

"Why not just sell out and to hell with it?"

He sighed, not a usual habit of his for it meant defeat, and in a way he was defeated because his options were limited. "To sell out would mean conceding everything I've worked for, eve-rything that dad and granddad worked for. It would mean con-ceding to the likes of George. This is another task that God has placed before me and it's personal. I hate saying things like this, but I have to win, my way. I just can't give in to the likes of George Archibald."

"Jeff, now don't get mad, but," she began, "Why not let dad-dy help?"

Jeff hated old man Howell, the ex-ambassador, ex-congress-man and vice president of one of America's largest photocopier manufacturers. Jeff and her father had fallen out over a silly allegation about ten years ago. At the time Andrew Howell was the American Ambassador to Hong Kong and word had it that IBM were to set up a manufacturing plant in the New Terri-tories. Even though it was only a rumour, Howell refused to comment one way or the other and several electronic companies ran away with themselves making plans for expansion to meet the expected demands from IBM. Some of the suppliers had ac-counts with the AAB and came looking for loans to fund the ex-pansion plans. Although he told them to wait and see, they went elsewhere as the expectations quickly got out of control. The whole thing ended when IBM announced that it was opening a new plant in Malaysia. Howell retired having dumped his entire shares portfolio during the height of the speculations. Naturally the reporters now turned their attention on Howell and began running stories that he had refused to comment to increase speculation and drive up the value of the shares he held.

Howell was in London when the story broke and rang Jeff to see if he could trace the source of the story, so that pressure could be brought to bear to have it retracted and an apology printed. Jeff was furious with Howell's audacity in calling him. Jeff politely pointed out that he had asked Howell to issue a clarification statement which would have prevented the speculation in the first place. And he had lost customers over the incident, his anger boiled over and he said that he wouldn't be surprised if the alleged story was not the truth. Those were the last words the two men had ever spoken to one another. Howell had tried on several occasions to rectify matters with his son-in-law but despite Stephanie's pleading, he refused to speak to old man Howell.

After what seemed like an age to her he finally spoke. "Steff, I'm staring defeat right in the face, and if I go to that man I'm excepting defeat, I'm not sure I could live with myself if that happens."

Jeff was filled with indecisiveness and knew that he was in serious trouble. Could there be a way that Howell could help him out? And if there was, would he be willing to swallow his pride and accept Stephanie's father's help?

Just then the phone rang.

CHAPTER TEN

The first contact Dillon made with Stern was short and to the point. He rang him at home, it would have been around 7.30 am in New York and Stern hadn't left for the office.

"The proposition looks healthy, can we talk?"

"Try Ocean Towers, the Pan Asian Computer Information Centre on Connaught Road. The man you're looking for is Shui Lui, he had helped us out in the past. I'll be either here or available on the car phone for about the next hour."

"See you later." Dillon had replied and hung up.

Now waiting in Shui Lui's reception, Dillon prepared himself for what he was going to say to Stern. The bank was not only a prime target for a takeover, but it wanted a takeover. He could see their problem. Come '97, Hong Kong went back to China. The choice facing business was simple, pack up and move elsewhere or stay and chance being able to work within the new regime.

It was a straightforward gamble, and perhaps if the Hong Kong entrepreneur recognised that the lust for the gamble was just as important for him as the lust for profit, then the Chinese Take Away would suit them just fine. The potential profit in the gamble equations made the motive to stay all the more attractive to many businessmen, and then, of course, there was the golden opportunity to pick up some nice little business as other, more faint hearted individuals, pulled out.

It meant gambling everything, the risks were great, the Chinese could confiscate everything. They had done this before, but the trick was to set it up just right. Set aside the cushion and gamble just enough so that if things went wrong the cushion was there to soften the impact, the cushion being a few million tucked away somewhere safe.

The door to the office opened and Mister Shui Lui walked out to greet Dillon. He was Chinese with a serious business like smile and he introduced himself to Dillon formally with a polite bow.

"I'm sorry I kept you so long, Mister Dillon, but at this time of day with office opening in New York, I sometimes get tied down with unfinished business from 'their' yesterday."

Shui Lui was around 35, extremely well dressed and very well spoken. He had attended business school in London and later returned to Hong Kong where his father operated as a Stock Broker. His company, PACIC Ltd, operated an information exchange and forwarding service linking up with most of the big computer bureaus around the world.

Hong Kong was the centre of the universe for many Chinese but for the business information service, it was definitely centre of the earth. What PACIC Ltd did was to pull in information from one side of the world and store it until the information was needed on the other side when the offices opened. PACIC made a living out of the fact that on one side of the world it was night time while on the other side it was day and business as usual.

"Unfortunately, this is rather a bad time of day for us, with New York about to open and London about to close for lunch, so you will understand if I am called away." He indicated his beeper.

"I understand, Mister Shui Lui, this is not a problem." Dillon replied not really concerned whether or not he was called away.

"You wanted to use a secure line, if you would care to follow me."

He led the way through a double set of glass doors. On the way though, Dillon felt his hair rise as the air suction overhead removed any loose particles, cleansing them for the carefully controlled atmosphere of the computer rooms. Even though it was gone seven o'clock in the evening the banks of computer terminals were all staffed as incoming information was sorted and stored for later transmission to various parts of the world.

Shui Lui showed Dillon through another doorway at the end of the computer room.

Here was a smaller room with only two terminals both active but unattended.

"This one should do, I can link you via satellite to your destination." Shui Lui sat down at the terminal and worked at what seemed like the speed of light, within seconds he had transferred this terminals duty to another terminal.

"Okay where do you want?"

Dillon told him but he already suspected that it was his HQ in New York. What Shui Lui did was to use the computers ability to seek and find a compatible system in New York within the Orrang Banking system that could then convert the digital signal back to speech within the banks own phone system. The signal would be relayed by satellite in digital code form using part of the computers own memory.

"Okay, you can go ahead and dial you number now." Shui Lui said handing the phone to Dillon and indicating the numeric key pad to the right of the computer keyboard.

When he had left, Dillon keyed in Stern's car phone number.

"Yeah." Came the harsh reply almost immediately.

"Morning Ed, how's the weather in New York?"

"Don't know, ain't had a chance to look out the window yet."

Dillon smiled visualizing Stern in the rear seat of the blacked out Caddy going through printouts as his chauffeur sped towards the city.

"I think we've got a live mover here. I presume you've been filled in on the banks portfolio?"

"Yeah, I've been going through it again since you phoned, it looks pretty attractive." This coming form Stern was a recommendation to buy.

Stern was only 29 years of age and during his short five years with the bank, he had become known as 'the Procurer', he acquired things. He had gotten himself a reputation as being a hard young man in a hurry. Some said that Orrang himself should look out, but that was usually said by people who didn't know either Orrang or the World Trade Bank, which he owned and ran like a personal home. No one quite knew though if Stern had ambitions or was just ambitious, and few cared, for the main thing with this man was to stay clear.

Dillon liked him and knew that Stern would never cross him because Dillon had thumped him once after Stern had acted like a spoilt school-child. Apart from their personal feelings, Dillon knew only too well that Orrang wanted him within the bank where he could be controlled and watched, for outside Dillon could be dangerous, he knew too much. Dillon wondered about telling Stern that Bordes-Aitcheson wanted a takeover bid but he had decided against it, for the simple reason that Stern was such a prat that if he knew Bordes-Aitcheson wanted a bid, he would stall on any offer just to unsettle the principle and try and force him down in price. The last thing Dillon wanted to be responsible for was to give Stern the opportunity to blow his trumpet in New York and besides Bordes-Aitcheson was a small fry compared to Orrang, not much sense in making him smaller.

"We could take over here if it interests us." Dillon started.

"Of course we're interested; it would be a straightforward share purchase not a buy-out and we're certainly not interested in a hostile-bid situation. If we can acquire say 30-40 percent of the shares with management agreement and place some key people in there, we could visualise some potential growth in that sphere of the world."

"What about '97?" He just had to ask the question because considering the fears of the 'Chinese take-away' he had seen here, he found it difficult to understand the WTB's wish to get involved in Hong Kong.

"What about it? The Chinese are suffering right now, they can't feed their own people, and they need to attract western businesses, they have to open themselves up. Hong Kong is their stepping stone to the west. Where there is a long term element in the particular investment, there are short term gains that out-weigh the long-term risks."

"Oh?" Dillon prompted when he realised that Stern was not going to elaborate further.

"Well hell, let's put it this way. There's been a change of leadership in China, and a change of outlook. They are relaxing the rules, there is free trade getting in there. They are expanding their whole industrial base, they have begun to manufacture product that are not essential, but are luxuries, hell you can even buy a TV set now in China. They are about to become a consumer society. Can you imagine the amount of technology that they are going to need to catch up with western production techniques and who is best positioned to supply them?"

In the silence, Dillon felt that he had to reply so he said, "Hong Kong!"

"Yeah, and what's that going to do to the profit levels of companies trading in Hong Kong?"

Again the silence so Dillon had to answer. "Sky-rocket?"

"Exactly, but the problems is that Hong Kong business has become used to supplying them with goods other than luxury. So with proper marketing over there and the right directives to the local business community, I believe that Hong Kong should turn to China to increase its exports of goods, such as luxury goods. Why if this thing was handled right, Hong Kong could double, treble its exports to China. And what's that going to do for the business sector in Hong Kong?"

"Boom." Dillon took the prompt.

"And who makes money in a boom?"

"Banks."

"Business banks, that's why I want the AAB because they have the business people of Hong Kong and we can redirect them to look at China with a new vision."

"Then we buy?" Dillon asked.

"Hell yeah, we buy in say 30-40 %, enough to be able to have the influence we need to put someone on the board, and place key people in the bank there who can organise the marketing for the existing business customers and hell, when other guys see what we are doing, they are going to want a piece of the action and they are going to move over to the AAB, right?"

"Sounds good to me." Dillon replied, a little bemused with Stern who hadn't put a foot wrong in the last five years and he had made a lot of money for the WTB.

Dillon was a gut reaction man, he was not into long term planning like Stern, but Stern had proven himself very successful in forecasting the markets and being able to take a different view to others and see the impact of something going on that meant change and quite often scared the hell out of ordinary people.

"Can you handle the purchase of the shares?"

"No problem." Dillon replied.

"Okay, we transfer $200 million to the AAB tomorrow morning to be used as collateral to purchase shares. You and Olli check out the brokers and get back to me this afternoon, hell, what time is it there now? 8.10 right? Okay so you're going to have to come back to me at the same time tomorrow. By that time I'll have the 200 million transferred. Now I've got a short-list of brokers here, but you've got a better view there on the ground, Okay, you come back with a list of say three of the most reputable and if one of those are on my list we go for them, Okay?"

Dillon agreed his heart beating a little faster at the prospect of some action.

"Okay so when we've got the shares we settle up, I'll come over and finalise the arrangement, Okay?"

"Okay."

"GTI." With that Stern signed off.

Dillon switched off the mains to clear the computer and left the room.

Outside there was far too much activity for anyone to pay him any attention so he went out to the reception where Shui Lui was coming from his office with a string of computer print-outs. He waved to Dillon and apologised but New York had just opened and the price of zinc had fallen another three points on the overnight close, he had a duty to pass this on to some customers so he couldn't stop and he left.

Dillon made his way back to the Mandarin. Olli was going to love this, Jesus a few days wheeling and dealing on the stock market was something worth looking forward to. Dillon had experienced it a few years ago in Wall Street when Orrang went after a bank in the States, he didn't get the bank but he made a fortune forcing up the price of the shares in a pitched battle with the president of the target bank only to dump when people began to say that the shares looked overvalued. But then again Orrang was like that, he'd go after something and if he saw that he couldn't get it he'd push it to the limit then pull the plug leaving people stuck with very expensive shares on the way down, more often than not it would be the very shareholders who didn't want his control that would be stuck with the over-valued shares.

He arrived at the Mandarin and went straight to the bar where Tina and Olli would be waiting.

"Scott, Jesus, have you heard?" Olli turned to Dillon, a worried expression on his face and fear in his eyes.

"Hear what?"

"Tom Maxwell, he's been killed." Olli exclaimed.

*

When Dillon got to the hospital, Bordes-Aitcheson came over to meet him. There were two well dressed Chinese standing near the window of the waiting room, they both turned to look at Dillon when he entered.

"Am I glad to see you?" Bordes-Aitcheson said.

"Is he dead?" Dillon asked straight, never having been able to find a nice way of beating around the bush.

"No, he's alive, but only just. He's lost a lot of blood, they say that if he survives tonight he may live, but what mental shape he will be in, they couldn't say."

"If he survives he may be a vegetable?"

"Something like that. I'm worried, not just about Tom, but about Clair, his wife. She hasn't been contacted yet. She wasn't at home. I've left message all over town, their squash club, the golf club, with every friend of hers I could think of."

Bordes-Aitcheson was in a pretty bad state, he was more shook up than Dillon could have expected.

"Who are those two? Cops?"

"Yeah." Dillon noticed that Bordes-Aitcheson shot him a stare that said, I've something to tell you, can I trust you?

"Let's go over here." Dillon led the way to the furthest end of the waiting area, away from the two cops. "They're just plain clothes cops?" Dillon asked quietly feeling that part of Bordes-Aitcheson nervousness was due not just to the presence of the two cops, but who they were.

"One is." Bordes-Aitcheson sat down. Dillon followed knowing that he was about to be let into a secret.

"I've gotta know I can trust you?"

"You can."

"You're not to repeat a word of this to anyone, no one."

"I said you can trust me." Dillon said forcefully, not in the habit of repeating himself.

"Okay" Bordes-Aitcheson sighed. "The taller one is Chief Inspector Allen Lee of the fraud squad." And he went on to relate the conversation of the morning with Lee about Oversees Unit Trust Bank and Harry Chan's deal with AAB.

"And Lee thinks that Chan's banking problems could somehow be linked with this attack on Tom?"

"Why else would he be here? I don't particularly want to talk to him but if I don't he's goanna go off half cocked getting all the wrong ideas."

"Who do you think attacked Tom?"

"John Sing would be my prime suspect, wouldn't he be yours?"

"I'm not so sure about that, did you speak to Tom after we left you office this evening?"

"No why?"

"We were talking, the four of us, Tom, Tina and Olli, and we figured out just who was the first to know about the discovery of the ledgers. Tina got the key to the safe from Maylay."

"What?" Bordes-Aitcheson gasped his mind racing.

"You think she informed Archibald?"

"That's the way it looked this evening. Tom went over to Kowloon when he realised that he had two unfaithful people over there."

"Jesus Christ, what a bloody mess!"

Above the general noise of the corridor, a woman's racing step could be heard approaching. Bordes-Aitcheson turned to look at the door. Then he saw her, Clair. She looked frantic; she saw Bordes-Aitcheson and raced to him. He rose and she fell into his arms.

As they held each other in the embrace, Dillon began to ponder on something; not a word had been exchanged between them. She was shaking but as he half held her firmly, she began to calm down. Quite a few minutes passed before they released each other, she was red faced and tear stained. He was flushed but still reassuring.

"He's alive." Bordes-Aitcheson said calmly. She just closed her eyes. They sat down again and for a while no one spoke, the tension and uncertainty evident. Then she realised that the two men were cops, she turned to Bordes-Aitcheson.

"Who are they?"

"Detective Chung and Chief Inspector Allen Lee"

She studied the two men again for a moment; they glanced over occasionally but made no effort to approach. "I should see the doctor." she said finally.

"Come on." Bordes-Aitcheson got up and taking her hand, led her out.

Dillon considered the two cops, they were unusual in that they didn't appear to want to interview anyone, it was almost as if they were there to observe.

Allen Lee looked at Dillon and nodded, he returned the gesture feeling that Lee was looking for an introduction.

"Are you related to Mister Maxwell?" Lee asked from across the room.

"An associate, you might say." Dillon replied only too well accustomed to this blatant type of prying questions.

"Oh, from the bank?"

"Sort of." Dillon could see that Lee was getting a little angry.

"Did you see Mister Maxwell today?"

"Yeah."

This type of question and non-answer session went on until Bordes-Aitcheson returned by which time, Lee was rightly vexed.

"Ah Jeff, could I have a word?" Lee asked.

Bordes-Aitcheson was not in any mood, he was visually shocked and not in a state to stand up. Dillon went to him and helped him to a chair. Bordes-Aitcheson looked up at him; there was disbelief and an apologetic gaze in his eyes.

"My God, I never seen anybody like that, he's as white as a sheet and, god, I don't know, shrunken. He looks terrible, the, the doctor says he may not make it. He's just not responding to the treatment." Bordes-Aitcheson hung his head, and then shook it slowly. "What the hell will I do if... Jesus don't let him die, he's the only man I could ever truly trust. He was like a brother to me." Jeff was distraught and Clair consoled him.

Lee and the other cop were still hanging around so Dillon took Lee by the arm and led him toward the entrance to the waiting room.

"I'm sure that you can appreciate that this is not a very good time to be asking questions. Why don't you call in the morning and we'll set up an interview, Okay?"

"I realise that, but a crime has taken place, and I have a job to do. This is most misfortune." Lee feigned sympathy.

"Jeff is as much in the dark about this attack as you and I are, you know yourself that when something like this happens, you need clues. Let Jeff sleep on this, get over the shock and then he can begin to think about who might have a reason for doing this."

Dillon was still holding Lee's arm and continued through the doorway into the hall. He retained a firm hold on Lee's arm that gave Lee the impression that now was not the right time to press the issue.

"Very well, I will call Mister Bordes-Aitcheson first thing in the morning and I expect that I will receive his fullest co-operation, is that understood?"

Dillon stared at him for a brief moment slightly taken aback by the sudden tone of voice, and then he felt the presence of the other cop and knew that this was not the time.

"Okay, I'll make sure that is done." He felt that this was the most appropriate thing to say. Sometimes, just sometimes, it's best to eat humble pie.

But fuck it, it wasn't easy. Dillon thought.

CHAPTER ELEVEN

Dillon rang the hospital at 8 o'clock the following morning, but all the nurses on duty would say was that there was no change. Next he rang Tina's room, no reply so he figured that their date for breakfast had not being changed and they would all meet for breakfast in the Mandarin.

He then rang Jeff at home; the maid answered and said that the Honourable Jeff had already left for work.

Dillon finished dressing and went down to the morning room. Tina and Olli were already there.

"Morning."

"Morning." came the chorus. The two familiar faces cheered him up.

"We figured you were on your way, the receptionist said you were on the phone, so we ordered breakfast for you."

"Thanks, how are you this morning, ye were gone before I got back last night?"

"Well we thought that if Tom was real bad, you would have stayed on at the hospital and to be quite honest with you, I was plain tired." Olli explained.

"Today's the day then?" Tina said.

They both looked at her; she glanced at each of them in turn, realised that they were not on the same wavelength and added, "We take over a bank." she said in a secretive whisper.

"Yeah." Dillon sighed,

"I'm not so sure that this is going to be a good day for Jeff. I think he misses Maxwell more that he's prepared to admit. He was close to tears there last night."

"It must be a hell of a blow to the guy to suddenly find that someone wants to kill one of your best friends and business friend at that." Tina pondered.

"I wonder who he's going to appoint as manager of the Kowloon branch?" Olli asked thoughtfully.

"Are you applying for the job?" Tina asked light-heartedly but from the look on Olli's face, he was serious.

"He's gotta have somebody over there."

"Let's give the guy a chance to catch his breath." Dillon said.

The waiter arrived with breakfast. Orange juice, tea for Dillon, coffee for the two Americans and bacon, egg, sausage, fried bread and toast. The presentation was splendid and just the type of thing to start off the day.

"We've really got to make a start on purchasing some of those shares." Olli said.

"Right, first we gotta find a stockbroker."

"Already checked out the scene. Looks like our man is Philip Thorn of Thorn North and Crenshaw Company. They are a relatively new outfit set up about ten years ago. North is Australian, Thorn and Crenshaw are English and a little younger."

"A bit of a whiz kid Crenshaw, spends a lot of his time in New York chasing deals on Wall Street. Thorn expects Crenshaw to cut ties with them shortly. I like them; they're young, energetic and keen for business. I got the impression from talking to Thorn that they have no ties or allegiances to anybody, so, that for me makes them a good bet. We don't want to tie ourselves in with an old company who have friends and owe favours."

"Sounds good to me, but will Stern approve?"

"Want me to handle that?" Olli asked.

"Sure, give it a shot." Dillon replied.

"Well then, we can start this morning." Tina suggested.

"We'll need to confirm to Thorn that the 200 million is lodged with the bank. Once that is done, we can start buying."

"You know what's going to happen with those shares once we start?"

Dillon hadn't mentioned to them about his conversation with Jeff the previous evening and he toyed with the prospect of telling them now. The problem was that Jeff's speculation was just that, speculation about the other bank falling and his plan to make a bid for it. If Stern got wind of the chance of the second bank, it could just stall the deal. This was something Dillon didn't want.

He just didn't agree with a 'wait and see' policy, he believed in diving right in. And besides that, he liked Jeff. Dillon had seen all too often situations where the big guys stood back from a deal because there was some uncertainty about it. Meanwhile the small guy burnt and in the final breakdown, it was usually the small guy that ended up with nothing and the big guy got the lot for nothing. Jeff had told Dillon at the hospital about George and he speculated that George would indulge in a little vengeance by dumping his 7% on the market this morning. At the time he thought of it, it was something Jeff had to do, he had to force George off the board, but afterwards Dillon had realised just how big a gamble Jeff was taking. By forcing George off the board, he was inviting him to sell his shares, in so doing he had to force the price down. Jeff didn't say, but Dillon knew that he just didn't have the capital to buy the shares himself so was he not leaving the 7% vulnerable to buying by Narrow Investment.

Dillon for the life of him couldn't figure it, until this morning. The thought occurred to him that George's stock was registered and that anybody buying them would have to re-register the shares in the new owner's name. Whereas the stock already owned by Narrow Investment was probably Bearer certificate issue so that no name need to be registered. Therefore the true owner need not notify the bank as to who they were. Jeff could be using his altercation with George to force Narrow Investments into the open. It was one hell of a gamble and it struck Dillon as something Stern would do, he was risking the 7% to find out the names behind Narrow Investment. But now everything was changed. The WTB was on the scene to pick up any loose shares. Was Jeff gambling that the WTB would come on the market and to help their bid, he had forced George to sell, thus unsettling the market.

Dillon couldn't quite figure which way Jeff was playing it. So for the time being, he decided not to tell Tina and Olli about the other bank.

"If we can pick up 10% before the price starts to rise, at least we will have saved some, right?" Olli said.

"There's Penderville's 7% there right away that I'm sure we can pick them up with a little persuasion."

"What's that?" Dillon's ears pricked up.

"Tuesday but you were too tired, remember?"

"Can we cut through the bullshit?" Dillon asked emphatically.

"Sir Percy Penderville owns 7% of the stock. The guy is getting on in years and wants to retire to England. But," He paused to pour himself another cup of coffee. "But?" Dillon prompted.

"He's broke." Olli replied.

"Eh?" Dillon looked at Tina.

"It's true; the guy got slaughtered on the stock market in the crash of '83. The guy was just after purchasing a load of shares about a month before the crash. He panicked during the crash and sold out, losing a fortune. His own business took a nose dive and went bang. He had to borrow from the AAB to stay afloat. Now Jeff's too nice a guy to pressure him but he owes the bank $1 million and with little prospect of repaying. The guy is in shit but he's too damn proud to sell out. He just won't give in."

"You said something about 'a little persuasion'."

"Yeah well, let's put it this way. We figure that if the right guy was to go to him, real friendly, and suggest that he part with his shares at a fair price, he could pay off the bank loan and have a fortune with which he could retire to England."

"Who am I?" Dillon asked.

"Mister Right" Tina replied. Her eyes held his again for a brief moment, then broke away; there was work to be done.

*

Jeff arrived at the bank around 8. He was not in a good mood; things were not going right for him. He was about to enter into the greatest deal of his life, one which would secure all their futures.

But he was hit with one problem after another. The bloody ledgers, John Sing, Maylay, Tom Maxwell, George Archibald and now Stephanie. He had gotten up early this morning, well he had to. He got an early call for the bathroom, brandy always had that effect on him but hell, he had been drowning his sorrows last night when New York came through for him and gave him something to celebrate, and so a little more brandy went down. Unfortunately, it came up again this morning.

But what the hell, it's not often you get US$20 million out of the blue. he thought.

Eight years ago during a trip to London, he met a cousin of Sir Percy Penderville, it was one of those, 'don't forget to look up Lady Penderville when you're over there, old chap' things which afterwards Jeff was very sorry he did. The old woman, at the time was in her 80s and never married, took Jeff in as if he were one of the family. She was a nice old woman if a little doddery but she had a huge warehouse complex lying idle in London dockland. The place was a mess, old, run-down and disused warehouses from the war era. Over a bottle of sherry one evening she said to him that the site may be a nice little long term investment. Jeff asked how much and the woman said £50,000 Sterling. He thought that this was an agreeable sum and bought the warehouse.

For the past eight years it was one of his worst investments, but now the London dock area was being developed again, not as Dockland but as a residential and commercial area. A couple of months back after reading of proposal for the area, he placed the two and a half acre site on the market.

He had gotten a few enquires during the two months but nothing really extraordinary. Then one day about two weeks ago, he got a call from a company in New York looking for development potential in London. He knew the site was worth £5 million Sterling so he asked for US$20 million; the Americans flew over, had a look and phoned him last night confirming the deal. That was the only bit of good news he had all year and Stephanie wasn't even there to share it with him.

When he woke this morning she was gone, God only knows where. She hadn't said a word last night about going out and there were no messages left this morning. She really could be the most infuriating woman from time to time; she never thought of him. Stephanie always went off and pleases herself leaving him to worry about her. There was nothing he could do; he had to go to work so he left a message with the maid for her to phone him when she got in.

Kay Herbert, his faithful, reliable secretary was there when he got to the bank, as he had asked her to be. Ruxton was also present.

"Morning."

"Hi." she replied, knowing from his face after ten years that he was pushing himself against the clock.

"You got coffee going?"

"Sure have." she replied.

"Good, get some cups and come into the office. We got some stuff to get organised before we open the doors this morning." He motioned Ruxton to follow them in and when they had all settled down with a cup of coffee he told them about Tom Maxwell, John Sing and George Archibald.

"My God, what stirred up all this?" Kay asked.

Jeff didn't know just how much they knew about the ledgers so there wasn't much point in telling them.

"What matters right now is where we go from here."

Ruxton nodded in agreement.

"I want you to go over to the Kowloon branch and assume control" Jeff looked at Mister Ruxton who straightened in his chair for a moment, then seemed to realise that he was taking the place of a dead man and he slumped slightly again.

"How is Tom?"

"They said this morning that he may just pull through, but he had lost a lot of blood. The next 24 hours will tell if he is to recover completely."

"Is George going to sell his shares?" Kay redirected.

"I would expect so." Jeff replied, then after a moment he added.

"I want to make sure he does, I want you to contact all the board members and confirm that they will be present for the scheduled monthly meeting at 11 o'clock this morning. Don't take 'no' for an answer."

"Yes, Jeff." Kay replied immediately.

"Before you go over to Kowloon, transfer $78 million into my personal account."

Ruxton shot a deathly look at Jeff.

"Seventy eight million?" he gasped.

"Yes I've got some money coming in from America to cover it; it's just short term, a week or so."

"You're sure you can cover it, you know that the board would require collateral."

"Don't worry about it, it's Okay, I've just closed a deal for US$20 million for the site on Dog's Island in London"

"Okay now, nobody over there knows about Tom Maxwell, so you will have to watch your step. Just keep an eye on everybody and call a staff meeting for lunch time, but don't call it until, say, twelve o'clock. Now we don't know who attacked Tom Maxwell, neither do the police, I haven't spoken to them, so they know nothing about John Sing."

Jeff felt that this was enough to worry Ruxton, no point in mentioning their doubts about Maylay.

"Will Sing be there?"

"I don't know, technically he's still on the payroll until 5 o'clock this evening, now if he doesn't show for work this morning, then we can call the police" Jeff watched their reaction, and both seemed to react as if that was favourable. Now remember, whatever you hear or see today, don't overreact, just stay cool. A lot of things may happen, say nothing to nobody save me. Understand?"

"Yes" Kay said immediately, but Ruxton was more hesitant.

"Okay then, transfer the money and then get over to Kowloon, Scott Dillon should be there sometime this morning, and don't worry, you can trust him."

Ruxton nodded and left.

"Should I start now on the board members?" Kay asked.

"It's as well." Jeff replied, he watched her leave. Jeff picked up the phone and dialled Eric Ratner's home number. The phone rang three times, then it was answered, just as he expected. The Ratner's had a phone in every room of their magnificent Spanish style villa on the shores of Aberdeen. June answered the phone.

"Morning June, this is Jeff. Is Eric there?"

"Howdy Jeff, he's in the shower. Got a minute?"

"Sure, how are things with you?"

"Pretty good, we've just got back from Tokyo, you know."

"I'd heard you'd gone, or were going. How was your trip?"

"Shitty. Jesus we think Hong Kong is bad in rush hour but hell, Tokyo is rush hour all day long, it just never lets up. We were there for five days and you know, we never seen the sun once. The first two days it was cloudy, misty and hot and the other three days there wasn't a breath of wind and we had smog all the way and hey, we had an earthquake. Jesus it was great, it was around noon, and everything started to shake, shit it was like one great vibrator. I felt like sitting on the pavement and enjoying it. Eric thought it was great, he said it was like the crash of '83 all over again. But hell if you go to Tokyo and they don't have a quake, complain to the tourist board. It's just great, one of the best experiences I've ever had. In fact, it's the closest I ever came to having an orgasm."

Jeff couldn't contain himself any longer, he just burst out laughing. June had to be one of the most open women he had ever met; she was a constant bubbling energy fountain. She had the weirdest way of looking at life, Jeff put it down to the fact that Eric kept her supplied with so much money to spend that she turned back to life to find pleasure. Eric and June's place was the all season's open house, they had four children, but if you visited there was always someone popping in. They had four girls aged between 16 and 20 and there was a constant queue of cars at the entrance. They were not like other Hong Kong millionaires who put up a barrier around themselves. Eric adored the girls, even though he had no son to carry on the business for him he knew that May, the second last and named after June, but before her if you understood the Ratner's logic, would take over the business. She had the flare and the talent and took after her father more so than any of the other three.

"How is Steff?" June asked when Jeff settled down again.

"Oh, that bloody woman, I don't know. I haven't seen her in a while." Jeff knew he could tell a part truth to June and she wouldn't read anything into it or get serious.

"Oh my God, you don't think she's playing golf again?"

Jeff knew what she meant. About two years ago Steff had taken up golf with a vengeance and she was inclined to do things like that. But they usually faded after the initial enthusiasm wore off.

"No, I don't know what she's at this time."

"You're Okay as long as it's not 'red ball'."

This was Hong Kong in-talk for women chasing man.

"She gets enough of that at home, I hope." Jeff replied quickly although the thought of Steff having an affair had never crossed his mind. Those types of things only happened in Dallas or Dynasty.

"Oh, here's Eric, look after that little lady of yours, eh?"

"Sure thing June, we'll probably see you at the mid-summer ball tomorrow night?"

"We'll be there. Here's Eric. Bye."

Eric came on the line. "What's happening, man?"

"Morning Eric, got'a minute?"

"Got five. Shoot!"

"There's a possibility that a large block of shares are going to hit the market this morning or within the next few days that I wanna buy."

"Who's?" The question was purely academic.

"AAB."

"Price range?"

"I don't want to let these get into the wrong hands so I'll go HK$23, but I expect that the price will fall once they hit the market. It's going to be a fine balance to know when to buy" Jeff said.

"That's why you came to me." It was honest statement.

"Correct."

"Method of payment?" Eric asked.

"My personal account. There's $78 million there as from 5 minutes ago."

Eric was silent for a moment. "That solves that problem, Okay. I'll send a messenger over with the forms for you to sign."

"Okay, I'll see you later." Jeff replied.

"Let's have lunch at the Mandarin, Okay by you?"

"Fine, 1 o'clock"

"Gotcha." Eric hung up.

Eric Ratner was one of the liveliest stockbrokers in Hong Kong. He was a one man outfit, no partners just himself and two juniors to do the bidding and buying on the floor of the market. But he was extremely good at his job and he chooses his clients. He didn't just take any buyer or investor, he knew all his clients personally and only dealt with those he liked. He drove the biggest BMW that could be bought with all the possible extras and personalised number plates. That was Eric.

*

Dillon and Olli followed Shui Lui though the computer room to the small room at the end where he promptly set up the computer line for them.

"Now, gentlemen, you may make your call, please excuse me. You can let yourselves out when finished." He bowed politely and shut the door behind him.

"Let's do it." Olli said expectantly.

"Ah, just a minute." Dillon sat down and faced Olli, he had to tell him about Archibald selling out, time was crucial now. If Archibald dumped this morning, the price would fall and if Dillon hadn't gotten the power of buyer by the open of business this morning, those shares could slip to Narrow Investment.

"How do you feel about Jeff?"

Olli was surprised by the question, but he shrugged his shoulders.

"The guy's Okay, why?"

"This thing is not as straight forward as we first thought. There's a complication in the deal. George Archibald has been forced to resign from the board and there's every likelihood that he'll dump his shares on the market this morning."

"That's great." Olli replied. "So we've got shares to buy straight away. Hey, they may even drop in price, all the better."

"There's another complication, Jeff thinks that another bank is about to collapse. He thinks he can buy that bank at a knock-down price."

Olli took sometime to think that one through.

"I don't see a problem there. We acquire AAB at their current share price, if we're lucky and fast, and in the meantime, AAB acquire this other bank which will shove up AAB shares and if Stern decides to pull out, he offloads shares with a high mark up value. Good business. No problem."

"You don't think that Stern would hang back and wait and see?"

"I shouldn't think so, it's not his style. Well I don't think he needs to know anyhow. After all, it's not a complete takeover or buy-out we're talking about here. We're merely taking a stake in a bank with a view to placing key personnel into it with a view to building the bank up to a worthwhile asset. Now I know that Stern has his own ideas for the bank but hell, we can't expect to prevent the board carrying out an acquisition if we only own a percentage of the stocks. We can mention it in passing if you like but I don't think it's gonna affect Stern's decision."

Dillon contained his relief at Olli's optimism and just in talking it through helped alleviate some of the doubts he had about the deal. Dillon swung around in the chair and dialled in Stern's home phone number.

After some static pauses, the phone began to ring. On the second ring Stern answered.

"Dillon here, how are things in New York?"

"Cool and wet. What have you got for me?"

"Oliver." Dillon handed the phone piece over.

"Hi, things are developing faster here than we thought. This guy is really making life easy for us. There was one bad apple on the board, but Bordes-Aitcheson shoved him off, now that creates one small problem. The guy is holding 7% and we think he's going to dump this morning, so we've gotta be in a position to buy within the next," Olli glanced at his watch, 8.30.

"Forty five minutes."

Olli held the phone set out, Dillon could hear Sterns tiny static voice.

"You should have US$100 million there in the bank this morning. There's another 100 million going Friday, all that remains is to get a stockbroker, Dillon was to look after that today."

"Yeah, so he said. So when things developed last night and this morning we had a council of war, and I think we found the guy, Philip Thorn of Thorn, North and Crenshaw." Again he held the phone out for Dillon to hear.

"I had them on a list of ten but not in the top three, I've heard of Crenshaw over here, he sounds as if he's full of shit."

"He is, that's why we've gone for Philip Thorn, they expect him to cut loose from Crenshaw." Olli grinned at Dillon, knowing that they had cracked it; he had said just what Stern wanted to hear.

"Okay, go with Thorn. We've heard rumours here that a bank is in trouble over there?"

They looked at each other slightly shocked, but then anybody who paid as much attention to bank news as Stern did would be able to smell the signs of money being shifted.

Dillon took the phone. "It's true, Bordes-Aitcheson was telling me about it last night, he thinks it could be open to a bid. He is going to try and take it over"

"How much does he think he's gonna' need?"

"One hundred million." Dillon calmly replied.

"US?" Stern enquired.

"Yeah."

"Can he do it on his own?"

"I don't think so; he doesn't know yet just how bad it is."

"Okay look, I'll transfer another 100 million first thing in the morning. You should already have 100 million. If the shit hits the fan today you're just going to have to bluff your way through. Let's just hope that it doesn't happen for another day, if it does, lie, act as if you got a billion on hand. Bordes-Aitcheson can phone me if necessary to confirm the money is on its way. He is just going to have to back you on this. Okay?"

"Okay."

"GTI." Stern signed off.

"Let's go appoint a stockbroker." Olli said enthusiastically.

Chapter Twelve

Don Ruxton was only slightly apprehensive as he unlocked the main door to the AAB bank on Nathan Road, Kowloon. He stepped into the silent building and locked the door. After checking the alarm system, he went first to the telex machine. There were some overnight messages. He tore off the paper, folded it and headed towards Tom Maxwell's office.

It was 8.35, 25 minutes before any staff were due in and Ruxton wanted a little time to look around and familiarise himself with Maxwell's filing system before he had to face the staff. Although it was more than likely the most of them would have heard the eight o'clock news, which was the first bulletin to mention the assault. But he still felt that he had to address the staff, make sure that no unnecessary rumours got a head start. He sat at the desk and went through the telexes.

Of the five received overnight, three were ordinary transactions but the other two were a little more alarming.

One was from a London bank requesting the transfer of depositor's funds to an account in London. The amount called down was almost the entire account. Two million HK Dollars. The second one was the same situation except this time from a German bank acting on behalf of a major international company that had large deposits with the AAB.

"What the hell is going on?" he asked himself. He reached for the phone and buzzed Jeff's extension over on the Island.

"Yeah?"

"Jeff, I've got two requests on telex for major withdrawals together. They come to over $4.8 million."

"Christ, who are they?"

"Equinox Ltd. in Germany and John Lismore in London."

"Christ almighty, the word must be out about the OUT Bank and they're pulling their money from Hong Kong."

"Then it must be true, Chan's bank is in trouble."

"Look Don, leave that to me. I'll telex them back for confirmation. Let's see, it's what time now, 1 a.m. in London so they won't be open for business until 4 o'clock our time. We've got seven hours to see how things develop here. If this is a result of speculation about the OUT bank, then it's going to be a bad day here because if they've heard it in London, they'll know here. What reserves have we got over there?"

"Hold on," Don switched on the IBM and keyed into the holding account. "Just over $22.5 million."

"Yeah." Jeff was checking the reserves according to his IBM. "There's just over 100 million here. Now look, if there is a run, tell the staff. Wait, you were going to call a staff meeting?"

"Yes."

"Okay then, alert them about the danger of a run and tell them to double check every withdrawal. Use the terminals, let queues form if necessary, but tell them not to overdo it. We don't want to panic people, the general public may not even have heard about OUT. Let's hope so, eh?"

"What a day to have to stand in for Tom."

"And late opening as well." Jeff laughed nervously.

"Shit, I never thought of that."

"I'll call you before opening time."

Don hung up and stared at the telexes. "Gosh, $4.8 million and we haven't even opened for business yet."

The door bell rang. Don's mind was elsewhere as he walked through the bank towards the door. He turned off the alarm, turned the key in the lock and pulled the door open.

*

Jeff was studying the IBM screen anticipating the likely effect on the Holding Account that a depositor run might have on the balance sheet. He had been thinking about it overnight but had not been overly concerned because he figured that most of his depositors were investment of institutional deposits. If they were panicking already on rumours and speculation, however, then what hope did he have when the news hit the street and the small depositors came looking for their money? His thoughts were interrupted when Kay buzzed him. He stabbed the intercom button on the phone.

"Yes?"

"Detective Chung to see you."

Jeff muttered under his breath, but he knew that Chung must have been persistent to get past Kay. "Okay send him in." He stood up; Jeff hated the idea of being looked down at by a cop.

The door opened and Chung strode arrogantly into the office. Jeff motioned him to the chair. Kay shot Jeff a glance of apology and closed the door. When Chung was seated Jeff sat back down.

"What can I do for you Detective?" Jeff ignored the formalities.

"I was hoping we could get this over with at the hospital last night."

"I'm afraid I wasn't in much condition to talk to you last night. Tom Maxwell was a very close friend."

"That's what I understood and I would have thought you would be anxious to see his attacker behind bars as quickly as possible."

Jeff knew he was stumped so he kept quiet; he wanted to get to the point and get this over with so he let Chung have his little victory.

"When did you last see Tom Maxwell before the attack?"

"He was here around 4 or 4.15 yesterday afternoon." Jeff had decided last night to give the police everything that might be relevant.

"When you say here do you mean in this office?"

"Yes, we had a meeting here?"

"Yourself and Tom Maxwell? Was there anyone else present?"

"Yes, John Sing, that's our assistant manager over at Kowloon and Scott Dillon, he was at the hospital last night."

"And the purpose of the meeting?"

"To sack John Sing." Jeff put it as bluntly as possible.

"For what reason?" the cop enquired without showing any surprise almost as if he had already known.

"Well it's a slightly delicate situation and there's an ongoing internal investigation. I think it would be wrong of me to make any unsubstantiated allegations against John Sing at this stage. Once our investigation has been complete and if I feel that the result of it would assist your enquiries, then of course I will make a report available to you."

"But you said the meeting was to sack him, so you must already have a conclusion drawn."

Jeff hadn't seen that one coming; he had dug a hole for himself and had fallen in.

"Yes, the purpose of the meeting was to sack him, needless to say he denied the allegations made against him, so I asked for his resignation by 5 o'clock this evening. In the meantime we are carrying out an investigation, so in the event of his not resigning we hope to have the evidence which will justify his dismissal."

Detective Chung stared at Jeff intensely. "Who was the accuser, or should I say the-"

"I know what you're getting at, it was Tom Maxwell that reported John Sing to me."

"You think John Sing is responsible for the attack?"

"I've no doubt whatsoever about it."

Chung nodded but there was suspicion in his eyes. "Of course, it would solve your problem about proving any allegations against him."

Jeff picked up some sheaf of paper off the desk and began to tidy them by pounding the ends of the sheets on the desk.

"Well Detective, I've taken enough of your valuable time, so if you'll excuse me I'll allow you to get back to your duties."

Chung was startled by the abrupt and sarcastic dismissal. He rose, bowed and left.

That was going to be one problem out of the way for the rest of the day. Jeff figured. They would probably arrest John Sing and hold him for the day at least and interrogate him. That would keep George'y boy busy, sweating in case Sing sang and mentioned his name. But then, what if Sing hadn't attacked Tom, but that it was really Maylay as Dillon suggested? Christ that was crazy. Then he wondered if either Sing or Maylay had showed up for work. Only one way to find out. Jeff punched the key phone for the extension to the Kowloon bank. It rang around 3 times without answer; just then the door of the office opened and Kay came in.

"Sorry, Jeff, but I think you should see this" She held out a telex message. Jeff stared at her, she was shaking, he had never seen her so unsettled before. He took the telex and read it.

*

Dillon had gone back to the hotel to change into a lighter suit after he and Olli left the PACIC offices. The morning was developing much hotter than he had expected. It was around ten past eight when he got back down to the reception and Charlie Chan was waiting for him.

"Mornin' Boss."

"Top o' the mornin to you Charlie, you're going to save me a taxi fare. I've got a visit to make."

"No problem boss, where to?" Charlie said enthusiastically as he led the way down to the car.

"You know where Sir Percy Penderville lives?"

"Sure boss, get you there in ten minutes, no problem boss." Dillon got into the back seat of the black air-conditioned Merc, relieved to be in the coolness of the car. Charlie fired the engine and almost immediately started swearing at every other driver in sight.

Pretty soon they were heading out of Hong Kong central and started to ascend the peak. The early morning fog was replaced by the humid haze that hung around the summit stubbornly.

"Is it always this hot?"

"No boss, this pretty shitty. Soon go away when rain come, maybe today, maybe tomorrow, never mind" They drove on in silence now, there being only the occasional car for Charlie to watch carefully, just in case they needed a lesson in their parentage.

"You with the bank long?"

"Oh 'rong time boss, ' rost count of years.'

Dillon nodded, figuring the maybe Charlie didn't want to talk. They were on the western side of the Peak now and Charlie slowed the Merc and drew up at an entrance gate. Charlie got out and pushed open the apparently unlocked gate. The house up the drive was ancient, perhaps a hundred years old and could have stood on the English countryside. But as they drew closer, Dillon could see that the place was not well maintained. The once magnificent fountain and flower beds were now dried up, covered in bird droppings and overgrown.

"I wait here, boss." Dillon got out and went up to the door. Just as he was about to ring the doorbell he heard footsteps on the gravel to his right.

"Hallow." an elderly woman wearing a white summer frock approached.

"Ah hello, my name is Scott Dillon. I was hoping to see Sir Percy Penderville?" Dillon greeted the old woman. Time had ravaged her face, but he could see a proud woman hiding in her eyes and her stance.

"I'm Lady Penderville. What do you want with my husband?" She looked at the black Merc and probably recognised it as being from the bank.

"I'd like to talk to him about a business proposition that would be very beneficial to him."

"Percy is far too old for business propositions, young man."

"I represent some people who would like to purchase his shares." He knew he shouldn't be talking out here with her, but he felt that she would have to approve the deal too. She had that air of decision about her, she was not the type of woman to leave her man to it.

"Well at least you're blunt, young man. And I dare say that if I was to ask you, how much per share, you would undoubtedly say, more than sufficient?" There was a hard knowing grin on her face. She went to the door and opened it.

"If you lock a door, bad minds think you have something worth locking up. If you leave it unlocked, those minds think you're either not far away, or you have nothing worth stealing. We leave them unlocked, you can make your own mind up as to why."

She led him into the enormous reception area. As he followed, he looked around realizing that this was once a centrepiece of Hong Kong social life, but now it was obvious that the halls were far from hallowed.

Light rectangular patches showed where great paintings once hung. The only pieces of furniture in the reception hall were a phone desk and a hat stand. She led him through a narrow corridor off the hall and through into the kitchen. Only here were the signs of things as they were in times past. It was a long narrow kitchen with sinks and washing area against the exterior wall.

Sunlight poured through the many panes of glass across the room to the three solid fuel cookers. He could visualise times past when perhaps 20 people worked in this kitchen preparing meals for the guests out in the great dining hall. But now it was a sad reminder of better days. In the middle stood a long working table made of beech and probably as old as the man sat at the end of it, staring back at him.

"This is Mister Dillon, Percy. He says he wants to buy your shares." She pulled out a chair for Dillon near the old man. He nodded his head in thanks and sat down turning to face Sir Percy. Time hadn't been as unkind to him as it had been to his wife, he still had tight tanned skin but his eyes were sad and had a bloodshot permanency.

"Who gave you the impression I wanted to sell?" he asked studying Dillon closely. His wife now sat opposite.

"Nobody, but you have the single largest individually owned stock after Jeff."

"Just who do you represent?" Lady Penderville enquired.

"A group of people who wish to purchase a share in AAB, it's a friendly bid, Jeff wants to reduce his share considerably because he is far too exposed personally and my people want to establish a foothold in Hong Kong."

"And who are ' Your People'?" she repeated.

"Because of the delicacy of the situation here in Hong Kong at the moment, I'm not at liberty to divulge their name just yet. However, if you require reassurance as to the nature of the bid you can, of course, call Jeff."

"How much of Percy's stake do you want to purchase?"

"The lot."

They looked at each other, and then she looked back at Dillon. "We couldn't give you a decision here and now, even if we agreed on a price."

"Well, that's your decision, but I cannot make any commitments on price, at least until I know I can buy straight away. You see, there are things happening on the market right now that could affect the price of all shares." He had both their undivided attention, now for the killer blow.

"I couldn't tie myself down to a price that may drop by 10 o'clock"

They both stared at him, but he felt that there was more concern in her eyes than in his.

"What exactly do you mean by that?" she asked.

"Just what I said." He had to shake, he felt sure that he had made the case perfectly clear, but just in case he reworded it.

"Unless I get a commitment to an understanding before I leave here this morning, I cannot guarantee the price." Again he paused and considered both of them. "Things are going to happen this morning that will effect the price of your shares. My people want this to be a friendly bid; it would not be seen as such if the current shareholders got less than the current price. We are prepared to bid 50 cents above the market value."

"What's going to happen?"

"Can we just say that things are going to happen, if not this morning or later today then certainly tomorrow. It would be unfair of me to enter into the exact nature of the speculation."

"Mister Dillon," Sir Percy began angrily. "I have never liked half truths or the unscrupulous use of rumours to bring pressure to bear on me. You will not have to concern yourself, old chap, with agreeing a price this morning unless you clean up your act and stop beating around the bush."

Never one to backtrack apologetically Dillon forged on. "Do you keep in touch with your banking contacts?"

"Yes, of course." Sir Percy snapped.

"Well then you've probably heard the rumours around town?"

"I say, if you know something that we don't, either inform us or don't, whichever suits yourself, but for God's sake get on with it, man!"

"You probably have already heard but if you wish for confirmation I will supply it. There is talk that a major bank will collapse very soon."

"Would you like tea, Mister Dillon?" Lady Penderville rose and looked at him expectantly. Either the conversation was over, or ' time out' was being called. He nodded.

"Do you follow cricket Mister Dillon?" Sir Percy asked.

"Ah, I used to but I'm afraid we don't get much news of Lords or the Oval in Wall St." He smiled disarmingly.

"Are you one of these Wall Street Chappies then?"

"No, I don't work on Wall Street but my boss does. He's a whiz kid."

"I thought they were called ' Yuppies' or some-such nowadays."

"He probably calls himself a Yuppie." Dillon agreed.

Sir Percy pondered a thought for a moment, "So you don't follow cricket, damn pity. Don't meet enough people to have a good old wag with anymore. You know," He turned to look at Dillon in the eye. "There was a time when you met white men regularly here now it's all changed. These young people are mixing with the 'slanties' as if they were equal. Now I say that's just not right, old chap." Sir Percy's face was twisted in disgust with the very thoughts that he was evoking.

"They let them in everywhere now you know, bars, hotels; you can't even have a white's only club anymore. Good lord, what has the world come to? I mean, there was no one here when we arrived, not a one, there was no one on this island when we came here first and when we began to build and trade they started to flood into the place. Now look at it, there are millions of them and we are less than one percent. Damn Governors we've had here, lilly liveried lot of damn socialists giving away our way of life to the 'slanties'. When I see how much this place has changed, there are times I could just catch the next ship."

Lady Penderville placed the milk jug, some cups, sugar, spoons and a plate of scones on the table.

"Now, now, Percy, you know you shouldn't get overly emotional about our little friends." She caught Dillon's eye and winked. Then nodded towards Sir Percy. Dillon figured that the message she was trying to convey was, 'play along'.

"They do get around." Was all Dillon could think of to say.

"They breed you know, I thought Catholic's had the monopoly on reproduction records, but these Chinese will out number every other race in the world by the year 2013. Just imagine that, every other person you meet will be Chinese. And, they only have 27 surnames." Sir Percy shook his head slowly realising, as if for the first time, the implication of the facts and figures. Sir Percy suddenly changed tack as if something else was now more pressing.

"How are things back home?" Dillon overlooked the fact that they had just been talking about Wall Street, home was England and it seemed as if Sir Percy's mind was there right now.

"People are making money in England now for the first time in years. People willing to work that is, and property has picked up for the first time in a while"

"I read *The Times*." Sir Percy grunted.

"Then you know that the stock market is on the move?"

"Yes I do." Sir Percy eyed Dillon suspiciously; he knew now that Dillon knew just what he wanted. He wanted to get the hell out of Hong Kong and back to England where money meant something. Here it was just monopoly money, it was treated as if you could get any amount of it, if you went broke you could start again. Okay for young men, but when you're pushing seventy? And he was offering 50 cents over market price. Which will probably fall with the crash of Harry Chan's bank. So P.B. Gunn had been right when he said yesterday that the OUT was gone. But there was nothing Sir Percy could have done, His AAB shares had always been the family silver. He just couldn't place them on a falling market, they were given down to him by his father, he couldn't panic sell.

"Fifty cents above market value is tempting, you're Ladyship." Sir Percy said to her.

"I leave all these things to you, Percy." she replied offering Dillon a scone.

"Well what would your advice be on the matter?" he persisted.

"If there's trouble coming and Mister Dillon is offering 50 cents above market, I would be inclined to sell."

"There you are, Mister Dillon. We sell, by George."

"Okay let's get onto your broker then."

CHAPTER THIRTEEN

"What the hell is going on?" Don Ruxton stared at John Sing.

"Don, I need to talk to someone, everything's gone crazy."

"You're not kidding." Don shoved the door closed, against his better judgment, and led Sing into his Maxwell's office. To say he had been surprised to see Sing at the door was very mild. He hadn't expected to ever meet Sing again after what Jeff had told him this morning when he had asked him to hold down the Kowloon branch.

Don Ruxton had little time for Sing, for although Ruxton was Eurasian, he was second generation whereas Sing had a Chinese mother. Ruxton's father was Eurasian but his mother was Portuguese so he always said that he was better bred than Sing.

"Everything's going crazy, Don. I didn't know who to talk to." He was silent for a moment then said, "Does Jeff think I attacked Tom?"

"What do you think?" Don was trying hard not to show his fear; he didn't even want to be in the same room as Sing.

"It looks bad, eh? But I swear to you on my mother's ancestors that I did not attack Tom" He starred right into Don's eyes.

"I'm sorry John, but if you're innocent you should go to the police."

"I know, I know." Sing almost cried. "But if they don't believe me and they have no other suspect, I would just be the easy scapegoat for them. You know how they are, they collect as much evidence on the suspect they have rather than do the hard work of finding the real attacker."

"I can't see what options you have John."

"I could find the real culprit." he suggested helpfully.

"Where would you start?" Don asked trying to think of how long until other staff arrived.

"I'd start with George Archibald, after all it was him who was most interested in finding out about the ledgers and you know that he came here Monday evening after Tina Bolger found them."

"I heard that, yes."

"You know who told him in the first place?"

"No." Don replied nervously, not wanting to vex Sing. He needed to keep him calm and wait for someone to come.

"It was Maylay; she phoned him and he then came and asked me if it was true. What could I do? He did get me my appointment, I owed him that much. But I had no idea that this would be the result. I cannot understand how it came about that Maxwell would be attacked, unless," He hesitated for a moment.

Ruxton glanced down at the executive pad on Tom Maxwell's desk, he just couldn't look Sing in the eye and he just wanted this over with. Then something written there caught his eye.

"Unless," Sing was saying, "Tom found some connection between Maylay and George Archibald and confronted them. Something which could be used against them?"

Ruxton was not listening, he was reading Tom Maxwell's scribble on the note pad. It read, 'George Archibald, Territories Freight and Shipping CO, and Maylay Dulles?' A circle had been drawn around all three names.

"What do you know about Territories Freight and Shipping Company?" Don suddenly forgot this fear of Sing.

"George's company? Not a lot really, why? What do you mean?" Sing replied, puzzled.

Ruxton didn't know what he meant himself. "It's written here, look."

Sing rose and went behind the desk and looked at the writing.

"What can it mean?" They both starred at the note unable to make a connection. It didn't make a lot of sense, as far as they knew there was no connection between George and Maylay, and certainly no connection between the bank and Territories Freight and Shipping, for that account was with Lloyd's. The company had no connection. George himself had an investment account with the AAB but apart from that none of his business accounts were with the AAB.

"Perhaps Jeff could make a connection." Ruxton suggested.

"Or Tom Maxwell."

They looked at each other thoughtfully. Ruxton reached for the phone.

"What are you going to do?" Sing asked.

"Tell Jeff about this."

"Will you tell him I'm here?" Sing studied Ruxton sympathetic eyes.

"That's up to you, but for your own sake I think you should turn yourself in."

"Tell him I'm here but ask him not to call the police; I'd like to stay away from them for as long as possible."

"Okay John."

*

Bordes-Aitcheson hands trembled as picked up the telex and read it once more.

For the attention of;

JR Bordes-Aitcheson

AAB Bank Hong Kong.

Date: July 16/85, time 2.45 p.m.

Place: New York.

Our man Scott Dillon recommends buy.

I can now confirm interest.

US$100 million being forwarded, you will have it by noon your time.

Further money available if required.

Have a nice day.

Stern

WTB

New York.

So now he had money to deal with, or, rather the Americans had money to deal with. The intercom on the phone buzzed.

"There's a William Straff here from Eric Ratner's Office."

"Ah good, send him in."

Kay came in followed by Straff. The man was 23 years of age and dressed like the new breed of young powerful executives.

"Morning Jeff." he said with assumed familiarity. Kay closed the door as she left.

"Morning." Bordes-Aitcheson replied with a generous amount of politeness. He didn't like this new breed of brash new kids that had sprung up around the fast changing Hong Kong money and stock market. The financial area was once controlled by careful refined old men but that had all changed now with the new instant knowledge technology that the computer had brought to the whole Financial Market.

"Some stuff for you to sign. I understand you're in the market for some stock?"

From Straff's statement, Jeff knew that the young man was fishing for something and wondered did this kid figure that there was percentage here, or was he just passing time?

"Yeah I'm chasing stock." Jeff replied leafing through the papers.

"You have heard the rumours?" Again this sounded like a snooping question.

"About what?" Jeff acted surprised.

"The OUT is trading down heavily, even before opening."

Jeff glanced at his watch, five minutes to nine, five minutes to opening and the market was nervous already. "How bad?" Jeff enquired; buying the OUT bank may be easier than he first thought.

"They are down 50 points already. The word is that there's going to be a meltdown" Straff said confidently.

"What's the reason?" Now Jeff was the one fishing for information.

"Harry Chan has disappeared; he wasn't at the golf course this morning."

Harry Chan played golf every morning without fail; it was like, his way of waking up. This was major news.

Jeff studied the 'Buy Form' on his desk, it was blank, he knew he wasn't expected to fill out the name of the stock he wanted to buy. Normally Eric would take care of that entering 'AAB' against 'name of stock' and Eric would also enter the purchase guide-lines, but now?

Now, now everything was changed. If it was true about Harry Chan having disappeared and the OUT being down 50 points already, then there would be a general knock-on and all stocks would fall. The problem was a very basic one, in that it was going to be a very jittery market.

It was an accepted fact that things in Hong Kong had never fully recovered from the '83 crash fuelled by Britain's careless approach to negotiations on the very future of Hong Kong and the Chinese investors were notoriously nervous about their hard earned money. With only one year to go, a fortune lost now may never be recouped. With the OUT bank teetering on the verge of a major crash which would undoubtedly cause major problems for all bank shares, the investors would undoubtedly cut their losses and dump shares, thus forcing the value of stock down even further. The question was, would this just be a readjustment of value or would it be as Straff suggested, a major 'Meltdown'. If it was a Meltdown then this was no time to go buying stock, he could loose a fortune not to mention the value of his own 40% which would decrease in value with every point dropped.

"Look William, I think I'd better talk to Eric again before I go ahead with this."

"That would be my advice; it's not a particularly good time."

Straff rose to his feet. Jeff watched the young man leave the office and then picked up the telex again.

Where the hell does this development leave our plans? he thought.

The phone interrupted his thoughts.

"Yes?"

"Jeff, this is Don"

He listened to what Don had discovered written on the desk pad.

"Maylay Dulles?" Jeff replied thoughtfully.

"Perhaps the connection is on George's wife's side."

"Aggy? And Maylay Dulles?" Jeff again replied thoughtfully.

"What was her maiden name?"

"I don't know, it's never occurred to me-"

"Maybe Tom found something out-"

"Are you suggesting that Maylay may have attacked Tom?"

"That's what we think." Don said 'we', Jeff picked up on it.

"We? Who's there with you, Scott Dillon?"

"John Sing."

Bordes-Aitcheson stared into space, fear suddenly filled his gut. If John Sing was there then had the phone call been forced on Don?

"Are you Okay?"

"Sure, John says he didn't do it and I'm inclined to believe him."

"Has Maylay showed up yet?"

"No not yet, Jeff. I think the police should be told about our suspicions, about Maylay. They're looking for John and she could get away clean."

"Okay I'll phone Detective Chung, he was here this morning. So I guess I'd better set the record straight." Bordes-Aitcheson considered telling him about the latest on the OUT Bank but decided that Don had enough on his hands for the moment.

He signed off and hung up. The phone buzzed immediately.

"Hallow?"

"Jeff, Nora Conlon here."

"Morning Nora." She was the doctor on duty last night at the hospital.

"You were right; there was another attack this morning."

"Jesus, did they get him?" he gasped in disbelief.

"I moved Tom as you suggested early this morning, the gunman shot up the ' John Chan' in Tom's room.

"Thanks be to God." Jeff let out a sigh of relief. Now his worse fears were confirmed, something big was going on; the very fact that there was another attempt was made on Tom's life proved that. "Er, how is Tom this morning?"

"Still unconscious but the signs are a little better this morning. But Jeff, there's going to be hell to play here over this. There's one policeman dead and another wounded, the place is a mess."

"Did they get the guy?"

"He was wounded but he got away. They got a good description of him and figured that they will get him pretty quickly."

"Jesus what a mess!"

"The police are pretty pissed off right now. They are asking questions about why we moved Tom and put a ' John Chan' in his place. They want to know who authorised it and why. They say that we set up those two policemen for nothing. There's going to be trouble over it."

"Okay Nora, I'll handle it. I'll get in touch with the Chief Superintendent. Look I'll come over there just as soon as I can."

"I'm off duty now anyhow; I just happened to be here a little later then normal this morning so I'll just go home and stay out of reach for a few hours."

"I'll call you later." He hung up and buzzed Kay.

"Get me Allen Lee on the phone." While he waited, his private line rang.

"Hallow" He fully expected to hear a familiar voice, but it wasn't anyone he ever heard before.

"Good morning, Honourable Bordes-Aitcheson. My name is Diver Ho and I have information that will be of great interest to you."

"Do I know you?" Jeff said suspiciously, wondering what the hell this was about and how did someone he didn't know get his personal number.

"Beg pardon, Honourable Sir, we have never met before. But information very important, oh very much. You wish to meet?"

"Well I don't know about that; I'm very busy this morning." Jeff wanted to get rid of this person, but at the same time, the puzzlement of this man's 'important information' caught his interest.

"Information makes your day, maybe make your whole week. Very important, you see."

"Okay, can you come to the bank around 12.30?"

"Very good, Honourable Sir, you not regret." The line went dead. He replaced the phone and it buzzed immediately.

"Allen Lee here."

"Morning again Allen."

"Morning." Lee replied and Jeff thought there was suspicion in his voice. The noise in the background was unusual to say the least.

There was a discreet knock on the door.

"Just a moment Allen," He cupped the receiver and called "Enter" Kay stuck her head around the door.

"He's at the airport." She pointed to the phone. He nodded and uncapped the receiver.

"Allen, sorry about that. Am I keeping you from something?"

"It's Okay go ahead." But Jeff knew something was going on, what the hell was he doing at the airport, he waved Kay forward.

"You've probably heard about the attack at the hospital."

"Oh." Lee replied and Jeff figured he hadn't.

"There's been a bit of a cock up; I had Tom Maxwell moved last night but apparently no one told your people. Seems that a ' John Chan' was left in the room that Tom was in. Well hell, it was just a mix up but one of your guys is dead."

"What?"

"One of your men got shot in this morning's attack, didn't he?"

"Sorry Jeff but I don't know what you're talking about, I'll check this out and get back to you. Where are you at?"

"The bank." Jeff said and let Lee hang up first. Shit this was going to be real trouble. He hadn't told the cops about his suspicions that there might be another attempt on Tom's life, now a cop was dead.

Yeah, he figured, *there's gonna be big trouble.* Jeff looked up at Kay. "Very odd, he didn't know anything about it."

"Has there been another attack?" Kay gasped.

He told her about the call from Nora Conlon.

"So, Tom's Okay then?"

"Yes, but I wonder why Lee is at the airport?"

"I thought it rather odd, when I phoned police HQ. They told me he was out at the station there. When I got him and put him on automatic stand-by, then I realised that you might be interested to know where he was but you had the other line tied up. So I couldn't tell you in time."

"Doesn't matter, I wonder why he's out there?" Jeff's stomach was in turmoil good and proper, he didn't know what question to try and tackle in his mind first: Tom's attack; the shares; the mysterious phone caller; Dillon; Don; Sing and Lee at the airport.

Shit, this was going to be one fuck-up of a day. Jeff thought.

CHAPTER FOURTEEN

By nine o'clock that Thursday morning, the heat out in the street was oppressive. It was with relief that the employees of the Hang Seng Stock Exchange took their positions at their respective computer consoles. Little did they know that within two hours the heat on the street would seem like a gentle summer breeze compared to the frenzied panic that was to grip the Stock Exchange that day. In a matter of hours, trading had wiped 50 points off the value of OUT shares but that was nothing to what was to come.

When the market opened the values were adjusted and the phones began to buzz with sell orders from all over the Colony, putting even more pressure on the prices. Last night the word was that the bank was in trouble, this morning the word was that Harry Chan was not at the Golf Club and now at nine he was not at his desk. Chan was known to be a meticulous time keeper and was regularly at work at eight. The signs were not good and those keen market watchers wanted out, just in case. And then there was the Bear Gambler. These people who played the market purely for monetary gain. Buying and selling stock for the gain, not for any of them believing in the value of the stock itself. They can buy or sell stock and have up to 14 days to settle their accounts, but in this case they had only five days as the end of the accounting period was the following Monday. But as everyone was to know later that day, a day is a long time in the Stock Market. In the case of the OUT shares that morning, the Bear would offer for sale shares that he did not necessarily own in the hope that he could buy them later at less then he offered them for sale. With the shares that morning trading at $22.50 and obviously in for a fall, the Bear would offer for sale a quantity of shares at anything less then the $22.50 that they were trading in at that moment. He then had until Monday morning to produce them. In the meantime, he hoped to buy them at much less than the current price.

The buyers this morning were the unawares of life. Most brokers would have standing orders to buy all sorts of shares, from the outside investor to the existing and determined OUT shareholder who believed in the bank and refused to accept that their shares would fall. And then there was the small time punter who had a few dollars to invest and would have a buy order with his broker. The OUT bank's own broker would have instructions to pick up any spare shares to help fend off any sudden panic, but his buying would only stem the drop for a short while. He couldn't prevent the floodgates.

By five after nine, it became obvious that there were far more shares being offered for sale then there were orders to buy. So the sellers reduced their asking price, the shares hit $21.95, a drop of 80 points on last night's close. The number of buyers receded. All other banks also suffered although not to the same degree as the OUT. By ten past nine, AAB was being offered at $22.40 down 10 points. Those brokers handling mainly industrial shares watched in anticipation of the jitters hitting their area. It became obvious after just a few minutes of trading that a fairly major realignment of the financial sectors share values was about to happen.

Most trading posts had their computers set up in such a way that when shares fell below a certain value a warning would flash on the consuls and the order to sell would place the shares on the market automatically and reduce the price to sell. The problem with this system is that it creates its own momentum and can take some time to be noticed and then stopped. The computers were already flashing the sell sign for OUT shares and just then nobody paid too much attention to the computers and anyhow, nobody cared as they were to busy selling them themselves. But later it would matter.

*

Sir Jerald Lawson was the 'senior' partner in the Stockbroker firm of Lawson & Lilywhite - a long established firm with little or no interest in the ultra modern stock-market. They had no computer link up with the Hang Seng stock-market for one very simple reason: Lilywhite was to retire in two months time and Lawson intended to 'Sell On' the brokerage firm. Although Lawson was the senior partner, he was much younger then Lilywhite.

When he entered his office at ten after nine, his young secretary had a message for him.

"Sir Percy Penderville rang; he asks that you ring him back 'Rather urgently'."

What does Sir Percy want then he wondered as he dialled. The old goat still owes me money, maybe he has come into an inheritance.

Sir Percy answered the phone.

"Good morning, Sir Percy, Jerald Lawson here. I received a message to call you. How can I help?"

"Ah Jerald old chap, how is Lily and the children?"

"Fine, fine and how is your good lady wife?"

"No change still got green fingers I'm afraid. What news do you have from the stock market this morning?"

"What section?" Lawson became suspicious.

"The banking sector."

"Well I think it's still there. Of course, there are always rumours," Then as an afterthought, he added, "But as you know, I don't pay any credence to rumours. Our great Empire was not built on rumours."

He heard Sir Percy cough his disapproval and waited.

"I say, old chap, you know those AAB share's I have?"

"Yes." Lawson straightened in his chair expectantly.

"Actually I rather thought I would dispose of them."

Lawson sat bolt upright. The last time he had checked on AAB, they were something around $23. He didn't know off hand but he knew that Sir Percy had a sizable amount of them, at 1.5% commission.

"I say." he stammered.

"Oh?" Sir Percy asked suspiciously.

"No, sorry, old chap, I was just thinking out loud and do you plan to sell the whole lot?"

"Yes, the lot."

Lawson almost dropped the phone.

"Okay, Sir Percy, I'll get right on it." Lawson said into the phone trying to conceal his excitement.

"Just one other thing."

"Yes?" Lawson replied suspiciously.

"There is a, ah, shall we say, understanding with a certain party that they alone will buy the shares."

"Oh? Do you want this deal conducted privately?" If this was so, Lawson knew that would cost more and would need the approval of the Chairman of the stock Exchange.

"There shouldn't be any need for that. It can be done on the open market, provided that the right party purchase. You know what I mean, old chap?"

Lawson did and he didn't like it. It was slightly unethical.

"Leave that to me. They will contact you." Sir Percy hung up.

The market is based on speculation and opportunism: in other words you see someone buying a large block of shares, then he knows something. Either the shares are undervalued or the guy is trying a takeover. Either way they are going to rise in value, so you grab a piece of the action, but this under the counter deal looked like an attempt to control the price. He wondered if he still had any AAB stock.

It took a few minutes but Lawson found them, 2,000 AAB shares that he had bought some years ago for around $14 each, so selling now at a profit of $9 a share, that's a profit of $18,000.

"Well that's made my day." he muttered as he gathered up his briefcase and headed for the outer office.

"If anyone is looking for me I'm down the Hang Seng for the rest of the morning." He left the office and rode the elevator down.

Lawson avoided eye contact with people in the event that they could read anything in his expression, for he felt sure that his inner thoughts would show through. The deal would be Okay if the market was sluggish, but for the last 18 months, it had been positively 'Bullish' ever since that near fatal crash of '83, but now it was hard to know. Lawson kept reminding himself that he may not get away with it as seven percent of AAB was a huge block of shares to move.

Normally the way one would go about it was that one would spread it around a number of stations so as not to cause suspicion, but one fell swoop, it could be dangerous. *Seven Percent, Good Lord that was an awful lot!* Lawson thought. Then he recalled the fun and games there had been back in '83 over about the same amount of shares. Bordes-Aitcheson had phoned to ask if Sir Percy had sold any of his shares. The relief in his voice over the phone had been obvious when he learned that Sir Percy hadn't and now Lawson wondered if this mysterious group that Aitcheson mentioned were the same people that had bought that 8% back in '83? Perhaps he should call Bordes-Aitcheson and let him know.

Then he recalled another conversation some time later with another member of the board of AAB, George Archibald, asking him much the same question and Archibald had asked to be informed if Sir Percy ever wanted to sell his shares.

That's what I'll do. he thought, *I'll phone Archibald and let him know, as a matter of courtesy.*

It was 9.25 when Lawson got to the stock exchange and the first thing he saw was unlike anything he had ever seen before. On the way in, he met Nigel Chambers, an old friend from way back. Nigel was the main broker for the OUT bank and they had known each other for more than 20 years. Lawson saw Nigel coming down the corridor and stopped to talk to his friend to get a feel for the mood of the exchange this morning.

"Morning Nig' how are things?" he greeted.

"Jer' sorry, can't stop. The fucking world's coming apart."

"I say, what's going on, old chap?" Lawson enquired, surprised by his friend's near panic.

"The OUT, the bottom is about to fall out of it. Harry Chan has disappeared, he's not at his desk and he hasn't been seen since yesterday evening. The speculation is that he's flown the coop. The market is in one hell of an up-roar; all the banks are taking a hammering. Shit and it's like '83 again, only worse. In '83 there was a danger of panic due to outside influence, but this is internal for Christ sake. It's a bank that's gone wrong and that's going to effect us all." Chambers shrugged his shoulders at him and brushed past.

Lawson stood there for a moment trying to collect his thoughts. What the hell was old Percy up to? Did he know something? Or was this pure chance? One thing was for certain, it would not now be easy to sell the AAB shares, if what Nig' said was true.

He ran up the corridor now to his tiny office overlooking the floor of the exchange. Brokers were not allowed on the floor of the Hang Seng exchange, but they could observe from communication offices overlooking the floor. Even through the glass partition he could feel the tension down on the floor: many operators were standing watching the huge wall monitors that displayed the current price of shares that was the average, struck between the sell and buy prices being offered.

Although still not too familiar with the computer system, he paged through the screens until he found the OUT shares. They were being offered at $20.95. From the console, he could see that, that was a full 180 points down on last night's close.

He quickly found the AAB shares, they were being offered at $22.15 down 35 points.

He flicked through the rest of the 60 or so publicly quoted banks, and all save the Hong Kong & Shanghai bank were down at least 30 points.

Christ this was a major fall and the markets had just opened! Lawson thought.

He was just about to pick up the phone when it rang.

"Yes." he said into it.

"Hi there. This is Philip Thorn here of Thorn North & Crenshaw. I understand that a certain party wishes to part with some shares."

"Ah, yes, I, ah believe that that is the case." Lawson was in somewhat of a quandary; did he go ahead with the deal or advise Sir Percy to wait and see if this thing blew over and the market recovered. Or did he go ahead and be damned? Of course every moment he waited meant that he lost money, as the selling price reduced and that meant less commission for him.

"I act for Sir Percy Penderville, if that's what you mean?"

"It's certainly a buyers market at the moment, eh?"

"It would seem that way, but as I understand it, my client and yours have an agreement."

Lawson wanted to conclude this transaction as quickly as possible so as to maximise his commission, especially now that the values were falling and nobody was going to pay much attention to the deal.

"Can we set up a meet?" he enquired.

"That's what we're paid for. Let's say fifteen minutes in the Criterion across the road," Philip Thorn suggested. Lawson thought he detected a sense of sarcastic joy in Thorns voice.

"Okay, old chap, but I may be a few minutes late."

"Suit yourself. Take as long as you like."

Lawson hung up quickly.

That little prick, he thought, *he was enjoying this.* He had heard of Thorn, of course and had met him on a few occasions but never went out of his way to talk to him. Thorn was one of those new upstart whiz kids that the new modern Stock Exchange had attracted like flies. He despised the type; they drove around in BMW's as if they were an extension of their vital organs.

He picked up the phone again and dialled.

"Territories Freight, Good morning." came the brisk reply.

"George Archibald please, Jerald Lawson here."

"One moment, please." the person on the other end said in a sing-song reply. Then came that infernal obnoxious jingle, ' London Bridge is falling down'. He often wondered if the moron who invented this device was totally deaf and that this was his revenge on society.

"Morning Jerald, what can I do for you?"

"Morning George, I just thought I'd give you a buzz about something that's come up this morning."

"Fine, go ahead?"

"Well you recall that you phoned me some time ago about Sir Percy's shares in AAB and you asked me to call you if there was any change or movement."

"Yes, I recall a conversation to that effect." George Archibald sounded cautious.

"Well, this morning I got a call from Sir Percy, he wants to sell his entire AAB portfolio."

"What, the whole seven percent stock?" George gasped down the line.

"Yes, the whole lot. I can't understand why he is doing it. It doesn't make sense, especially the way the market is this morning."

"Oh and how's that?"

"Well the market's taking a tumble, the OUT is in trouble. It's down 180 points this morning, the AAB is down 35 points. Now's just not a good time to sell."

"What's behind his move then?"

"I don't know, but the entire stock is being bought by one buyer. There has been some kind of deal struck."

"What's the present position, what action have you taken to conclude the deal?" George asked.

"Well I've got a meeting with the buyer's broker in fifteen minutes."

"Can you stall, for say, another ten minutes or so?"

"I guess I can, but I say, old chap, I only called you because of our prior conversation. You do understand, this is strictly confidential. The only reason I called is because of my loyalty to the AAB. I know the problems you had back in '83 with that eight percent that was picked up against your wishes."

"I appreciate that and thank you, Jerald, but if you could hold fire for twenty minutes I'll get back to you. Where are you?"

"The Hang Seng, my number is-"

"Hold a sec. Jesus, who keeps taking my fucking pens! Ah, Okay, shoot."

Lawson gave him the phone number and hung up. "I'll show you, Mister Philip Thorn." Lawson muttered to himself resolutely. He glanced out at the floor for the umpteenth time. In all his years there he hadn't sensed a foreboding on the floor of the Hang Seng stock exchange quite like this. The crash of 83' was predictable, inevitable almost giving the way the British had barged into the negotiations, but this was different, like everyone was waiting to see who blinked first. The phone buzzed.

"Lawson here." he snapped.

"Jerald, George here, we have a battle situation. We're going after those shares and can you back down from the deal with your friends?"

"I say, old chap, that's jolly good news. I like to see the AAB board members putting up a fight. I'll meet with these people and see what they're offering and then I'll know exactly how I can break the deal they struck with Sir Percy."

"Good. Get right back to me. I'll wait at this phone, Okay?"

"Tally Ho." Lawson said as he replaced the handset.

CHAPTER FIFTEEN

Jeff decided that he needed to clear up the matter of the accusation that John Sing was the main suspect in the attack on Tom. He tried both Chung and Lee but neither was available. So he dialled Central HQ and asked to speak to William Gualt. After a few minutes he came on the line.

"Hallow" Gualt sounded like a man under pressure.

"Good morning, Chief Superintendent. Jeff Bordes-Aitcheson here. How are things with you this morning?"

"Morning Jeff, what can I do to help you?"

"Well actually, I've called to apologise to you and the police in general."

"This sounds serious."

"I'm afraid it is. I've got to say that I ordered the movement of Tom Maxwell last night at the hospital-"

"I'm afraid I'm not up to date with what is happening at the hospital. I'm expecting Detective Chung at any moment now. All I know is that we lost a man there."

"Okay, I may as well tell you what happened."

Bordes-Aitcheson told Gualt everything about the hospital move for Maxwell.

"I'd be inclined to say you did the right thing. The most paramount thing is to insure the life of the subject. It's a pity that you didn't tell us though; we did lose a man there."

"I'm very sorry about that and if I can make things right for his wife, he was married?"

"Yes he was, for a few years."

"Any children?"

"Yes, two."

"I'll see them right, I'm sure that Tom would want that. You do understand that I was just thinking of Tom's safety? I had no idea that the killer would strike again. It was just a precaution, you understand?"

"Of course I do, perfectly understandable; it's just unfortunate that a good policeman had to get killed."

"There's just one other thing. I spoke to your Detective Chung this morning and I may have given him the impression that I suspected that John Sing was the culprit in the Maxwell case. Apparently that is not now the case, John Sing is currently in our Kowloon branch and we suspect that Maylay Dulles is the real culprit. She was Tom's secretary, she hasn't shown up for work this morning and it seems that she either had something going with George Archibald, which Tom found out about, or she just went off the head"

"Did you say, Dulles? Isn't George Archibald's wife's maiden name Dulles?" Gualt asked thoughtfully.

"I never knew that and I should have. Jesus, Aggy Archibald and Steff are good friends. I just never had occasion to wonder about her maiden name. They were married before Steff and I met them, but hold on a minute," Jeff said, obviously pondering. "I always thought that Aggy was English. Wasn't her father supposed to be an Earl?"

"He was, John Dulles's father was, Foster Dulles, the fourth Earl of Pembroke. Old man Dulles came to Hong Kong way back, and met his future wife, Aggy Kim, and shortly after the marriage-"

"What did you say her name was?" Jeff asked.

"Aggy Kim, her mother was Lo-Xian Kim or Kimberley-"

Jeff suddenly interrupted, "This Aggy Dulles, or Kim, that you mentioned, you said her mother was Lo-Xian Kimberley? What was her husband's name?"

"Jason Kimberley." Gualt replied and suddenly Jeff could no longer hold the phone, he tried to mouth the 'Good Buy' but it didn't come out.

Bordes-Aitcheson sat at his desk and stared at the frayed leather bound diary. What Gualt had said deeply shocked him, but helped to set things straight in his mind. He was not a man to wonder about the improbable, he got on with life. When his father died back in the Forties he had appointed a very good friend of the family, Hewlett Campbell, to run the bank until such time as he was old enough to take over. When Jeff turned eighteen Hewlett sat him down one evening and told him that his father had kept meticulous diaries for the period when he ran the bank. Hewlett told him that one day he may need to refer to the diaries and showed him where they were. At the time Jeff had no interest in the past and was too consumed by the future to even wonder what they might contain, but now, it was different.

Bordes-Aitcheson now looked at the diary of the man that was alive in 1898 and who took over the running of the bank, the Bordes Wanchai Bank, as it was then known. With trembling hands he opened the diary.

Arthur Aitcheson arrived in Hong Kong in 1891 from a banking background in London. His father owned a jewellers shop and had progressed into banking in England, but Arthur wanted more excitement in life than sitting behind a counter in Whitehall waiting for people to come to him, he wanted a faster life. So when he decided to emigrate the choices were: Ireland where the pickings were rich but the climate bad; America where the weather was great but the pickings dodgy because there was a threat of war with Spain; Australia where the pickings were good but the weather was unbearable or Hong Kong where the pickings were great and the weather tolerable for most times of the year.

When Aitcheson arrived, he met an old banking friend of his fathers whose name he had been given as a parting farewell from his old man. He was offered a job as manager; he took it while awaiting passage to Australia.

He quickly realises that there was an opportunity here, for the owner still used old banking methods, methods that had been outdated in London for over ten years.

He set into the task with a vengeance and watched the owner go slowly silly. In those days, banks operated on much looser systems then they do now and Aitcheson soon had control of the investor's funds. He ran up some incredible lending figures, leaving the bank in a position that if there was any major problem, it would go under. The bank didn't, but its owner did. On the old man's death bed, Aitcheson forced the owner to sign over the bank to him until such time as his only son was old enough to take over. He did, but the son never lived long enough to take over. He died mysteriously soon after his father. Aitcheson became the proud owner of the bank, with a little assistance from the owner's old wife, who just adored young Arthur and the attention he poured on her. He quietly took over full control of the bank and began to amass some valuable assets.

He saw the future and knowing that he had nothing to lose, as the bank was not his by inheritance or purchase. Arthur gambled heavily with depositor's money and won. He became known as the "borrower of Aberdeen".

Within just five years of arriving in Hong Kong, he had built up a very successful business. In 1896, he turned his attention to a competitor, Geoffrey Bordes of Bordes Wanchai Bank. In those days there were not too many takers for long term shares in banks in Hong Kong, as Merchantmen were seen as the big profit makers because they could turn over their goods in a very short space of time. So even if the British Empire had to leave, the Merchants didn't stand to lose too much. Whereas banks were seen as long term investments and they couldn't turn over quickly enough. Coincidentally, the banks shares were not in big demand. Aitcheson, coming as he did from a banking background, had a different outlook. He began buying shares in the Bordes Wanchai and nobody paid too much attention. Least of all Geoffrey Bordes. Bordes saw Aitcheson as a new breath of life in the Banking Sector, and viewed his purchase of shares as a vote of confidence in his operation of Bordes Wanchai. They became quite good friends, or so Bordes thought. His view changed when in early 1897 he realised that Aitcheson had amassed nearly 25% of the issued shares, which was nearly equal to his own share.

Aitcheson's interest in Bordes Wanchai was born out of his frustration in his own inability to attract the big Merchantmen, where the real profit was. The acquisition of Bordes Wanchai would give him access to their accounts. But his bank did not have the capital to make an open assault on Bordes. The only way that Aitcheson could do it was to acquire the shares that would give him the Chairmanship of the bank.

Late in 1897 the row between the two men flared during a board room battle. The other shareholders had no idea of the hatred that had built up between them and in the resulting argument, sides were taken. Aitcheson offered more profits, Bordes offered stability, the majority of board members sided with Aitcheson. They wanted profits too and that meant that their dividends paid more. Bordes knew he was beat. Aitcheson was voted onto the board and he made life hell for Bordes, eventually forcing him to stand down as Chairman in July 1898. Bordes had an even greater problem facing him, his health was failing rapidly and his son, being only five, was too young to take his place on the board. He wrote to his brother in England and convinced him to come and take his place on the board until such time as the son would be old enough to take his rightful place on the board of Bordes Wanchai Bank.

Ronald Bordes came to Hong Kong in early 1899 and stood in for his nephew. He was himself quiet a wealthy man and began buying into the bank. Ronald Bordes himself had no children and his wife had died some years earlier, that indeed was part of his reason for moving from England to get away from the memory of her. He took a liking to young Anthony Bordes and made his succession on the board as his goal in life.

Aitcheson realised what was happening, he could see what the Bordes were up to and knew that he couldn't ward off the challenge forever. Aitcheson had only one child, a girl called Bessie and no matter how much he tried, he could not have any more. He had been taken by a bad fever in 1900 shortly after his new wife gave birth to the girl and the fever had done him more damage than the best doctors of the time could find.

After many years of trying he knew that he could not be the father of a son to follow in his footsteps. He tried to make peace with Ronald Bordes but failed. Ronald told Aitcheson in no uncertain terms that his days as Chairman were up. But he

fought on making the Bordes Wanchai Bank the most successful merchant bank in the Colony.

However, apart from one branch in Kowloon which was
opened in 1912, he never expanded the bank. With the presence of Ronald on the board, he could do nothing out of place.
When Anthony became of age in 1914, he replaced his uncle on
the board. Aitcheson had despite himself, come to like young
Tony and welcomed him on the board. At the time Bessie was
16 years of age and a very attractive girl and her hand had been
sought by many of the wealthiest fathers in the colony for their
sons but Aitcheson had turned down all offers. He had one last
gambit to play. If he didn't have a son to take his place then the
next best thing was to have a daughter married to the Chairman of the bank.

He took ill shortly after Tony joined the board but he stubbornly refused to stand down as Chairman until his term had
run its course. Tony was naive on the finer points of running
a bank and while he had gotten the position of manager as a
concession from Aitcheson when he joined the board, he was
deeply concerned about the day to day running of the bank. He
couldn't legally make decisions about new loans or extra facility
without having to refer to the Chairman. He and Ronald had
tried to have Ronald appointed acting Chairman, but Aitcheson
scuttled the meeting by sending Bessie to act for him. He had
19 months to run in his term as Chairman and it became obvious that he was going to insist on making things as awkward as
possible for them.

Bessie disagreed with her father's actions but had to obey his
command for as she told Tony, she had been brought up to be
obedient. A relationship developed between the two. Ronald
wondered about Bessie, for his attitude was once an Aitcheson
always an Aitcheson and that would never change.

The situation at the bank was becoming impossible: they
were losing business as people wanted an instant answer. They
were used to dealing with a small personal bank where they
could go and ask for a loan and get a reply, but now they had
to wait for days even a week. For if Aitcheson was not well, a

board meeting had to be called. Everything came to a head one evening and Tony went to confront Aitcheson with the threat that as manager and major shareholder, he was going to call an Extraordinary General meeting.

Bordes-Aitcheson read the diary entry for the 12th April 1914 with interest, for although the diary was that of his grandfather, this, the last entry was written by his mother. He had no idea just how close Arthur and his daughter Bessie were, but they were far closer than his father, Tony Bordes could ever have imagined.

Bessie waylaid Tony Bordes that evening when he entered the Aitcheson house. She took him into the library and sat him down. She made small talk while she got him a drink. Her entry in the diary read something like this.

"My father wants me to like Tony, I do not mind, he is quite nice and is a handsome man.

When I asked him to come into the library, he was extremely mad. I had never seen this side of him before, except that day when I turned up at the board meeting when he was trying to have Ronald appointed Chairman. He was angry then but he was pleased to see me. I could see that in his eyes, they danced all over me. I enjoyed the dance too, but I never let him think that I thought him good enough for my Dad. I know that Dad is near the end, Dad knows too.

Dad's dying wish is that I marry Tony Bordes and keep his name in the bank. I suppose that that is what I should do, for I owe everything to him. I know that he always wanted a son, but unlike some fathers I have seen, he never hated me for not being the son he wanted. I know that mother was very unhappy before she died because she felt she had failed him. Mother never said as much, but I knew. Dear Mother, you have not failed him for I will do what he asks. I will marry Tony Bordes, that will please Father and I know that it will please me. I may not be the son he wanted but I will make him proud of me, I will not only marry Tony, but I will insist on retaining the name Aitcheson.

We will be known as Bordes-Aitcheson and our children will be named this way also. And I am sure that there will be many children, enough to make Dad proud."

Bessie side-tracked Tony that day back in 1914, she concluded her father's diary by writing,

"Dad, today I became a woman, and do you know, it's not such a terrible experience after all."

Bordes-Aitcheson leaned back in his chair and turned his eyes unseeingly up to the ceiling.

So that was his mother, the mother he never knew. He didn't feel the tear at the corner of his eye; he was oblivious to the room around him. He had never thought to question his father about his mother's past; all he knew of her was that she died at childbirth, giving birth to him. What must he have meant to her bearing him at her age, she must have been 42 years when he was born? His father never spoke much of her, but then again he never asked.

Now he understood the 'Bordes-Aitcheson', what it meant to her and how much his father must have loved her to retain the name after her death. They must have tried for more then twenty years to have a child and when the child came she died. He was amazed at how important children were to them in those days, now it is so different, if you are having problems having a child there is artificial insemination and all sorts of things that can be resorted to.

While Bordes-Aitcheson found the past enthralling, the diary had not cast any light on Jason Kimberley. He closed the diary and went to the shelf where he had found it, scanning through the old books and documents stored there touched only by the cleaning ladies for years. He found the row of Company Minutes for the period 1895 to 1910.

The first two made no reference to Jason Kimberley, but the minutes of the board meeting of December 1897 showed something of the hatred between Aitcheson and the Chairman.

Aitcheson had just concluded a deal with three Chinese traders. The deal was widely known of in Hong Kong prior to the board meeting. One member faithful to Bordes, accused Aitcheson of financing deals which was to the detriment of the Merchantmen. The traders were to supply goods to the Portuguese traders in Macau, but they needed a line of credit to set up a supply of produce.

Leonard Paterson, a board member, was directly effected by the deal because he lost the trade of the Chinese to the Portuguese and he was most upset. He questioned Aitcheson in no uncertain manner and was backed by Bordes. They maintained that by moving the trade to Macau that the British and the Bordes Wanchai Bank was losing money because of Aitcheson's action.

Aitcheson would have none of it. He maintained that he was making profit so the Crown was making profit. It was unfortunate that Paterson should lose out, but had he not stepped in then. Both the trade and the banking requirement would have gone to the Portuguese had he not acted as he did.

As it was, all they lost was the trade but they would still benefit from the profits.

Bordes had erupted in anger and he lashed out at Aitcheson with a vengeance. They were here at the pleasure of the Crown and they owed the Crown their pledge to conduct their business in such a manner as to produce the maximum possible benefit to the Crown. Bordes said that anyone who would back a deal between the Chinese and the Portuguese was a traitor to the Crown. Aitcheson took exception to this remark, but to everyone's surprise he did not ask for satisfaction. He merely replied that he would take pleasure in seeing Bordes off the board.

The minutes of the meeting of June 1898 told another story. Aitcheson was not present for he had been called to Macau at short notice. Bordes informed the Board that he had approved a loan to one Jason Kimberley for 12,000 guineas, on foot of the lodgement of the deeds to most of the lands of the area then known as the New Territories. There was no importance placed on the deal as the British were concluding a 99 year lease with the Chinese and this other deal between Kimberley and the Chinese would only mean royalty payment to Kimberley during that 99 year period, no one raised the issue of what would happen after the lease ran out. There had been no questions and the meeting had concluded earlier than normal. The following month all had been peaceful at the board meeting, as it was the one in which Bordes gave his farewell address.

Strangely there had been no reference to Kimberley's loan in any future board meeting. This had to be unexpected, as there were several board members who were known supporters of Aitcheson. Bordes-Aitcheson studied the minutes one last time before returning them to their place where they had rested for many, many, years. So Bordes had granted a large loan to Jason Kimberley as a parting shot, now his Grand-daughter had tried to kill Tom Maxwell. Why?

He must check on whether or not Kimberley ever drew down the loan. It was rather ironic that his action of bringing in the WTB experts should trigger off the finding of the ledgers and the attack on Tom, considering that his two grandfathers had fought over, just the topic he was now considering, expansion.

On foot of lodgement of the deed to the New Territories, the thought kept coming back to him. If the deeds were lodged with the bank in 1898, then what happened them since? He had been all through the documents on deposit with the bank at one time or another and he had never seen them. It was, of course, possible that this was a joke played on Aitcheson, the parting shot.

Still he would have it checked out.

The most important thing now was the threat from Archibald and Maylay. Did Tom find out something so sinister that they had to kill him to prevent him from telling anybody? If so, what could that be? The only reference that he knew of to Jason Kimberley was the Ledgers, and the board meeting of June 1898. He could find no reference to either Kimberley's loan or the deeds after that, so what did Tom find out that caused his attack?

*

The Criterion Bar and Lounge was the "in" place for the Yuppie set from the Stock Exchange across the road, it was very up class and expensive. It was owned and run by Lo-Xian Maltbie.

Philip Thorn was well known there and Lo-Xian greeted him personally. She, like her sisters was an early riser so as to get a good start to the day.

"Good Morning, Honourable Philip. What can I get for you?" she asked as she eyed the two men with him.

"Morning Lo, I think three of your famous coffees would do to start." Thorn turned to the others, "Have you guys had breakfast yet?"

They had so they settled for the coffees and headed for a booth.

"What time did Lawson say he'd be here?" Dillon asked checking his watch.

"He should be here in a few minutes. Old Lawson is reliable, if nothing else." Thorn replied.

He looked at the man opposite him, he was about his own age, the other guy Dillon, had gone to the phone.

"What's behind this deal?" he enquired.

"We just work for a guy that likes to acquire things." Olli replied.

"And this guy also runs the WTB, right?" Thorn suggested.

"You've heard of Edward Orrang?" Olli made sure that his voice expressed the amount of surprise that was befitting the situation.

"And Dillon is the King Dick right?"

"I don't follow you."

"Dillon is the Head Chief in the Asian operation?"

Olli got his drift and nodded after looking over his shoulder to ensure that they were not being overheard. Of course Dillon was the main man, but the instructions came from on high, Dillon was more like the Wide receiver. Thorn was beginning to get up Olli's nose, the reason being that he stood to make big money from this deal and all of a sudden he was getting too nosey.

Olli saw Dillon as a father figure, the coach. The man you turned to when things were not going to plan. He was the strong man, the guy that sorted things out when they had gone wrong.

He felt that he thought for Tina as well when he figured that they were safer now that Dillon was here.

"So where the hell is Lawson?" Olli asked irritably.

Thorn glanced at his watch and then at the door expectantly. "He's not renowned for his punctuality, but this is ridiculous. I don't understand why he's not here."

Dillon came out of the men's room into the short hallway that leads back into the bar. He stopped there just outside the door and pondered on something that had been bugging him for some time now. Bordes-Aitcheson had mentioned the possibility of him buying shares. All very well, but he didn't have any funds in Hong Kong. So the thought occurred to him that he should transfer in some money to lodge in the bank to use to speculate on the shares. He had just over $425,000 in his deposit account in New York and what the hell was he saving it for, the rainy day? This was the rainy day, this was the day he had waited for, the golden opportunity to lash out and try and make it a half million, or perhaps more, if the stock market reacted like it should with the news of the take-over by the WTB, the stocks in AAB should soar. But what if something went wrong?

"Shit." he muttered as he looked for the phone.

Just down the hall was a coin phone. He made a sudden decision to call Jeff and ask him to transfer money from his bank in New York. He searched for loose change in his pockets as he approached the phone. He found the coins he needed and reached for the receiver. It rang just before he could pick it up.

Dillon hesitated a moment or two, wondering if someone would come to answer it. Then he figured that it may be a call for someone in the bar and the bar staff being bar-staff would probably not bother their arse to come and answer it so he reached for the phone.

Just as he was about to take the receiver off the hook the ringing stopped. Like anybody answering a phone he still picked it up, figuring that there may still be someone on the line waiting for a reply.

"Is Paddy there?" a voice said.

He was slightly taken aback and thought for a moment to formulate just how he should explain that he didn't know who Paddy was and that this was a bar and did the caller want someone's name called out.

"No he's not, who's calling?" another voice replied and Dillon realised that there must be an extension in the bar and it was answered there. Dillon made to hang up.

"George, is that you, Lo-Xian?"

Dillon stopped mid movement and brought the receiver back to his ear. Now his senses were on full alert. *George? George Archibald?* He wondered.

"Yes George, good morning."

"Morning, I was looking for Paddy."

"Pat's not here at the moment. He's gone over to Reilly's for some stuff, but he should be back in a few minutes."

"How long, exactly?"

Dillon thought he detected desperation in George's voice.

"Ten, fifteen minutes no more. What's the panic?"

"We've got a green light on the Grand Plan, Jason has just given the go-ahead. Apparently there is a big fall coming on the market this morning. The OUT bank is about to go belly up and shares are falling rapidly and to crown it all, Sir Percy bloody Penderville is about to sell his shares to that American crowd that are in AAB at the moment. They are supposed to be meeting Lawson to clench the deal but Lawson is stalling until I get back to him, so I need to talk to Paddy to confirm that the money is still there in the secret account. The money that we're going to need to buy Sir Percy's shares."

Dillon could hardly believe his ears; he let the receiver drift away from his ear.

Betrayed! By Lawson, the bastard. Dillon said in his mind. "Shit." he cursed.

"Who was that?" George asked.

"Their must be someone on the other extension." Lo-Xian replied.

"For God-sake, quickly, find out who?" George shouted.

Dillon let the receiver dangle loosely and turned away from the phone. His immediate reaction was to get away from the phone so as not to be discovered as the eavesdropper. He couldn't care less about whether or not they confirmed that there was an eavesdropper; there was nothing that he could do about that. They would have heard the receiver being replaced anyway.

Right now he couldn't face the boys back out in the bar, this new development was a shit-load of trouble. This prompted him to turn into the toilets.

"Bastard." he muttered as he closed the door in the cubical after him.

Moments later he heard the outer door bang open. He flushed the toilet and opened the door adjusting his clothing as he left the cubical. Lo-Xian herself was standing there looking at him.

"Am I in the wrong toilet?" he enquired, stopped in his stride.

"No, I am." she replied, her suspicion easing a little.

He returned her stare. "I hate to grope, but is my fly undone?"

"Sorry, I was looking for one of the bar-staff, a new guy. He's been sneaking off from work. I thought he might be in here. Again, sorry." She turned and left letting the door slam after her.

"What the fuck is going on?"

CHAPTER SIXTEEN

Lawson reached for the phone at last. He couldn't quite figure the angle of attack to take with Sir Percy, how to get him to break his deal with Thorns clients. As he sat there in his little office overlooking the floor of the Stock Exchange it came to him. It had been there all along, the share index screens gave him the answer.

"Yes." Percy said. Lawson flinched at the sound of Sir Percy's voice.

"Sir Percy, Lawson here again." He detected rather than heard the sigh at the other end of the line.

"I didn't expect to hear from you for another few hours at least."

"Sorry about that, but I just thought that you should know that the market is taking a pounding this morning, shares are dropping like-"

"Good thing we're selling early then." Sir Percy cut in.

"That's what I'm calling about, there appears to be some hold-up. Your buyers failed to show up at our meeting that I arranged. I'm here in my office waiting for them right now."

"What, I can't understand it. He seemed so keen to buy." Sir Percy gasped.

"Who Sir?" Lawson enquiry tentatively.

"The American, Scott Dillon."

"Who is he?"

"I don't know exactly. He said he acted for a group of people who wanted to take a stake in AAB."

The idea came to him out of the blue. "Could he be part of that same group that grabbed that 8% share of stock back in '83?"

Lawson didn't want to push it, let Percy put some of it together.

"The blighter."

"Do you think it could be the same people?" Lawson could but hope now that he had sown the seed that would spur Percy on to his own conclusion.

"But he said it was a friendly bid, Jeff approved. He said Jeff was going to reduce his own stake"

Lawson had had a little time to think now and it occurred to him to ask a question that had crossed his mind when Percy first phoned him.

"Why did you decide to sell so suddenly?"

"Dillon said that things would happen pretty fast this morning. He was in a hurry to get the shares."

"Perhaps he knew that this crash was coming and figured he could pressure you into selling knowing full well that by the time we got the deal set up that the shares would fall in value, therefore he got his hands on a large block of shares at knockdown price."

"The blighter."

"Good thing I phoned you."

Sir Percy didn't reply. Lawson waited for a moment but still there was nothing. He hoped that Sir Percy wasn't having a heart attack.

"Sir Percy, hallow?"

"Yes, sorry I was just thinking."

"About what?"

"England, funnily enough. I cannot understand why he would stall; he was going to pay 50 points above the odds." Percy sounded forlorn

"Look, Sir Percy, I think I can get you another buyer" Lawson ignored the 50 points above the odds, because that made no sense Why offer that when the market was falling?

"Oh, who?"

"I can't say just yet, I just remembered a phone call I got back in '83, I think I may have a buyer. Can I get back to you?"

"Yes, yes of course, old chap."

Lawson hung up. Let the old git sweat for a while. Anyhow it would save George a fortune.

But what about my commission? he thought with a wry grin. George would look after him. Wouldn't he?

*

Tina was a little apprehensive just being there, a whole lot had happened since she was here last. But right now it scared the hell out of her.

As she had approached the bank this morning she saw Maylay cross the street coming from the opposite direction and also heading for the bank. Tina moved into the cover of a doorway and watched. But Maylay stopped upon reaching the footpath. At first she thought that Tina had somehow sensed her presence, but as she watched she realised that she was watching someone else altogether.

John Sing had reached the door of the bank first and reached up to ring the bell. A little over a minute later the door was opened and after a moment's hesitation, he went inside. She couldn't see who opened the door as they were out of her line of sight. Maylay began to walk towards the bank but slowly, obviously deep in thought, then suddenly she turned and walked much quicker, now straight to a teahouse just a few doors from the bank. Without giving the situation too much thought, Tina followed her to the teahouse. The inside was a little like the street outside only here the people weren't moving so fast. It was packed. Even with the crowd that was there a waiter managed to pick her out and handed her a menu and she placed an order. Tina moved into a corner well away from the door. Maylay had gone to the public phone but Tina couldn't make out the number she punched in. The conversation was very short for she hung up and sat near the phone, at a table with two young girls who looked like office workers.

Tina eyed the phone thoughtfully, something just occurred to her. The phone was a digital push button type with 12 keys, 10 were digit keys the other two were function keys and one of those was a re-dial key. If she could get to the phone, she just had to hit the re-dial key and whatever number Maylay had called, would be re-dialled for her. Then she would know who Maylay had spoken to. It could be important because she was obviously deeply upset at the sight of John Sing. Tina couldn't figure out what caused Maylay to be upset other than to assume that seeing Sing meant that he was not in police custody and would seem to indicate that he was not a suspect in the attack on Tom despite the sacking yesterday. The sudden change in direction and then the phone call would seem to indicate that something Maylay had assumed had changed. Maybe it was as simple as she suspecting Sing and seeing him there, Maylay feared he was up to no good and she phoned the police.

Tina thought about leaving, but what the hell she was just having a cup of coffee.

The waiter had other ideas; he arrived with a tray of food. While she toyed with the food, she suddenly realised that it could not have being the police Maylay phoned as she had dialled a seven digit number. The police are only a three digit number. About 15 minutes later, a young Chinese man entered the teahouse and joined Maylay at the table which had since been vacated by the two girls. Tina had seen him pass in but hadn't paid him much attention but now she re-adjusted herself on the seat so that she could watch without looking to obvious.

The youth was in his early 20s about 5ft 6ins tall, above average for Chinese, but this guy was tough looking. He wore a sleeveless black shirt and shorts. He looked vaguely like one of the guy's that had followed her on the MTR the other day. She tried to remember now as she glanced occasionally at their table. Tina had recognised Wei-Ming all right at City Hall, it was funny really, Wei-Ming was not the one that had stared at her on the MTR, yet he appeared more frightening. The second guy, if this was the same guy, was the one that had stared, and she was not as scared of him. The eyes seemed softer she recalled, it was more like he was admiring her, yet she was not sure that this was the same guy. Tinawww.hotmail.com was not going to look too closely at him to find out. They seemed to know each other well, they leaned into their conversation like lovers.

The conversation was short lasting only two minutes, the youth rose and departed. Tina turned away, shortly afterwards Maylay too followed him out into the street. Tina jumped to her feet and rushed to the phone, luckily no-one had used it. She hit the re-dial button, her hand was shaking. The phone rang and rang, she began to breathe more evenly and the threat of having to talk to a stranger was beginning to fade. Then she heard a click.

"Hallo" a Chinese female voice said.

Her heart was pounding, who was she talking to? "Ah, hallow, I ah," She reached desperately for something to say.

"Who is there please?" the voice asked.

"Sorry, I was looking for Sue." Desperately Tina sought something clever to say.

"There is no Sue here, so sorry must have wrong number." the voice said dismissively.

"Wait, what number are you?" She grasped at a chance.

"This is 6579854."

"I am very sorry I must have dialled the wrong number" Tina did her best Chinese accent.

"Bye."

"Six, five, seven, nine eight, five, four." she muttered to retain memory as she fumbled for a biro and something to write on. Finding the biro, she wrote the series of numbers on the back of her hand. Now what was Maylay up to? The person that answered the phone was not involved in business as there was no company name mentioned, so it had to be a private number and it was obviously local as there was no first digit to indicate a dial code, plus, it looked like the person who had answered Maylay's phone call had shown up here within a few minutes.

Maylay, where was she gone? She caught the waiter's attention, paid the bill and rushed out onto the street. Maylay was standing at the door of the bank, just up the street. Moments later, the door opened and she went in. Tina looked around the street as she went towards the bank but could see no sign of the man who met Maylay in the Tea house. Tina continued to examine the passing crowd while she knocked on the door of the bank. She was petrified, her palms were sweating and she could not hold her hands steady.

Suddenly the door opened behind her, one of the counter staff had opened it for her.

"Good morning, Miss Tina," It was Su Lee, a nice Chinese girl, her warm greeting turned to concern when she realised that she was in a state of anxiety. "Are you Okay, Miss Tina?"

"Yeah I'm fine." She brushed past her after checking that Maylay was not in sight.

Tina went upstairs to the office that she was using yesterday. Once alone in the office, her adrenalin began to subside and the fear took over. She had been surprised at her own calm in the teahouse, but then she had been in control. There was no immediate threat to her, there had been people around, she was in no danger. But now in the sanctity of the office, she realised that she had been spying on a probable murderer. Reconstructing what she had seen, told her that Maylay had been shocked to see John Sing entering the bank. So that said, that meant Maylay expected Sing not to be there, did she expect him to be in police custody? But the fact that Sing was free and at the bank reporting for work as normal meant that she, Maylay, was now in danger and what did Maylay plan to do about it? Why did she phone that young Chinese woman? And who was the girl on the phone and was she connected to the guy that met Maylay in the teahouse?

To hell with it. she thought, she had things to do. Tina would tell Dillon, he would figure it out.

First the ledgers, she wanted to photocopy the relevant pages and then double-check to see if there was any reference at all to the deeds. She placed the ledger on the desk and opened it at the bookmark. Someone must have moved the mark; she couldn't find the reference to the loan. Tina checked the dates but there appeared to be a page missing. On closer examination, she made out the remainder of the page right in at the seams. Someone had cut out the page!

"Now why the hell would anyone want to do that?" While she wanted to keep an open mind, one name popped up: Maylay. Tina wanted to get to hell out of there. What if Maylay discovered that she found out about the missing pages? God and she had to go to her for the keys of the file room to search for any reference to the deeds.

"The hell I will." she muttered as she made for the door. Bolger knew exactly what she was going to do, get someone else to ask her for the keys.

Su Lee was the cashier who had let her in and had seemed to like her, so who better to ask.

"Hi Lee." she greeted her as she approached.

"Hi, Miss Tina, are you sure you are Okay? You look pale."

"No I fine, I was out late last night."

She smiled knowingly, and then the smile turned to concern again.

"That was terrible news about Mister Maxwell?"

"Yes that sure was a shock, but I hear that he's going to be Okay. Hey, can you get the keys to the file room?"

"It's already open, Hwan is down there."

"Thanks see you later." Tina said with great relief. She went down the stairs that led to the file room just below the manager's office. Hwan was just about to lock the door.

"It's Okay, I want to go through some stuff."

He handed her the key, exchanged the usual pleasantries and went back up.

Alone now, she surveyed the file room. The room was at the end of a short corridor at the bottom of the concrete steps. Off the corridor were three other doors: one led to the vault, one led to the safety deposit box room and the other was a small storeroom. The file room itself measured some 10ft wide by 20ft deep running from back to front of the bank itself. Floor to ceiling height was about 8ft. The three walls away from the door were lined with free standing steel shelving units.

Tina examined the shelving first to see if there was any form to the filing system for the boxes. Each shelf held boxes of files, each box had a 'from-to' date in it and was in order. Tina followed the dates backwards through the '70s back to the '40s. Obviously the boxes were not as well loaded the further back she went. The boxes were well labelled from 1945 on but prior to that, the labelling was a bit scarce. It was obvious that any labelling on pre-war material was removed, apparently to protect clients from the unwelcome examination of the occupying Japanese forces. She decided to start with the war years and work back; she placed the key on top of the nearest shelf.

"Okay Jason Kimberley, where are you?" Tina began at the first un-labelled box, not that she expected to find anything relevant in the box for 1944, but merely as a matter of verifying that the box she expected to be 1944, was in fact, just that. The next box was 1943 and so it went. Everything was in order all the way back to 1920. Then the next box was from 1918, she marked the boxes with the correct year and removed a box further along so that she could make room for 1919. The box she removed she placed on top of the filing shelves. The next few boxes were in proper order and then she found 1909 was out of place, so she pulled it out and put that on top of the shelves unit alongside the other box. As Tina pushed the box back, she heard something metallic slip off the top and clatter down the back of the shelves. She shrugged her shoulders and continued on with her search.

She found 1919 and double checked the contents but everything was in order so she put it in place, and also got 1909 sorted out and got the other box back into its rightful place. Now everything was in order and she was down to the turn of the century. Strangely enough, that particular box was pretty well loaded. With her curiosity aroused, she examined the contents.

As she leafed through the faded, carefully handwritten and some typed documents from 1900, it amazed her that a lot of colonists had entrusted valuable documents, guarantees and the likes to the bank, strangely to be left there for 85 years. One file that she spent some time over included many stocks and shares in, perhaps, long forgotten companies. She passed the file back to the box and the box back to the shelf. The year 1899 seemed to have quite a lot of deeds of covenant, lease agreements and purchase documents, many signed by the Governor or the Colonial secretary. It was obvious that in that year a lot of land was purchased from the government.

Tina took down the box for 1898 with a certain amount of trepidation. If she didn't look in the box, the document could be there, but if she looked and it wasn't there then her time was wasted.

She began and again there were loads of land exchange, purchase or lease documents. But all were government or Crown, two private individuals or companies, none were Chinese.

Bolger was about to give up. She was down to the very last document and lifted it out of the case, her heart beating a little bit faster. The document was a typical old legal one, foolscap size and folded in three, length ways. It was bound by a piece of string. Carefully undoing the knot she unfolded the paper. Her heart stopped, she couldn't breath, she froze staring at the document.

The woman closed her eyes for a moment; she felt a tear swell up. The document that Tina had sought had finally been found. The name leapt out at her, Jason Kimberley. The document was an internal bank document, a standard loan approval form, pre-printed but with blank lines for name, date amount etc. The document was dated May 24th 1898 and signed by Jason Kimberley and Jeffery Bordes. The amount of the loan was 12,000 Guineas.

"Jesus H," she muttered, that was a hell of a lot of money in those days.

There was a hand written note at the bottom of the document.

Security, Lo-Wok deeds.
300 G, - 28th May, Box key.

It didn't make much sense, but the important thing was that she had found something. Tina found a folder and placed the document in it to protect and conceal it and returned the box to the shelf. Her excitement reached fever pitch, eager now to show the document to Olli and Dillon, she headed for the stairs. That was when she remembered the key to the door.

"Shit what the hell did I do with it?" she snapped angrily as she searched her pockets. Calming herself she retraced her steps from the time she came down and meet Hwan. She placed the key in her shirt pocket, but it wasn't there now. The key had a large metal tag, like hotel keys so that it wouldn't be lost or carried out of the hotel inadvertently. When had she taken it out of her pocket? When she had taken out the biro. Of course.

"On top of the shelf."

Tina felt around the top of the shelf, as she couldn't see for they were just a little too high.

She tried climbing up but felt the shelves coming away.

"Something to stand on." Tina found a strong crate in the store room and brought that into the file room. She looked all around the shelf top but there was no sign of the key. That was when she remembered the metallic sound of something falling down the back of the shelves.

"Shit." She stepped down of the box and moved it to one side then tried moving the suspect shelve unit away from the wall. It moved easily enough, as the floor was very smooth.

Bolger got it forward about 2 feet, leaving enough room for her to look behind the shelf.

Sure enough, there it was. She pushed the unit forward a little more so that she could get in behind and reach for the key. She grasped the key and was about to straighten up when she noticed the recess in the wall. The recess looked to be about a foot deep, two foot wide and about 6 foot high.

Strange. she thought, perhaps it was a shelving recess that was made redundant when they outfitted the room with the newer shelving. "Let's check it out."

After pushing the shelf unit a little further away from the wall, she got a better view and there was much more light allowed to fall into the recess. Now she could clearly make it out.

It was a disused doorway.

CHAPTER SEVENTEEN

Tina stood there looking at the door; she had a flash-light in her hand, appropriated from the storeroom just up the hall. The door itself had a simple dead-bolt, it was a bit rusted over but a stiff tap from the butt end of the torch broke the seal of rust. Now it slid stubbornly over.

The door was a heavy wooden type painted over several times, but it was obviously not opened in many, many years. She pushed hard against the door but it refused to budge, Tina put her shoulder to it and heaved. It gave a little. With a few swift kicks, both gave way. A shot of pain went up her leg, and a cloud of dust came out of the open doorway. After a few seconds, the first wave of pain passed and she put her foot back on the floor, it hurt like hell but she could put pressure on it. She moved into the doorway and shone the light into the abyss. Beyond was a small narrow area much smaller then the file room.

The walls were bare stone and the area was bare save for a few wooden shelves on which were what appeared to be reams of paper, un-boxed.

"What the fuck?" she said to herself. Despite the fear in her heart and that little paranoiac voice telling her to get the hell out of here, she moved painfully and carefully into the tiny room.

The paper was covered in a slimly damp dust but upon examination, revealed that they were no more than leftover letter-heads that should have been dispatched to the dump years ago. Probably because of fear that the letterheads might be used for illegal purposes, they were left aside possibly with the intention of burning them at a later date. There was nothing of interest here so she gave one more swing of the torch. Tina thought that she detected something out of place on the furthest wall. The woman couldn't be sure what it was that attracted her to examine the wall more closely. There was just something, the texture was not right or the colour, not that it was possible to detect colours as such the place was devoid of colour, it was a sixth sense thing.

When she touched the surface, she knew that it was not stone. Tina tapped with her knuckles, it sounded hollow. She examined the whole area then for any sign of a crevice where a hidden lever might be. Why, she thought that there was one she couldn't explain to herself, but the woman had seen Raiders of the Lost Ark and The Temple of Doom and this just seemed to be a situation where such a device might be. There was no hidden crevice with a lever that operated some mysterious device that rolled away this false wall. So she pushed against it and it just moved away from her.

Now panic set in. "Shit" she gasped, wishing that she hadn't found a way of opening it.

Now what to do? Do I go on and see what's beyond this obviously secret panel? Her curiosity told her, "yes" but the paranoiac voice said "no".

With sudden and determined clarity she turned and limped back out onto the file room.

With the key that started all the trouble, she locked the file room door, from the inside.

Tina did not want anyone, anyone, sneaking up behind her. Bolger went painfully back into the tiny dark room and shoved the panel the rest of the way open. Ahead was a low narrow passageway with bare walls. The passage floor was damp and apparently un-trodden on for perhaps 50 or 60 years. The dust and dirt just lay there like a spray painted finish, not level, as the floor was bare stone but the layer hugged the contours of the stone evenly. The passageway was about 2 feet wide but seemed to narrow considerably just ahead. She moved forward to examine, shining the torch up and down.

This was something totally weird, a concealed passage, why? she thought. *What was this passage for? Where did it lead? Who constructed it? Who concealed it? And what the fuck am I doing there?* The brave woman turned to go, took just two steps and stopped.

Where she thought the passage narrowed was, in fact, a very narrow series of steps, flat stones jut out of the wall, no more then 10" wide going back up over her head. There was another passage overhead going back towards the ground floor level. The beam of light could not penetrate all the way back into the dark recess above. A tiny voice told her to take a little look, just a peep, but a big voice told her to get the hell out of there. Strangely enough, the little voice won.

She turned back and approached the steps. Carefully she mounted the steps, they were damp and slippery, but by pressing against the wall opposite the steps, Tina managed to climb them safely. She now stood in a passage above the tiny secret room, and she imagined that she would be on the same level as the floor level of the bank proper, in other words, street level. This passage was no more then 15" wide and she had to move sideways along it. One thing for sure, the man for whom it was built didn't have or expect to have a weight problem. She figured that it was a good thing that she was not a big-breasted girl.

It seemed to her that she had gone quite a long way down this passage, but in actual fact, it was no more then 10 feet from the top of the steps. It came to an abrupt end, just a dead stop.

No up, no down, 'no' straight ahead either. However, on closer examination, she found that the obstruction in front of her was wooden, and it had a handle on it. She pulled on the handle, nothing, so she turned it, it moved reluctantly. She sensed rather then felt the release of the locking device. Tina pulled the door. There were signs of light ahead now, less then a metre away, a single shaft of vertical light, a crack in a wall, the gap between a door and a doorframe? The light was dull, it was not sunlight and she could hear voices. Her brain had to do a 180 to fathom out where she was.

She was standing in the rear of a closet in the manager's office and the voices she heard was that of Don Ruxton and John Sing. Her first impulse was to open the door and walk out into blessed fresh air, but part of her brain said no, this was a secret best kept secret for the time being. Besides, Sing might still be a threat. It was best to keep this quite until she talked to Dillon.

She closed the door carefully and walked down the passage. Once down on the sub-floor level again, Tina decided that she'd had enough adventure for one day and began to retrace her steps back to the file room. "What the hell was this passage for? What purpose did it serve?" she muttered. Apart from the passage up to the manager's office, where did the other part of the system go to? She stood still for a few moments thinking about the purpose of this passageway. "Shit." she muttered as she turned again and made her way back into the darkness.

This time she passed the steps and continued along the passage, it was becoming narrower now, not wide enough for her to walk forwards without turning sideways. In the beam of the torch, she saw what appeared to be the dead end of the passage, for a wall cut straight across from left to right. She checked the ceiling for any openings as she approached the wall, but there was none, just the rotten timber the builders had used to case-in prior to concreting over the ceiling.

Just when she was about to turn back, Tina noticed that there was an opening to the right, not very wide, no more then the width of the present passage. Tina had to place her head right up against the end wall before she could look into this passage. Beyond the first few metres of the new passage going away towards the front of the building the passage began to widen out. Even from here she could see that the passage also rose quite sharply. Although pensive, she took a deep breath finding the air stale and mucky and squeezed herself through the opening. The steps began almost immediately as the passage widened out. Tina was no engineer but she figured that the reason that the passage was so narrow at the corner must have had something to do with the need for structural strength at that point to carry the weight of the building above. Tina examined the floor, or rather the steps as she proceeded up them, for any signs of marking, footprints, scrapes or anything that showed that the passage was used in recent times. There was no marking of any description, it was obvious from the thin layer of dust and spiders webs that this had not being used in years. The surface of the steps was, of course, telling her that the passage was not used very often.

At the top of the steps, she found some crumbled pieces of paper, on closer examination they turned out to be old newspaper fragments. They were not cut-out sections just random pieces of torn paper. She checked each piece in turn to see if she could find a date. Tina had become so engrossed in her task that she forgot her desire to shine the beam forward every few seconds to check that no one was coming.

As she realised her mistake, the woman gasped and shone the light up the passage, as with each time she had done it before there was nothing to see. Her heart was pounding in her chest, what exactly she expected to find she did not know. She focused her attention to the scraps of newspapers. Tina finally found a scrap with a partial date on it from November 1941. The heading underneath mentioned the war. The piece of paper was very faded and yellowed and the print was barely distinguishable but from what she could make out, the article was about the invasion of the Korean Peninsula by the Japanese. Tina folded the scrap carefully and moved on along the passage.

About 20 metres ahead, she sensed rather than saw, at first, a tiny shaft of light high up on the right hand wall of the passage. As she got nearer, Tina realised that there was indeed a tiny slit set in a small recess at the very end of the passage. As she stepped into the recess the woman realised that there was noise coming from the slit which was about 3 feet by 2 inches wide. The reason for the recess became apparent also as from here, a person could look down on the people within the bank proper. The other possible reason for the slit and indeed the whole passage system could be a primitive form of air ventilation. However, Tina suspected that it was for the former purpose as if it were for ventilation, the warm air raising from the floor of the bank would become entrapped in a kind of vacuum being held in the passage by cooler air coming from the lower levels of the passage at the rear of the bank. It would appear that the person that had the design of the bank commissioned had it in mind that he would be able to spy on either his customers or staff, or both.

She turned away from the slit and found the sudden impact of the darkness quite frightening and had forgotten about the torch. Having let the beam of light drift towards the floor, she brought the torch up just a little too quickly and she knocked it off the wall. To her dismay, the light died.

"Shit!" she shouted in horror. "Work, fuck you." she muttered to the torch. Tina fiddled with the switch, the light shot to life, momentarily blinding her as she had it turned towards her face. It scared the hell out of her and almost dropped it. She had actually turned it off when she snapped it after hitting the wall. Her breathing was very erratic and she felt light headed. She though she was about to faint.

"Calm yourself you fool" She leaned back against the wall opposite the recess.

Tina was angry for allowing herself to become so uptight considering that she was in no danger whatsoever. She was a grown woman and she was still afraid of the dark. In frustration she banged her head of the wall behind her. Tina wished she hadn't. The woman suddenly realised that she had banged her head of what she thought was a stone wall but it was not a stone wall at all. In fact, it was a timber panel or a door.

"Oh no. Not more secrets? Shit." Tina turned slowly to examine the spot. She brought the torch up for the beam to bear on the spot where her head had hit the 'wall'. She had been so intent on examining the slit in the wall opposite initially, that she never noticed the wooden panelled recess on the other side. There was a small slot just large enough to get your four fingers into what obviously acted as a leverage point to open the panel which was floor to ceiling and about 24 inches wide. The panel or door refused to budge at first but then gave a little. She had to step right back into the opposite recess so as to open the door fully. It opened to the left thus blocking off the passage and escape. Had she realised that she would not have delved any further. When she had the door fully opened, she shone the torch up to see what lay beyond. At first she wasn't sure if her eyes were actually open for what she saw looking at her did not make any sense. Tina shook her head vigorously to wake herself up, how the hell could there be a body of a man standing there looking at her, although the eyes had long since sunken back in their sockets and she did not introduce herself.

Tina just closed the door as calmly as possible and ran like hell with total disregard for the pain she was inflicting on her body as she pounded of the narrow sides of the passage. Tina was not aware of having fallen down the steps, neither was she aware that she nearly crushed her ribs when she became wedged in the passage where it narrowed near the corner. Nor did the panic-stricken woman notice banging her head off the protruding steps that led up to the office above. She also did not know that she was screaming at the top of her voice. Tina was through the first of the secret rooms now having firmly shut the panel painted to look like the rest of the walls in the room. She rushed into the file room and slammed shut the door to the secret room. Tina pushed the filing shelf back into place and after checking that everything looked as it was unlocked the door.

"There was no body." she began to tell herself trying to block out the sight of the un-seeing eyes, the dry brown leather skin, the disintegrating clothes that was once a business suit. "Pull yourself together, there was no body. Why are you bleeding? Bleeding?" She examined herself; the knuckles of both hands were bleeding as was her forehead. She had to get out of here and clean herself up. The toilets were on the way back up to the main floor so she should be able to get there without being spotted.

Tina retrieved the one file that contained the loan approval document before leaving the file room. The torch she returned to the store. The young woman made it to the toilets without meeting anybody. She glanced at her watch she had lost all track of time. It was just 10 o'clock, so they were opening the bank. When she looked in the mirror, she realised just how much a mess she was. Bolger looked like someone who had been in a fight with a Doberman Pincer.

"Let's get cleaned up and back to work. Got to go and see Dillon. He'll love this."

The cold water on her face was a blessing, it was like a long cold drink after spending the day in the sun, like a 'Bud' in the desert. She felt much better.

"Now let's go and meet some living people. Shit, there was no body, Okay?"

*

Dillon got a hostile reception from Percy. The old Englishman came to the door and went straight onto the offensive.

"I no longer wish to hear anything you have to say, Mister." Percy began to close the door but Dillon placed his left hand on it.

"Give me a hearing, old chap; at least explain why you re-neged on our deal?"

"Very well then, I'll tell you. I've seen your type before, I've heard of your 'Raiders' out of bloody New York. You tried in '83 to get your hands on our shares. Well Old Chap, we thwart-ed you then and we'll thwart you now. You think that the only reason I'd sell is for the money, well you're wrong. I'll wait, I'm not desperate. I'll wait and sell to an Englishman, not a bloody Yank and that's another thing, that was ours too until a pack of bloody convicts and despots from all over Europe took it away from us."

"What the fuck are you talking about?"

"America, New England, as it was as it should be. Well I'm glad that Lawson didn't wait any longer for you, because I fig-ured out what you were up to trying to buying my shares on a day the market is falling, trying to get them cheap-"

"Percy, you're talking shit!" Dillon interrupted angrily, he had enough of Mister Nice Guy. "Firstly it was Lawson who stood us up and if he showed up when he should, you would have got top dollar for your shares, plus 50 cents per share. Secondly, we got no shares yet, we're trying to stop the people who stole those shares in '83. *They're* the raiders, we're trying to save the bank and thirdly, I'm not a fucking Yank. I'm Irish and I resent being called anything else. What's more I'm the closest thing you're going to get today to an Englishman to buy your shares."

Sir Percy lightened his stance a bit. "But Lawson said,"

"Lawson is in cahoots with the '83 crowd."

"Why? Why how dare you make such an accusation against a good Brit! Why I'll have you know that Mister Lawson is a highly respected member of the community."

"Lawson is a double-crossing son of a bitch. He is in with Archibald and Paddy Maltbie and Jason Kim." Dillon was angry, angry with the double cross and angry with, well just about everything.

Sir Percy's chest suddenly fell back into its normal position; the wind had gone out of his sails.

"Perhaps you should come in," Sir Percy stood aside to let Dillon pass. "Come into the library."

Penderville led the way into a high ceiling Victorian room.

The walls were lined with books; every inch of the wall was covered with leather-bound volumes.

"Large collection." Dillon commented as he accepted the offer of a chair.

"Law gathers references like the Chancellor gather taxes."

"Law? You're a solicitor?"

"Nothing so lowly, old chap. QC, Queens Council, Barrister at law. I was attached to the Governor's office when I came out here as a lad - a junior assistant to the Public Prosecutor's office. I got a taste for law and went on to do a BL."

"Were you in private practice?"

"Yes, eventually. I stayed in the Prosecutor's office for many years, I knew Geoffrey Bordes-Aitcheson, Jeffery's father and he asked me to join AAB as legal adviser. I was already a shareholder; I was offered a place on the board so I joined the AAB."

"But you did go into private practice?"

"Oh yes but some years later. I always retained my interests in the AAB. You see my father had been out here some years before Mother came out, he was a merchant, you know. Nowadays they call them Export Agents. Father purchased goods from the mainland and sent them onto England. Bamboo and exotic plants were his specialty."

"Bamboo?" Dillon was puzzled.

"Yes, strange the things that people in the old country were fascinated with. Bamboo had been a trade commodity for many years of course, but no one specialised, you understand? Bamboo was just filler for the cargo ships. It was light and much in demand in the theatres for making lightweight props that could be moved easily when they changed the scenes, you understand? But father had seen some Bamboo furniture but it was very scarce in England. So he came to Hong Kong and began buying the stuff and shipping it home. Made a fortune, the Gentry couldn't get enough of it. Apparently they had a fascination with the stuff, it was so light. Every lady wanted a chair that she could move around without placing a strain on her girdle. The Chinese had little use for chairs, of course, they sat on the floor, the peasants that is. Of course Bamboo was used here for a different purpose altogether, scaffolding for building work, still used for that to this day. Just look at the building work around here, all will be using Bamboo."

"I never noticed."

"Anyhow, old chap, father had invested in AAB, he had known Jeffery's grandfather, Arthur Aitcheson."

"Aitcheson? I thought you said that Jeff's father was Bordes?"

"Yes, Anthony Bordes, Bordes married Arthur Aitcheson's daughter, Bessie. It was a marriage designed to stop the two men fighting. Bessie retained the Aitcheson name in marriage."

"Why the feud?"

"Goes back a long way." Percy told Dillon as much of the story about the battle for the bank as he knew. Much of it they had already figured out. Dillon figured he needed to reclaim Percy's trust and let him waffle, plus it helped confirm much of what they had uncovered.

"So you see now why there was a feud and why Jeffery got the name Bordes-Aitcheson"

"There certainly are some great stories in the history of Hong Kong; it must have been an interesting place at the turn of the century."

"My father loved it, he never asked to go back to England. My mother didn't see it that way, but she was a loyal wife. She supported him in whatever he did."

"And you? How do you feel about it?"

"I'd gladly die here if it wasn't for those damn Chinese coming in to take over in '97, I'll be damned if I'll be buried in a place that will be controlled by China, bloody Commies walk on your grave you know, just to disturb your spirits. Damn Pagans."

"Now about those shares." Dillon had places to go, people to do.

"Ah yes, well perhaps I was a little premature in my judgment. Damn Lawson, lying little beggar. But not to worry, we'll conduct our affairs without him." Sir Percy smiled.

"How about a broker? Have you anyone in mind?"

"Yes, P.B. Gunn is a good friend of mine I'll have him organise it for me. Who is your Broker?"

"Philip Thorn."

"Never heard of him, but P.B. will organise it, leave it to me. Ah, care for a drop of Port before you go?"

"Well, I, ah, oh what the hell, why not?"

"That's the ticket old chap; let's celebrate the deal this time."

Dillon winced at the thought of a drink at this hour of the morning, but it was as well to please the old git.

*

Diver Ho had gone to the doctor last evening, not the Chinese Healer who could have healed just about anything, but he did not have anything to heal. The purpose of the visit was to get one of those invaluable pieces of paper that said you were sick. Most unusual system the English brought to Hong Kong, the

Excuse Cert. So he had got an Excuse Cert and sent it to his employer.

Now he was on his way to see Ho Chan. He had told his father last night about the discovery. His father was a fearsome man. He worked as a fisherman and spent many hours a day on the sea. He would be gone to work at dawn and would not return until dusk, thus even as a child, Ho did not see much of his father.

Senior Ho had come home at 11 o'clock looking very tired. Ho had waited until after he had eaten before approaching.

He told them everything, every move, about following Ho Chan to Macau, about the letter it's contents, everything.

Suddenly his little sister wasn't listening anymore. She was looking at the door to the bedroom where Ho had opened the letter. Ho continued on talking about going to the city hall where he found out about Mad Jason, and he did not notice his little sister slip quietly away to the bedroom.

Once in the room she turned on the bare light bulb hanging from the centre of the ceiling and ran to the bed. She got down on the floor and searched under the bed but she could not see it.

She remembered seeing it, a small slip of paper with a number on it. She had picked it up and turned it over, but there was just the number and a name, nothing else, and then she had thrown it away again. It had meant nothing at the time but now, now that she knew that Elder Brother had opened the letter in this very room. Then perhaps the slip of paper had come out of the letter, and perhaps it was a secret code. A code to more treasure. It had to be here somewhere, but it was so dark under the bed. She slid in further and passed her hand back and forth in front of her feeling the bare wood floor.

There was a downside to the story, when Ho's father heard the part about him selling a copy of the letter to Ho Chan he insisted that Ho take the original letter to the Locksmith.

So to fulfil his father's wish he was going to see Ho Chan to give him the original letter.

He approached the shop and saw the silver coloured Toyota Crown double parked just outside the entrance to the upstairs shop. He noticed that one of the car's doors was open. Diver Ho made a mental note of the number plate just in case he happened to hear of the car being stolen.

He turned into the hallway and was about to climb the steps when he heard the commotion at the top of the stairs.

"Come on, old fart, move or I shall place the tip of my boot in your smelly hole with great motion."

Ho stopped in surprise as a youth appeared at the top of the stairs. Ho Chan was directly behind him being shoved by yet another youth.

"Out of the way, scum. This place is closed for business!" Headboy Kim shouted down at Ho.

Ho backed down the steps and out into the pavement.

"What do you want with him? Who are you?" Ho asked his mind racing.

"Get out of our way unless you want to meet the Aberdeen Tongs." Headboy Kim ordered arrogantly.

"Tongs? Who are Tongs? You are not Tongs." Ho did not believe them.

Suddenly a serrated edge dagger appeared as if from nowhere and touched his cheek.

"Who is now Tong?"

"You would appear to have a good case." Ho replied as he moved back slightly, away from the blade's tip. But he was still not convinced. He was himself a member of the clan in his own area and he had never heard of the 'Aberdeen' Tongs.

"I am Tong. This man is wanted by the head of our cell and you will not interfere if you value your life." The threat had now become rather menacing so Ho backed off. Perhaps there was a new cell in Aberdeen calling themselves the Aberdeen Thong.

Ho Chan had remained silent during all this, he just stared at Diver Ho. Now he was bundled into the Toyota Crown and driven away. A few passers-by had stopped to watch what was happening, although no one offered to intercede. In fact, there had been quite a few people hanging about until the Tongs were mentioned then most went about their business. Ho, however, was not satisfied that they really were Tongs, and even if they were, what did they want with Ho Chan?

Ignoring the stares from the few remaining onlookers, he looked around for a taxi.

He could see none, but there was a Hi-ace van just down the street with its rear door open, a delivery van. Ho walked up to the driver's window and glanced in. The keys were in the ignition.

He opened the door and sat up into the van. The engine fired first time; he moved the column shift into first and hit the gas. It took off with a jerk and half the contents of the van shot out the back door.

Ho was not too familiar with this type of gear shift so he went along in first gear to make sure, firstly that he got away from the scene of the theft and secondly there was a set of traffic lights coming up fast and he wanted to make sure that he got through them before they changed.

He did both, but the engine was revving dangerously high. Once through the lights he chanced changing gear, he pulled the column stick towards him but forgot to ease off the accelerator, the result was that the gears grounded but engaged and the van shot forward even faster. Another few boxes shot out the back.

He was on Wing Lok Street and heading east towards the junction with Des Voeux Road. Ho knew that once out there the traffic was going to be heavy and slow so he had time to get used to the van. Once he had the Crown in sight in traffic where they would not be able to lose him, he could relax, and perhaps even close that back door so as not to attract too much attention. The last thing he needed was to be stopped by the police to be told that his door was open.

Now he began to wonder about the driver of the van calling the police. But that would not happen for some time, assuming that it would take the driver of the van a few minutes to phone the police and then another few minutes before the police got a description of the van on the radio to the patrol cars. So all he needed was to get the door closed, and that could be done once he had sighted his quarry and got stopped at a traffic light.

He was in a clear run of traffic now where he could see the silver grey Toyota up ahead, so Diver eased back on the accelerator and looked at the gear change again. Logically, if first gear was forward and the second back then third had to be forward again but he would have to move the stick either up or down. He tried down; it was a good decision, the engine sounded a lot quieter now and he was within two cars of the Toyota. He began to relax.

They approached a set of lights, he prayed for them to change before the car got to them but they didn't, so now he prayed for them not to change, but they did. The first of the two cars in front of him went through on the amber but the second one braked. He was in the same lane as the car in front so he shot into the inside lane and accelerated ahead. The light was red by the time he hit the intersection and cars on the crossing road had begun to move. Diver Ho hit the steering wheel for the horn but couldn't find it, so he went through with his heart in his mouth. One car was well on top of the changing light and was first forward; Ho swerved and just missed him. Ho drove away from the intersection to the sound of blaring horns. Ho looked down at the centre of the steering wheel, where was the horn? He pressed different places in the centre of the wheel but heard no horn. This didn't make sense. Then he looked at the lever on the right hand side of the steering column, there was a button on the end of it. He pressed it, a tiny 'beep' was heard. That wasn't going to be much good to him, so he was going to have to stay close to the Crown especially near traffic lights.

The Toyota was only one car away now and approaching another set of lights, Ho was ready this time, he pressed the accelerator on the Hi-ace and shot past the car in front. Now he was behind the Toyota, only about ten metres back. They went through the lights together. The main junction was coming up with Des Voeux Road, and to his horror the lights changed to green, no chance to shut the back door. Boxes of stuff had been falling out all the way along Wing Lok Street and this was drawing a lot of attention to him. He had not looked in the rear vision mirror once, now he did and to his amazement, there were white clouds of dust all up along the street. It did not make sense. Both vehicles had to veer left onto Des Voeux Road and Ho heard the boxes move in the rear of the van. He could visualise the box flying through the air. He looked in the mirror this time. Two cardboard slid out the back and tumbled across the street. A great cloud of white dust exploded from the boxes on impact.

As he drove away the cloud completely engulfed the intersection and all that could be seen was brake lights fading into the cloud. Ho could not figure out what was going on, so he just concentrated on the driving. All the way along Des Voeux Road Central past the Mandarin Hotel and up onto Garden Road past the U.S. Embassy, not one red light did they catch. He followed them around the Peak and down into Aberdeen.

As they drove down, he began to wonder what he would do when they got to where they were going and who were they anyway? He thought at first that it might be something to do with the sovereigns, but if that was the case then why did they not take him also for he had been there when the transaction was done. That was presuming that these men were the same men from Antiquity Chang. But no, these were not the same men, this was something that Locksmith Ho had gotten himself involved in. Maybe it was as a result of the letter. If so then it could only be of interest to Jason Kimberley's ancestors and it must be them that are somehow involved in this for it could not be the boss of the bank for he does not yet know. Not until I tell him. If this is so, if all this is because of the letter then are the Kimberley's not placing a great value on it and should he not perhaps be more careful when dealing with the Gwi-Lo, Bordes-Aitcheson, perhaps the letter is worth more then I at first thought.

The car slowed as it approached the Golden Moon restaurant. Diver Ho stayed well back and watched. The Crown turned slowly around the side of the building; he lost sight of it momentarily. Easing his foot off the clutch, Diver let the van roll forward until he could see the car again. Ho had heard of this place. It was not for the poor people in Hong Kong. This place was for the rich. But then was he not rich too? Did he not have many thousands of dollars?

The two thugs dragged the old man out of the car and walked him around the side of the building and up wooden steps. Half way up, Ho Chan looked back, Diver Ho knew that the old man saw him. The thugs led him along the veranda to a secluded door and went inside. He was afraid to follow for he felt vulnerable having to climb up the steps that led up from the beach. The stairs were very close to the patio door through which the men had led Locksmith Ho. If he tried to go that way he could be seen. Ho decided to wait and see what happened, but first he had to get rid of the van for the police would surely be looking for it. He drove it to a side street and got out, went around to the back of the van and reached up to close the back door, that was when he saw the flour. This gave him an idea. He closed the back door of the van, but it refused to stay shut, he tried several times but the hinges must have been damaged and the door was out of place and just would not close. Ho left it like that and jumped back into the driver's seat.

In the cab he got a clipboard and a delivery roster sheet with about 20 entries. There was only a few entries with a quantity and delivery dates entered up against them. Obviously the driver had only started the day. He made a fresh entry for an urgent delivery for the Golden Moon restaurant. They needed flour quickly. Special order, just phoned in this morning. He started the engine and drove back to the restaurant. He opened the side door of the van and took out a box.

This was a good plan, Ho thought as he turned towards the building.

With a box of one kilo bags of flour on his shoulder and the clip board on top, he shut the door of the van and headed for the restaurant. He figured that there must be an entrance at the side to the kitchen. There was, amid containers and sacks of garbage, a clearance in the middle of which was the open door. The kitchen was practically deserted except for two cleaning ladies; they glanced up and saw a guy with a delivery and went about their business. Ho walked deliberately through the kitchen into a short hall away from the double doors that obviously led to the dining room.

Off this hall were a number of doors, he ignored the most immediate ones; they had signs on the doors for toilets and store room. The one that interested him the most was in the middle of the corridor for it had no sign. He walked up and opened it. Ho was standing on the veranda overlooking the beach. To his right was a large open patio window; further along was the French door leading back into the restaurant. To the left was a wooden stairs leading to the veranda above.

This stairs was at the opposite end to the one that Ho had been led up, by going up this one he would not be seen by the men that had gone into the room. He left the box on the floor and with clipboard in hand he climbed the steps.

At the top, the veranda ran the full length of the building. Ho went on tiptoe along the wooden floor, now approaching the patio door. It was open and he heard voices. He did not recognise the voice of the person that was speaking. Whoever it was said,

"I found the letter most interesting, oh very much so. However, I was most disappointed that it was not the original." Diver Ho was shocked to hear the words, the old fart had shown the letter to someone else. The voice continued.

"Did you know that it was a mere copy?" Still no reply, the old fart must have made some gesture for the voice said-

"Well, this is worse than I feared. Now we have a third party lie. You know what I have to know?"

Then a shot rang out. Diver Ho tensed himself and took a step away from the doorway. The reverberations were still ringing in his ears when he heard the old fart say.

"If ever to pull trigger near Ho Chan again take better aim. For if you do not kill me next time I will kill you."

"I must apologise for my son, I promise you he will never again do that. He will never miss again. Now to this stubborn matter of who gave you the letter, please do understand, I will find out who gave you the letter. I must have the original. I do not bluff. But we are both businessmen."

There was a pause and then the voice spoke again.

"You must make money and I, too, must make money. But I have made my money. Perhaps if I were to give you some of mine you would be more disposed to give me what I need to know. Are we perhaps getting close to understanding each other?"

"Perhaps?" He heard the old fart say.

"Very well then, you supply the name and where we can find this man and I will give you $10,000."

"Paltry sum, for such valued information."

On the veranda, Ho knew in his heart and soul that Ho Chan would give them the information, he was a worthless fart who would do anything for money including selling his own cousin's son.

Not at all honourable, like his father's side of the family. He knew now that he had to get home and get his money and leave Hong Kong for this Man would follow him until he got the letter, and perhaps even then, he would kill him. So Ho decided to get out of there. He turned slowly and began to move away. He forgot the clipboard.

He had placed it on the post at the top of the stairs and now moving away carefully watching the window to be sure that he did not come into the line of vision, he hit the clipboard. Ho grabbed for it as it went over the edge but he missed it and it went clattering down the stairs.

Now he moved fast and careless. Ho heard running steps as he rounded the corner of the building. There was no one around so he ran flat out into the car park. He heard the running feet still behind as he ran to the van. It was still there. Diver Ho grabbed the door handle and yanked the door open. The keys were still in the ignition and the engine fired first time. The frightened cousin had left it in first gear so it just took off jerkily, swinging the steering wheel around making a wide arched turn in the street. He heard them pound on the side of the van.

Suddenly there was an increase in the noise level. In the mirror he saw to his horror the back door open. He'd forgotten that. There were shouts as he heard and then sensed a body, jump into the van. In the mirror he saw a shape, no time to worry about it now must get up the gears and get away from here, which way did the gears go? Yes back for second.

The van shot forward, with the driver vaguely seeing the shape being thrown backwards; now he was hanging on grimly at the open door but with nothing to hold onto and totally off balance. Ho tried to watch him fall out, and then the van hit a rut as he came out of the street.

He turned back to what was happening ahead and the shock hit him that he was heading straight across the road through the scattering crowds but heading straight for the docks. He swung the wheel and the van slewed wildly knocking over fish stalls sending produce flying in all directions.

The van came to a halt at last and Diver knew there was still danger. He glanced back and the shadow was gone. Diver Ho got the van into first gear and ignoring the roars of abuse from the crowd, he began to move away as the van got showered with rotten fish and damaged vegetables.

Suddenly there was a big thump and something hit the van. He looked back and there was the shadow again, this time well inside the van down on all fours moving forward. Ho could think of only one thing to do. If the guy wanted to come forward towards the front of the van, Ho decided to help him. He put his foot hard on the brake.

As will happen with vans with the engine being out over the front wheels, the back of the van came up at the same time as it came to a halt. The raising action of the back made the man in the back light and he shot forward hitting hard against boxes of flour. Some burst, filling the back of the van with white dust. Ho figured that would keep him quiet for a while so he slammed hard on the accelerator again. He got into second gear and kept the accelerator down hard. The shadow was still there but laying in a disorganised heap. He was beginning to climb out of Aberdeen when he saw the Toyota Crown in the rear vision mirror. He had begun to think along the lines of going straight to the police with the shadow in the back of the van to help him explain his actions.

But now with the Crown back in pursuit, he did not have time to think about the police. To make matters worse, the shadow was beginning to come around.

The car was closing fast up the hill and he did not have the power to race them. The road was narrow and littered with bends so the Crown had no chance to overtake. However, the slow climbing was giving the shadow a chance to get his act together and he began to move slowly forward, this time he was being super careful. Ho used both sides of the road, to keep the van rocking to prevent the shadow from coming forward and also to keep the Crown back.

There was a problem, however; because of the hill he could not keep the speed high enough to cause enough sideways motion to throw the shadow around enough. The crest was approaching and he willed the van on, he looked around the cab for something to hit the shadow with, but could find nothing. The crest was but 200 metres away now but the shadow was almost close enough to reach up and grab the bar behind the seats. Ho swerved from side to side again but in doing that, it acted to slow the van down further, but it did not slow the shadow. He had his feet firmly wedged in front of the rear wheel arches.

He was almost there; he glanced back only to see the white shadow's hand reach up for the bar. He swung his left hand back and hit him as hard as he could, but it was not enough and he knew it. He was on the top now and the van began to gather speed. He swerved violently one time to try and dislodge the shadow; he got knocked around a bit but did not lose his foothold. There was nothing for it now but to go flat out. There was a bang on the side of the van. While he had been intent on the shadow, the Crown had come alongside. He swung the van away and then back viciously hitting the car around the passenger door at a slight angle. The Crown backed off; the hit had also thrown the shadow about a little.

A blaring horn brought his attention back to the front, he narrowly missed the oncoming car by centimetres. He was doing about 80 KPH now and the Crown began to come along side again.

Ho watched the Crown and kept edging it over towards the edge of the road. A horn sounded ahead, Ho looked up, there was a car coming no more then 30 metres away, he swung back onto his own side of the road, the Crown did not have the opportunity. The driver hit the brakes and the car went into a slide, straight into the oncoming car. The cars impacted at a combined speed of around 100 KPH the result was a mess: the Crown was still spinning as Ho rounded the corner, going too fast and not watching what he was doing.

"Shit!" he exclaimed. The bus was crawling, Ho braked and swerved at the same time.

The van slewed broadside, by sheer reaction Ho countersteered and that stopped the van from going into a complete spin. As it was, the bus hit the rear driver's side of the van, it crumpled but bounced off and spun the other way. It was as if Ho just stood still and the van went around him.

It did a full 180 and the passenger's side rear now hit the back of the bus. Ho did not notice the white shadow being catapulted out the rear door along with perhaps 100 kilos of flour in the form of a white cloud.

The body was thrown some fifty metres down the hill, the man tumbling uncontrollably, somersaulting through the air like a rag doll only to come crashing unmercifully down to the hard surface again and again. He was dead long before he came to rest.

The white cloud slowly descended back to earth.

CHAPTER EIGHTEEN

It was just a little cooler up on the Peak than it was down in the business district. Even though the air was cool and crisp, the tarmac on the road was hot. The inside of the van was hot.

Ho came to and tried to figure out where he was, what had happened? The dust and smoke had settled now and the bus driver approached the van.

"Are you Okay?" he asked in Cantonese. Ho nodded painfully, beginning to remember what had happened. He turned back to the interior of the van but there was no sign of the shadow. Then he saw the open back door. Diver Ho tried to open his door but it was jammed, but the passenger door was Okay, so he got out that way.

By now, the passengers had begun to disembark from the bus. There was not much damage done to the bus as it had been stopped by the time of the impact. Two passengers went round the van and stood looking down the road, talking excitedly to each other. Ho was on the same side of the van as the two passengers and curious about them, he asked what they were looking for. They had been sitting at the rear of the bus and could have sworn that they saw a man thrown out of the back of the van, during the crash. Ho began to run stiffly down the hill, the two passengers following. About 50 metres away in a lifeless bundle of blood and torn skin lay the body of the shadow. The woman passenger screamed on recognising the shape of the body. Ho told the other passenger to take her away.

Alone now, he turned the body over but the face was unrecognisable, being covered in blood and torn pieces of flesh. The nose was practicably gone, only cartilage remained. The clothes the man wore were shredded as if he had been attacked by a madman with a knife and slashed unmercifully. Ho remembered the Crown and turned away from the body and went back up the hill, past the van and bus.

As he approached the upturned Crown, he examined the interior, there was no body. He went to the other car and the lone driver was slumped at the wheel. Ho pulled open the door and examined the man. He was alive but his head was split open on the forehead.

A car pulled up and two men came toward the crashed car.

"What happened?" a Gwai Lo asked.

"There has been an accident, this man is badly hurt and there is no one in the other car." Ho replied looking up at the tall Gwai Lo.

"I will call for an ambulance." said the second man who was Chinese.

Ho looked at the Gwai Lo and said, "Nothing can be done for this man, best left to doctors. Very important that I get to Central as quickly as possible. Can you give me ride? I will pay."

"Okay we'll give you a lift. Are you sure you're alright? You're bleeding." The Gwai Lo touched Ho's forehead.

"Not important, must get to Central. Please help."

"Okay fella take it easy, I'll get you there."

The Gwai Lo took him by the arm and led him back to the car.

*

When Tina Bolger had a chance to get her thoughts together over a cup of coffee in the teahouse just up the street from the bank, she decided what she had to do. First there was the matter of the missing pages from the ledgers; they had been stolen, probably by Maylay as she was the main suspect for just about everything that was going wrong right now. Second, the deed had to be in the bank, if not, then over in the Island branch. If they did exist and Kimberley's descendants were told about them, then they would have a case for re-negotiating leases for all the property in the New Territories. That was in the short term. In the long term, surely the Chinese would have to enter into discussions with them as the legal owners? This would have to throw open the whole position of the Colony again. On the other hand the bank, being the current holders of the deeds as security, may have a case to claim that the deeds belong to the bank and therefore the bank would have to negotiate with the Chinese. If the bank could prove that they owned the property, then the bank overnight would become one of the biggest banks in Hong Kong. Either way there was going to be speculation in the shares of the bank because a legal case would have to be fought as to ownership. And the void would generate the speculation in the shares. The speculation could be fierce, considering the current mood in Hong Kong; it was possible that people would jump at any possibility that might indicate that somehow the Chinese take away could be thwarted. They were going to go for the optimistic view hoping that the Chinese would ease their position at least.

All this led Tina to believe that a little flutter on the stock market would be a good bet.

"Let's just suppose that the deeds can't be found?" she asked herself. Then even if the deeds themselves were lost, they could be reconstructed, the fact that they existed at one stage was enough proof. In effect, the deeds could be re-built. The only uncertain thing was the effect their existence would have on the future of Hong Kong. Third, now she had a new tack to follow at least, the secret room and passages were put there for a reason and from what she could recollect, the bank on the Island was the same design as this one here therefore, the secret room and passages may be there also.

This brought her onto thinking about investigating that room. It was Okay here but in the main branch it was much busier and it was unlikely that she would have such privacy in the file room. So for that reason she would have to ask Jeff's permission. Now how to ask the man without telling him what you were doing. So it was a job for Dillon, he seemed to have struck a cord with Jeff, they seemed to get on quite well and she knew that Dillon would find a way of doing it.

Dillon was like that, if something had to be done he just went and did it, and to hell with the fall-out. Fourth, even though she didn't want to think about it, who was the man whose body she found? How long was the body there? Was he killed there or carried there? Either way there was the last question, who killed him? The body was obviously there for many years. Tina was no expert but she suspected that the body had to be at least ten years dead, maybe much longer, maybe even from the time of the Japanese occupation. She couldn't recall just what the style of the suit was, but she thought it was double breasted, that would seem to indicate a period of time around the war years.

That would indicate that it was placed there around the time that Jeff's father was in control of the bank. That in turn begged the question could Jeff's father have known about the death of the man? It was hard to imagine how he could not have known. For surely it would have being very dangerous to attempt to place the body there when it was obvious that the owner of the bank would be aware of the existence of the passages and was likely to discover the body.

Then there was the rope? She tried to picture the body again, it was not difficult, the image was etched in her mind's eye for all eternity. A cold shiver went up her back as she thought about it; thank God it did not fall out on her like it normally does in the movies. The rope, Okay it was tied around the man but not around the neck as you might expect. No, it was tied around the man's chest like it would be if you wanted to raise or lower a person from a building or a cliff. She suspected that the rope was not used to raise or lower the body but to drag him through the passage, for it was so narrow in places that there was no way that the body could be carried or dragged without the aid of a rope. So the guy was slugged elsewhere and dragged up the passage and hidden in the closet. So that begged the question, where was he killed? Probably in the bank and there was no place to take him without being seen so the logical place to hide the body was in the secret passage were he would never be found, because no one knew of the existence of the passage except for the owner of the bank. That led her back to Jeff's father. What anger or betrayal led him to kill the man in the first place? Had the man any form of identity on him.

"Shit, I should have looked." She glanced up from her pondering and looked at the three Chinese staring at her from the next table. She went red in the face; she had completely forgotten where she was.

My God, have I being talking out loud all the time? She couldn't have been.

"Sorry." she said to them and got up to leave. Tina decided to go back to the bank and phone Dillon.

It looked a perfectly normal morning in the bank; the doors were open now and a good few customers were in, but she noticed that there were only two tellers on. Every other morning there were at least four tellers on duty.

She crossed the floor and went behind the counter and into the inner office. Maylay was at her usual position like as if nothing had happened. She hadn't seen her this morning, after she entered the bank and she doubted if she had seen her at all. She didn't look up when she entered.

"Good Morning." she said but knew there was a croak in her voice.

"Oh, Miss Tina."

Tina looked as if she had seen a ghost. "Good morning. I hadn't expected to see you." Maylay stared at her. Tina wanted to avoid any further conversation and made towards Tom's office.

"Are you alright? You are all cut," Maylay asked, suddenly seeming concerned as she rose from her seat behind the desk.

"Why's that?" Tina ignored her comment on her appearance.

"Sorry, I just meant I hadn't expected you to come in." Now Maylay seemed puzzled.

"I still don't follow you?" She turned to face her, defiant now.

"Well with all that's happened, poor Mister Maxwell and all. I thought that you would stop your work until after the funeral."

Did she really think that she had killed him? "He's not dead." Tina replied, she could not control her venom.

"There was another attack at the hospital this morning. Mister Ruxton just told me and Mister Maxwell has been shot this time."

"What?" Tina could hardly believe her ears.

"Is true, some gunman, probably the same man that attacked him last night, shot him in the hospital, just over an hour ago."

"Good God!" Tina gasped.

"It's just terrible, poor Mister Maxwell. But what happened you?" she said again.

"I'm fine; I fell down the stairs is all."

"You should go see a doctor with those bruises." She eyed her sceptically.

"I will. Is Don in here?" She gestured to the office.

"Yes he is, would you like me to call a doctor?"

"No I'm fine, I'll check with one later." Tina went through to the manager's office. Sing was still there with Ruxton. They both stared at her.

"Jesus, that's terrible about Tom!" she said as she closed the door.

Ruxton put his index finger over his mouth and beckoned her over to the desk.

"He's not dead, it's just a story that was fed to Maylay and Jeff has a plan to trap her." Don stood up and came around the desk.

"What happened you?"

"Never mind that. What the fuck's happening?"

"Sit down I'll tell you. Are you sure you are all right? You look terrible."

"Forget it; tell me what the fuck is going on?" Tina snapped impatiently.

When she was alone, Maylay reached for the phone and dialled the same number as she had earlier from the teahouse. What had happened to Tina Bolger? How did she receive those injuries? The phone was answered.

"Sue, has Tommy returned there yet?"

"Yes mother." came her daughter's polite reply.

"Do you wish to speak to him?"

"Yes please." For many years Maylay had instilled the need in her daughter for politeness. Now she wanted to scream at her to get that useless no good son of a Gwai-Lo to come to the phone and explain what he had done, but she held her temper and waited patiently while he came.

"Hallow, Honourable Mother" Tommy said.

"Did you do as I said?"

"Yes. I called my esteemed cousin in the Royal Hong Kong. All he knew was that Detective Chung was leading the investigation into the attack last night and this morning on the Gwi Lui. He could not contact Chung to find out who they suspected for the attacks. He knew nothing of John Sing. I told him the story you told me about Sing stealing money from the bank and he said he would tell this to Chung when he sees him."

"You did not see the other Gwai-Lo that I spoke to you about?"

"The American girl? No I did not see her, I will return to the bank shortly and follow her as you asked."

Now Maylay's mind was in complete turmoil. If Tommy had not attacked Tina and inflicted those injuries on her, then who had?

"Be careful, I do not want you detected, understand? I just want to know who she speaks to." Maylay said and hung up as Sui Le came into the office.

*

Jeff had to do his own brain-storming this morning, there was no Tom to help and throw ideas about. However, by 10 o'clock, he was quite confident that the actions he had decided on were the best he could do under the circumstances. Earlier he had phoned William Gualt back.

"Bill, how are you?"

"Fine Jeff and you?" Gualt replied expectantly.

"Look, Bill, I'm sorry about hanging up on you before."

"That's Okay, think nothing of it."

"It's just something you said, about Jason Kimberley's descendants and particularly Maylay Dulles. I've gotta tell you that, that came as a complete shock to me."

"Oh, how's that?" Gualt enquired.

"I don't know whether you know it or not, but I asked George Archibald to step down from the board of AAB yesterday. I didn't know at the time that Tom had been attacked. Rather ironic, isn't it, that I oust George and that his sister in law tries to kill Tom." Jeff paused to allow Gualt time to think this through.

"Ironic. But what sparked off the dispute with Archibald?"

Jeff told him everything about the finding of the ledgers through to Sing's dismissal and the confrontation with Archibald.

"Hmm, did you tell this to Detective Chung?"

"Not all of it. I've only just heard from John Sing and I'm now convinced that he had nothing to do with the attack on Tom."

"I see, you realise that this is quite serious, Jeff?"

"I understand that, but the reason I called you was because Maylay Dulles is in our Kowloon branch at this very moment."

"Can she be kept there?"

"I think so; I might have a plan to trap her."

"Yes?" Gualt prompted.

"If, as I suspect, that she is either the culprit or the instigator, she will act in a certain way if certain information is fed to her. Now here is what I suggest," He went on and laid out the plan that he had hatched.

"Okay, I'll go along with that. It's unethical but it could cut down on police work, and we're having a busy day here today."

"Oh, how's that?"

"Harry Chan, he's been arrested trying to leave the Colony with US$5 million." Gualt decided to give this to Jeff if his idea for Maylay Dulles worked he deserved something.

"Shit, it's true then, he really is gone belly up."

"Afraid so." Gualt replied.

"What's going to happen with the bank?"

"The Colonial office is looking after that. They have been expecting this for some time. As I understand it, the Bank of England is going to send in some people to tidy things up. The bank won't be opened for business this morning, to protect the deposits and also give people time to settle down until the Bank of England decides on just how to deal with the situation. I guess that, that will take a few days, so by then the panic should have died down and they can carry out whatever reorganization is necessary."

"They won't let it just be closed down?"

"I don't think so, this is an actual bank we're talking about and even the Bank of England will not let a bank go. That would undermine the whole banking system."

"What about the shares. I understand that they are taking a pounding this morning?" Gualt asked.

"Tough luck I guess. That's the speculation side of the business. That's up to the Stock Exchange." Jeff was thinking that everything was going according to plan. This was all good news. But he hadn't expected the Bank of England to act so fast, but then he hadn't expected Harry Chan to be picked up either.

"What's Chan to be charged with?"

"We haven't decided yet, but he'll probably be charged initially with fraud. That'll keep him in custody for a while."

"How bad is the position at the bank?"

"I gather from what Bowers says that the situation is quiet bad, the reserves are dangerously low, something in the region of 40 million."

"Jesus, they wouldn't last half the day."

"That's why the bank may not open."

"Has that decision not being taken yet?"

"It may have, I don't know. Bowers is over there right now with the Bank of England people."

"It sure as hell is going to be one hell of a day."

"Yeah, and I'm afraid it will get worse. Look, Jeff, I'm going to have to go. I've gotta go and write charges against Chan. I'll get Detective Chung to get back in contact with you when I hear from him."

"Okay thanks, Bill."

Jeff considered the time to be right to make a move on the OUT. Their shares were on a major fall, and chances are that there would be no one interested in taking a gamble and thankfully the Bank of England had not made any direction on the issue of the shares. So it would be up to the Stock Exchange itself to decide on whether or not the shares should be suspended from trading. A lot depended on the Chairman of the Stock Exchange, Paddy Chin Lee. Chin Lee was known not to like Harry Chan's methods of conducting his business. So it was quite possible that Chin Lee would not suspend trading in OUT shares. He phoned Chin Lee at the Stock Exchange.

"Good Morning, Paddy."

"Jeff, good morning. What can I do for you?" He sounded like a man under pressure.

"I hear that things are hot down there. How are my shares doing?"

"Hot. I would say boiling, there is much activity here." Chin Lee punched at his keyboard and the bank's listing came up on screen.

"You're holding Okay considering, let's see, AAB are trading at 21.90, down 60 points. You're holding as good as the other banks, in fact a little better then most. Some banks are down as much as 90 points except for Hong Kong and Shanghai for some reason; they seem to be holding better, they are down just 30 points."

Jeff knew that HK & Shanghai were a particularly privately owned bank with little or no shares on public offer. So with only a small percentage of shares on the market they traded lightly. Most of the shares were owned by a group of Shanghai businessmen.

"And the OUT?"

"The computers are not able to keep up with the fall. At the moment they are being offered at 18.25, wait, $18 even. The bottom has fallen out of them."

"What are you going to do?" Jeff asked calmly, but inside he knew that his time had come, the shares were now way undervaluing, for even though there was a reserve shortage in the OUT, they still had a good asset base.

"Nothing, absolutely nothing. Harry Chan has abused his clients and depositors for too many years already. He is a major shareholder, so are his brothers. They are dumping shares themselves, why should I worry about protecting them. No the OUT shares can continue to fall to the bottom, if necessary. That will ensure that Harry Chan and his friends do not get any money out of their shares. That will ensure that they never get off the bottom again."

Jeff listened in disbelief to the venom in Chin Lee's voice; it surprised him that the Chairman should allow his personal feelings to influence his decision.

"Ah, Jeff, by the way, this is completely off the record. And I do not expect to ever hear my words quoted." There was strength in his voice that Jeff hadn't heard before.

"I'm surprised you even had to mention it. I thought you knew me better."

"Yes, of course. Sorry, Jeff."

"No problem, Paddy. Tell me how low do you think those OUT shares will go?"

"I do not know, Jeff, they may keep on falling to nothing, but personally I think that they will hit about $10 by the end of the day's trading."

"That bad, huh? And poor Harry is in custody, he probably can't even get in touch with his broker to dump his shares."

Jeff heard the 'Huh' of joy in Chin Lee voice; this was good news to him.

"Unfortunately, it will drag down other financial sector shares as well."

"That's only to be expected. Well thanks for the information, Paddy. I'll probably see you tomorrow night at the Toxin charity thing?"

"I will be there. See you, Jeff." Chin Lee hung up.

Ten dollar a share? he thought, the OUT could be bought up for less then 200 million and all he needed was 51% for complete control. He could pick up the 51% for less than 100 million.

The icing on the cake was the Chan Building, worth $250 million alone. He had the contact with the Chinese who were interested in the building, but only if Harry Chan was not the owner. Thrown into the bag were the 44 branches that the OUT had, 12 of those overseas.

"Shit, the deal could make us one of the top ten banks on the Island." he muttered to his shadow. "And drive our stocks over $40 a share or higher."

But he was depending on panic to drive the OUT shares down and there was no better way to cause panic than to give the arrest of Harry Chan a little publicity.

He reached for the phone and dialled the number for Keith Wells. Wells came on the line after his secretary.

"Jeff, nice to hear from you, what can I do for you?" he greeted, suspiciously as ever.

"Just a friendly call, Keith. Heard any news of Harry Chan this morning?"

"No except that he's not in his office"

"He's not in his office because he's in police HQ. But I thought you knew that?"

"I didn't, are you sure?"

"Christ maybe the police don't want it known, yet. Perhaps it's best I shouldn't say anymore?

"Jeff, old friend, old buddy, old pal, you know something, that for some reason I don't. That bothers me and undermines my reputation as the Profit Prophet. Now I knew that Harry Chan was in deep financial shit but I didn't know that the police had acted. Now what gives?"

Reluctantly Jeff gave him as much information as he knew was enough to get Wells on the trail of Harry Chan. Jeff figured that Wells had more than enough time to establish the facts and include the report on Chan's arrest on the one o'clock news. That in turn would trigger the mass panic that would drive the

OUT shares through the floor. If things went according to plan he could buy the OUT by close of business today. But it would be best left until morning when any shareholders left, would offload to anyone willing to buy at a knockdown price. Then he could start to buy, buy fast and in huge quantities. So fast, that it would take the market some time to spot the move and react by upping the price. With some luck he could pick up 4 or 5 million shares before anyone became aware of it.

The danger was the Bear Gambler; the guy who didn't have any OUT shares at present but offered them for sale when they began to fall with the expectation that he could buy the shares much cheaper later in the day. So he would be in the market for shares at the same time as Jeff moved. Still he shouldn't cause that much of a problem. He may pick up a few thousand shares but that shouldn't effect the price too much.

He could plan out his attack with Eric Ratner at lunch. First though would come the board meeting in about a half hour, at 11 o'clock. He didn't expect any trouble at the meeting, especially now that Archibald was gone off the board. In fact, had he not been ousted it was quite possible that he would have attempted to scuttle Jeff's plan. But most of the board members were aware that he intended to go on the acquisition trail. The subject had been raised at every board meeting for the past 18 months and had been first suggested at the second last AGM. It had been carried unanimously and he had made a point of raising the prospect of a takeover at all subsequent board meetings. It was called Item 17 and each time it was mentioned, it got carried without opposition.

Now, however, the time had come and he had butterflies in his stomach just thinking about the prospect of taking the bull by the horns. But he felt that with the prospect of being able to unload the Chan Building to the Chinese more or less straight away would sway the board members.

After his talk with Gualt he had decided to call Bowers at the OUT. It was not easy to get to talk to him, but finally he got through.

"Morning, David, you're a hard man to track down."

"Sorry about that but we've got problems here. You've obviously heard?" The tension was obvious in Bower's voice.

"Yes I had heard. How bad are things over there?" The question was casual, well, as casual as he could force himself to be.

"I don't mind telling you it's bad. It will be public knowledge by the end of the day anyhow."

"Are you going to open the bank for business?"

"Christ no. The reserves are disastrously low. We would have to close the doors by noon. There's a crowd outside already, but we've got the police handling the situation. We put up a notice that there was a small fire early this morning and that the bank will re-open after lunch, I don't expect too much trouble."

"Just how low are the reserves?" He knew the question was presumptuous and there was just a little too much anxiety in his voice.

"Jeff, is this a polite business enquiry? Or are you just nosey? Or have you something else in mind?"

"Thank you, David-" Jeff retaliated in a friendly tone.

"But yes, you're right as usual, I do have alternative motives."

"Oh, and what might they be?"

Jeff knew he could trust Bowers. He was one of the old stock, his parents were practically native Hong Kong having come to the Colony in the '30s, his father being in the services.

"I may be interested in the OUT." he said, confident in the knowledge that this would be like a bombshell to Bowers and also a huge relief.

"You're having me on?" Bowers laughed cautiously.

"No, I'm deadly serious; I am interested in taking over the OUT."

"Shit, do you realise what you would be facing here? Once you open the doors there would be a mad rush."

"I don't think so, David. Once we guarantee the deposits, I think the depositors will settle down and wait to see what happens."

"*We?*" Bowers asked, the suspicion obvious.

"Of course, the Bank of England will have to step in anyhow so would it not be better for you to have someone there that is going to operate the bank as a going concern? I think that once people see the confidence I have in the OUT they will wait, and especially as the Bank of England will be guaranteeing the depositors money. Okay some money will move, that can't be avoided, but I'm confident that it can be pulled back from the brink."

"And the assets?"

"Naturally some would have to be disposed of, but that would be par for the course."

"And the monies from the sale of the assets?"

"Straight into the reserve, of course."

"How much could you guarantee straight away?"

"We've got over one billion in reserves. As you know, we've had a few good years and we're flush at the moment," Jeff held his breath. The reserves figure was exaggerated.

"What would be the exposure for the Bank of England?"

"Well let's say that if the run went over, say 20 million, they step in and guarantee 50 cents in the dollar, we guarantee the other 50."

"I do not think that they would go for a figure as low as 20 million, it may need to be 50."

"Ah come on, if the run goes to 49 million, I'm left holding the can and the Bank of England looks good but had done nothing, come on now, David."

"Well that's down to yourself and the Bank of England, I'm just throwing figures around. The other thing that might cause some problems for them is the probability of asset stripping. They would want some guarantees?"

"Appreciated, but I must have a free hand to dispose of assets that I feel are of no worthwhile benefit to the bank or the shareholders."

"I feel that they would expect that a reasonable level of assets would be maintained."

"Oh I'm not suggesting selling off everything, but there are a few projects that would have to be abandoned and disposed of."

"Have you seen their balance sheet?"

"Not yet."

"Can you come over?"

"No, I've got a board meeting in 20 minutes and anyhow, I think that if I was seen over there just now, might cause premature speculation." Jeff knew that this would give Bowers ideas.

"You're planning a stock market buy-out, you bastard?"

"David you know me better than that. I'm not an opportunist."

"I'll send someone over with the balance sheet."

Jeff could hear Bowers laughing as he hung up. Now all he had to do was to line up the Chinese to buy the Chan Building.

Chapter Nineteen

"AAB, good morning." Kay said in a bright and cheery tone, although she would have preferred not to have answered one of the general phone lines. But all lines were light red meaning the staff that normally answers the general lines was busy.

"Good morning, I would like to speak to Mister Bordes-Aitcheson please." the male caller said.

"Who's calling please?"

"Jason Kim."

Kay paused for a moment, then recovered and replied.

"One moment, please. I'll see if he's free."

Kay buzzed Jeff and told him who was on the line, there was silence from Jeff for a few moments then he said,

"Okay, let's see what he wants."

"Putting you through." Kay said and waited for the line to go red and replaced the phone.

"Jeffery Bordes-Aitcheson here. How can I help you?"

"Jason Kim here, I wish to move my accounts from my present bank and would like to talk to you about that."

"Okay, can you give me some idea of your banking requirement?"

"I operate a business account for the restaurant; we have a current account and a deposit account. I also have some personal accounts and investment accounts."

"Which of those are you considering moving?"

"The business accounts firstly, then perhaps the personal accounts. Who knows?"

"The business accounts, what is your requirement there?"

"Our current overdraft is for $50,000, but being a cash business it's rarely overdrawn."

"Is that your only requirement for the restaurant?"

"I also have a requirement for the use of a safety deposit box."

"That's no problem. Would you like to call into the office and have a look at our facility? I would be glad to show you around." Jeff wondered if he should meet with this guy or not, it's like sitting down with the devil, but what the hell.

"Very well then, I was going down to Central shortly. Perhaps I could call in, say, an hour?"

"That will be fine. If I am not available, my secretary will show you the facility, I have a board meeting at eleven so if I am unavailable you will understand."

"Yes, of course, but I should like to meet you. But perhaps some other time."

"This meeting may be over in ten minutes, but it may drag on for an hour. You know how these things go?"

"No I do not; you see I do not have a board to answer to."

"Lucky you. As I say I may see you when you call. My secretary will know what time I'll be free."

"Good, hope to see you then."

Jeff replaced the phone and wondered what the hell Jason Kim was up to?

*

Dillon got back to the Stock Exchange about 10.45 and could sense the tension and panic the moment he walked in the corridor that led up to the offices overlooking the exchange floor. Everybody that he met glanced at him expectantly then realising that he was no one they knew, the eyes darted away and they went on frantically looking for someone to tell them that everything was all right, that their world had not come to an end. In the midst of all this he saw Olli, wide eyed and obviously enjoying all this.

"Hi." Then Olli looked more closely at Dillon's face.

"Are you all right?"

"Oh I just had a few too many Ports." Dillon shrugged it off.

"How'd you get on with Percy?"

"No problem. He's got a new broker working on the job right now, I expect that the shares will hit the market shortly."

"Let's get up to Thorn's office then."

He led Dillon to the left and up the broad staircase onto the viewing area above the floor.

"It's crazy out there." Olli shouted.

The noise level coming up was amazing. The area below was about half the size of a football pitch. Directly beneath where they stood were five rows of monitor banks that stretched from one side of the area to the other. The monitors were manned by the Dealers; they took the instructions over the phone from the brokers. Each Dealer had a Runner who took the orders from Dealer to Dealer. All along the left wall was a huge electrical digital board that flashed the current selling price of shares along with their name and quantity on offer.

At present OUT shares were being offered at $17.90. AAB shares were being offered at $21.75, there were about 120,000 shares on offer. They went along to Thorn's office. It was small, had a phone, and three comfortable looking chairs.

"G'day sport," Thorn greeted mimicking the current ad craze for Fosters Lager.

"What's happening, man?" Olli asked, in his most impressive Valley Talk.

"Say, "What"?" Dillon said.

"What?" Thorn looked puzzled.

"You said it, man."

"Okay quit the shit; we've got a deal. The shares should be coming up shortly." Dillon brought them back to reality.

"Right we'll hang tight and just wait this time. What did ya say to Lawson?" Thorn asked Dillon.

"I just told him he was a bollocks and that he would be hearing from the practices committee."

"That'll fuck 'em." Thorn replied.

The phone rang. He answered and held a short conversation then hung up. They looked at him expectantly.

"That's our man; he's putting them on the market in fifteen minutes." Thorn glanced at his watch. It was 10.50 am and that meant that the shares would hit the floor at 11.05.

"When do you issue the order to buy?"

"Sutherland will phone us one minute before he offers them for sale, then we give the order and fix the price. That will be the going market price plus 50 cents, no one will be able to react fast enough to offer more. Within a minute we should be able to buy all 800,000, plus that 120 or so odd thousand currently being offered for sale." Thorn glanced at the electric board. 122,300 were now on offer. The asking price moved out a further five points. The OUT was down another five points, to 17.85.

"At this rate of going, the OUT will be ten bucks by lunch."

"And by close of business?" Dillon asked thoughtfully.

"A good investment." Thorn replied.

Dillon could see now what Jeff was planning, this was what he meant by buying a bank. He would be able to pick up those shares for half price, but of course it was a huge gamble. The shares could continue to fall and the position at the OUT may be beyond recovery. It may not be possible to restructure the thing. It was like buying a pig in a poke.

"How bad does a bank have to be before it is insolvent?"

"It must have a realistic level of liquid assets, in other words, it must be able to call in money to cover a percentage of its deposits. Not 100% you understand, that would make banking impossible, but it must be able to meet the demands for about a third of its deposits at the very worst. The problem with the OUT is that it continued to invest in Hong Kong where prices had practically stopped increasing. Long term investment is now no longer thought to be a good risk here because the returns are short term."

"What about the 50 year changeover the English are pushing for. Surely that would lengthen the value of the investments?"

"The Chinese are deliberating that; they insist on the change-over period being ten years but at the end of the day, they know that to hold onto the investors they will have to give in to the 50 year changeover. The problem they have created for themselves is that they insisted on the 10 year changeover from the start, the problem being how to back down without losing face."

A buzz of excitement from the floor below distracted them. Suddenly the red coats were stopping, now they spoke to each other. The last one spoke to the next then he spoke to the next and so on. Dealers stood at their monitors and roared at the runners, sheets of paper were thrown on the floor, Dealers held their heads.

"What the hell is going on?" Thorn was already on the phone, below Dealer Chin turned and looked up at Thorn's office. Thorn glanced at his watch as he hung up.

"Chan was arrested this morning; it's just been on the 11 o'clock news."

They turned back to the electric board, suddenly the price changed. Instead of being $17.85, it now became $17.

"Shit, that's the biggest drop all morning."

The electric board now showed over six million shares being offered for sale.

"How many shares are there in OUT?" Dillon asked.

"Around 20 million." Thorn looked at him, but he just looked at the board.

"So at top value they'd be worth around 400 million?"

"That was the value put on the bank by the stock market, yes."

"So that six million shares represent over 25% of the value of their issued stock." he said thoughtfully.

"It's almost time." Thorn said looking at his watch.

*

King met Gerard in the hall, both were in a hurry.

"Bloody murder in there this morning." Gerard said.

King did not really intending to stop and talk, Gerard was a bit of a nuisance.

"Rather, but a good morning for making money, eh? As they are apt to say locally, 'Never mind.'"

"So, what is happening in there this morning?" King asked politely.

"Where have you been? The place is falling apart for Christ's sake."

King had been caught in conversation, and as much as he disliked Gerard, he just could not resist catching up on the latest gossip.

"I've been out playing golf. I wouldn't be in now either but I promised someone I would buy some shares for them this morning. Actually I did rather well in the Captain's competition, just one shot off the first prize, bloody fifth hole again. I had 20 footer for a birdie but it just slid past. Six inches past, bloody bad luck, eh?"

"They really should do something about that green, it's far too uneven, and what did you go around in?"

"Seventy nine"

"That's damn impressive really." Gerard seemed genuinely impressed.

"Yes I suppose, but I should have come in with 78. What's being happening here?" King changed the conversation. Gerard told him about the fall of the OUT and the effect on the market.

"How are the AAB faring?" King asked.

"Not too bad really, they are at $21.70, are you interested?"

"Well I have an order to buy."

"Many?" The question blatant and probing.

"A few, enough." King was not forthcoming.

"Actually I may be selling AAB this morning."

"Well then we shall be trading paper, eh?" King said.

Just then Gerard checked his watch. "Sorry, old chap, gotta dash."

The Monarch, as was King's nickname, was just a little annoyed that Gerard hadn't giving a little more information about how many shares he had to sell. After all, he was in the market for the AAB shares for Narrow Investment Company. He went back up towards his office but met Paul Sam on his way and had something to conclude with him.

"Paul, good morning. It's all go around here?"

"Morning Will, it's a bit of a mess here all right. What's new?"

"Nothing, I just wanted to see if we could reach a settlement on that Retail Centre down on St George's Place."

"Ah yes, I think there may be progress on that one. Want to come inside?" Paul Sam gestured towards his office just a few steps away.

King checked his watch, he had the deal to do for Narrow Investments. The plan was that when the AAB block belonging to Sir Percy came on the market, he would hold off buying for a few minutes, as such a large block would force the price down, then he could pick them up later at a lesser price and at a considerable saving for his client. And he knew that they would not be offered until he got a call from Lawson, so there was no rush. He followed Paul Sam into the office and glanced out at the display board on the main floor of the exchange, the amount of AAB on offer hadn't declined, so it was safe to assume that there were no buyers out there for AAB. In fact, the amount of shares on offer had increased to over 122,000, plenty of sellers but no buyers. So he could relax and wait till they go below $21.00.

"Okay I've got a few minutes. Let's talk."

It was 11.05 a.m.

"They're early." Thorn gasped looking at his watch again, he reached for the phone.

"What's going on?" Suddenly they were on their feet looking at the electric board. Now there were 922,000 AAB shares and there was a buzz of excitement from the floor below.

For a brief moment everybody stood looking at the board, they all knew that the worst was about to happen. They expected to see OUT shares being offered in large blocks, they were being dumped, but AAB? This was a serious turn for the worst; for that amount of shares to be offered meant only one thing, a major shareholder was dumping AAB.

Now Dealers began to look in horror at the AAB shares that they held personally, with this amount of shares the price would surely drop, like the OUT. Was this the beginning of the end? For if a major shareholder of AAB was dumping then did it not mean that others would follow? And then other bank's shareholders would dump also.

In the office, Thorn looked at Dillon. "If we wait the price will drop. What do you want to do?" He still held the phone cupping the mouthpiece.

"I made a deal with Sir Percy; I'm not going to play the market so that the price falls; besides it's not my money. Buy as agreed."

"Buy AAB." Thorn shouted into the phone.

They saw Dealer Chin leap to his feet and roar the buy order. For a moment everybody on the floor of the Hang Seng looked at Dealer Chin.

Was this guy crazy? everyone thought. He was buying while everybody else was selling. It did not make sense, but it must be a mistake. There was almost silence while they all looked at Dealer Chin, silence on the floor of the Hang Seng was relative of course, it could be compared to the sound of a 747 landing as compared to taking off.

A historic coincidence now took place, Gerard, acting for George Archibald had placed the 800,000 AAB shares on the market as instructed. Dealer Chin, acting for Dillon, assumed that the shares on offer were the shares being sold for Sir Percy and shouted the buy order. Chin's Runner pounced on the Runner acting for the Dealer acting for Peter Gerard. The deal was done in the blink of an eye, Chin's Runner did not know the owner of the shares, nor did it matter to him. He handed the slip to Chin who then wrote the receipt. Dealer Chin examined the name and was shocked.

All around him there was pure pandemonium, every Runner acting for Dealers selling AAB converged on Dealer Chin's Runner. The computer had by now been re-adjusted and the buying price for AAB shot out to $22.00 from the $21.70 it had been only a moment ago. When Dealer Chin realised that the shares were not Sir Percy's, he reached for the phone and rang Thorn.

"These shares we buy are not from dealer we expected, these shares come from Broker, Peter Gerard. He never acts for Sir Percy."

"Okay." Thorn said,

"Let's not panic, so we bought the wrong block of shares"
He hung up.

"What the fuck is going on, and who the hell is Peter Gerard
acting for?"

"What's wrong?" Dillon asked.

"I don't know, those shares we just bought were not Sir Percy's."

"What?" Dillon gasped.

"So who the hell did they belong to?"

The phone rang, Thorn snapped it up.

"I don't fucking know. Were they not your shares?" Thorn
gasped looking in disbelief at the other two men. "Okay, hold
on." Thorn turned to Dillon cupping the mouthpiece. "What do
we do now? This is Philip Gunn on the phone wondering what
he should do. He has Sir Percy's shares. He wants to know does
he go ahead and sell the shares. Do we buy?"

"Yes, we made a deal I'm not going back on that again; we've
got the money to cover it. Let's go for it!"

"You got it!" He un-cupped the phone.

"We buy." He slammed the phone down on the cradle.

A moment later, the pandemonium erupted again as the
800,000 new shares came up for sale. By now the other dealers had copped on to what was happening and the AAB price
moved out a little further to $22.30, but there was no shares
available for the Runner descended on Sutherland's Runner
and grabbed the dockets. This was the arrangement in the first
place, but the Runner hadn't looked twice when the first block
of shares came on the market. He just charged at the guy with
his hand raised with a sell slip.

"Well you now own 18% of AAB." Thorn said after talking
to Dealer Chin on the phone.

"Shit man." Olli released a sigh of relief.

"Shall we go for a drink?" Dillon was feeling a little light-
headed, Percy's port was beginning to wear off.

The time was 11.09am, Thursday June 17th.

CHAPTER TWENTY

There were 21 steps and then 10 paces to the door of the board-room. Kay Herbert was sat at her temporary position outside the door.

"Are they all here?" He asked not really seeing her.

"All except George and Tom. Clair is here though."

"Good. How is she?"

"She seems fine; she says the news is better this morning. She was at the hospital; Tom regained consciousness about an hour ago, but slipped back again."

"Did he speak at all?"

"No, but the Doctors say he will probably be Okay now."

"Thank God for that." He went towards the door Kay rose and followed him in.

During these meetings Kay usually sat in and took notes, but this morning she expected to have to leave early if she got a call from below that Jason Kim had arrived.

"Good morning." Jeff greeted.

There was a chorus of greetings. Sir Denis White approached Jeff and taking him by the arm led him away from the board table.

"Look Jeff, I know that this is a rather bad time for you, what with losing Tom and everything, but I've got some problems myself, financially that is, if this is anything to do with raising further funds, I won't be able to support you."

Jeff turned to look him in the eye. White was a strange sort of a bird, he was 58 years of age and had the blackest head of wavy hair that Jeff had ever seen. He came to Hong Kong in the '50s with a little money to invest. He had done insurance in his home town of Leeds in England, so it was only natural that he would fall into the insurance business in his new land.

White was relatively successful and had made a lot of money by the late '70s; unfortunately, the '80s were not so kind to him. He had got caught badly in the recession and had dropped a lot of his wealth by 1983 and then the stock market crash of that year virtually wiped him out. Jeff had seen his personal bank account go from 30 million savings in 1978 to less than one million in 1983.

That year Jeff thought White was a goner.

"No it's nothing like that Denis. How bad are your problems?"

Jeff shifted the conversation slightly, although he was disappointed that White would not be available to support him if he was needed.

"It's nothing serious lad, don't worry about it. I'm just heavily committed right now."

"Okay, you know Denis that if you ever need help I'm available. Don't hesitate to contact me, in fact, I'll be pissed if you don't."

White chuckled and patted Jeff on the back. "Don't worry, lad, I'll be knocking at you door one of these days to take you up on that offer."

They went back to the table; the others had sat themselves down in their usual positions. Clair and Key sat side-by-side deep in conversation. He interrupted them.

"Hi Clair, I hear Tom is on the mend."

"Yeah he's looking much better today. You know, I haven't been in church for over five years, but I went this morning. You know it must have done some good, I felt a lot better afterwards and then when I went to see Tom, he looked so much better. And then you know," She stopped for a moment to wipe a little tear from the corner of her eye. "He woke up, it was just for a moment. I don't really know if he could see me or not, but God it was ever so good to see his eyes again. The doctor, Pierce is looking after him. He said that he was going to be all right now. I could become hooked on the church again."

"That's terrific, Clair. Do you think you can handle this?"

"I think I can. Is there anything you want me to do?"

"No just follow my lead."

He straightened up ignoring Kay's stare and went to the chair. The murmur of conversation died slowly as he sat down and opened the folder Kay had left there for him. Apart from Kay, Clair and White, three others sat at the large oval oak table. To his left were Alistair McMorrow and Alex Sapherio. Down the far end of the table and on his own was Howard Humphries.

There were two vacant chairs; one was between Sapherio and the end and was normally occupied by Sir Percy. He insisted on sitting there as he had his back to the window.

Deep down Jeff knew he was going to miss old Sir Percy; he used to come out with some of the most ridiculous statements but always amusing. The other vacant chair was normally occupied by George.

"Thank you for coming this morning. I must apologise for insisting, but as you will see, it was most important that we all convene as quickly as possible. Firstly let me offer our sympathy to Clair Maxwell, but we also have some good news. Tom is recovering nicely and let's hope that he will soon be back on his feet and among us again."

Clair nodded her appreciation and the others added their good wishes.

"Now let's get the minutes read. Kay, would you be so kind?" Jeff eased back in the chair. He knew he had them in the palm of his hand; their curiosity would keep them engaged.

Kay read the short minutes; these board meetings had become a mere formality.

"A vote was taken on resolution 17 and once again passed unanimously."

Jeff felt that this was the most important piece to come out of the minutes, for Resolution seventeen was the one that gave him carte blanche to do just what he had already started. He watched them as they listened; all were at ease except Howard. Humphries was a bigwig in publishing.

Kay was finished the minutes; they were proposed, seconded and adopted.

"I know that you are all busy men, but I do need a forum for what we will discuss here this morning, and I wanted everyone to be aware of what is going to happen."

He knew that this was going to be difficult for some of them, not least of all for Denis White.

"Now to the purpose of the meeting, but first a word of caution, I would remind everyone, that the first and foremost priority of this board is the future of the AAB bank. You will hear things this morning that are being revealed in the strictest of confidence. Should any of these...matters get out before we've carried my proposals, then the proposals may be for nothing. It's extremely important that you tell no one about what you are about to hear. Not for 24 hours. That's very important; do I have your agreement on that?" There was no way he could enforce such a gagging order but maybe, just maybe they would agree. He looked at each of them in turn and waited for a response. There was puzzlement on their faces, but each one in turn nodded. Humphries was last for Jeff's gaze. He held Jeff's eyes for what seemed a long time, and then finally he nodded.

He had all their attention. You could hear a pin drop.

"Firstly, two resignations from the board."

There was an audible gasp from the members.

"Sir Percy has disposed of his shares in AAB. Well I assume that he has by now sold the shares, I understand that he intends, to return to his native England, I wish him well in his new life" Jeff watched them. Humphries natural nose for a story made him suspicious.

"Yes, I'd like to second that, but is it not just a little bit strange. I was talking to Sir Percy only last week and he never mentioned his leaving. It's a bit sudden." Humphries looked determined that he was going to find an answer to this unexpected announcement.

"Sir Percy was made an offer he couldn't refuse. He made it known to me some time ago that it was his desire to move out of Hong Kong and return to his native England. I was approached by an interested party looking for AAB shares in fairly large blocks." Jeff knew that this was going to be a bombshell to them.

"What are you saying?" Humphries seemed almost indignant.

"What do you think I'm saying?" Jeff retorted innocently.

"You directed buyers to Sir Percy?"

"Yes," Jeff replied and glanced at his notes then continued before Humphries could come back.

"George Archibald has also resigned from the board." This was the second shock. The silence was immediate, and short lived. It was as if a grenade had exploded under Humphries.

"What, what the hell is going on here, Jeff? This is like a communist party purge. What the hell did you call us here for, to ask for our resignations?" Humphries was so angry that he was practically foaming at the mouth.

"If you think that's bad, Howard, listen to this. I've Okayed a bid by the World Trade Bank to buy into the AAB." Suddenly all Jeff's fears were gone, now he was no longer unsure of the course of action to take. Right now he was on top of the world, full of confidence and felt that everything he did would turn to gold. He had been afraid of this meeting earlier, especially when Tom has not here to back him. Right now he held his own destiny in his hands and apart from Humphries, he felt that he would have the backing of the Board.

"The World Trade Bank?" Humphries gasped and sat back down. It was like someone had hit the back of his knees and he just collapsed in the chair. That changed everything, drastically.

"That's right, they have decided that they would like a share in the Hong Kong market and they see us as a likely partner for the future. They have already, or will have shortly, purchased Sir Percy's shares and it is my intention to sell them part of my share by the end of the day they should have up on 30% of our stock."

"You didn't consult us?" Humphries was calm now; Jeff had to strain to hear him.

"Resolution 17 passed at our AGM two years ago and carried at every meeting since. Kay would you read Resolution 17 please?"

Kay was ready; he had told her to have it at hand. "Resolution 17. The Chairman is hereby authorised to examine and pursue any course of action to improve the assets of the company, in particular, seek any likely partnership with a local or overseas bank. To proceed to enter into any partnership without having to consult the board further if time is of the essence to conclude a deal."

"Yes, yes," Humphries said, "But surely this is a little sudden and why did George resign? He was very actively involved in the bank; there was never a hint that he had reason to leave."

"No, he didn't have a reason to leave but I found one for him. I don't think that this is the place to discuss the matter. I feel certain that if you were to talk to George he would give you the reason that he would want you to hear." Jeff was trying to be diplomatic, but also giving them just enough to realise that it was not just a case of George wanting to leave, but having to.

Humphries seemed suitable confused, so Jeff turned to White and the others. He wanted to get on with this, the most difficult part was yet to come and the part that he couldn't very well pass off as being done within the authority as set out in Resolution 17.

White was on the verge of busting out laughing, he obviously enjoyed watching Humphries being licked, not that he was licked yet, just confused enough to keep him thinking.

"Pity we didn't know about this sooner and we could have bought some stock. The value is bound to rise when this becomes known." White said with a broad smile.

"Alex, what's your opinion?"

"I go along wi' Denny here. Sounds a' good too' me." Sapherio had never really mastered the English language. He was about 40 and had come to Hong Kong in the '70s on his way to Australia, met a woman and fell in love.

"Alistair?"

"I dina' see any problems, laddie. If we make money on the deal then that's one of the things we have to live wi'."

"Good that's carried then?"

"Now," Jeff studied his notes, now for the wild card. "There is, as you know, something of an upheaval on the market this morning, namely the collapse of the OUT bank. Apparently Harry Chan has been arrested."

There was a gasp from around the table.

"The shares are falling rapidly, at the last check they were down to 17.80. Now does that suggest anything to you?"

"Someone is losing money fast?" White suggested helpfully.

"Also true, but does it give you any ideas?"

They just stared back at him, some of them puzzled; Humphries alone had a very suspicious look on his face.

"What does it suggest to you?" Humphries threw it back on Jeff.

"Well to me it looks like a bank on its knees. But it could also offer the opportunity of a lifetime."

"What the hell are you saying now?" Humphries was thinking fast, Jeff could see it on his face.

"What do you think I'm saying?" Jeff replied angrily, annoyed at this arrogant manner of Humphries.

"If you're thinking what I think you're thinking, then…it's crazy."

Jeff realised that he stopped short of saying, 'You're Crazy'.

"Perhaps." Humphries said. But Jeff could see the chain being pulled, he was thinking fast.

He disliked people that said *'What are you saying'*; he had just said it, did they have a diminished mental ability or are they just so thick that you have to keep repeating it until they got it.

He had to be in full control. Humphries was the biggest threat, if Jeff dismissed him outright, the others might think that Jeff was indeed crazy and while they might not cross him they might not back him, so the thing to do was to hold fast against Humphries and try to convince him, whether he did or not was irrelevant, for in trying to convince him he may persuade the others in the process.

"It may sound crazy to even think about taking over the OUT, but someone will, and at a knock down price. Just look at their list of assets." He passed out the photocopies of the accounts that Bowers had sent over.

He watched them examine the balance sheet and the profit and loss sheet. He found himself attracted to the sheets himself.

If the bank could be picked up cheap and only 30% of the assets disposed of, then they would have enough money on hand between the two banks to stave off any run that might still occur after it was known that the AAB had bought the OUT.

"Good photocopier, laddie. Wha' make is it?" Alistair McMorrow was trying to be funny.

"It's one of these "buy now pay later jobs"." Jeff replied, trying to be casual.

The others were still reading; McMorrow was finished because he was a speed reader at least that was what Jeff hoped. White finished, he turned the copy over as people are prone to do for whatever reason. He checked that the others were still reading then looked at Jeff.

"They look good, what happened them?" White enquired.

"Harry Chan, that's what happened them. He did silly things."

Humphries grunted sarcastically without looking up. Jeff got the message. He thought that Jeff was about to do silly things.

"Their reserves are dangerously low. How long will they last?"

"The Bank of England is in there at present. They didn't open this morning."

"Ah," McMorrow heard that, "So the wee reserves are still there? Well that is considerate o' them. How long ken' they stay closed though?"

"Until they decide what to do, the Bank of England won't let the bank be closed."

"How much this cost us?" Sapherio got right to the point.

"There are 20 million shares; I suspect that by the end of the day those shares will be selling at $10 a share, so to buy a controlling interest we would need about $110 million. That would give us just over 50%, enough to put in our own board and start selling assets. They have over one billion in assets, their shares were undervalued as it was. That was as a result of the crash of '83, and I think I can dispose of assets worth 250 million straight away. That would give us plenty to starve off any likely run straight away. But I suspect that when it becomes known that the AAB has bought the OUT, then people will wait and see what happens."

"And if they don't wait?" Humphries asked.

"Then we have the Bank of England to guarantee the deposits."

"You've spoke to them about this?" Humphries was surprised.

"I spoke to the Colonial Office."

"The AAB would not be at risk?" McMorrow seemed genuinely interested.

"Unlikely. The opportunity is too great to miss; the likes of this may never come again."

"So what you're saying is that an American bank is interested in taking 30% off us and we take 50% of a failed bank?"

"You're getting real good at this, Howard."

"And you're getting just a bit too cocky for you own good, Jeff."

"Howard, if you don't mind I'm going to be perfectly frank with you. You've been on this board for eight years now. You are a minority director with more to say than most members of the board, both you and George Archibald have defied me and the other board members on several occasions when there was not a full attendance of the board. You have run rough-shot over me and other board members. You are probably the wealthiest man here and to be quite honest, I do wonder what the hell you are doing here." Jeff knew he had gone too far, whatever about not needing Humphries on the board; he did not need him against him, at least not for 24 hours.

"I can only assume that you consider this slumming or something to that effect. I mean what are you worth? I have to ask because as you only keep a token account here I don't know your full worth?" Jeff eased his tone and tried to make it more jovial. He was looking him dead in the eye now and while Humphries was just a little taken aback earlier on, he seemed to realise that Jeff was just having fun with him.

"You're right, of course, Jeff. I've gotta admit it," He knew he had their attention. "I'm slumming."

They laughed but it was more to break the tension than mirth at Humphries humour.

White had realized long ago that Jeff didn't like Humphries, Jeff was like that, and he did not suffer fools easily. White had no time for Humphries either, he remembered the time his business had almost gone belly up, and Humphries paper had been none too kind to him. And Humphries was so thick that when they met sometime afterwards Humphries hadn't even apologized, didn't even seem to realize that his paper had hurt White. That was an indication as to just how insincere the man was. He thought nothing of insulting a man in his paper and the next night having a drink as if nothing had ever happened. Just plain thick!

Knowing Humphries it was quite possible that he hadn't realised that Jeff was taking a swipe at him.

"These assets," White tried to get them back to the matter on hand. "Will the Bank of England allow us to dispose of them?"

"They understand that the OUT is asset heavy and liquidity light so they understand that a certain amount of assets will have to go, they accept that. They don't want the headache of the day to day running of the bank because they realise that they may have to hold onto the bank for quite a while. But apart from the assets here in Hong Kong, the OUT has overseas offices and they own the building, some of them in prime locations: London, Bonn, Paris, New York, Singapore, Tokyo, Los Angeles, to name just a few."

"What about here, how many branches?" Humphries asked.

"Forty four in all. We could close half of them, again the buildings they don't own outright they have long term leases. We could sub-let."

"What would be our maximum exposure?"

"Fifty million if the worst came to the worst, 50 cents in the dollar. But I'm confident that when it's known that we've bought it, the depositors will stay put and give us a chance. Plus the news that a big American bank has bought into AAB, then investors will want to get into our shares. The value should soar."

They all considered this for a while; it was a huge gamble, but if it worked and it might, just consider that the WTB was buying into the AAB. When people heard that a big American bank was buying into AAB then the AAB must be sound.

"So our maximum exposure would be $150 million?" Humphries voiced his thoughts.

"Correct, that's if the worst came to the worst. Personally I don't think it will come to that."

There was silence now as each man considered his personal risk.

"How do you feel about this?" Jeff wanted some feedback.

Again the silence, they looked from one to the other, either wondering what to say or hoping that someone else would start. But it was Mister Negative that began.

"My opinion is that we should wait and see what happens. I think it is too big a risk to rush into this. If the Bank of England is already in there, I suggest that we wait and see what their findings are. It may well be that the OUT is beyond recovery. We should not buy a pig in a poke." Humphries said. But the conviction just wasn't there, Jeff knew from Humphries' voice the way he was thinking and the conviction just wasn't there. He doubted his own assertions. Humphries didn't have his mind made up and maybe he wanted someone to persuade him.

Jeff was not going to waste his time trying to persuade him so there was no point in arguing. In the end, he felt he didn't need him. If White, McMorrow and Sapherio backed him, he had the votes. In fact, he could get away with just any two of them.

"Alex?" He wanted the doubtful out of the way before he came to White. He believed that White would back him, for White needed Jeff's help most of all.

"This very strange too me. I not understand this, 'Pig in poke'. What for you say this?" Alex turned to Humphries.

"I think," Jeff cut in before Howard could answer; he didn't want him talking Alex around.

"What Howard is worried about is that he doesn't fully understand the opportunity that exists here." Jeff knew that he was playing with fire taunting Humphries like this, but he needed to convince the others that Humphries was not a true businessman like the rest of them.

"What Howard fails to see is the answer to all our dreams has come at once. We are a minnow; we are a small bank with two branches; that's not really a bank in the modern business community. What we have to do is grow and expand. If we were to undertake an expansion that would give us let's say, 20 overseas branches and say 10 branches locally, the capital cost alone would be in the region of $30 million. Then we would have to advertise and attract business, which could take two maybe three years and at what cost? A conservative estimate might put the cost at 50 million. That's $80 million, gentlemen, just to start to make money. We know only too well what will happen in '97. We decided long ago that we have to do something about it. We have to expand, that was the reason for 'Resolution 17'. Now I'm not the type of man to abuse my power, I could have gone ahead with the purchase of the OUT without referring to the board. It would have been fully within the powers given to me by 'Resolution 17', but I realised that this was too big a move to make alone. You've gotta realise that this will place a huge responsibility on my shoulders; the re-organization alone will take months. There will be job shedding in the new company; there will be asset disposals; there will be complete re-structuring of their accounting practices. There will be travel. I will have to visit all the overseas offices and see first hand the business being conducted. Then there will be the massive task of tying the two banks together. There will be staff problems, there will be resentment from the staff of OUT. Last of all, there will be the huge gamble, I could go down the tube on this one. I could lose everything that I have worked for and my father before me and my grandfather before him. At my age that's not the sort of thing that man does. But having said that, I cannot stand by and watch everything I've worked for go down the drain as it surely will in '97. I'm prepared to gamble everything I have on this venture. But then this colony was built on gambles; everyone in the business community in Hong Kong lives on gambles. That was what made us great. We can show the rest of the world that we are prepared to face into the future confident that we businessmen in Hong Kong can take on the impossible and carry the weight of the world on our shoulders and stand tall. And all I ask is your support. Will you support me, Alex?" Jeff was at his best.

"By Joss, yes I wi' support you." Alex was visibly moved by Jeff speech.

"Alistair?"

"Ach ai', laddie. 'Tis' against me better judgment and me nature to' risk money, but if ye' are half as good as ye' say ye' are, then by God I'll back you."

"Denis?"

White was silent, his eyes were locked on the sheet of paper on the table in front of him. They all knew his position; his past problems were public knowledge. But were the problems 'past'? Was he still in financial difficulty?

Finally, after what seemed like an eternity, he looked at Jeff.

"I've been down before, as you all know. It's not that bad, you know. I guess I could live through that again, yes, I'll back you, damn it!"

"Thanks, Denis. You won't regret it." Jeff turned and looked at Clair.

"You know how Tom feels about this. I cast his vote in favour of the, well whatever you call it. Is it a resolution?"

"I guess it is now." He looked at the lonesome figure down the far end of the table.

"Howard?"

"I'm against it, you know that, but I will not be the lone dissenter. I'll back you, but I want the minutes to note my reservations."

"Well let's see if your reservations are still in existence in say, six months? Jeff said. Jeff glanced at Kay; she nodded and made the note. "It's so noted. Now can I call for a show of hands just to make it official? The proposal is that we proceed to purchase

at least 50% of the shares of the OUT bank at the most opportune moment."

"Seconded." Alistair said as a matter of form.

"Show of hands?"

All hands were raised, it was deemed carried. They began to
shuffle and gather themselves up.

"Very well, but your stock market dealings should be conducted with that consideration in mind." He knew that he was
giving them tips, if they hadn't already thought about it. If the
AAB shares doubled they would all be wealthy men. If they
bought shares now and held on until the dust settled then sold
on at the adjusted price, they would make a nice profit.

"And finally, as I said at the outset, I would like to remind
you that this discussion here this morning should be considered
highly confidential, at least for 24 hours." He looked at each of
them in turn. It was important that none of this got out prema-
turely, as it would effect the price of the OUT shares.

They nodded their acceptance one by one.

"Right that concludes the business for today, gentleman and
ladies. I move that we adjourn this meeting."

"Seconded." Alistair said.

They got to their feet and Clair was first to join him.

"This has been brilliant, Jeff. Now I can understand why
Tom comes home so fired up sometimes."

"Only sometimes. I must look at his schedule; maybe he's
been underworked."

"You know, he would have loved this." she whispered. "That
Humphries is a right pain. You sure handled him well." White
approached.

"Jeff, you're a mighty man. You know, I came in here this
morning expecting you to be looking for more money. What
with the way things were going on the market this morning?
And you know. I was sorry that you didn't ask for more money
when it was all over. You handled Howard brilliantly. Good
lad." White shook hands and bid his farewell to Clair and Kay.

Alistair came up next. "I'm buying AAB. See you tomorrow
night." He was like that, not much to say. Then he to was gone.

Alex also said something to the effect that he was fully confidant in Jeff's running of the bank, then he left.

Humphries was the last to go. "You're a crazy son of a bitch. You might just do it. You don't mind if I say 'I told you so' if you don't?"

"Not at all." Jeff replied confidently.

"Catch you later, kid." Humphries said then he too went out.

"Well that's that." he said as he sat back down.

"Well done, Jeff. That was the best ever." Kay said, "I'll get back to work. Why don't you have a drink, relax for a while? You've got no appointments for a half hour and I'll cover if anything comes up. See you in a while-" then she looked at Clair and asked, "-you coming?"

"Yes, I'm going back to the hospital to see how Tom is getting on. I'll see you later Jeff."

When he was alone he sat back down and a lit a cigarette. He put his feet up on the boardroom table and enjoyed the nicotine top up as the adrenaline rush subsided. These moments are what life is worth living for.

CHAPTER TWENTY ONE

Kay Herbert returned to her desk just a little high after the meeting. Her life behind her desk had few real highs, and most of the board meetings she attended to take notes were run of the mill and boring, but this one was different. Jeff had been brilliant; she had wanted to laugh when he asked Humphries if he was slumming. It was such a brave thing to say to him, he was a very powerful newspaper mogul and could hurt the AAB if he took a mind to. But she figured that Jeff figured that Humphries wouldn't publish anything that would damage the bank as it would hurt his own shareholding. It called 'biting your nose to spite your face'.

The phone distracted her.

"I wish to speak with Mister Bordes-Aitcheson. This is Detective Chung"

Kay held her breath, she didn't like Chung. He was an abrasive little cop, he had been arrogant and aggressive this morning when he called to see Jeff and was not going to be persuaded that Jeff had not got the time to see him. Why was he now calling again?

"I'm sorry but Mister Bordes-Aitcheson is at a meeting. Can I help you?"

"No," came the curt reply. "When will he be available to talk to me?"

"He has a number of appointments between now and lunch time. Can I get him to call you after lunch?"

"No, I will be out of the office. I will call again later" He hung up without waiting for a reply.

"Little shit," Kay said into the dead receiver dismissing Chung, she was not even going to mention his call to Jeff.

The phone rang again.

"Halloo. Speak to Sin Sang Bordes-Aitcheson. Ching Neih."

She recognised the voice, he had called earlier and spoke to Jeff. It was Jason Kim.

"Sorry but Jeff is in a meeting at the moment. Can I help?"

"Never mind, I call to let him know that I late for appointment. Will be 15 minutes late."

"That is Okay, I will tell Jeff, who shall I say called? Just to confirm."

"Jason Kim. Joi Gin."

"Joi Gin." she said and hung up. She glanced at her copy of Jeff's appointment schedule, she had Jason pencilled in for 11.30, it was now exactly 11.30. At least he was prompt.

The phone rang again.

"Kay is Jeff free?" It was Don from the Kowloon branch.

"Still in that meeting. Can I help?"

"It's Maylay, she's asked for the afternoon off. She says she is upset by Tom's death, I need to talk to Jeff because there is something going on here." Don sounded nervous.

"Like what?" Kay enquired.

"Well, you know this new phone system we have where you can just hit a button on the computer and you can monitor the call, the destination of outgoing calls and the source of incoming ones?"

"Yes."

"Well I just did it by chance and Maylay is making and receiving an awful lot of calls. I mean *a lot*."

"So what do you think she is up to?"

"I don't know but TS & F are making a lot of calls to Maylay and vice-versa. There are also a lot of calls to a local number here, but we have been unable to trace it. We tried entering it on the local network but no name came up against it. It may merely be un-listed, we would have to get someone inside Telecom to get the information on what the name and address of the subscriber is."

"Have you tried ringing it?"

"Yes, it sounds like a private house. A teenage girl answers but she is giving nothing away."

"Okay I'll have Jeff phone you the moment he comes out of the meeting."

At precisely 11.45, Jason Kim was shown into Kay Herbert's office. She smiled and exchanged greetings with him while suppressing her surprise at his appearance. She expected a Chinese, this man was not Chinese. He was over six foot tall with flaming red hair and light blue eyes.

"I am sorry but Mister Bordes-Aitcheson is still in that meeting. He did explain that he might be held up. Perhaps I can look after your needs?"

"Indeed." This was a very embarrassing situation for Jason as he could not very well decline her offer of help and he did want to meet Bordes-Aitcheson face to face so that he could get a feel for the man that he was shortly going to be in conflict with.

"I can wait if you are otherwise occupied."

Kay recognised the discrete refusal of her help; he wanted to deal with a man not a woman.

"Thank you for considering my heavy work load. Shall we give Mister Bordes-Aitcheson five minutes and if he does not come out of the meeting by then, I will show you around. That is what you required?"

"Yes." Jason replied surprised that Bordes-Aitcheson would have told a lowly secretary what the intention of his visit was.

She was entering information into a computer via the keyboard, she typed very fast he noticed. She glanced at him as if she felt his eyes on her. When Kay caught his eyes, she smiled embarrassed. He smiled politely and turned his attention to the table of magazines in front of him. The clatter of the keyboard continued, he chose the topmost publication and sat back in the chair glancing at her as he leaned back.

Bordes-Aitcheson breezed into the office. Jason had been daydreaming, he rose after placing the magazine on the table, and he bowed slightly, as Kay Herbert introduced him to Bordes-Aitcheson who returned the bow equally as polite.

"Sin Sang Kim, welcome to the AAB." Jeff said reaching out his hand.

"Pleased to meet you, Sin Sang Bordes-Aitcheson." Jason took the hand and equalled the strength of the grip.

"Please come through to my office." Jeff gestured towards the inner door. Jason led the way while Jeff asked Kay to bring coffee.

In the office they sat down, Jeff in his usual place where he felt totally in control, at his desk.

"Weather most extreme." Jason began as was the custom to enter into small talk to allow the conversation to drift into the matter at hand.

"I was watching the forecast last night and they predicted very warm weather with the threat of thunderstorms."

"Most unpleasant, feel that weather at present conducive to typhoon conditions."

"That's just what we need." Jeff commented with a certain amount of irony.

"Very bad for shorefront."

"Indeed. How is you business, the Golden Moon?" Jeff enquired to bring the conversation back to the business at hand.

"Most rewarding, of course. Golden Moon very well established as one of most prestigious restaurants in Hong Kong. Very good clients-" Jason said proudly, "-of course the quality and service is renowned, you do not frequent yourself?" Jason said pointedly.

"Unfortunately, I do not get to eat out as much as I would like to and I must be seen to support my own customer's establishments. However, perhaps all that can change after this morning."

"Yes indeed." Kim seemed taken aback by the comment, like he had left an opening.

"You will appreciate that the AAB is renowned for being the businessman's Business Bank in Hong Kong. We specialise in this area and offer one of the best services available-" Jeff gave his bladi blab' chat about the bank and concluded with, "-small can be beautiful." Jeff finished his standard sales pitch.

"Most impressive indeed." Jason seemed suitably impressed.

"How much did you plan to place on deposit?" The question was so direct that Kim looked startled.

"I have some cash that I wish to move from its present position and I shall consider placing it on account here. I also have some valuables in my possession which up to now, I had not thought about the security of. However, recent events have made me think seriously about their value and security. Therefore I would need the use of a Safety Deposit Box. I presume that you do have such a facility?"

"But of course, we have some of the best facilities in Hong Kong."

"And perhaps the oldest?" The question casual, a smile on Jason's face.

"Well not quite the oldest, our original Safety Deposit Boxes were fitted in 1896. However, they were out of date so we upgraded them in 1946 after the war."

"Very interesting" Jason said casually, but Jeff thought he saw something else in his eyes.

"How much had you in mind for lodging on account?"

"Ah, you do stick to the point."

Jeff smiled innocently.

"I was thinking in the region of $10 million."

"Well I am sure that we can offer you a very good rate for that most generous amount." Jeff looked taken aback. "Perhaps you would like to see our facilities?" Jeff enquired.

"Yes would like very much to view security arrangements and examine Safety Deposit Box system."

He asked Kay to hold the coffee for ten minutes while they took the guided tour.

Jason looked most impressed by what he saw as Jeff led the way down to the basement level.

"As you can see we take great care to ensure that no point is overlooked in our security arrangement. We have total video coverage of every part of the bank. No one can enter or leave without being picked up on video."

The camera system was new, just installed last year and had a revolutionary new housing system. The camera itself was mounted in an explosion-proofed clear PVC housing. The purpose was simple, by housing the camera in a 'Glass' enclosure thieves could not get at the camera lens to prevent it picking up images by spraying paint on it. The enclosure has a cylindrical shape and an outer layer that revolves so thieves spraying paint over the lens area would be caught out as the sprayed area would then move away from in front of the lens. At the back was a tiny wiper so as the enclosure turned any paint would be wiped off as it passed the wiper.

Jeff was showing him the vault; the massive steel door was closed at the moment and was on a time lock so he couldn't open it just then. When they entered the Safety Deposit Box room, Jason's interests seemed to rise.

"Ah this is of much interest. How many safety deposit boxes do you have?"

"Five hundred. They are the two key types; our security man holds one key, the customer the other. Both keys have to be presented at the one time. We check the signatures. When everything is in order, he then unlocks his side of the combination with his key and the customer unlocks his side. The customer can request the security man to remove the Safety Deposit Box or he can choose to do it himself. There are privacy cubicles which the customer can use to examine the Safety Deposit Box without being observed. There is only one security camera here, up over the main entrance door; it is used only to check who comes and goes and to ensure that no one tampers with other people's Safety Deposit Boxes."

"This is most reassuring. You said earlier that the first Safety Deposit Box system was introduced in 1896. What has happened to the contents of those Safety Deposit Boxes?" The question seemed casual as Jason surveyed the room while talking for the sake of talking.

"Well that happened while my grandfather was in charge of the bank. I would imagine that customers were advised about the new boxes and they moved the contents." Jeff was slightly puzzled by the question and made a mental note to check it out to see if any reference was made to that in the day book.

"Let me just speculate for a moment." Jason looked directly at Jeff. "If one of those old boxes was not claimed, say the contents had laid there for years and no customer came to move the contents to the new Safety Deposit Boxes, what would have happened to the old box. Presumably you would not be able to open it. What would have happened to the box?"

Jeff mused on this for a moment. "I don't honestly know. I guess that the box would be stored somewhere."

"Ah, so any old box might still be in existence?"

"Possibly, why do you ask?"

"I have a collection of artifacts, rare items from the turn of the century which I have built up over the years. I have collected them at auctions and antique shops. When you mentioned the old Safety Deposit Boxes earlier, I thought that I may be able to acquire an old Safety Deposit Box for my collection. Never mind."

"I will check that out and see if we do have any left laying around."

"I appreciate your generous offer, I would be very grateful."

"I would like to see the collection some time."

"I can arrange this; you feel that the old boxes may still be in existence?"

"Possibly, there is a store room that has not being used for years; I'll have one of the staff check it."

"So much trouble. So sorry."

"Not at all, anything for a valued customer."

"I may even find some other artefacts that is no longer of value to you but may be of interest to me." Was this a discrete hint that Jason would be present when the store was examined?

"Yes, I will arrange that." Jeff answered, but the alarm bells were ringing in the back of his mind, Kim's queries were too persistent to be pure coincidence.

"But back to the matter at hand. What I have seen impresses me greatly and I will indeed make use of your services. I shall arrange to deposit money with your bank. You might make whatever arrangements are necessary."

"Thank you for your confidence. I will be most happy to facilitate all your requirements should you decide to do that. Shall we go back up and have that cup of coffee now?"

When Jason had gone Jeff considered the significance of the visit on the same morning that he had learned of his ancestors granting a loan to Jason's ancestors. If the deeds were lodged in the bank, where were they now? Was Jason's interest in the old Safety Deposit Boxes as he stated or had it something to do with the deeds? But then how would he have found out about them? On the same day as he had discovered the reference to the loan to Jason Kimberley? It was not possible that he could have discovered the existence of the loan and the deeds through the same source as Jeff did. Jeff had not mentioned it to anybody, so the only logical conclusion that he could come to was that there was another source of information. Someone else had discovered that Jason Kimberley had done a deal with the old AAB. The question was who? And one name kept coming to mind: Maylay Dulles! How was it that Maylay kept her connection to George Archibald through marriage secret all those years? For what purpose? Why should they keep such a secret?

Everything that had happened had occurred since Tina Bolger had discovered the reference to Jason Kimberley in the ledgers over in the Kowloon branch. Maylay must have passed on the information not only to George but also Jason Kim. Now Jason wanted to know the whereabouts of the old Safety Deposit Box system. The deeds had to be in the bank somewhere? It was the only possible answer.

He referred again to the bank's Day Book where all relevant activities were recorded.

There were two Day Books covering the year 1940, that was when the old boxes were changed to the new system. The first reference to the Safety Deposit Box's was on February 6th of that year. Tony Bordes noted that the board had approved the expenditure needed to convert the old Safety Deposit Box Room into a new vault and construct a new Safety Deposit Box Room in what was then the staff room. It would then be necessary to restructure the second floor area to accommodate a new staff room. That was a major restructuring program so the plans must have being prepared by an engineer. If that was so, then there must be drawings submitted, in which case they must also be in the bank. "Father never threw anything away." Jeff muttered, making a mental note to look up the plans which had to be in the general store room or the file room. He flicked through the pages of the Day Book; work started on the new Safety Deposit Box room on February 13th and finished on April 28th 1940. There was a reference to notifying customers of the change late in April and a further reference in May to the need to place advertising in the local paper as some customers had not come in to transfer their valuables. Work was due to commence on the new vault in May, which was to be constructed in the old Safety Deposit Box room so it had become imperative to have all the old boxes cleared out.

The next reference in the Day Book was of the start of work on the new vault. Jeff got his father's diary of that year and leafed through the pages for the early part of the year. There were many references to the construction work that was going on, including the names of the contractors, engineers and architects. It was in May that the Boxes themselves were mentioned in any detail.

'Must make decision on what to do with unclaimed boxes.'

Was written on the top of the page on May 3rd. On the 8th he wrote,

'10 days to claim the contents or boxes would be moved.'

Jeff calculated that this was probably a reference to drawing up copy for an advert in the papers. On May 24th a series of numbers were written in the diary.

'123, 135, 279, 300G, 368, 468'

This was written on the top of the page, and on the bottom it said,

'Boxes stored temporarily in old store.'

"Old Store?" Jeff went through the rest of the year carefully but there were no further references to either the Safety Deposit Boxes or the 'Old Store'. He had never heard of the 'Old Store' in all his time in the bank.

He went through to Kay's office.

"Jeff, you have an appointment pencilled in for 12.30 with a Diver Ho. Is there any change on that?

"Ah, I'd forgotten about that. No, it still stands as far as I know. I haven't got a clue who the guy is, see if you can get information out of him when he arrives."

"Okay, I'll give him the third degree before I let him in."

"Thanks. I'll be in either the File Room or the General Store Room."

"By the way I got a call from Philip Thorn while you were with Kim; they bought over 1.7 million shares on the stock market this morning."

"Wow, 1.7 million? Jesus Sir Percy only had 800,000. Where did they get the rest?"

"Philip seems to think that he bought George's as well."

"What?" A smile of disbelief on his face.

"Yes, he thinks he bought George's as well as wiping up all the other shares that were available, we're trading at £23.50 a share."

"Wow, well if that doesn't make my day, nothing ever will."

"I thought you should know." she smiled.

"This is going to put the cat among the pigeons."

He was in really good form when he reached the File Room, so much was going his way right now that it was almost embarrassing, almost! He didn't expect to find the drawing here and it only took a few minutes to eliminate this room from the search.

In the General Store Room he found what he wanted quite easily. There was a large cardboard box marked 'plans and drawings'. There were ten drawings in all. He decided to bring them all back to his own office and examine them there.

Chapter Twenty Two

Dillon was feeling the effects of Sir Percy's port and then the three Blackbush he had drank since coming over to the Criterion Bar and Lounge, was starting to have an effect. Olli and Philip Thorn who were deep in conversation when Dillon noticed this big man standing behind the bar starring at him. Dillon looked up at the big fella.

"How's she cutting?" he said in an Irish accent.

"A 'right, and yourself?" Dillon replied in his best brogue.

"Ah, could be worse. What part of the 'auld country are ya' from?"

"Galway." Dillon replied, the surprise showing on his face. This guy had him tapped; he must have recognised his accent.

"I'm from Mayo me'self, Belmullet. Blacksod Bay to be accurate."

"You can't get much further west then Blacksod Bay." Dillon replied he heard the Irish in London talk of Blacksod Bay.

"You know it?"

"No but I've heard of it."

"That was enough for any civilised man." He leaned on the counter getting intimate.

"A Yank once stopped in Belmullet looking for direction to the 'scenic route'. Well he was told that one way was Blacksod Bay and the other way was Ireland. He say's, 'What's beyond Blacksod Bay? Well yer'man say's, 'A bloody awful lotta water, and then America'." The big fella laughed and Dillon saw the funny side to it.

He stuck out a big callused hand. Dillon took it and shook hands.

"Scott Dillon." he introduces himself.

"Paddy Maltbie. Are you anything to the Dillon's from around Tuam?"

"Nah, my old man left Ireland years ago. I was born in America, but we came back to Ireland when I was very young. I grew up around Barna."

"Ah, nice place." he commented politely.

"In the summer." Dillon corrected.

"A bit like Blacksod Bay." Paddy Maltbie replied.

"Yeah." Dillon commented. Why did this man that George Archibald wanted to talk to earlier in the day come over to Dillon and indulge in small talk? He figured that the probing would start shortly.

"You're new to Hong Kong, aren't ya'?"

"Yeah, just got in the other day." He was going to play along, this was going to be interesting.

"Are you staying long?"

"Two weeks."

"Holiday or business?" The questions were casual, just conversation to fill the time.

"A little of both." He decided to throw the guy a little.

"What do you think of the place then?"

"I like Hong Kong, it has got balls."

"Great place to do business. What line are you in yourself?"

Dillon almost laughed, it hadn't taken him long. "I'm an Assessor."

"Insurance Assessor?" He seemed surprised.

"No, bank!"

"Ah, banks, now there's an interesting subject."

"Oh, how's that?"

"Well with everything that's happening around here this morning, bank's tumbling and all. You're not involved with the OUT bank, are ya'?"

"No."

"Which one are you dealing with?"

"Anglo Asian" Dillon replied he deliberately avoided using AAB. Paddy Maltbie would know.

"Good bank, pity what's happening to them."

"Oh, what's that?" Dillon was puzzled.

"Word has it that they're being taken over."

"By who?"

"Are you really working in there?" Maltbie seemed genuinely surprised.

"Yeah, but I didn't hear anything about a takeover."

"A load of their shares just changed hands, about 15 %. Now that's a strange thing in a falling market."

"Do you follow the market then?" Dillon asked.

"Well not really, just that I hear talk, a lot of stockbroker types come in here, but I do follow AAB shares. You see I've got some of them myself. Three percent in fact. With the price rising like it is, I might sell them. If I could find the right buyer." Maltbie turned away as if someone caught his attention.

"I'm wanted up there; I'll be back in a minute." He went further up the bar.

Dillon looked at Olli and Thorn, they had heard.

"What's he up to?" Olli whispered.

"I don't know, but I'm going to find out before we leave here."

Maltbie was filling a drink nearby so they let the conversation drop. But Dillon's interest was heightened. He seemed like a friendly sort of chap, but Dillon knew that the Irish could be a slippery lot, especially the natives of the west coast. He also suspected that Maltbie recognised that Dillon was reluctant to talk so he had thrown the mention of the AAB shares that he wanted to sell as a bait to get familiar. Then he had moved away, the perfect ploy to insure that Dillon would be stewing while he was away. He would expect Dillon to be only too willing to talk when he returned.

This was all assuming that he was reading the situation correctly and that he knew who Dillon was. For he expected Lo-Xian to have told him that Dillon was probably the one that overheard her phone conversation with George. She will also have known Philip Thorn and it would not have taken much for her to put two and two together and come up with the conclusion that would have linked Dillon with the AAB and the dealing on the Market across the road.

"What do you know about this guy?" Dillon asked Thorn when Maltbie moved away again.

"He is a wealthy man. He does plant and machinery. He came out here about fifteen years ago, as he says himself, to get away from the Irish Persecution in England when the troubles began in Northern Ireland. The English, much to their surprise, discovered that they still had a presence in Ireland. That's what he says. He made his money working on the tunnel. His story is that he came over here with a pick and shovel and a few hundred dollars in his pocket. He saw an opening for a dump truck hire business during the work on the tunnel. So he bought a second-hand dumper with his savings and hired it out to one of the contractors on the tunnel. He was getting good money on hire so he trained a young Chinese to drive it and went and bought another one. He became a plant hire mogul. By the time the tunnel was finished, Maltbie had built quite a good business for himself. The tunnel set him up and he has just grown ever since. He is tied up with George Archibald through marriage, his wife Lo-Xian is a sister of George's wife.

"Who's for another drink?" Olli asked.

"I should get back across the road and see if we've picked up more available shares." Thorn said looking at his watch.

"Okay, we'll probably catch you later then; we've gotta try and track down Tina" Dillon said.

Thorn got up and with a wave of farewell to Lo-Xian and Paddy he left.

Maltbi moved back down the counter mopping the top as he went casually approaching the two men. They broke off their conversation as he neared.

"As I was saying, there are funny things happening over there this morning. A guy was just saying up there." He motioned to the other end of the bar. "That the OUT bank shares are at an all time low. Yet the AAB are rising at a great rate. There has to be something going on, hasn't there?"

Dillon looked him dead in the eye. "Sounds like that to me too."

"Has to be a takeover bid, doesn't it?" Maltbie tried again.

"Ah well, there could be other reasons too. Shareholders confidence in the chairman, expansion plans, better than expected results. There could be any number of reasons."

"Bullshit," Maltbie replied. "That might be acceptable in normal times, but one bank alone going against the trend of the entire market. Credit me with some cop-on."

There was a touch of anger in Maltbie's voice which surprised Dillon.

"Can't keep much from a Paddy, ha'?"

Maltbie overlooked being called 'A Paddy'. "I fucking knew it! There's a bloody takeover and you're part of it, right?"

"I can't say anything; company loyalty and all that."

"But you're not denying it, are ya'?"

"No comment." Dillon replied with a smile, but he was reassessing his opinion of Maltbi. He had figured him for a George and Kim lackey, but he could see in his demeanour that he was thinking profits.

"That sort'a makes my 3% sort'a valuable, doesn't it?" It wasn't a rhetorical question.

Dillon nodded.

"You interested?" Maltbie asked. This one was rhetorical.

"No." Dillon replied quickly enough to tell Maltbie that that wasn't the real answer.

Maltbie's face fell a mile, then it turned briefly to anger until Dillon added, "Not personally, but I might know someone who is."

"Oh yeah?" Maltbie's feelings were hurt, he had offered his valuables and was turned down.

"Who's your broker?"

"Why?"

"Well if your broker was to get together with Philip Thorn, you know him? The guy that just left?

Thorn is offering over the going rate at the moment."

"How much over?" Maltbie enquired anxiously.

"Fifty cents."

"Jesus, ye're generous."

"Thanks," Dillon replied.

"You'll have to improve a lot on that."

"It is a falling market, as you said yourself. There is only one buyer on the market and I know for a fact that they are not making a takeover bid, merely a stake. My tip is to sell; they are not buying the AAB."

"What the hell is the point in a stake in a doomed economy? It's short term investment at the very best and why should anyone want to invest short term just for a stake? No it must be takeover or nothing."

"You see? You've just proved my argument, why would anyone buy into a bank in Hong Kong in a doomed economy unless? Big banks think different to the rest of us human beings. They have their own ideas, they see Hong Kong as a doorway to China, the largest single populated market in the world. I can tell you for a fact that they are not looking short term investment, they are looking at the AAB as long term input into Hong Kong in partnership."

"I find it hard to believe that, but then again I'm a sceptic. I'm Irish."

"Two true statements one after another. You sure you're Irish?"

"Sure I am. Me mother, she was Orange, me father, he was Green." He mimicked the old song 'The Sash'.

Dillon finished his drink and stood up. "Well, old sport, I gotta get along, little doggy. See you again."

"Sure drop in anytime."

Olli followed Dillon out onto the street. The weather was even hotter then when they went in, or maybe they had become too accustomed to the air conditioning in the bar. They stood on the sidewalk, Olli waiting for Dillon and Dillon waiting for inspiration.

"What was that all about?" Olli asked.

"That was a Paddy trying to make up his mind. And trying to figure out just who was telling the true story."

"What now?" Olli shrugged his shoulder, pushing Paddy thoughts to the back of his mind.

Dillon was deep in thought, not deep thought, just superficial thought. He had just spent an hour in a bar before midday waiting for something to happen, but what? What the hell did he have to do here, his work was done, he had started the process, the brokers had taken over and it was their ball game now. There was nothing for a hard nosed tough-guy left to do. The potential threat from this, no longer mysterious. Narrow Investments had not developed. There was no secretive society pulling the rug from under his feet after each clue was unravelled. There was no Godfather figure lurking behind a shroud of deceit.

Wait a minute, Dillon thought. *There was!* A name had suddenly entered his mind.

"Jason Kimberley!" he gasped.

"Ah there is life after half a bottle of Irish whiskey." Olli said.

"Not a lot."

"What had you got on that cunning mind of yours?"

"I war' thinking that it was about time that we started to kick some ass."

Oh no! Olli thought

"I'm going back to the bank, I want to talk some stuff through with Jeff. What are you going to do? Stick with Thorn?"

"Actually I was thinking that we haven't heard from Tina in a while. I wonder how she got on over in Kowloon this morning?"

"Why don't you give her a call from Thorn's office?"

"That's a good idea, I'll catch you later." Olli got the message and headed for the Exchange.

Dillon signalled Charlie and the black Merc' was at the kerb in a flash.

On the way back to the bank he thought about how he could wrap things up here. Basically the job was done; Stern had wanted a stake in AAB, well now he had it. The bank wanted to swallow a rival, now that was going to happen real soon. The OUT was ripe for picking. So the only loose end was Jason Kimberley and Maylay. Once they were dealt with, he figured that he was done here.

The car came to a halt. Dillon got out of the Merc' opposite the bank. Charlie had wanted to hang a u'ie and pull up at the kerb but Dillon had had enough of Charlie for now. It was quite likely that Charlie would hang a u'ie in front of a charging tank.

"I see you 'rater, Boss." Charlie shouted as Dillon closed the door.

Five too many drinks were going to Dillon's head in a big way and he just wanted to have a quick word with Jeff about buying some shares, organise the transfer of the money from New York and buy the bloody things. He might as well get in on the action. After that, he wanted to go back to the hotel and have a nap. He thought that it was a pity Singapore Girl wasn't around so that they could go for a dip.

His head hurt from the drink. He was waiting for a break in the traffic to cross the road when he noticed Tina across the street approaching the bank. He got the break in the traffic and crossed just as Tina came near the door of the bank. As Dillon approached he realised that something was amiss. It is hard to explain how he knew, he just had a sense for this type of thing. It might have been the way that Tina walked, the way she held her head, the eyes darting or perhaps it was the clenched fists. Whatever it was, there was a huge sign of relief on Tina's face when she saw Dillon.

Now her walk slowed, and she moved her head to one side as if nodding, but sideways, her hand up in front of her chest and motioned with her thumb backwards.

Backwards? What the hell was she up to? Dillon thought, puzzled. They were still about 20 metres apart on a fairly crowded pavement Dillon's instinct told him to check the faces behind her.

None were familiar, the faces milling about meant nothing, except one. About 10 metres behind Tina was a face looking not just straight ahead but looking at Tina, his head was tilted slightly back like a man looking for someone. His pace was the same as Tina's, he even slowed to match the pace when he realised that Tina had slowed.

Dillon gestured Tina on past the bank as he stood on the edge of the pavement looking up at the bank as if examining the facade, or perhaps looking for a street number. He kept glancing at the "Face", a name Dillon had given to the man tailing Tina.

When Tina passed by, she quickened her pace. The Face matched the pace again. This indicated that he was indeed following Tina. When the Face came alongside Dillon, he stepped forward and hit the Face hard in the guts. He doubled up in shock as much as pain. Dillon reached down and grabbed him and pulled him out of the flow of people.

"Are you all right?" Dillon asked loudly. The few people who had actually noticed the guy apparently stumble, quickly lost interest once they realised that someone was taking care of the man. He supported him with one hand while he patted him on the back with the other and glanced around to seek out Charlie. He spotted him and whistled. The Merc' roared into life and shot out onto the traffic and came to a screeching halt at the kerb. The rear doors handle not six inches from Dillon's left hand. He opened the back door and shoved the Face into the rear seat; he put up no resistance. He was trying to get his breath back.

"What happen', Boss?"

Tina jumped into the front seat. "Who the hell is this guy? He has being following me since I left the Bank in Kowloon and I think Maylay had him follow me." Tina was obviously highly anxious and was breathing very fast.

"Calm down everybody and get us the hell out of here." Dillon shouted checking the people on the pavement to see if anyone was watching them but apart from the odd casual glance, no one seemed to have paid too much attention to what had happened. Dillon had a tight grip on the Face's arm holding it behind his back high up where there was little or no chance of the Face breaking the grip. Dillon frisked the Face as best he could with his free hand, all the time watching his expression which remained stone faced and seemingly un-emotional. He showed no fear.

"He has being following me for nearly two hours. I have been trying to shake him but I had to give up. He just follows, like shit sticks to the back of the bowl."

"He stuck now." Charlie said.

"Take us around the block, Charlie."

"Okay fella', start talking." Dillon watched him but he made no move to look at Dillon or made any effort to talk. Dillon hit him square in the ear with his clenched fist. The Face screamed momentarily then quickly controlled himself and remained silent. Tina winced and turned away.

Dillon raised his fist to hit him again. He held his fist close to this man's ear and the Face tensed himself and moved his head away as far as he could.

"No speaks Gwai-Lo. Please no hit."

Charlie turned his head and smiling said something in Cantonese to the Face, before turning his attention back to the road ahead. The Face seemed to realise from what Charlie said that he was trapped and the tension drained from his body. Dillon felt the resistance ease in the wrist that he was holding. Dillon made a motion to hit him again.

"No!" he shouted. "I speak. What you want to know?"

"Who sent you?" He started with the easy ones.

"Not know answer. Boss phone me, tell me follow American from bank. See where she go, who she meet."

"Why?" Dillon snapped angrily.

"Not know. Please not hit Lee."

"Who's Lee?"

"Me Lee" He sounded surprised.

"Everybody in Hong Kong is Ree, Boss." Charlie said.

Who the hell was Ree? Dillon wondered, then he remembered Charlie's speech problems with his 'L's'.

"Is he lying?"

"Probabrey, he is gang member. See tattoo on back of hand, is sign of Tong, maybe not. No way to terr' Tong wirr never terr truth, bad men."

"Who Boss? Who is Boss?" Dillon corrected himself, having listened to Charlie for to long.

"Ko Lee Tong" The Face answered quickly. Too quickly.

Dillon glanced at Charlie in the rear view mirror, his face showed concern.

"Who is he?"

"My Boss."

"Okay, smart ass, Boss of what?"

"Run Harbour Nights."

Dillon glanced again at Charlie.

"Bad prace, Boss. Night club in Aberdeen, prace to buy White Powder. Very bad."

"Is this guy a dealer?" Dillon enquired.

"Maybe." Charlie replied.

"What is your name?"

"Tommy Lee, Boss."

"Charlie, get hold of directory enquiries and find out the phone number of the Harbour Nights. Let's find out if Mister Tong knows our friend here."

Charlie dialled the number and spoke to the operator. While they waited to get the number, Dillon told Charlie to head for the tunnel. He noticed that Lee tensed up at the mention of the tunnel. Was it that he suffered from claustrophobia or did the tunnel mean something else to him. Strange, because the only reason that Dillon wanted to go to the tunnel was that there was some derelict sites on the waterfront on the Kowloon side where he could carry out a little un-observed interrogation. Did Lee also suspect this or was it that he was just claustrophobic?

Dillon relaxed his grip on the wrists so he could re-position his hold.

Lee moved so fast that Dillon was caught completely off-guard. Lee hit him with his right fist on the temple and jerked his hand free, he turned sideways on the seat and before Dillon could protect himself, and he brought his left leg up and kneed Dillon on the chest, knocking the wind out of him. Then on the backswing the propelled his leg towards the front of the car and caught Charlie on the back of the head with his heel. Charlie jerked away from the blow and hit the side window losing control of the car; it swung violently to the right as Charlie slumped at the wheel. There was a sickening crash of metal as the Merc hit the car travelling next to it.

Tina reached for the wheel to save them but Lee lashed out with a vicious blow that was meant to hit the side of her head with his lethal left leg. Tina had expected that she would not be spared and had a little more time to react then the two men so she kept her head well away from Lee. The kick missed her by inches.

Dillon had just about got his breath back and seeing the opportunity he reached for Lee's leg. Lee was momentarily off-guard and balance as he was in the act of bringing his outstretched leg back. With all the strength Dillon could muster, he grabbed the leg just below the knee and drove it as far back towards Lee's torso as he could. Lee exhaled air and screamed at the same time; above the noise a distinct crack could be heard. Lee collapsed into a bundle on the seat in agony.

The car was still racing forward with the traffic, Tina doing her best to steer while trying to pull the unconscious Charlie up in the seat so that she could take his foot off the accelerator. She had to divide her attention between watching the road and glancing down to negotiate getting Charlie's leg away. Car horns blared at them making the need to be calm and concentrate all the more difficult. Dillon saw the problem and though still groggy, he leaned forward and caught Charlie's shoulders and pulled him upright in the seat. Tina released the foot from the accelerator and immediately the car slowed just as they were about to rear end a slower car in front of them. Tina slowed the car down and eased it over into the inside lane. It came to a jolting halt when she moved the stick to park.

They both sighed a breath of relief and sat back, that was when Dillon got the blast on the side of the temple; he slumped away toward his own side door. There was almost total darkness around him but in his desperate senses, he knew one thing for certain: if he did not take care of Lee they were all in big trouble. He had never before encountered a man who could fight so well in such confined space. Dillon knew that he was slumped in the rear seat and he knew that Lee should be somewhere to his right. He heard a door opening and heard Tina shouting; he shook his head to clear the drowsiness and reached out to where Lee should be. Dillon grabbed the arms that he found, although he could not yet clearly see the arm was taut and rigid. Dillon reached up for where the head should be he expected a hit but none came. He found the head, it moved away. Tina was still screaming, but the screaming was somehow muted. Dillon left his left hand where it was, he was holding hair, and he drew back his right hand and lashed out with all his strength at whoever's head was in the vicinity of his left hand. He hit something hard, a skull, there was a grunt. He hit again and again and again. Finally the target moved he had no idea what he was hitting although his vision was beginning to return.

A blow hit him, not hard, it was more desperation then anything else, he slumped back in the seat again but this time he moved his legs, he brought both of them up and lashed out. He hit something and it moved. Dillon tried to pull himself together and began to cross the seat, his vision was still only coming back slowly, he could see Lee now, he was standing up outside the car, he felt Lee's hands on his head, then around his neck. He lashed out with both feet; Dillon was still in a sitting position. His legs collided with Lee's knees and the strangulating pressure released.

Dillon took the opportunity to lash up with his fist at where Lee's head should be, he hit something, and then he reached out and grabbed at his belt with the intention of pulling him against the door frame of the car. Lee resisted and pushed against the roof of the car. Lee swung the door at Dillon catching him on the side of the head, Dillon released his hold on the belt, and suddenly there was a lot of free air around Dillon.

Lee's scream was accompanied by a screech of tyres as rubber tried to maintain contact with the road surface. The screech was momentarily relegated to second place as a sudden sickening short thump and the sound of crunching metal, a brief scream, the sound of breaking glass and then all noise seemed to stop. After a short few seconds came the thud.

Dillon pulled himself up and lurched out the door, turning drowsily towards the front of the Merc oblivious to the carnage behind as car after car thumped into the rear of the car in front.

The car that had hit Lee was stopped just beyond the front of the Merc'. The driver was in shock, a young Chinese girl, and she just sat there looking as if she hoped someone would tell her it was all just a dream. Dillon turned his attention to the road ahead, slumped on the road surface, a tangled heap of human wreckage, was Lee's body. Even as he approached the body he knew that Lee was dead. One leg was bent impossibly under the body; an arm twisted and shattered, the head at an inhuman angle. A pool of blood was beginning to form, oozing from an open gash in the side of the head.

"Shit." he muttered angrily and turned away sickened by the repulsive sight.

Ten years ago this type of thing wouldn't have bothered him. In recent years he had become a little more concerned about his own body. He had begun to jog a little and play golf and generally look after his own fitness and eat a little more carefully. He was not a health freak by any means, but he had begun to pay a bit more attention to his own fitness once he passed 40, he was at the stage in life where he was past the half way mark in his life span and if looking after himself meant prolonging that life span, then it was worth the effort. Becoming more aware of your own fitness forces you to have a little respect for all human life, even Lee. He had an existence too, he had a mother, a father, possibly even a wife and children even though it was hard to tell with the Chinese, Dillon thought that Lee was pushing 30. Seeing the crumpled body lying there brought sadness to his heart, there was no way that anything that Lee had done deserved the ultimate punishment - death.

People were starting to come from everywhere, then he looked up and realised the carnage that had been created, perhaps 20 cars had crashed as a result of the first accident. Now people, some of them angry, were moving forward to see what had caused the trouble. The car that hit Lee was being surrounded by people from the cars behind. He glanced at the Merc' and realised that neither front door was open. He ran to the driver's seat, Charlie was slumped over the wheel, Tina likewise was slumped in her seat but she was breathing. Lee must have being trying to strangle her. Tina was alive; he could see her breathing was erratic though, so it became imperative to get her to a doctor.

He ran around the car and slammed the back door shut. He was just a few feet from the driver of the car that hit Lee and someone was helping her. She was in a state of shock, sobbing and muttering. Dillon did not understand her words but he could imagine that she was saying that there was nothing she could do. The person consoling her turned to Dillon and said in broken English,

"What happed?"

"The guy just jumped out in front of her. There was nothing she could do." He moved around the car to the driver's side. His thought concentrating on helping Tina and Charlie.

Back up the road he saw a man coming through the crowd very fast, perhaps the driver of the car that they had hit when Lee hit Charlie. Dillon did not want to talk to him, for while they appeared to have no involvement with the accident that caused Lees death, the owner of the car that they had hit earlier could tie them up for some time until the police arrived. Dillon did not want to talk to the police for onlookers might have seen Lee fall out of the Merc'. It could be said that he was pushed out into the path of the oncoming traffic. That would be murder, or at least attempted murder or manslaughter. That was not the responsibility of traffic police but homicide. He did not need to have a run in with any more police, especially not the two he had meet after Tom was attacked yesterday evening. His conscience was relatively clear when he made the decision to get away from here as quickly as possible.

He opened the driver's door and released the seat reclining lever, letting the seat all the way back. That made it easier to shove Charlie into the back seat. He sat into the car and adjusted the seat to suit himself. The motor was still running so he engaged drive and took off. One or two people glanced at the Merc' as he drove slowly by the crowd around the body, but none seemed overly interested or agitated that he was leaving the scene of the accident. Realising that the tinted windows of the Merc' would have prevented anyone seeing the occupants, he eased down on the gas and gathered speed. He left the carriageway at the first opportunity and looked for a quiet spot so that he could check on both Charlie and Tina.

By the time he found a suitable spot, Tina was moving in the seat beside him. She coughed as she regained consciousness.

"Shit!" she gasped hoarsely.

"How do you feel?"

She nodded slowly finding it difficult to talk. Dillon checked Charlie and apart from bruising to the side of the head, he seemed fine. His breathing was shallow but regular.

"Fucker tried to strangle me." Tina whispered feeling her neck, she tried to cough but that hurt so she just leaned back on the seat and remained silent.

"I'd better get you to a hospital." Dillon said. Tina grunted and held up her hand slowly.

Dillon dialled Kay's number at the bank and asked for Jeff.

"Scott here, we have had a spot of bother." He went on to explain what had happened and why he needed to stay clear of the police.

"Jesus, this thing is getting out of control: first Tom, now Tina and Charlie and who the heck is this Tommy Lee?

"Lee is dead, what bothers me is who hired him to follow Tina. She seems to think that Maylay hired this Tommy Lee."

"We gotta talk. Where are you?"

Dillon looked around for a street sign; he couldn't find one and told Jeff so.

"Never mind, do you know how to get back to the bank?"

"I think so, but Tina and Charlie need a doctor."

"That's Okay, I'll have one here. You're on the Island right?"

"Yeah, we can be no more than 10 minutes from Central."

"Okay come back here. If you have any problems finding your way, just get a street sign and phone me. I'll direct you back. I'll have a doctor ready." He hung up and Dillon started the car and headed in the direction of the towers off in the distance. Scott figured that, that had to be Central so all he had to do was keep the towering building in front of the Merc'.

Tina was beginning to recover a little with each street that passed. She moved in the seat to make herself more comfortable and reached into her inside pocket and drew out the documents that she found in the file room.

"We must talk before you meet Jeff." she said hoarsely.

"Take it easy Tina; we'll get you help soon now." He felt so bad about the hurt she had suffered because he had let her down. "I'm so sorry about this."

"Don't understand. We must talk, look."

Dillon hadn't noticed the documents that Tina had taken from her pocket.

"What's that?"

"Jason Kimberley. They have his deeds."

"Who has?"

"The bank, they have the deeds to the New Territories."

"The AAB?" Dillon said in disbelief.

"Yes the fucking AAB!" Her voice just a little less hoarse.

Dillon pulled the car into the curb and grabbed the document from her hands and glanced through them.

"Good Lord, do you realise what this means?" he gasped.

"Yes, the New Territories belong to either Jason Kimberley's descendants, or to the AAB on default of the loan being re-paid."

"This could change everything. Tina, you're a beauty, give me five." He held up his hand for her to hit. She just stared straight ahead ignoring his hand. He was so high on the thrill of finding this document that he never noticed that she ignored his offer of shared achievement. He was examining the document again. Finally he turned towards her; her head was laid back on the headrest, her eyes closed. Dillon wanted to hold her and tell her everything was all right, that she wasn't going to be left alone again, that nothing else was going to happen. He felt his heart heavy at the sight of her obvious pain,

Jesus, how could he have let this happen? he thought. "Should we tell Jeff about this?" he asked softly.

"I'm not sure, there's more." she said.

"What?"

"I found a secret passage," She went on and told him the whole story, including the body. "Talk about skeletons in the cupboard." she concluded.

"Let's just say that these deeds are in the bank, where in the bank could they be?"

"It must be in the Hong Kong branch. I've searched everything in the Kowloon branch. It's not there. Deeds are not the sort of thing that a bank hides in the bottom drawer of a desk. These have to be stored and filed. So it must be held in a secure place with some reference to it, right?"

"Okay, so what does that leave us: the vault and the file room?"

"Possibly. I wondered about the reference after 'Security Lo-Wok deeds', the 'G 300' the date and 'Box Key'."

"Box, could that be a safety deposit box?"

"Could be. The only thing is why would Bordes place the deeds in a safety deposit box? These boxes are for costumers' valuables, not for bank valuables."

"Good point unless Bordes felt that the deeds would be safer there."

"That he was doing something that his partners would disapprove of? Could be. After all, Jason Kimberley was not the flavour of the month in Hong Kong at that time."

"I wonder just how significant the deeds were at the time. After all, the deal was just concluded between the British and the Chinese for the New Territories for 99 years. It may have been a fool's errand presenting the deeds as having any importance at the time."

"Not necessarily. If Kimberley owned the lands, the British only had the lease; they might have to pay him rent." she pointed out.

"Or those that sub-leased the land of the British."

"The courts would have to make the final decision on who paid what to whom."

"We need to find those deeds." he said resolutely.

"Fine, where do we start?"

"The file room I guess, and if everything pans out, we check to see if a similar secret passage exists in the Hong Kong branch."

"Okay." She wanted to say something more, but he turned his attention back to the road ahead and pulled out into the traffic, the moment was lost.

Jeff had buzzed Kay, briefly explained the call from Dillon and asked her to get a doctor.

Now he stared down at the plans of the Hong Kong branch of the AAB bank drawn in 1940.

They seemed just as he would have expected; the purpose of the drawings was to locate a new Safety Deposit Box room in what had been the staff room and convert the old Safety Deposit Box room into a vault room. There was very little in the way of structural alterations in the basement to accommodate the changes. The main work involved reinforcement of the existing structure. He then opened the drawings from 1906 and apart from different names on the various rooms, the layout was almost identical to the 1940 drawings. There were some minor changes in so far as there was much more detail in the 1906 drawings. In the earlier drawing, doorways were shown in great detail and it was while examining the details of one such drawing, that he noticed a written note.

'Refer to drawing No. 4.'

The note was tiny in comparison to the written detail on the rest of the drawing. He left the drawing aside and searched for the mentioned drawing but to no avail. Jeff thought this strange as all the drawing were numbered and were stacked in the proper order. Yet there was no drawing No. 4.

He returned to the earlier drawing and examined the note again. The note was located beside what appeared to be a recess in the old Safety Deposit Box room.

He examined the detail of other recesses in other parts of the building. At first they appeared to be the same but then he noticed that the wall thickness at the back of the recess was not as thick as the walls at the back of other recesses. Could it be that this was a door? But a door to where? The "door" was in the old Safety Deposit Box room and would have opened onto the lane behind the bank, not directly though, for according to the drawing there was an alcove at the rear of the bank. But that did not make any sense because the rear wall showed no alcove from the outside.

Something was wrong with the drawing. There had to be something wrong with it, maybe that was what drawing No. 4 referred to.

Jeff checked the most recent drawing and that did not show any alcove, so that was that then.

But why show an alcove where none existed? he thought.

The phone call from Dillon had thrown Jeff of his train of thought. While he had started out looking for the Old Store, now this mystery of the non-existing alcove had raised its head. There was no reference in the drawings to the old store. He had gone through them all and found nothing. Maybe his father had meant the Store Room, but then again he had never come across anything like safety deposit boxes in the store room. So what did he do with them? Bordes-Aitcheson felt that he knew every inch of the bank and the contents of all the rooms and offices and he had never come across any Safety Deposit Boxes other than what was in the new location. So had his father sorted out the problem of the missing owners of the uncollected Safety Deposit Box's or had he hid them somewhere else? And who owned them anyhow? This started him thinking about who actually owned the boxes, and he went back again to the list of numbers that he had found earlier. There were six sets of numbers. Five of them just had the numbers, but box 300 had the letter 'G' in front of it. What did the letter 'G' mean? He toyed with a hundred different words beginning with the letter 'G': "gale", "grant", "guarantee", "gold", etc. None meant anything. Of course it could have been the initial of the person who owned the box.

He was interrupted by the buzz of the phone.

"Jeff, a Sin Sang Ho to see you. Your 12.30 appointment. He has what he claims to be a very important letter for you."

Jeff remembered the instruction that he had left with Kay to find out as much as she could about his 12.30 before he was let in; she obviously felt that the guy was genuine.

"Okay, show him in." Jeff folded the drawings and placed them on the side of his desk.

The door opened and Kay introduced Diver Ho.

"Take a seat." Jeff bowed slightly and offered his hand.

Diver Ho returned the bow and shook hands before he sat down. Jeff was not in the mood for formalities so he came straight to the point.

"How can I help you, Mister Ho?" He dropped the formality of 'Sin Sang'

Diver Ho had had a very bad morning, after the crash he had gone home to calm himself. His little sister was still at home in bed with the fever, or so she said. This was her third day off school now with this fever that prevented her from leaving the house but not from leaving the bed.

She had followed him into his room and stood looking at him laying in the bed.

"What do you want, Little Sister?" he had snapped, immediately feeling sorry for being so harsh.

"You do not look well, Elder Brother. Are you ill?"

"No I am fine; please leave me. I need to rest."

"Very well, I will not make you mad; I will tell you later when you are better about the paper that fell from the letter you bring home." She turned expertly on her heels and bolted through the door.

He had jumped to his feet and raced after her.

"Wait, Little Sister, what paper?" he said desperately following him into the tiny room that acted as kitchen.

"No matter, Elder Brother. You rest, make yourself better."

"Little Sister!" he had said angrily.

"Not important. Just piece of worthless paper, never mind."

"Show me the paper." He grabbed her tiny arm.

"Please, let me go. I will give you worthless paper," She stepped back when he released her and she promptly produced the paper. "I would like to be able to watch television in my own room." she suggested. Ho stared at her. He reached for the paper; she withdrew it and looked at the fire, its embers glowing steadily in the hearth.

"Very well, I will buy you a TV, Okay? Now let me see the paper."

"Promise?"

"I promise that I will buy you a television, on my mother's grave, I promise."

"You break promise, I will never speak to you again."

"Promise?" More a question then a guarantee.

She did not understand the remark, but reluctantly handed over the slip of paper. He had glanced at it, and it did not make any sense, just Jason Kimberley's name, the words 'Safety Deposit Box' and number preceded by the letter 'G'. He had made a bad deal, but to be honest he had secretly intended to buy her a TV anyhow, for he knew how much she wanted one.

Now looking at Jeff Bordes-Aitcheson, he pondered again on the slip of paper, maybe it had some significance to him.

"Honourable Bordes-Aitcheson, I have in my possession a letter dated in 1898 from your grandfather to Jason Kimberley."

"A letter?" Jeff asked, puzzled. Ho removed the letter from his pocket and held it up for Jeff to see.

"So, why have you come to me with this?" Jeff was collecting his thoughts, this was obviously an attempt to extort money and Jeff felt that by playing casual he could get the letter quite easily, a few hundred dollars.

"So sorry, I think that perhaps Honourable Bordes-Aitcheson would be interested in letter about deeds to the New Territories. Never mind." Ho started to rise from the chair.

"Ah yes, the deeds." He paused, this all coming in the one day was a little too much. First the loan, then the deeds, then the visit from Jason Kim, the safety deposit box, the call from

Dillon about what Tina had found in Kowloon and now the deeds again. Perhaps the letter to Jason Kimberley from 1898 held a key to the mystery of the safety deposit box.

"Very well, let's talk about the letter. Where did you find it?"

Ho explained but left out the bit about the run in with Jason Kim and his Tong. Jeff listened patiently wondering if this guy had read the letter. Obviously he had, otherwise he would not know that the letter mentioned the deeds.

"Interesting story," Jeff said when Ho had finished. "So what do you want from me?"

"Ah so, much effort put into recovering letter, perhaps it is worth a reward." It was not a question, it was a suggestion.

"Well I suppose it is. Let's say $500."

"Ho feels that this letter is worth many times more than that, very important letter like I tell your good lady outside."

"How important? What can possibly be in the letter from 90 years ago that would have any bearing on today?"

"The location of the deeds."

"The deeds are here in the bank that is not news to me." Jeff bluffed; Ho's reaction would tell him if he was right. Ho looked mildly surprised.

"You have seen them then?" The reply was good, fast and presumptive.

"Ah ha, I do not spend my time looking at deeds." Jeff replied, realising that there was no point in wasting more time with this charade. He glanced at his watch, he had a meet with Eric Ratner for lunch and he did not want to hold Eric up.

"I've got a luncheon appointment, so if we can conclude the business at hand. I will offer you $2,000 for it. Take it or leave it."

"Worth at least ten?"

"Three, my last offer." Jeff rose expectantly.

"Eight."

Jeff glanced at the watch again, pulled on his coat, ready to go. "Four." he said.

"Six."

Jeff extended his hand in a gesture of farewell. "It was most pleasant talking to you but I fear that we cannot do any business."

"Very well, $4,500. Very poor reward for such hard work."

Jeff sat back down and withdrew his personal cheque book.

"Please, so sorry, but paper not of any use to Ho."

Jeff reached for the phone and asked Kay to get the cash. The exchange was made and they shook hands and Ho left the office. Jeff detected a little jump in Ho's step.

Alone now, he examined the contents of the letter, the slip of paper he left to one side.

The letter confirmed the animosity that existed between the two men, Bordes and Aitcheson. It also confirmed that the Governor was aware of the deal done between the Chinese warlord and Kimberley and that he was prepared to reach an agreement with Kimberley on royalties. Once the rush of curiosity had worn off, he re-examined the letter.

'I have placed the documents that you entrusted to me for safe keeping in one of our new safety deposit boxes in our bank. I have entrusted the key to the safety deposit box in the good person of Captain Formidable Wong who has personally delivered this letter.'

The documents that were mentioned had to be the deeds and they were somewhere here in the bank. The key to the safety deposit box was given to Formidable Wong who may or may not have perished with his boat. He suspected that the captain went down with the boat, for had he survived he would have made some effort to retrieve the contents, or at least would have told Kimberley that he was carrying a letter from the bank. It was obvious from the tone of the letter that Bordes had faith in Wong and trusted him with the letter and the gold. It would be unlikely therefore that Wong survived and failed to let Bordes know that the letter was not delivered. So Kimberley never knew that the loan was approved and that the first payment was released.

The loan of 12,000 Guineas was a very big loan, so Bordes must have had great faith in Kimberley and believed that the deeds were authentic and that Kimberley would have an income to repay the loan.

The appearance of Jason Kim this morning had to have some significance; he must have either seen or heard of the letter. Ho must have sold or given him a copy. Jeff wished he had not dismissed Ho so easily; he had a lot of questions to answer, like where was the key that Wong carried? Who had he shown the letter to? Where were the 300 gold Sovereigns? While he pondered this, he glanced at the slip of paper.

Jason Kimberley
Safety deposit box G 300.

So, he had been right, the documents were in box G 300 and it was Jason Kimberley's box, but he was still none the wiser about the 'G'. He looked back at the letter again, he could see no mention of the 'G' letter or any significance in it, unless it stood for the 'Governor', but the crown never held any type of account here.

He read the letter again from top to bottom. He looked at his grandfather's signature,

Geoffrey Bordes

He spelt his name with a G. Jeff looked at it again, no, it was not a mistake, Geoffrey Bordes spelt his name with a 'G', he examined the typed name and then the handwritten signature. There was no doubt, it was not a casual mistake, both printed and written names were the same. Now why would he do that? Was it a message to Jason?

Wait a minute, was the safety deposit box in Bordes own name? Jeff thought. If so, no one would ever find it 'cause they would be looking for the box in Kimberley's name. Of course, that would make perfect sense. If Aitcheson was opposed to the loan, he would destroy the deeds once he became chairman, therefore Bordes had to make sure that he never found them. He had been looking for a reference to a safety deposit box in the name of Jason Kimberley. Jeff had realised his mistake and knew then that it was no wonder he never found it.

CHAPTER TWENTY THREE

Diver Ho had left the bank in a state of high anxiety, not because of his conversation with Bordes-Aitcheson, but because he realised that the only person truly interested in the letter was Jason Kim. Ho had thought that Bordes-Aitcheson would pay a fortune for the letter, he was not interested whereas Kim was prepared to go to any length to get the letter, including kidnapping Ho Chan and ordering shots fired at Ho. This made Jason Kim very dangerous. Ho had decided that it was time to get away from his home. His thoughts now turned to his parents and family. He had to move them to a safe place.

Ho did not use taxis too often, he could not afford them but now he needed to hurry. If Kim traced him then he had no doubt that he would kidnap them also to force Ho give the letter, the original over to him. And he had sold the original. Diver Ho cursed his own greed. His honourable father was right about him; he was a greedy, worthless fart.

Now as he sat in the taxi speeding through the tunnel he realised just how stupid he had been. All that had preoccupied his mind was the money he could make from his discovery; he had not for one minute considered the implication of Kim's anger even after the scene at the Golden Moon restaurant. Ho knew that Kim was dangerous, he had proved that, yet Ho had not even considered holding onto the letter as it might just save his life. It was only when he walked out of the bank at last, free of all the treasures, every dollar extracted, that he finally felt empty. That was when he had realised that he had nothing left to bargain with. It was strange how the two thoughts had hit him at once, while he still had treasure, he could only think of the money he was going to make; now all the treasures were gone and all he could think of was holding onto something for his own safety. It was too late, it was all gone and everything from the chest was sold.

The fear was paramount now, he thought of all the things he should have done, should not have done. Perhaps he should not have gone to Ho Chan; at least he would not now be in a position of fearing Ho Chan giving his identity to Kim. Was Kim the head of the cell in the Aberdeen Tong that the kidnappers had mentioned so arrogantly back at Wing Lok Street? If they were Tong, then they were dangerous, very dangerous. If only he had something left to bargain with. Diver Ho pulled a copy of the letter from his pocket. The traffic was slow emerging from the tunnel so he had plenty of time to study the contents. Still the letter meant nothing to him, he could see no significance in the words and only one sentence meant anything.

'I have entrusted the key to the safety deposit box in the good person of Captain Formidable Wong who has personally delivered this letter'.

"Aiyee!" he gasped; the captain of the wreck had a key on him. The driver of the cab looked back at him in astonishment.

"So sorry, think out loud." Ho eased his mind and the driver turned back to the mess of traffic in front of the taxi.

Now things were clear, he must find the key, at least then he had something left with which to bargain with. His mind raced now; he must get to the waterfront and hire a boat. The taxi was emerging from the tunnel now, so he had to make up his mind quickly; go to his parents home or head for the boat people. He leaned forward in the seat and tapped the driver on the shoulder.

"Please, make change of mind. Must go to Yaumati. So sorry, must visit cousin in the Tanka." He watched for the driver's reaction, there was only a slight shake of the head.

"Very important." he held up a $20 bill, the driver reached back grabbed the note and indicated right. Horns honked and blared, the driver swore at everything in sight and steadily got over to the right lane for the turn onto Chatham Road.

What Diver Ho didn't see was that three cars back another taxi mimicked the sudden lane change manoeuvre amid a blare of car horns.

Now Ho relaxed again. The taxi continued up Chatham Road then turned right again, heading towards Yaumati, the home of the boat people. The taxi came to a halt at the dock. Ho got out paying the driver who did not hang about, he shot off as quickly as possible.

Ho heading down one of the wooden flotation rafts out into the Tanka. There was every size and shape of boat tied up or coming in or going out. Families lived here in poverty and squalor and stink. The temperature was in the mid thirties and what made life just bearable was the timid breeze coming in off the water. He finally found what he was looking for, an acquaintance who owned a motorised sampan. There was a little haggling and finally a price was agreed and a snorkel was thrown in for good luck.

The sampan was pushed back from its mooring position and the powerful motor kicked into life. The sampans bow rose in the water and the long paddle like pole which acted as a rudder steered them through the maze of boats. Once clear of the maze the boatman cranked up the throttle and they headed out to sea.

Maylay's stomach was in a state of turmoil, almost to such an extent that she got physically sick.

The staff was acting very strange towards her. She was getting the cold shoulder treatment and she was sure that they were whispering about her whenever her back was turned. Ruxton had told her that Tom was dead, shot to death in the hospital this morning.

So Wei Ming had done his job right this time. Pity he had to use the gun, something had gone wrong, he was only to use the gun if he couldn't inject Tom with the poison. That would have been difficult to trace and give her more time to organise her affairs and create a cover for herself. It was difficult being in the bank this morning but she had to be there to ensure that she had an alibi. She had listened to the news bulletins for information about the shooting but any that was given was strange and very vague. The newsreader just said that there had been an incident at the hospital in which one man was killed and another wounded.

Wei Ming obviously had to shoot the policeman guarding Tom. But there was no mention of anyone being in custody, so he escaped. That was good, now she just had to eliminate him and all the lose ends were tied up on the Maxwell thing.

She had to reach her sisters and let them know but first Maylay had to see Tommy.

Maylay entered the block of apartments and went straight to the stairs. She ignored the bank of letter boxes; there would be nothing there for her today, nothing that mattered now. She was a woman in a hurry. Her apartment was on the second floor. She had the keys out long before she reached the door, she was about to let herself in when a man emerged from further down the corridor.

She stopped and stared at the figure. Wei Ming approached her.

"What happened?" She stared at him; there was something about his movements that bothered her.

"There were two cops at the hospital, I was told there would be only one, your information was wrong."

"Well that's what I was told, come in" She unlocked the door and left it open for him to follow.

As he began to step into the apartment the door to the stairwell door closed, Wei Ming hesitated for a moment and glanced towards the stairwell door. It had a small glass window in the middle of it, but Wei saw no movement. Satisfied, he stepped through the apartment door.

Maylay wanted to conclude the business as quickly as possible and went into the kitchen and removed a small wooden box about the size of a shoe box from a cupboard. She took the box to the kitchen worktop and opened it. Inside was a metal security box. She removed it and unlocked it. She had already counted and bundled the five thousand dollars that was due to Wei Ming. There were five bundles of money in all and all were made up to the same value. There was also a 9mm Berretta hand gun. She put the gun in her handbag and carried the bundle of money out into the living area where Wei Ming waited.

He had seated himself in a chair; he began to stand up and grimaced as he did so.

"Are you hurt?" She noticed blood on his shirt when his jacket fell open as he stood up.

"The cop got lucky, never mind" Wei Ming was standing now.

"This may sound like a foolish question but did you seek medical help for the wound?"

"I have a first cousin who is a nurse, he fixed me up, he says the bullet is not in a dangerous place, it will keep until I get out of Hong Kong, never mind"

"You know that I am disappointed that you made such a terrible job of following the Bolger woman yesterday, you should not have gotten caught"

"It was Tommy's stupidity that gave us away; he just kept staring at her on the train"

"Where will you go?" She changed the subject quickly for Wei Ming was right, Tommy did act a little foolishly at times.

"Home, it is not safe to be in Hong Kong just now, there is much police activity, and they do not like it when one of their own is killed"

Maylay just nodded and handed him the bundle of money. He thanked her bowed and left.

When he left she quickly began to pack her things anything that she could carry that was of any value to her. Her plan was to travel to Macau she had friends there who would put her up for a few weeks so that she could lay low until this blew over.

The phone rang; she looked at it briefly and considered not answering it. But maybe it was Tommy.

She hadn't heard from him since she met him in the teahouse this morning. She had given him the task of keeping an eye on

Tina; he was to follow her but stay well out of sight. Wei Ming had already given himself away yesterday so Tommy had to be used.

She reached for the phone, but it wasn't Tommy it was Wei Ming. What the-

"You are being followed by a cop"

"What, how do you know?" She gasped.

"When I left the building I thought I spotted someone following me. Then I got a chance to see his reflection in a window, it's a cop called Chung, I know him"

"But you said he followed you?"

"He followed me from the building, but he defiantly didn't follow me to the building, he had to have followed you here"

"Where are you now?" Inside Maylay was horrified, if the cops were onto her then how would she get away?

"I'm right across the street, the cop is on your side of the road, he's reading a note book, and he is pretending to be looking for an address or something"

Maylay went to the window and looked down at the street. There was not a great deal of pedestrians and she saw the cop straight away. Damn her luck.

"I will take care of him for you but it will cost extra" Ming was saying. But Maylay was thinking if the cop had been following her, now he would follow Ming. She had to think fast, she didn't want to make any promises about more money; she had to get away with what she had. She could not very well go back to the bank to withdraw money from there. But there had to be a way to make Ming do the job, or else lead Chung away from her.

"What do you want me to do?" Ming pressed.

"Lead him away from here, can you lose him?" Maylay was desperately thinking of a way out.

"Do you think I am some kind of worthless Tanka, of course I can lose him, but when I do he will just come back here, he knows where you live," He pointed out.

That hadn't occurred to her. Right now she needed to get that cop off her back; the problem was as Ming pointed out he

would come back here once given the slip. Did this cop work alone or did he have a partner? She scanned the pedestrians again but saw no one loitering about, but everyone on the street was on the move.

"I can not stay here all day" Ming pressed again.

"Lead him away from here," She finally said.

"I can do this for another five" Ming said obviously seeing an opportunity for a fast buck.

"But I do not have that sort of cash on me." Maylay threw that out to see what would happen.

"When can you have it?"

Suddenly Maylay saw the answer, why had she not thought of it before.

"The house of Kim is good for the money" She said and waited.

Apparently this gave Ming pause for thought; the mention of the House of Kim would send a shiver down Ming's spine. The underworld knew that Jason Kim was ruthless, but also benevolent to those that acted in a manner that pleased the House of Kim.

"Then it will be done, I am sure that the head of the House of Kim will think kindly of Wei Ming"

"I'm sure he will" Maylay sighed with relief.

She watched as Wei left the phone box and hurried down the street and turn into an alleyway then she saw the cop follow, moments later to her horror she heard the shots.

While she feared the possibility of being discovered, it was never a real and present danger, it was something for the future, something that might happen might not. Now the danger of the police actually arresting her was very real. There was no way that she was going to be held in police custody, she felt weak at the very thought. Freedom was very important to her; she needed to be able to move about without hindrance or restriction. The thought of being locked up in a cell was akin to being dead, she would prefer that. In her haste she was not sure she had packed her revolver, she hurriedly looked through her purse, yes it was there, if it came to it she would use it on herself, she would not be taken into police custody.

She scribbled a note for Mary and Tommy and turning her back with finality, left the apartment.

"Now for George" She thought to herself and again touched the bulk of the revolver in her purse.

Police cars were everywhere on the street, she ignored them and walked up Kimberley till she found an empty taxi and hailed it. The taxi made a U-turn when the driver heard the destination and headed towards Nathan Road. Maylay looked out the back window not really realising that this was the last time that she would see the street that she had lived on for over 20 years.

Chapter Twenty Four

"Shit happens." They were together again in the staff room over the foyer of the bank. Tina had related 'the happenings' to Olli since they had seen him last. He had gasped when he heard of the death of Tommy Lee that was when Dillon had said, 'Shit happens.' They had gotten the once-over from the doctor, apart from bruising they were Okay. Charlie had a large black eye, but apart from that there was nothing serious.

They were alone now and debated what to do next. The unsaid was harder to discuss. Should they tell Jeff about the secret passage, and their suspicion that a similar one existed here in the main branch?

"Jesus, you must have got an awful fright?" Olli said to Tina.

"You kidding?" She was still shaken, the bruises red and moist looking. Dillon watched her; he was surprised at her strength, her resolve. He didn't know any other woman who could have gone through what she had just experienced and not become freaked out. She was quite attractive actually, he had thought when he saw the doctor examining her. He had never really looked at her as a woman, well, never looked at her as being attractive in the sense of being available. Not that she was available, of course; he knew that she was happily married. But right now she was somehow vulnerable, less at arm's length; she was somehow nearer to him. He found it difficult to explain to himself exactly what had changed, probably nothing had changed from her point of view, but from his side it had changed. He now wanted to be closer to her, to be in her company, to protect her. Tina had gone through a lot these last few days: being followed; attacked; lost in a dark secret passage; found a dead body; been in the same room as a killer and watched a man die. Well Okay, she hadn't exactly seen Tommy Lee die but she was there. He felt sudden guilt for exposing her to all that. He should have been more observant, he should have realised that she was in danger when she found the ledgers. Especially after she was followed on the train yesterday.

Now he made a secret self-agreeing pact, she was not going on any more adventures on her own.

"So do we tell Jeff?" Olli said, bringing Dillon out of his train of thought.

"Tina?" Dillon asked, wanting her opinion now on everything.

"He deserves to know. However, the information hidden here may be more damaging then even the skeleton over at the Kowloon branch."

"What do you mean?"

"Well let's just say we find something truly devastating here. I don't know what, but the man that was running the AAB when that guy was stashed in the Kowloon branch, was not playing with a full deck. He was obviously deranged, he could have done anything, hidden anything. Just suppose he has more bodies stashed here. God only knows but suppose, where does that leave us if something is discovered that effects the bank?"

"It's no skin off our nose." Olli said.

"Isn't it?" she asked. Dillon watched her, she had a point.

"We did recommend a buy to Stern." Dillon stated.

"Exactly and now if we turn up any more skeletons, we will look like asses that did not do our job properly."

"Shit, I hadn't thought of that." Olli admitted.

"So we investigate this passage, if it exists, on our own without authorisation?" Olli asked.

"I should think so. Where do we start?" Dillon asked Tina.

"Well, I found the door in the file room."

"Are you fit to start, or would you like to rest up for a while and tackle this tomorrow?"

"I don't think that I could sleep tonight wondering what was down there." she said resolutely.

"Olli, would you cover the file room for us while we are inside?"

He looked disappointed that he would not be going with them into the abyss but nodded anyhow.

"Okay. Let's do it then."

*

The Mandarin was packed for lunch, but Eric Ratner was early and had a table booked. Jeff joined him, his anxiety high and obvious.

"What's the matter with you? You look like you seen a ghost."

"I think I have," Jeff had decided that he was going to place his faith in Ratner and show him the letter and get his reaction. "But first let's order."

Ratner was puzzled and suitably intrigued. He caught the waiter's attention and ordered the Chef's special.

"Okay, give?"

Jeff withdrew the letter and handed it to Ratner who glanced at the letterhead and gasped when he saw the date.

"Jesus H," Ratner stuttered.

"Read."

He did in complete silence, his attention totally riveted to the document. Oblivious to the noise and commotion in the restaurant. While the Mandarin was renowned for its tourist visitors, it was high class tourist that visited here as the prices were geared at the big spender - business and government clientele. The office worker did not eat lunch here unless it was on the boss's business account, a working lunch, so the clients were big stuff. Jeff knew many of them by name and the usual lunch would involve much table hopping and many G&T's. However, this was not a usual business lunch. This was different, so Jeff did not table hop and he drank brandy. He needed its blood thinning power to prevent him from passing out.

"Mother of Jesus!" Ratner said when he had finished reading the letter for the third time.

"This is genuine, right?"

"Absolutely, arrived by special delivery just a half hour ago."

Ratner looked at the letter again, "Presumably it was not delivered by Formidable Wong?"

Jeff managed a laugh and shook his head. "Some kid called Ho walked in off the street and sold me the letter, I never thought to ask where he found it, well not exactly and he said that he found it in a sunken Lurca. That's all he said. Jesus, I thought nothing of it at the time. It was only when he left and I read the letter that I realised that there was much of importance in the letter, I mean if the deeds are really in the bank..."

"Then you're worth a bloody fortune, assuming that this Kimberley hadn't repaid the loan?"

"No, don't you see the point. This is the irony of the whole thing. He never drew down the whole loan, he only got, well didn't get, the first 300 sovereigns. It was sent to him but the Formidable Wong died with his boat, Kimberley never got his loan, but the bank had dispatched it to him."

"Woo, this is something else, so you have the deeds then?"

"Yes and no, we have them somewhere in a safety deposit box. Only it is the old system and my father would have stored them somewhere when the new system was introduced in the '40s."

"There is no record?"

"There is a record of the box number, but no indication as to where the actual box is stored."

"You've got to find it. The deeds are going to be worth a fortune."

"And after '97?" Jeff prompted.

"The Chinese, would they recognise the deeds? After all, they repossessed all the land titles after the revolution."

"But they couldn't repossess that what was not in their control at the time. It was under lease to the British and they could not know of the deal done with Jason Kimberley and Lord Lo Wok, so they could not repossess the title."

"Good Lord!" Ratner gasped.

"Good Lord Lo Wok." Jeff prompted. "There might be a case in International law. Yes it could be contested, it is reasonable, Jesus, this is going to throw the whole negotiation into disarray."

"And send the value of stock and land through the roof."

"Woo, this is heavy. Everything is up for grabs then if you can find those deeds."

"I'll find them, even if I have to pull the whole bloody bank apart."

*

Olli had commandeered two emergency torches from the store room while Dillon got the keys from Kay.

"What happened you?" she enquired examining his bruised face.

"Had a run in with Chinese student of extreme bad manners."

Kay looked puzzled but knew when a man doesn't want to give information away. She opened the drawer of the desk and produced the key to the file room. She asked Dillon to sign for the key.

In the file room they studied the shelving.

"The shelving is arranged the same way," Tina said examining the furthermost shelf on the right hand side of the room. "This one should just pull out" She added and began to tug on the unit.

"Wait." Dillon went over and got his hands under the middle shelf and pulled. The unit moved a little on the smooth concrete floor. Olli joined him, while Tina covered the door. Now with their combined strength, the shelf unit finally moved away from the wall and clear of the unit beside it. Dillon glanced into the space behind. There was a perfectly smooth plastered wall. No recess as Tina described in the Kowloon branch.

"Nothing." Dillon said and glanced at Tina.

"You sure?" She joined them and examined the space herself. She tapped the smooth wall; maybe this one was plastered over. But the tapping did not produce any hollow sound, just that solid click of concrete.

"It may be in a different position, this bank is older and maybe the walls are thicker?" Dillon suggested and began moving the adjoining unit. But still no recess, the sound was the same.

They moved each shelf in turn, but there was no recess and no hollow sound.

"Shit, I felt sure that there would be a similar room here, but I guess not." Tina said disappointed with the failure.

"Wait a minute, didn't you say that the passage also led up to the manager's office?"

"Yes," she replied excited, but then frowned, "That means we have to tell Jeff."

Dillon glanced at his watch. It was 1.15 p.m. "Lunchtime, he may be at lunch. Doesn't he take a late lunch?"

"Yes, of course." Tina replied.

Kay was still at her desk guarding Jeff's door.

"Do you mind if we use Jeff's office for a while. I've gotta phone New York."

"Yes, of course, no problem. Jeff should be back about 1.45. He's lunching with Eric Ratner."

"Thanks," Dillon said handing back the key to the file room.

They filed into Jeff's inner office and Tina immediately went to the cupboard set back into a recess in the wall and opened the doors. Dillon joined her and on his hands and knees he leaned into the cupboard examining the back wall which was made of timber. He tapped the timber, there was a very hollow sound but he could see no way of opening it. There was no latch of any description in sight. He pushed the panel; it moved a little but no more than that.

"Wait a minute." Dillon said remembering a secret passion of his youth: fine cabinet making.

He remembered being at a loose end one weekend in Seattle where there was a craft exhibition on and to kill a long dreary weekend he decided to go and view some of the craft on display. It was one of his other ambitions in life to be able to make fine woodwork and he was attracted to the fair. There he looked in amazement at some of the beautiful pieces that was on display. He was particularly taken by one craftsman from Santa Cruise, California who had some of the best furniture on display. His specialty: hidden compartment and the clever methods of concealing the locking devices to the concealed compartment. The man's name was Robert Carter and his work was famous. He sold by mail order all over the States at very high prices.

Now Dillon applied his knowledge as to how Carter would conceal the locking device.

The obvious was out of the question. He sat back on the floor having removed the few pairs of shoes and two boxes of assorted items from the floor of the cupboard. The back was about 48" wide and 60" or so to the bottom of the one and only shelf. The timber back was made up of 4" wide laths running from top to bottom. A strengthening piece ran across at about 36" high, apart from that there were no other protrusions at all. The bottom of the cupboard was the usual stand up type found in the base of any cabinet or wardrobe. He turned his attention to the bottom, same type of timber, only not as well selected; here was a knot hole, not very good. Knot hole, or a way of lifting the bottom panel.

Expecting failure he reached in and sticking his finger in the knot hole, he tried to move the bottom panel. He expected to have to use force, so when it came away easily he was caught off guard and fell back on his ass. Ignoring the sniggering of the other two, he straightened and looked at the exposed aforementioned locking device.

"Well, what do you know?" He turned back to Tina and smiled; she smiled but quickly broke the stare. He reached back in and moved the latch; the doors swung open revealing the dark abyss.

The joints were perfectly mated, the doors were no more than 3 ft high just to the 'cross' strengthening piece, which helped conceal the top edge of the doors.

"So we have a secret after all." Dillon said, reaching for the torch.

"Close this after me. If Jeff gets back make some phone calls, to anyone. I'll knock three times, and then get Jeff out of the office on some pretext. That will give me a chance to get out. We'll face Kay later. Okay?"

"Fine." Olli said in a tone that conveyed his disappointment in being left as sentry while they went to the frontline.

"You don't think that you're going in there alone, do you?" Tina asked with a 'don't you dare' look on her face.

"Come on, you've being through enough."

"I found it in the first place, Mister Dillon and I'm going in" She turned on her torch and got down on all fours and crawled past Dillon. He had to avert his eyes from her ass as she went past him. Despite all the bruises and the smell of disinfectant off her, he still found her presence so close to him almost intolerable. The look was not lost on Olli either, he frowned.

Dillon followed her in and pulled the doors partially closed behind him. He saw the shadow of her hunched frame ahead of him silhouetted by the torch she carried. He had to concentrate to keep his thought off her.

Tina gasped suddenly.

"What is it?" he whispered.

"It's just that it's different here. There should be steps leading down, but there are none, just a drop. There's an old ladder, but it's on the floor below. I don't know how far the drop is, maybe eight feet."

"You could break your neck. You'll have to turn, can you?"

"Can you?" she shot back the question from the darkness beyond.

"I doubt it, but you're smaller then me. You might be able to turn, or I could let you down by holding your ankles." His heart was in his mouth, just the thought of holding her upside down was enough to drive him crazy.

"I'll turn." she said, almost as if she could read his mind. Tina backed up to give herself room to turn, her ankles passed between his hands without touching. The first he knew was when her backside bumped into his face.

"Dillon!" she shouted.

"What? I didn't know you were coming." He could have bit his lip, worst thing to say.

She didn't react; she just moved away and began her efforts to turn. The passage was only 2 feet wide by less then 30" high, but she managed to make the turn. They were face to face now less then 12" apart.

"What are you playing at?" she said coldly.

"Honest to God, nothing. I didn't see you coming, I swear."

"That's the second time you've said that and I can tell you, Dillon, I don't like those sort of cracks." She barked his name and there was a determination in her eyes that told him he was barking up the wrong tree.

"I liked the crack I felt." He couldn't help himself, it just came out. He felt like a school kid being scolded by the teacher, and yet he couldn't help himself. She was actually smiling at him, what was in that deep devious mind of hers. He could never figure out women.

"Dillon, you're full of shit." she said and began to back away from him towards the drop. He couldn't see her now as the torch was blinding him. He moved forward wanting to help her, hold her hands while she was lowered to the floor below.

"I'm not full of shit; I'm 98% water. I feel offended" Dillon said sulkily.

"Build a bridge, get over it." she replied.

She was being a little bit too female aggressive so he let it go.

"Here, hold my hand. I'll lower you down."

She had her belly on the edge, ready for the drop. Tina held up her free hand, he grasped it and held on firmly as she lowered her body over the edge.

"Okay, I can reach the ground." She relaxed her grip on his hand. He didn't let go straight away,

"Are you sure?"

"Yes, now would you please let go my fucking hand?"

Dillon did finally, he shone the torch down into the tiny corridor below, it was not much wider then the one they had just left. In the beam of the torch he could see that the passage in front of him disappear into darkness. By putting his head well out over the edge, he saw that there was a passage going back underneath the present one on a lower level.

"What are you waiting for? You scared?" she said.

"No just stupid."

Tina let that pass; she just stood there watching him.

"Would you mind placing the ladder against the wall?"

She grinned, wondering if he remembered. Tina had stood over it, knowing that her shadow would conceal it. She stooped to pick it up, that was when she saw him starring at her with black menacing eyes, she screamed. Tina barely heard the shout from above and the crash of a body and suddenly arms were upon her, grabbing her and pulling her away, throwing her back against the wall, then he was in top of the scurrying intruder, flaying out with the wooden ladder hitting him again and again until he lay motionless on the ground in a rapidly spreading pool of blood.

Then he was back to her, holding her trembling body in his strong arms. They stood like that there for what seemed an eternity. He never once released his grip on her. Tina was safe now and the intruder was dead.

"I hate rats." she said finally.

"Don't talk, you'll be Okay in a minute, an hour, a day, a week, I can wait. I can stay like this for ever."

She pulled away from him, looking up into his eyes; the beam of the two torches cast a strange light on his face. He had killed the rat for her. But how had he gotten down so quickly?

"How did you get down?"

"I fell; I'm good at that that makes it two falls in one day."

Tina was puzzled, he was not hurt, and how did he manage that without getting hurt?

"What do you mean, 'two falls in the one day'?"

"Well I fell for you twice: once with my body and once with my heart." He tilted his head slightly and moved closer to her.

"Jesus!" She stopped; he was going to kiss her. Their lips met in the dank air of the passage. He released his breath through his nose. She just held hers, she expected roughness, a hard long kiss, but it was nothing like that. It was soft, gentle like the kiss you give your baby before you put it to bed. She had to stop this, she was going to be sick. This was not meant to happen, and she was not ready for another fall, not yet.

"Stop it." she said, breaking away from him and turning to lean against the wall.

"I'm sorry. I shouldn't have done that, it's just-"

"This is crazy, you know that, don't you? I'm married for fuck sake."

"I know that. I don't understand rules." he said simply.

"Snap out of it!" Tina said as much to herself as to Dillon.

"We've got a job to do." she added.

"Okay, I'm sorry, Okay? Let's get on with it, which way do we go?"

She picked up her torch and shone the way.

Tina led him back towards the small room off the File Room. This was where they should have entered if everything was the same as the bank in Kowloon. The door from the passage to the little room was no opposition. It was red rotten, it just fell away to her push. He had offered to do the pushing, she just ignored him and pushed the door.

In the little room she found much the same as she had in Kowloon: stacks of old letterheads; some wooden boxes containing loads of old stuff; newspaper cuttings; photographs and a few leather bound notebooks, some with entries, and some without. They spent about ten minutes going through the stuff but there was nothing that they could see that had any importance.

Dillon grunted and turned his attention away from the box he was examining. What he now became interested in was the access to this room.

"When you entered the 'copy' room in the Kowloon branch which way did you enter the room?"

Tina was examining a press cutting from 1940 and had to draw her attention away,

"Pardon?"

He repeated the question.

"Oh, let's see." She cast her mind back; the rooms were of similar size, long and narrow as she entered. Tina turned her back to him facing the rotten door. She turned back to face him and shone her torch past him, showing the wall opposite the rotten door.

"Yeah, that's where the door entrance was in the Kowloon bank."

He turned and examined the wall closely. There was no sign whatsoever of any door ever having being there. The brickwork was in perfect condition and the entire wall had the same type of brick, no signs whatsoever of the doorway being closed up years after the original building. These things can be spotted, a different type, style or size of brick being used in any part of the wall would indicate a modification to the building, but there was none.

"From the way you described the bank in Kowloon, and this bank is very similar. There should be a second entrance. If this room was in the original plans, then the entrance could not have been through the passage that we came through. No, that would not make sense. The guy that drew up the plans for the bank must have had another entrance to this room and the passage that we came through was for covert entry by the owner to check on staff or files or whatever. The guy that came up with this design was paranoiac at the very least, if not downright distrusting and evil. He had to have an entrance to this room from the bank proper."

"Okay I can accept the logic of that; only thing is, where is that entrance?"

"That is the $64,000 question, honey."

"Don't call me 'honey'!" she snapped.

"Sorry. Jesus Tina, don't be so touchy! Look I'm sorry about that out there, it's been building up since I've seen you again the other day. I just recalled the fun and bullshit we have when we meet."

"That's not the problem." she said not looking at him.

"I know you're married." He gave a shrug like that was the most important thing in the world.

"It's not just that. It's not even that." Tina muttered.

"Well what is the problem?"

"God no, if only you knew."

"Knew what? For God's sake, Tina, talk to me!"

"That's the problem, I'm afraid to."

"Why? Call me stupid, but I cannot understand why you are so cold to me now after all the fun we had the last time we met."

"Men," In the shadow of the light thrown from the torches, she rolled her eyes to heaven,

"You really can be so blind."

"I honest to God don't know what you are talking about; I made no passes at you then. I didn't say or do anything to upset you!"

She was silent for a few moments and then she released a deep pent-up breath.

"Maybe that's the problem." Talking riddles.

"What are you saying? That I should have made a pass? Christ, I had no idea that you had any feelings for me at all. I thought you were happily married, that we just got on as friends that we could have talked to one another until the cows came home."

"Yeah, the bullshit, that brings the cow's home. You said that that night in Bahrain" She was smiling now, an ironic smile.

"And why are you so reluctant now?"

"Things have changed my marriage is on the rocks. Oh I could give you a litany of things that have changed. Basically I'm afraid of an affair with you. I'm afraid that you may be getting into this for the short haul, the quick fling. I don't need that right now, not with you." She looked him dead in the eye.

"Tina, I don't know whether I just want an affair with you or spend the rest of my life with you. I can't make a rush decision. All I know is that I like you company, I can talk to you, with you. I've always admired you as a friend, as a woman, boy what a woman. I wanted to be close to you that was all that mattered. I never thought of making a pass in Bahrain because I never wanted to do anything to upset the friendship. But seeing you these last few days, especially today, the way you coped with the agro, the danger, Jesus I was so pissed when that guy hit you. I felt responsible. I was here to protect you and I let you down. I just felt so bad about that."

"You didn't let me down, far from it. You were there when I needed you, and God I was so glad to see you outside the bank.

You have no idea how I feel for you, but I'm afraid of how you see me. I do not want a fling. I want something more solid, I want a relationship with you. There, I've said it."

"Whoa, that's good for me. You don't know just how much I want that. I just never thought that you would want me."

She came into his arms again and their lips met. He held his breath, he wasn't sure that he really was feeling the way he felt, how could this be? The first kiss was like nothing he had ever experienced before. Oh, he had kissed dozens of women, but he never held the kiss in any great importance in the scheme of things. The kiss was something that women expected, perhaps they got high on that, but he was far more basic in his desires. He wanted to play with their bodies, the kiss was merely a formality he had to go through. But this woman was different, she had the sensuality of Munroe, Jamie Lee Curtis and Bessinger all rolled into one beautifully sensual mouth. All thoughts of where he was, gone. In each others arms, the passion was high, dangerously high. His hands began to roam. Her back was curved and taut, her bottom perfect mounds of sensual flesh. His hands were now on her bottom, his ran his fingers into the valley. She moaned her breath short and sharp, breathing through her nose now as the kiss was long. Tongues searching probing deeper, beyond deep, almost to the extent of pain at the base of the tongue.

His hand now below the valley, moving further forward reaching for the softest tissue, even through the jeans she wore, he could feel the moisture of her. He suddenly grabbed her there with strength and lifted her clean of her feet. She broke the kiss and screamed with pleasure. Her head was now beside his ear, her breath short and rapid, he could feel the warmth of her breath in his ear, it felt good, and it drove him crazy.

Tina moved back off him, still in the air and pulled at his shirt buttons, some opened, some popped, and she didn't care. He pulled his free hand out of the sleeve, then holding her lower body against his belly, he changed hands and pulled the other hand free. The shirt fell to the floor. She reached for his belt, he had to break the hold and let her onto the ground. Quickly now, breath short and sharp, hearts pumping, she released his belt. He pulled his trousers off kicked them away, he turned to her blouse ripping the buttons almost together. Tina leaned back, his arms around her waist and she pulled the blouse up over her head. His hands groped at the bra, the hasp clip no match for his impatience, he pulled the bra forward. Tina leaned back again and pulled her arms free of the bra. Dillon flung it away over his shoulder. She giggled, a girl again, like the first time, nervous, petrified, yet abandoned his lips now were at her nipples, the left one first then the right. They were already hard, now they rose to an unbelievable height.

Now his lips and tongue explored lower down past her belly button. His hands reaching up thrusting between her legs, hurting her and driving her crazy with joy and ecstasy. Now his hands reached for her jeans unfastening, tugging, and pulling them down.

"I want you." she gasped, he moved back up slipping his pants off.

His hand went to her panties, they were light silk, no resistance they were torn off with a quick tug. She was naked, high and ready for love, she gave herself to him.

Afterwards they stood there in silence except for their rapid breathing. He stood there leaning against a pleasantly cool wall, her legs around his waist, he was still inside her, she moaned as the hardness began to recede, she wanted him to stay there forever.

She had just had the best sex ever, she had peaked three times, and she wanted to savour the moment. He had come like a giant seemingly caught in a trap, he roared and surged thrusting deeper and deeper inside her, it was beautiful, the feeling of his ecstasy released.

She closed her eyes again as he kissed her ear lobe his tongue going into her ear hole. She moaned again. It was not possible, she couldn't come again.

Later they dressed themselves in silence, neither had any concept of what time had passed. Dillon watched her dress.

"I've got to tell you, Tina that was undoubtedly the best ever."

She didn't reply, instead just leaned over, kissing him gently on the cheek. He examined her face and smiled.

"Okay then, let's go explore this passage." she said.

"I thought I already done that." he replied a smirk on his face.

"Come on, dick."

"Oh you do say the nicest things." He followed her, the torch on her ass, he just couldn't help looking at it, and it was probably the best ass he had ever seen. From the shadow cast by the torch behind her she knew what he was looking at, so she wiggled it, just a little bit. She heard him groan, an animal groan.

They reached the corner of the passage just as it was in Kowloon. It was just as tight to get around, she led the way. He followed saying that this was as tight as she was.

"Let's put the sex drive in neutral for a moment. Let's get done what we have to do." she said.

"There's only one thing here that I want to do." Dillon replied.

"Please, Scotty, let's just get this checked out and get out of here. We can go back to the hotel and fuck like rabbits then if you want."

That animal growl again and he smiled at her like a spoilt child, then he got serious and nodded.

"I'd like that."

Again she turned and made her way up the dark passage. It was just as Kowloon, the damp steps, not worn, very unused. They ascended what seemed like ten feet and then the passage levelled out but only for a very short space. Now the incline was quiet slight, the floor of the passage slippery. As they went forward, the floor rose so much that they had to stoop to save their heads from the ceiling.

Finally when she could see the dim light ahead that obviously came from the slit in the wall overlooking the foyer of the bank below, she had to drop to her knees as the floor had risen so much. Ahead was the tiny alcove where she had found the body in the other bank but now the space between the ceiling and the floor was so small that they had to crawl on their bellies.

"This is different from the bank over in Kowloon. I could walk all the way to the alcove. I can't understand this."

"This bank is much older."

"And colder. Jesus the floor is freezing!"

He had noticed that too. It was strange, the walls were cool but the floor was very cold. In a way it was a relief, for it helped reduce the temperature in the passage.

"I might be able to make it to the alcove but I doubt if you will." Tina said stating the obvious.

"Okay but be careful. If there are any more bodies, just ask him to hold on until I lose some weight."

"Just be careful where you lose it." she replied, unable to turn to see the look on his face.

She crawled forward, inching her body like a snake knowing that she was ruining her clothes, but the blouse was ruined anyway. Tina eased her head cautiously into the alcove. There was by now, less then 15 inches of space from the floor and ceiling, but beyond the narrowness of the alcove entrance the floor dropped away sharply to the level that she would have expected it to be. She would be able to stand up once she got through. Tina immediately turned her head to the left; the same type of cupboard as she found in Kowloon was here also. She couldn't face finding another body; the woman backed away from the small opening.

"Move back, I'm coming back." she whispered to Dillon.

"What did you see?" He moved back down the passage.

"What, what?"

"It's Okay, I didn't see anything. It's just that the same cupboard is there, the same as the one I found the body in over on Kowloon, I'm scared of opening it, Scotty."

He reached out his hand turning the torch away from her face so that she could see his hand, she took it and squeezed.

"Can I make it through?" he asked patiently.

"No way, I can barely make it. The floor drops away, I'll have to go all the way through and stand up on the floor before I can open the door. That's what scares me, I'll be trapped. I won't be able to get away quickly if there is anything nasty there."

"Come on, there can't be another body. Jesus, are you sure I can't get through? Let me try."

"Scotty, you won't make it, not a chance. I can barely get my head through, let alone the rest of me."

"Well I'm not losing any part of you. It's not worth it, let's get out of here."

"But the deeds, they're too important. I've gotta make it, I must." she said resolutely beginning to turn.

"Tina, wait, I feel so bloody helpless and you have no idea what this is doing to me. Most times in my life it has being an advantage being big, now it's a disadvantage, I want to rip up this bloody floor and crawl in there instead of letting you go in there alone."

"Come on you're going to be right there behind me, right? Ready to pull me out." She leaned over and kissed him then she turned and crawled back up towards the small opening.

Tina was not really afraid of what she might discover; it was more the potential fright that scared her. It's like being at the Hitchcock movies, you just know you're going to get the shit scared out of you. Still it was these few minutes alone in which she had to crawl into that confined space and squeeze through the small opening, then drop to the floor four feet below, and then open that bloody door. What lay beyond that door? Was there another skeleton? Or were the deeds hidden there, the deeds to the greatest riches of all time, the ownership of the lands of The New Territories?

"Come on, there's buried treasures in there." she whispered to herself finding courage.

Tina was at the opening, she put her head through then brought up her left arm, it was difficult, but she managed it. Dillon's new girlfriend was going to see if she could open the door without having to go all the way through. The woman recalled that from the Kowloon bank, the door just had an opening the size of the palm of her hand into which she had inserted her fingers to pull open the door. This one was the same, she could barely reach it. Tina got a fingertip to it and squirming her finger, she managed to establish a hold on the door. She pulled, but her force was directing the pressure in the wrong direction, towards her. Tina needed to pull the door straight out at right angles to her present position. There was just no way that she could do it from out here. Bolger felt Dillon's reassuring touch on her feet.

"Okay, I'm going in, cover me." She mimicked the words of all the great cowboys.

"As the dick said to the condom." Tina heard Dillon say. Bolger started laughing and in her fit of laughter, she pulled herself in and collapsed onto the floor below.

Tina was still giggling when she opened the door. Looking into the recess she saw no 'body'. Now she erupted in laughter, so much so that she almost cried, collapsing onto the floor laughing.

"What is it?" Dillon asked his head just visible through the opening.

"Boxes!" she spluttered out.

Dillon couldn't see as the door was blocking his view.

"The safety deposit box, G300?"

"Yes, and more, there are four, five, six, six bloody boxes!"

Tina reached in calming herself and examined the boxes. There it was box number 300.

She pulled it out, her laughing subsiding. Now Tina handed it up to Dillon, it was heavy but the woman could handle it. Dillon moved back and grabbed the box and moved down the passage until such time as he could pass the box behind him, then he went back up to help Tina. She had pulled the other boxes out and left them on the floor and then closed the door.

"Come on, give me your hand. Let's get outta here."

"Okay, Okay, here take these boxes." She passed up the next one, it was even heavier.

"Oh fuck the rest of them, let's get going." Dillon was impatient to open the box marked 300.

"No I'm not leaving here until we get all these. I'm never coming back here again."

Finally he moved the last box past his side and scurried back up to the opening one last time.

Tina was standing there at the opening, the torch shining up at her face. She was radiant.

"Beam me up, Scotty." she said giggling.

He pulled her up through the opening; her blouse was totally destroyed. By now more black than white. They were head to head laying on their bellies in the dark passage.

"Well Missy, I guess this is it, the moment we have being waiting for."

"What, what?"

"Take the money or open the box?"

"Let's open the box."

"Good decision, Missy"

Laying on his back, he kicked the boxes down the passage behind him until he could turn and look at the boxes. With her leaning on his shoulder, they examined the box. It was not like the modern boxes, where two keys are used to open the outer door and the box is then removed and the box itself opened by the owner. This more primitive type is locked using the key held by the owner. The bank just hands over the box to the owner. So Tina and Dillon couldn't open the box.

"Okay let's get out of here and open the box."

Tina slipped, losing her balance, grabbing onto Dillon for support. He was in the act of turning and lost his balance and slipped on the slippery surface and landed with a thump on his ass. Tina survived the support of Dillon, giving her time to balance herself and now she stood there looking down at him, worried at first then laughing at his disposition.

"I guess that, that is the third time today that you've fallen for me"

"I guess so." He rolled over onto his stomach to raise himself; the torch was just inches from his face, shining into him.

"What the fuck?" Dillon was looking at the 'floor' of the passage, the surface was reflecting the light of the torch, yet it was not wet. He had decided early on from the stone steps further down that this passage was not used too often. How could there be a shine off the floor that was neither damp nor worn smooth?

"What's wrong? Are you hurt?" Tina asked. The surface intrigued him, it was very cold, it was made up of a layer of smooth bricks, or so it seemed. Dillon rose carefully, now shining the torch more closely. The 'bricks' were perfectly formed, not with a coarse concrete surface but with a smooth shiny metallic surface. Shiny, he looked again, it was only shiny where his shoe had slipped, and the rest was a dull grey colour. Looking more closely, he saw scratches where the boxes had scraped the surface. The scratches revealed bright streaks of shiny straw colour.

The hair stood on the back of his head, what he was looking at was metallic brick, ingots, camouflaged to look like an ordinary stone floor surface. He used his fingers to find a crevice between the 'bricks' ingots. Desperately now he found a gap in by the wall and worked the ingot loose. He held it up to the light and looked at the underside. A stamped impression confirmed it; the floor was covered in gold ingots.

Dillon stood back now and moved down the passage, he didn't even notice that he hit his head on the ceiling. Tina was flabbergasted, unable to say the words reaching for the ingot and examining it. But how many were there?

They backed further down the passage the floor falling away all the time. Finally they reached the spot where the inclined floor began, they both stood up. Dillon and Tina shone the torches back up the passage and realised that the rise in the floor was because the ingots were stacked in such a way that with each row, the depth of ingots increased. Each row was stacked another ingot higher. At the furthest end near the cupboard, Dillon estimated that the ingots must have been stacked 20 high. There were hundreds of ingots, a thousand or more.

"Jesus, there is a fortune in gold here." Dillon whispered hoarsely. Tina followed his gaze now as they looked back up the passage towards the front of the bank.

"That's why the floor rose up to make the passage so low. Christ there must by over $100 million worth of gold here!" she gasped.

"And whose is it? How did it get here?" Dillon said.

"And who knows its here?" they both said simultaneously.

Chapter Twenty Five

Jeff hadn't returned to his office when they finally emerged. Olli was frantic.

"What took so long? I heard some funny noises after you went in. What happened?"

They exchanged lover's glances, content that their affair was the single most important thing in the world, to them. Consequences were of no importance, there was no future, only the present beautiful sensation of real attraction.

"I encountered a rat." Tina explained. Dillon smiled, now everything had a double meaning, so now he was a rat? That was cool.

"Is that the box?" Olli accepted the explanation without question, but he did feel that Dillon had got his way.

Now in the light for the first time, they all had a chance to look at the box. After wiping away the dust a gleaming polished mahogany rectangular box was revealed. It was protected at each corner by steel corner brackets and a steel reinforced strip protected the lock area.

"Oh yeah, well at least we hope so."

"So let's open it. Here, the letter opener." Olli took the box to the desk and using the letter opener, began to work on the box.

"Hold on a minute," Dillon commanded. "Let's think about this. If we open the box, how do we verify that it is genuine afterwards?"

"What do you mean?"

"If this document is as important as we think it is and has the implications that we feel it will, then its authenticity is bound to be called into question. No I think that we could use this document for a greater purpose."

Tina was staring silently at Dillon, a puzzled expression on her face.

"What are you getting at?" Olli asked.

"We have evidence that the document exists, we have the safety deposit box in which the document was originally deposited nearly 90 years ago. Suppose, just suppose that this document was to have an effect on the future of Hong Kong, then I think that this box should be opened in a blaze of publicity to ensure that the authenticity of it was not called into doubt."

They were silent for a moment and then Tina said, "You know, it could be turned into the publicity stunt of the decade. Remember the media hype about the opening of the chamber that was supposed to hold the treasures of Al Capone, or Legs Diamond or whoever it was? Do you remember that?"

"Yes, it got national, hell international coverage. This is like the finding of Tutankhamen's Tomb. Shit, publicity stunt of the decade? More like the stunt of the century!"

Olli was warming to the idea.

Just then the door opened, they all turned and lost in their own thoughts, they had forgotten about being in Jeff's office. He stopped just inside the door and stared at the three people looking back at him like three kids caught with their hands in the cookie jar.

'What's going on? What happened to you?" He was looking at Tina's clothes, she was covered in dirt and Dillon's clothes were destroyed too.

"We've being tunnelling, so to speak." Dillon replied. Jeff's eyes fell on the box on his desk; he pointed at it.

"What's that?" Jeff asked.

"G300." Dillon replied flatly.

"Jesus, where did you find it?"

Dillon explained while Jeff crossed to the desk and lifted up the box cautiously, examining it carefully as if it were some valuable, delicate piece of China.

"Secret passage?"

Again Dillon explained how Tina found the passage by accident in Kowloon and concluded that there might be a similar passage in this bank.

"That's fine, that's fine." Jeff held up his hand when Dillon went on to explain how they had planned to tell him but their curiosity had taken over and they found themselves in the passage without even thinking.

"Have you opened it? Are the deeds in here?"

"No, and don't know." Dillon answered both questions.

"Well let's get it opened!" Jeff snapped.

"Wait a minute, there is something we should consider," Dillon went on to set out their plan for opening the box in public. "Imagine the amount of publicity it would get for your bank?" Dillon concluded.

"But what if the deeds are not in the box after the build up of expectations? We would look foolish, it would be a great loss of face and face is everything in Hong Kong." Jeff said.

"Imagine what would happen to the shares in the mean time." Dillon was thinking of the shares he had bought this morning.

"But what would happen to them if the deeds were not in the box?" Jeff replied.

"It's worth the risk, the short term gain for the bank would be enormous - shares would go through the roof, confidence would soar, land prices would rise, property too. If we held off the opening of the box for say a month, just imagine what would happen? You yourself said that the Hong Kong entrepreneur loves to gamble." Dillon watched him closely, he was thinking. Jeff was silent for a moment, obviously weighing up the pros and cons in his mind of going public with the box.

"I'm going to have to think this over, there are implications, big ones. I'll explain it to you later. Why don't you come over for dinner tonight?"

Dillon looked straight back at him slightly puzzled but figuring that there was reason for the dinner offer, but then was he going to go without Tina? After all, it was her investigation that had uncovered the box.

"Okay, I'll talk to you later about that. But there is something else that you should know,"

Dillon looked at Tina and said. "Tell him what else you found over on Kowloon."

"I found a skeleton in the secret passage, from the remains of newspapers that I found there and from the clothes on the body, I suspect that the guy was placed there around 1941." Tina removed the newspaper clipping from the back pocket of her jeans and handed it to Dillon. "The date is clear enough and the article is on the war and the invasion of the Korean Peninsula by the Japanese."

"Oh my God," Jeff replied, suddenly looking weak and in need of a chair to sit on. "Oh my God." he muttered again.

"Do you know something about this?" Dillon was suspicious now, he had assumed that Jeff knew nothing of the secret passage or he would have searched there for the box, but now the news of the skeleton seemed to suggest otherwise.

"Not really, it's just that many years ago, I remember going through fathers papers after he died and I came across newspaper cuttings, just two. I remember reading the cuttings at the time with curiosity, not just the story, but also why my father should keep these two cuttings." He held out his hand for the piece of paper, Dillon handed it across the desk. "Yes, that is one of them, or at least the same copy, November '41. I have the other one in one of father's diaries from '41. This one spoke of the invasion of the Korean peninsula and the threat to Hong Kong. It was only a matter of days before Hong Kong was to fall. The other piece was published the morning that the Japanese invaded. The first piece chronicles the exodus from Hong Kong of some of the bigger businessmen in the face of the invasion force coming down through China. The local reaction was rather hostile to those people who were talking of fleeing Hong Kong. It was feared that much money would flow as well, this would effect everyone. No one likes to see money flow out of the Colony, even in the face of the Japanese. I recall that he had made a note on the bottom of the article to the effect, 'Need to guarantee the funds will be safe.' I thought about the newspaper cuttings many years later while watching a TV programme on the Japanese invasion of China. It was kind of ironic, because the program only made a passing reference to the invasion of Hong Kong; it was made by the BBC and concentrated more on the Chinese angle than on how Hong Kong was effected. I thought at the time that they mustn't have had archive film on the attack and occupation of the Island. But the footage was important to the world because the West wanted to see how the Chinese would react. As it was, the Japanese came so fast the Chinese didn't have time to react. I had meant to read my father's diary entries for those years to see how he handled it."

"Where are those diaries?" Dillon's question was blunt, more than he intended, but his excitement was mounting. Could there be a connection with the bullion and the occupation of Hong Kong? And where did the skeleton fit in? Was the bullion in this branch linked to the skeleton in Kowloon?

"Well, here in the office. Why?"

"It could answer a number of questions."

"What sort of questions?" Jeff was more than a little puzzled. "You hardly think that my father would have mentioned the skeleton in his diaries, let alone kill the poor bastard?" The anger was tangible, the question cutting into Dillon.

"Well I doubt that he would have mentioned the skeleton in his diaries and I doubt that he would have killed the guy. No, that's not what I'm on about. There's something else you should know."

"There's something else?" he enquired.

"Yes, but first, I really do feel that we should check your father's diary to see if there is any hint and I say that carefully, because I realise that your father may not have been aware that the body was placed there. However, it must be pointed out that your father must have been aware that the passages existed. It is also highly possibly that someone else knew of their existence, granted, but that person must have worked for your father."

"Dillon, I feel that I may begin to dislike you. I understand that the discovery of this body is a shock and a complication to everyone, but to start throwing accusations around 40 years after the event is a little much. Now you must admit that."

"This need not go beyond this room. It can be solved right here, but a body has been found. We must be sure that your father's involvement or lack of involvement is resolved once and for all beyond any reasonable doubt."

"Are you saying that this will be reported?" Jeff was aghast. "You're not suggesting that we ignore the presence of the body in Kowloon?"

"What's it going to prove?"

"That we have nothing to hide, a crime, presumably a crime has been committed. It may not be, it may be suicide, we don't know. But nevertheless, there is an investigation needed."

"I realise that this needs to be solved, of course, yes, but an investigation? Jesus, what are the papers going to say?"

"Fuck the papers, let's get this thing sorted out," Dillon was growing impatient. "Let's look at the diaries."

"Okay, Okay, mind the profanities, there's a lady present."

"I'm aware of that" He glanced at Tina, she just shrugged her shoulders. Jeff crossed to the shelves and after a brief search, found the diary, a bank diary from '41.

"Let's have a look." Dillon held out his hand. The handwriting was clear, concise and very much to the point. The diary was a personal record of appointments and events for the calendar year '41. Towards the middle of the year the appointments were heavy and there were several references to the threat of war with Japan and the effect it was having on business confidence in the Colony. Several appointment entries ended with the comment, 'Another depositor closes account.' There were also many references to newspaper reports about the level of the British forces in the Garrison in Hong Kong. Tony Bordes it would appear was not in favour of careless comment about the troop levels in Hong Kong as he felt it encouraged the Japanese to consider the taking of Hong Kong as a mere formality. As Dillon read through the entries approaching the end of the year, a few names appeared several times. He glanced back a few pages at one stage just to be sure, but there were three names reoccurring on a very regular basis, sometimes twice or even three times a week as he checked the month of October '41. He found at one stage that two of the men had appointments on three consecutive days, the names - Chandlers and Wilson.

There were no notes or entries made other then the actual name entry and the time.

"Jeff, could you check to see if these two men had accounts with the bank in 1941?"

He looked at the names and nodded. "Okay, it will take a little while," He reached for the phone and dialled an internal number. "Can you check the customer deposit accounts books for '41 for reference to a Mister Chandlers and a Mister D Wilson? Yes, Okay, if you find any reference bring me in the book."

"What are you expecting?"

"Well these two guys had several appointments with your father towards the end of the year. Well up to November anyhow; these appointments became more and more frequent at a time when many depositors were moving money out of Hong Kong. I suspect, from the amount of appointment's your father gave these men that they were big depositors."

"What's this got to do with the skeleton?"

"I don't know, maybe nothing, but just the sheer number of meetings is curious." Dillon went back to the diary. The month of November was very busy for another reason. Tony Bordes noted that all the new safety deposit boxes installed the previous year were now let out as people concerned for the safety of their valuables deposited them as the Japanese approached. Towards the end of November, the frequent meetings abruptly stopped. The third name that of one James Clavell continued to have regular weekly meetings with Tony Bordes, then on December 10th 1941, just a few days after the Japanese bombed Pearl Harbour, Tony Bordes entered a new name in his appointment diary.

"Foster Dulles."

"What? Jeff snapped angrily and snatched the diary. He read the name with shaking hands.

"Maylay's father?" Tina asked.

"Probably. My God, what the hell is going on here?" Jeff was obviously totally taken by surprise.

"I think that there is something you should know, we found something else in the passage here."

"What? Not more bodies?"

"No, gold bullion, probably worth $100 million."

"Oh, this is too much. Are you sure?"

"Positive."

"This is not possible, this can't be happening."

"I'm afraid it is happening, happened. I cannot even begin to speculate how it got there, but the reality is that it is there. Now we need to know how it got there and who it belongs to. Obviously all this happened before your time but someone left you a very messy legacy to sort out. Not only do we have a situation where the bank holds a deed as security that is not registered as an asset, but we also now have a massive amount of money in gold bullion that is not listed. The skeleton is the least of our problems."

"There's something else we should think about." Tina said.

"Oh no, not more."

"I have just been thinking. The box, 300, that had to be placed there prior to the gold bullion being stored there, for I could not imagine how anyone would have been able to get into that alcove after the bullion was left there."

"So?"

"Well the same person must have known about the passage, the person who stored the box must have stored the bullion and in doing so must have known what was in the box."

"No, my father wrote in his diaries that he hid the boxes that remained unclaimed in the old store in 1940-" Jeff explained what he had learned this morning about the boxes left over after the new system was introduced.

"So your father must have stored the boxes there in the alcove at the end of the passage?"

"Possibly, he referred to the storage place for the boxes as 'the Old Store'. I can't be sure one way or the other, but he did not know what was in the box. He had no idea. What does it matter?"

"If he didn't know, fair enough, but he must have known about the gold bullion. He obviously knew about the passage, he must have known about the bullion."

"I don't know the answer to that."

There was a knock at the door, Kay entered carrying a ledger. "Those two names you gave me to check on did have accounts with us back in '41, but they closed the accounts in November."

"Thanks Kay." Jeff replied absentmindedly, taking the book and examining the records.

"What happened to you?" Kay asked Tina looking at her dirty blouse.

"I got caught in a sewer, I must look a mess?"

"You sure do, I've got a change of clothes in my office if you would like to clean up?"

"I doubt if I will start a new trend with this outfit, I'll wash." They left together Kay asking what was going on.

"Jesus, they had over $20 million each on account and they just closed the accounts down on the same day. That's weird," Jeff said to nobody in particular.

"Not if they were worried about the Japanese invasion. It would make a lot of sense, it would be interesting to see where these guys went."

"We could check City Hall, there's bound to be a record. If they left the Colony it would have being registered with Emigration, there would be passport records."

"I've got a friend down at City Hall I can have him check."

"Of course, they might not have left the Colony at all. They may just have converted their money into securities or bonds and hid them." Jeff suggested.

"Or gold bullion?" Dillon said.

"And hid it here in the bank? But then they would have reclaimed it after the war."

"If they survived the war. Were there many people killed here during the war?"

"Yes, the Allies actually bombed Hong Kong after the Japanese occupation."

"The two could have been killed during the war and the money was forgotten about."

"Except that your father would have known about it."

"He died during the war, 1944 to be exact."

"Then it would all make sense. He hid the money for them in the safest place he knew and all three of them died during the war, perfect explanation. How about Foster Dulles, did he have an account with the AAB?"

Jeff turned his attention back to the ledger and examined the pages.

"You know this would add up. There's so much gold hidden in there, they are afraid to tell anyone, not even their families. During the war they go about their normal business, safe in the knowledge that even if the Japanese come after them, their money is safe. You know the Japs probably had informers and the names of the wealthy and influential would be gathered and handed over to the Japanese. I'm fairly certain that most people would have had time to make arrangements for the protection of their valuables, and these two guys came up with some kind of arrangement with Tony Bordes to stash the bullion-."

"Foster Dulles didn't appear to have an account with us," Jeff said after having checked the book.

"With his family connections I'm not surprised"

"This is the same Foster Dulles that is somehow related to Jason Kimberley?" Olli asked.

"From what I know of them, Foster Dulles came to Hong Kong in the '20s. He was an Earl or something, He married Jason Kimberley's daughter, Aggy. Their son, John Dulles, must be Maylay's father."

"The Kim's certainly have had some encounters with this bank," Olli remarked. Jeff was taken aback by the comment, and he starred at Olli.

"What's the problem?"

"It's just strange you should say that. I had a visit from Jason Kim this morning," Jeff said thoughtfully. Dillon stared at Olli; this was getting crazier by the hour.

"What did he want?" Dillon asked.

"He said he wanted to open an account here, but I felt that he was more interested in our old safety deposit boxes."

"Everyone seems interested right now. So what do we do about this box here, open it?" Olli suggested.

"Yes, it's strange." Jeff said thoughtfully, now he began thinking of his other visitor of this morning.

"I can see the smoke," Dillon said looking at Jeff.

"Smoke?"

"Coming out your ears, from the wheels turning," Dillon explained.

"No, sorry, I was just thinking about another man that came to me this morning. Here." He withdrew the letter that Diver Ho had brought to him. Dillon read the letter with Olli looking over his shoulder.

"Bit of a bloody coincidence this showing up now after we find the box."

"I only got it a few hours ago. It put me thinking obviously, but it might explain why Jason Kim showed up here this morning."

"You reckon that the guy showed the letter to Kim?"

"Why else would he come here talking about safety deposit boxes?" Jeff explained the Diver story.

"Jesus, there must be something in the stars or something that has got all this going at the one time."

"It's called Joss, destiny."

"What about this guy, James Clavell? Did he have an account here?"

"There's no reference to him in the deposit account book. I'll have Kay check during the afternoon."

"So what about the box. Do we open it or not?" Olli repeated, his patience coming to an end.

"No, I'm inclined to agree with Dillon. I think we should sit on this overnight at least. We can discuss it over dinner tonight." This last comment Jeff directed at Dillon indicating that only he was coming to dinner. Dillon glanced at Olli.

"Sorry I can't make it, I've got a date." Olli said, as ever the gentleman.

"Some other time perhaps?" Jeff was relived that they had gotten around the problem without having to confront it.

"I think it's time I met this Jason Kim." Dillon said.

After they left the office, Jeff returned his father's diary, well actually, his appointment diary. This was the official bank diary, not his personal diary. His father's personal diaries were comprehensive and a different matter altogether. His father was frenetic about matter being recorded for two reasons: one that a record should be maintained for future generations and two, that in the event of a dispute arising, he would have a record of what happened, rather than what people perceive to have happened.

From recollection, he remembered admiring the manner in which his father kept his records when on one occasion, he had reason to check on his father's diaries when a customer had quoted his father's promise made several years earlier to provide an unsecured loan which eventually fell into arrears. Jeff was left in the unfortunate position of seeking possession of a piece of property which the bank understood to be the collateral for the loan. The customer, a personal friend of the family, quoted chapter and verse of the conversation with his father, Jeff referred to his father's diaries and he had recorded the guts of the conversation which clearly stated that not only had he reservations about the loan but that he wished to avoid using the man's family home as collateral and instead accepted the deeds to a property in Kowloon which would not realise the full value of the loan in the event of failure to repay. However, when the man ran into difficulty, he tried to sell the property in Kowloon and would have gotten away with it except for the need to retrieve the deeds from the bank. Jeff refused to release the deeds because he suspected that the man would use the money to pay off other debts and ignore the AAB debt as he was a family friend. Despite the threat of court action, Jeff stood fast and eventually the man had to rearrange his finances and sell other property that he owned to clear his debtors. Many years later when the man was back on his feet, he finally sold the Kowloon property after paying off his loan to AAB and realised a bit of a windfall as the property was then in the centre of a major office development proposal.

The whole episode pointed out the need to keep a diary and Jeff had to admit that his father's fanaticism for record keeping was not just a habit but a necessity. Jeff kept his own diaries ever since having clearly seen the benefit of his father's ones, but his was not as meticulous.

Looking now at his father's personal diaries for the period of the war, he wondered just what lay in those pages. Surely his father was not a murderer, he was almost afraid to open the diary. But then so much had happened in the last few days, the peace and tranquillity smashed as one revelation after another unfolded. Starting with the news that someone was following Bolger, missing Ledger pages, long forgotten loans, Maxwell's attack, George's blatant attack on himself, the news of Harry Chan's arrest, the discovery of, well everything - skeletons, missing safety deposit boxes, gold bullion, the deeds. Everything had gone crazy, so what more could be waiting in these pages? He opened the diary and flipped through the pages searching for a reference to any of the men's names.

In early 1941, it was clear to everyone in the region that the Japanese were intent on war. An Anglo Japanese agreement reached between the three nations of America, Britain and Japan in 1920, limited the amount of warships that each side could maintain. There were to be five each for America and Britain for every three Japanese ships which infuriated the Japanese and lulled the other two nations into a false sense of security. And security in Asia was not a government priority in Britain in the years leading up to the 1940's. A proposed naval base in Singapore took 17 years to complete as the government in Britain changed from Tory to Labour and back to Tory again. The Labour government sought a League of Nations approach to defence rather than individual nations maintaining large military forces to defend their interests. And Britain's interests at the time were very global, and thus difficult to defend. Australia and India as well as large tracts of South East Asia, were within the Empire and local Military Forces were expected to offer resistance to any invasion force until such time as relief forces could arrive from Britain. At the time of the Japanese move on Indo China, an Aircraft Carrier was dispatched to the region but ran aground. In any event, it would have taken 70 days for the warship to reach the region. It took the Japanese much less than that to not only invade China, but come down through the jungle that British intelligence had classified as impenetrable by an invasion force. The main base being Singapore was heavily fortified on the seaward side, but because of the perception by the British military that invasion from the mainland side was impossible there was no fortification to halt the Japanese. While it was widely known that an invasion was likely in both Hong Kong and Singapore, there was little that the British could do but to offer the show of force by providing local, Australian and Indian, military divisions for both Colonies. America had not yet entered the war, so Britain fought on alone against the military might of Germany and at that time was deeply concerned about protecting the British mainland. All of Europe had already been overrun by the German war machine.

So in mid '41, the British Colonies of Singapore and Hong Kong stood alone, vulnerable outposts of an Empire at war with a mighty foe. Singapore was Japan's main aim; knock out the British base there with its heavy fortification and all of South East Asia would fall. The Japanese could not ignore Hong Kong though, for there was always the danger of the retreating forces fortifying the garrison on the island Colony and becoming more difficult to dislodge at worst, but even more unpalatable was the threat of a counter-offensive. It was imperative then for the Japanese to take Hong Kong and Singapore simultaneously.

British intelligence on the Island, although limited, knew for some time that the Japanese had infiltrators in the Colony. Ordinary citizens mostly, but with the purpose of gathering information on the military forces. One such operator was a Mister Oyez who offered a photographic development service. This particular operator would gather information by carefully examining the entire photo's he developed for the ordinary citizens in Hong Kong. Many photos were of no possible use to his Japanese masters, but the occasional gem would emerge like accidental or intentional photographs of military installations. He came to the notice of military intelligence when one soldier referred his services to his superior saying that Mister Oyez offered a special discount for military personal. It was an extremely good deal; any soldier wanting photos developed got a 25% discount. Naturally the word got around and eventually the chief intelligence officer heard of it and became suspicious. That officer was James Clavell and he was a personal friend of Tony Bordes.

Bordes wrote of Clavell.

"At first I did not like Clavell, he seemed to me to be an arrogant, particularly nosy person. He trusted no one, but then as I became to understand the man I realised that it was his profession I did not like. The man himself became quite acceptable and I invited him for dinner one evening. He seemed to like the Colony immensely; the weather seemed to suit him, he tanned easily. And while not a ladies man, the ladies seemed to find his company very acceptable. I must admit that I was rather nervous of him being in company with Betsy, she seemed to like him also.

I discovered his deep distrust for the Asians and the Japanese, in particular. I sensed that it was more than an uninformed ignorance of the races that provoked his dislike for them. Over brandy, I soon realised that he had studied the Chinese and the Japanese culture and attitude first hand. Apparently, although he did not go into detail, he suffered at the hands of the Japanese during the war between Russia and Japan when as a military observer on a Russian warship which was sunk he was captured and tortured. He did not elaborate and I did not push him, but I learnt to like and trust the man. When the Japanese threat heightened in '41 and it became apparent that they were about to invade, he advised me to hide whatever valuables I had, and a number of associates followed suit.

At that time it was impossible to predict what the future would hold. Tony Bordes did his best to prepare his valued friends and customers for what was to come. Many foolhardy ones refused to accept that the Japanese would invade or that the British would not arrive in force to ward off the invasion. The AAB was a very small bank at the time with only a handful of decent accounts of over a $1 million, but the few good accounts were very good ones, mostly old money from a previous generation handed down as a legacy. Some of these men would not know how to start a business let alone run one but their money meant that they were protected from the nasty world of fighting for a living. Two such men were Richard Chandlers, and a Damian Wilson. Both men were in their mid-50s and sons of two very wealthy merchants who made their money a half century earlier in the Opium trade initially and later in silk and tin exporting. Chandlers was a bachelor, Wilson a widower without any heirs and neither needed the money as the income they earned from directorships on their companies, kept them more than comfortable. They had no daily involvement in the business but attended board meetings just so they knew what was going on. They spent their time playing golf, canasta and roulette either on the colony or in Macau. With that sort of wealth, they never had to worry about what tomorrow would bring, but with speculation about the imminent invasion, they got nervous. A tomorrow without the money was dreadful. They approached Tony Bordes and asked his advice. He, acting on Clavells intuition, advised the men to convert the money to gold and hide it. This seemed the best option, for paper money would probably become worthless as would stocks and bonds. And who knew how the war would go? Just look at Europe, that war was going on for nearly two years. No, gold was the answer, but where to get such an amount? After all with the war going on in Europe gold was in short supply as many wealthy people converted their wealth into gold so as to avoid the worthlessness of paper money in the event of the war going the wrong way. The British Pound would be no good if Germany won the war and imposed the Deutschemark as the legal currency. Likewise the American Dollar was dubious as it was almost certain that they would enter the war shortly.

Luckily for them they had ready-made contacts that they had never thought of using. Bordes had the trust of James Clavell who would know where to buy the gold, and they had the export company with ships travelling the globe to carry back the contraband gold. Buying large quantities of gold would be difficult at any time but at a time of war, it is particularly difficult, especially large quantities. Gold at the time was valued at $35 a Troy ounce but sold on the open market at $40 an ounce. The purchase of $40 million was a major undertaking. The main producer was South Africa so it was to there that the three men turned with the help and guidance of James Clavell.

Clavells contacts revealed the name of a mineral dealer with connections in South Africa who could supply the quantities needed. The contact was Foster Dulles.

All five men first met in late August '41 in a private room at the Mandarin. Bordes made this entry in his diary.

"I had heard of Dulles, of course, his father was a wealthy man, an Earl, one of the landed gentry from England whose health required that he move to a better climate. He established a small mineral exploration and importation company on his arrival in Hong Kong together with his father. Why he should have chosen this particular activity I know not, but he either had contacts in the field or knew something of mineral exploration himself. His main interest appeared to be Zinc initially but he is known to have interests in rare minerals in Australia and South Africa. I have heard that he spends upwards of one month in each of those countries each year. I reserved judgment on him at our first encounter as he appeared to be somewhat stand-offish. This may have something to do with his slightly annoying speech impediment which resulted in his statement being extremely drawn-out.

After some initial concern as to the timing of the imminent arrival of the Japs, James set our minds at ease by stating that it was felt that the Japs had encountered some supply problems on the mainland that slowed their advance. He stated that we should have at least until November. We then moved on to the main matter at hand, could Foster Dulles supply the required bullion? We first asked for his credentials. Dulles stated that he had been involved with mining in South Africa for some ten years and during that time, had not only mined for his own company but also acted as geologist for other prospecting companies both in and outside South Africa. During his periods there he had established a number of contacts in the gold mining industry. He expressed confidence that the contact, who did not wish his name to be used, that he had spoken to just last night, could indeed produce the gold at the right price. When pressed for that price, he confirmed that we could expect to purchase ex-works at £37.50. The gold would be in ingots of 28 Lbs each, un-stamped at 90% fine or 22 carat. The terminology was somewhat over our heads, we found it difficult to comprehend him especially when he had such difficulty with the words. For instance, it took him nearly 10 seconds to say the word "carat".

He explained that his contact used a method known as "chlorine extraction" in which a chlorine gas is passed through crude molten gold. The chlorine combines with the impurities and the compound rises to the top and is drained off. The gold only begins to react with the chlorine when most of the impurities are gone. However, the process does not remove all traces of silver or bronze, thus it is classified as 22 carat and is therefore not as expensive as full 1,000 fine 24 carat gold which is presently fetching $40 an ounce on the open market, even though the current bench mark price was just $35 an ounce. If they wished to there were several foundries here in Hong Kong that could further refine the gold to full 1,000 fine or 24 carat.

We accepted his reassurances that the gold was perfectly acceptable, however, he did go on to say that the gold would not be stamped, in other words, it was not genuine gold bullion. It could not be sold to a recognised gold bullion dealer for trading on to legitimate sources. It could, of course, be sold to jewellers and other users of gold. A bullion trader may purchase it if he had a client who was prepared to buy knowing that it was not bullion. While this did not seem to bother Chandler or Wilson, I was a little concerned and decided to carry out my own investigation.

We then discussed the amount of gold that we needed. I explained that we wished to convert $41 million into gold. Dulles did not seem to be taken aback by this and carried out his calculation. Based on his figures, I also carried out the calculation.

$41,000,000 divided by $37.5 (per ounce) = 1,093,333 ounces.

As there are 12 Troy ounces in a pound.

= 1,093,333 divided by 12 = 91,111 Lbs.

As there are 28 Lbs in an ingot.

= 91,111 divided by 28 = 3,254 ingots. Our figures concurred.

Dulles then asked about shipping arrangements. We quickly confirmed that we would arrange the shipment from the port designated in South Africa. At our own expense, of course.

He enquired about his commission for making the arrangement. Very much a man to establish his own recompense. It was a question I would have liked answered much earlier as I would then be in a position as to how much we could tell him about the amount of money involved. Chandler and I spoke of this in advance of the meeting, but Chandler was of the opinion that we should find out his credentials first. I bowed to his wishes and allowed Dulles prove his worth before we spoke of his commission. I felt that it was somewhat of a fait accompli now that he knew just what was involved. However, I did insist that we kept the shipping arrangements to ourselves, that way there should be no fear of a double cross. We would use one of Chandler's ships with one of the most trustworthy captains and crews. It was felt that by doing this we had complete responsibility for the bullion once it left South Africa. We agreed to the payment of $50,000 as compensation for services rendered after much debate. Payment was to be made in two parts: 50% on conformation of the agreement and 50% on conformation of the authenticity of the bullion upon arrival in Hong Kong.

The shipment date was discussed and it was agreed that a ship at present in the port of Colombo, Sri Lanka would sail immediately for Durban. Chandler had already checked the location of the nearest ship and established just how soon the ship could reach South Africa. The captain and crew would be flown to join the ship in Durban and the present crew flown back to Hong Kong. Sailing time to South Africa would be 14 days and the return journey to Hong Kong would take 26 days. Dulles confirmed that the bullion would be ready for shipment on September 14th; this meant that the ship would have to tie up for a few days. Allowing one day for loading that meant that the ship could put to sea on the 15th or 16th at the latest. That then put the arrival in Hong Kong port on October 10th. This gave us over five weeks to organise the storage of the bullion. We did not discuss this in the presence of Dulles, of course.

The subject then turned to the matter of payment for the shipment itself. Dulles at first said that 100% would have to be paid up front. I was personally against this as I felt that we were totally exposed to fraud on behalf of the contact in South Africa. He then said that it might be possible to convince the contact by paying 75% up front and the balance on loading in Durban. I suggested that the risk was still very much in our hands; we would not have the reassurance that one, the shipment was genuine and two, that the shipment would not be hi-jacked at sea by mercenary elements that might have discovered the nature of the shipment from contacts in South Africa. I stated that I feared loose tongues. Dulles got my message and tried to reassure us that the contact was dependable and was well trusted in the bullion business. I accepted his reassurance but maintained reservations. I insisted that if the contact was genuine, he would not have any hesitation in providing credit for a percentage of the shipment, considering that he was after all, dealing with a bank that could supply a letter of guarantee. Dulles conceded that his contact might consider part payment on foot of letter of undertaking from the bank.

Once I got this opening, I suggested a three stage payment; 33% with the conformation of order, 33% on loading and the balance on authentication in Hong Kong and a letter of guarantee to cover this. He considered this for some time and said that he would put it to his contact. He then queried the currency and payment details. I had been prepared for this and I felt that the American Dollar was the only currency that was presently acceptable world-wide and I said as much. He seemed satisfied with that and I went on to say that we should fly to South Africa with the first stage payment and that the captain, who was to return the ship to Hong Kong, would provide the second stage payment. I had given the matter some thought and I felt that we could test the genuine nature of the relationship between Dulles's and his contact by the suggested method of the final payment. I will always remember the look on Dulles face when I said, "And the final payment will be hand delivered to you on authentication here in Hong Kong." At first, he appeared to grin, a nervous grin, and then he frowned as the implication sank in, and finally he laughed and nodded his head. I knew then that we could trust Dulles for he must have the confidence of his contact in South Africa. If he did not, the contact would not allow him to be the final collector. So I felt more confident that Dulles knew his contact well and had a good working relationship with the man otherwise he would not even consider putting the proposition to him. He also showed that he had the confidence of his contact. And on the other side of the equation, his presence at the final payment assured us that the shipment was indeed genuine, for were it not, then Dulles's life would be in danger, for if it turned out that the gold was not as represented, then we would be three very angry men and were likely to express our anger towards the most accessible person in the deal, Dulles.

There were some final details to be organised, like covering the transportation costs from the mine to the port, the port costs, exportation documentation and so on. It was at this point that Wilson queried the labelling of the crates and the description on the export documentation. Dulles had considered this and offered a viable proposition. Zinc was sometimes shipped in the form of ingots in similar crates. Such shipments were not unusual from the port of Durban. He shunned the suggestion of taking a port official into confidence, it was involving unnecessary people and increasing the risk of loose talk. He was confident enough in the suggested method, explaining that the port of Durban was extremely busy due to mineral exportation increased greatly due to the war in Europe. The volume of traffic had increased by over 300% during the last 18 months as the demand for metals and other commodities needed to build the planes, tanks and ships that were being lost at such a rate in the war that all mines were working round the clock. In such a hectic pace of movement of ships, one load would not be important; no one would notice one more ship. Loading would not take long so would not attract attention. There would be 102 crates with 32 ingots in each crate. Because of the weight, there could only be eight crates per pallet. He suggested pallets as it was the fastest way of loading and unloading. The shipment would come by train from the mine direct to the dockside. One carriage would be reserved for the gold. The carriage would be detached from the train and parked by the ship at dockside. The ships hoist could then lift the pallets directly off the flat top carriage and into the hold of the ship. He advised that the crates would not be man-handled as this would be time consuming and might attract attention as it would involve the use of two men to carry each crate.

I must say that while I had reservations about Dulles initially, I did have to admire the thoroughness to detail that he showed. I agreed with everything that he suggested and I intended to take some precautions of my own. I would be reluctant to allow the ship put to sea without some protection and to this end, I had already made some suggestions to Chandlers regarding having arms on board. But more of that later. We were satisfied with Dulles's arrangements and subject to conformation from his contact regarding the stage payment, we entered into a verbal undertaking for the purchase of the gold bullion. He was to talk with his contact and come back to us just as soon as he could."

"I later met with James and discussed what Dulles was suggesting. He too seemed impressed by the detail, but was nonetheless concerned about the lack of direct contact with the man in South Africa. If James had a name, he could have him checked out. The man could be a thief for all we knew, and that would put us in receipt of stolen property. Then James said something that I would never suggest. I would not manipulate him in this way. But he suggested it. He volunteered to use his contacts in the central telephone exchange to discover the name of the person that Dulles would phone. The call had to be made person to person, and the exchange name in South Africa would have to be given. This way, James would find out who the person was and would have him checked out. I was naturally very grateful to him and assured him that if there was anything he ever needed, he only had to ask.

Two days later Dulles phoned me to say that his man was prepared to accept stage payment backed by the letter of guarantee for the balance but that the payment method would be 50% up front and two payments at the intervals suggested of 25% each, and that the 50% payment was to be hand delivered to him in Durban by the principle person, presumably me, he suggested. While the thought of visiting South Africa filled me with joy, the reality of two days flying did not. However, there was the need to satisfy my two customers and if I did not provide the service, then there were others out there who would. I did not have to get the approval of the other two, this was the position that we would have accepted at the first meeting, but we felt that we should state our position in our favour and then retract from it to what we really knew was best for us. I told Dulles that I had been authorised to accept the conditions and to proceed with the transaction. I now had to prepare the letter of guarantee and the money for delivery. I asked Dulles when the money should be delivered, or more importantly when would the gold be ready. He asked me to arrange the flight for as soon as possible and let him know when I would be in Durban. He suggested a flight via Bombay and then direct to Durban. I would always be in British Territory he reminded me. I hadn't thought of that I must admit. He would arrange for his contact to meet me at the Gateway Hotel and he would then arrange to show him the gold field and refinery. This was more than I expected and was pleased that there would be more than just a flight in and out interrupted by a handshake in a dark alley and the parting with a large amount of money.

I had already made arrangements for the purchase of American Dollars. Once I had it all, I would then draw down four cashier checks for US$5 million each from four different banks. The reason for this was that I do not want to draw too much attention to the movement of large amounts of money. The Colonial office would be asking questions if they were to discover that $20 million was suddenly leaving the Colony, even if only for a short while.

James came to visit the day after the phone call from Dulles and told me that he had traced Dulles's contact in Durban. The man was a Jew called Cohen; this was not unexpected, for the Jews were very involved in the precious mineral trade. He was having the man checked out by the South African authorities. I mentioned the matter of the movement of such a large amount of money out of the Colony. All he replied was that the Colonial Office had its own problems and while the official position was that, it was not to be condoned. There was, however, a need to ensure that money in particular should not fall into the hands of the Japs. Forty million dollars would build a lot of fighter planes. So in our own way we were playing our part in the war effort."

The phone rang at his side and pulled him from 1941 back to present. Jeff shook his head reaching for the phone; he had been totally lost in the diary.

"Jeff, Eric here. I thought you'd like to know that your AAB shares are now pushing $23, the OUT by the way is on the floor, $12.50."

"A good result. Has trading finished yet?" Jeff glanced at the clock, 3.05pm.

"Yeah, the exchange just closed. How are you getting on with those deeds?"

"Well we found them, or at least I think we did. We got the box but we haven't opened it yet because Dillon was saying that we might be able to knock a bit of publicity out of it."

"Publicity? Jesus, you'll be able to milk this if you play it right. Where did you find it?"

"Long story. Why don't we meet after work for a drink?"

"Jeff, you mean to tell me that you're not rushing home to that long legged wife of yours to give her a quickie."

"Eric, you have about as much decorum as a Tom cat in heat."

"Yeah, yeah, that's why you find my company so irresistible. Speaking of Tom how is he?"

"He's fine. I haven't checked since before lunch, but the word is good. I'll probably swing by the hospital tonight to see him after dinner."

"Yeah, not a bad idea. I'll meet you there, we can have a few drinks afterwards."

"Sounds like a plan. I'll see you in the Mandarin at about 5.15."

Jeff reached for the calculator after the phone call and punched in the one million ounces of gold and multiplied it by the current price of gold - $640. The calculator produced an error. He tried again leaving out the last three zeros.

"Jesus H'." he muttered. The gold bullion stashed in 1941 was now worth over US$700 million.

CHAPTER TWENTY SIX

He tried not to think about the money, so much money, who owned it? It was depositor's money after all. But then again, did he not have the records that showed the deposits being closed? And what was the implication down the road? If the money belonged to the bank how it could be explained away? Did either Wilson or Chandlers have relatives who would inherit? Too much to think about! Concentrate.

It took Jeff a little while to get back into the period of the story. His father flew to South Africa via Bombay a few days later but not before James had reported back saying that as far as the authorities were concerned Amele Cohen was a genuine trader, he also gave him the name of military intelligence officer in South Africa that he could contact if he needed him. Thus assured he set out.

It was his first time out of Hong Kong, except for visits to nearby Macau or business trips to Canton on the mainland, so he recorded his thoughts and fears in the diary.

"There was much talk of the war among the passengers on the plane. I tried to keep the conversation away from the subject, but my fellow passenger seated beside me insisted on coming back to the subject again and again. I was thankful for the sound of the tyres screaming when they hit the runway in Durban. South Africa was much as I expected, hot but not as humid as Hong Kong. The hotel was pleasant enough if the room was somewhat smaller than I was accustomed to, still it was better than the hotel I frequented in Canton. I had expected Durban to be populated predominantly by blacks. I was surprised therefore to see quite a lot of whites on the streets

I was tired after the flight and slept well until the morning when Cohen called from the lobby. He was a short stocky man with white hair and what I would call a goat's beard. He seemed jovial enough and we talked quiet openly about the gold trade over breakfast. He enquired about the feelings in Hong Kong about the war. I explained as best I could why we feared the Japanese invasion. He seemed less troubled about the prospect of any invasion of South Africa by either the Germans or the Japanese. He explained that the feeling was that the Germans were bogged down in Libya with Montgomery's forces since April, and that they had spread themselves too thin on the ground. They were being held up in Russia after massive advances since June. Now with the onset of the Soviet winter, they were finding things a little difficult. He said he knew the Russian winter and that Hitler had miscalculated. He said that the Soviets would destroy the German forces with the onset of winter. For that reason South Africa was safe, as for the Japanese, they were concentrating on the Pacific region and doubted that they would turn their attention to the Indian Ocean for several years, even if they were successful. No, South Africa was safe, so while they had a huge mineral wealth as the prize, they were confident that as long as they sold to all and sundry, they were under no threat.

I found the man interesting to listen to. He spoke widely of the prosecution of the Jews at the hands of Hitler but he had left Germany years ago. He was fortunate that he had the wealth to leave when the intimidation started back in the early '30s. He had joined a relative in the gold trading business and had flourished. He was now a joint partner and they traded over $100 million last year. Even though margins were tight, the Americans, who controlled the world price of gold, had only allowed one increase in gold prices back in 1934. But you could still make a good living. While the present open value of gold was around $40 an ounce, the price fixed by the Americans was just $35. He could not see the sense in maintaining the price so low, because any increase would increase the value of the American reserves who were after all, the largest holder of gold bullion.

Later in the morning we travelled about 80 miles out of Durban to see the gold mine and later to see the foundry where the gold was being refined. He confirmed what Dulles had told us about the process, the method used and the carat classification. Our shipment was already being prepared. It was being stacked in crates marked simply, "AAB". Cohen took me aside from the guide and explained that when he was about to ship from the foundry, the false identification would be stencilled onto the crates. It was important that the foundry crew did not see the false stencilling as they might just let something slip. We then visited the section foreman who was in charge of the shipment. He was Dutch, by his accent, and name Van Horn. He appeared to accept the confidentiality aspects of the transaction and asked me no questions whatsoever, yet he answered my questions readily. He confirmed that the shipment would be ready to go in a few days; he had no problem about the date of the 14th. He would be the man to carry out the stencilling and impressed me with the familiarity of such procedures. He had obviously done many such operations before. He explained that he would personally carry out the work on the night that the shipment was to go. It would be done in one of the loading bays prior to the crates being loaded on the carriage.

I was well satisfied with the arrangements by the time Cohen had dropped me back to the hotel. Naturally we then spoke of money. He asked to see the cheque and explained that he did not want them that night, but would arrange to visit his bank in the morning and have the cheques authenticated. This was more than satisfactory. That night I dined with a companion that I met at the hotel bar and went to bed early. I was pleased to learn that Cohen dealt with Lloyds bank as one of the cheques was drawn on Lloyd's. It would take a day to verify them so they were left in the safe keeping of the bank overnight.

The following day he confirmed that everything was in order and my gold would be ready for transportation on the 14th. It was a strange feeling leaving Durban having left $20 million in the hands of a man that I had only known for a few days. In all, I spent five days in Durban and left just three days before the ship was due to dock.

The next reference to the gold was about two weeks later.

James called to the office today. I was busy as more and more people were closing accounts as the news of the Japanese's progress down through Lianhue Shan. Another force had already captured Canton so it was only a matter of time before they were ready to strike Singapore and Hong Kong. It was also assumed that they would launch a simultaneous attack on the American base in the Philippines. James was sure that the Japs were not yet fully ready. His informants had confirmed that the Japs going down through Kuala Lumpur were doing so on bikes and commandeering vehicles for transport. They were stretched out very thin on the ground. Their strategy seemed to be that they intended to attack all Allied Bases at the same time and have complete freedom in the area. The strategists calculated that the Japs feared a counter offensive from a single Allied Base left in operation, so the answer was take than all out together. As to timing, James said that the less optimistic forecast was for the end of November, the more optimistic suggest an invasion prior to Christmas. It was of course semantic, but it was also very annoying that everyone knew what was going to happen, but no one seemed to be doing anything about it. The British were otherwise occupied, we all understood that, but it was the attitude of the Americans who just sat on the fence confident that they would not be attacked. The American mainland was far too distant to launch a major attack on. And why had they not joined in with the British and the Allies to control Germany. Did Roosevelt really think that he could deal with a post war Germany in control of all of Europe? I could never understand the attitude.

I asked James about the danger to shipping. We had heard from the captain on shortwave, that he had departed Durban with full cargo. That was all he was told to say and not to report in again until he had cleared the Singapore Strait and in the South China Sea, unless something went wrong. Of course, then it would be too late. James said that as far as intelligence could establish, there was no danger to shipping in either the Indian Ocean or the South China Sea, as the Japs were concentrating on the Pacific Ocean. Any activity around these waters was purely commercial. Some Jap supply ships were detected along the Chinese coast, but they were almost all unarmed, or very lightly armed. The Jap's seemed to be keeping their heavy stuff for the attack on the Allied bases in the Pacific. This set my mind at ease, but I could see that James had something on his mind, so I asked him what was bothering him. What he told me greatly disturbed me. I had never for one moment considered the possibility that I would be of any importance to the Japs, but apparently I was being spied upon.

He informed me that the intelligence monitoring station had intercepted a message from our friend Mister Oyez which had mentioned my name and my trip. James had the job of reading all the intercepts and deciding which ones to pass on to London and he had come across the message that mentioned me. Naturally he was disturbed to learn of the collaborators' interest in me and while he regretted it, there was little they could do. They had begun to conclude that Mister Oyez was the co-coordinator of the collaborators in Hong Kong, but did not want to move against him until they had identified all or most of them. They had identified eight of them, but none of these eight could be providing certain information that was particularly damaging to Hong Kong which intelligence knew he had passed on to headquarters. If they were to hit them now, they would drive the rest of the collaborators further underground and might never catch them. Intelligence felt it was best to wait and clobber the lot of them together. James had ordered a watch placed on the bank to see if they could identify if anyone was watching my movement, or was the report of the trip just a once- off regular occurrence that they could have established from informers, either at the airport or in immigration. Just yesterday he had a report that I was indeed being watched. They did not yet have the identification of the person following me, but he reassured me that they would know tonight, with my help, of course. I asked him what he wanted me to do. The problem that they had was getting the spy into a position that they could either photograph him or find an excuse to arrest him. He suggested that they set a trap.

He asked me to meet him at the Mandarin at 8pm that evening, I agreed readily. I wanted this matter resolved as soon as possible. He also advised that I make no phone calls to anyone concerning the matter; there was the distinct danger that they had an informer in the central telephone exchange that could monitor my calls. If, as it now appeared, they had identified me for surveillance, presumably in connection with the money, then I was in great danger and should trust no one. He also told me that I would have around the clock protection. The matter was no longer private, it was now an intelligence matter and considering the amount of money involved, the Crown had an interest to ensure that the gold did not fall into the hands of the Japs to fuel their war effort.

I was of mixed mind that evening. I always feared that the very act of converting such a large amount of money into gold would have certain dangers attached but like a fool, I assumed that nothing like this could happen to me. I was just an ordinary banker, I did not get involved in underworld activities, cloak and dagger type stuff. Those were things that happened to characters in movies, Bogart and the likes. And on the other hand, I was confident with the reassurance James gave me that I would have protection, but protection from what? When I had time to think about it rationally, I surmised that even if the Japs had found out about the gold bullion, there was nothing they could do until such time as they actually invaded Hong Kong. Then they could look for the gold, but finding it would be another matter. The plan worked out was foolproof, it would never be found. There would be no recording of the transaction; I will make arrangements with the banks to ensure that the records are hidden for the duration of the occupation. This was something discussed recently at a meeting of bankers I attended. But more of that later.

James was at the piano bar where I joined him. He seemed relatively relaxed. He said that he had two police officers and one military intelligence officer outside. They had followed Tokyo, as they had named him, that evening after I finished work. He had followed me home and waited outside the gates of my home. After about a half hour, he was relieved by another man. This one was Chinese, they called him Peking. Peking was then relieved an hour later by Tokyo again. James said that while he did not have a second man at the scene, he had heard about the exchange of watch and had a car posted at the bottom of the road to the Peak and had picked up Tokyo again and followed him. That was their break, for he had gone to a house for about 40 minutes and then returned to the Peak again. Since then, they had identified the house and occupants. The owner was a Jap called Heto. They had no further information on him yet, but given time, possibly a day, they would know more about him than he knew himself.

He was outside now, waiting for me to leave. He laid out the plan that he had in mind. The most important thing to achieve right now was to distract the Japs from any conclusion that they might be drawing concerning my trip to South Africa. It was imperative that they did not know about the gold. We had to sell them some disinformation, convince them that the reason for the visit was entirely different. But what? I asked.

"What interests the Jap's more then money?" James said. I did not know.

"Secrets," he replied. I was curious as to how I could be involved in such a trade. James explained that he had thought of a scheme that might just fool the Japs. What he told me was so outlandish that it might just be a plot for a movie. He explained that one of the main problems that the British had encountered in the war with Germany was the need to distract or confuse enemy radar. The bombing of London and other major cities had prompted the efforts to confuse the enemy radar when approaching their target. A major radar research program was enacted by the military with the sole purpose of producing a method of delivering a system to distract radar. The program produced some results; cluster bombs that would be launched by ground artillery that on explosion scattered thousands of particles of alluvium oxide that reflected the radar beam. But the effect was only momentarily. Hundreds of such bombs would be needed to distract them long enough so that they would miss the target. For over two years, the programmers have been experimenting with electronic waves with suitable properties that would have the desired result. However, it's been concluded that this will not succeed with present day technology. That conclusion is not however well known, but the program is known of. What he was suggesting was that he create a story that we feed to the Japs that I was acting as an intermediary for a company in Hong Kong that needed rare minerals from South Africa to produce a machine that could produce the electronic beam. If we fed the story in pieces, we could in fact convince them that I was the victim of a well prepared and perpetrated fraud, a confidence trick. In other words, I could be presented as being innocent and of no threat or interest to the Japs. This scenario interested me, for it was now obvious to me that unless I could convince the Japs that I had no involvement in anything to do with either gold or anything else, I would end up in trouble once they invaded. He went on to explain that he had conceived the notion that he would instigate the creation of a completely fictitious character, a university professor who would have stumbled onto the process while experimenting on x-ray technology. He then approached a company, that too will have to be fictitious, but he could arrange that very quickly. The company has the technology to produce the machine, he just has the formula and one successful experiment to offer, but the company executive is convinced and approaches me for finance. I'm convinced of the success of the machine and agree to finance the shipment of the rare minerals needed. Of course, the minerals are worthless, the company does not exist and the professor is a fraud. The imaginary executive will be the culprit, and of course, will flee Hong Kong after the shipment of worthless Zinc arrives and the final payment is made.

The story will be fed in stages, allow Tokyo to follow you to the dummy company, meet the so called executive, the professor. We'll have a background set up for all these, the people you will meet will be military intelligence personnel. We can produce reams of documentation, we can supply some disinformation material that we used on the Germans, let it fall into the hands of the collaborators. That will convince them that you are completely taken in by the fraud. Then after the ship is docked and unloaded, we expose the scheme.

James seemed very confident of his plan, so much so that I suspected that he had an ulterior motive. He was certainly going to an awful lot of trouble to protect our interests, and the suggested use of London documents. While at first it impressed me greatly, I began to wonder how he could have explained the need for them to London. Surely such documentation would be highly classified, or was it just that now that they had been used once on the Germans they were no longer classified? Unless, of course, the Germans believed in the theory and were themselves wasting valuable resources to produce the machine. This was the first time that I had doubted anything James suggested and while I needed his assistance, I was not going to endanger our relationship by questioning his judgment. Could it be that when he informed London they decided that this was an opportunity to send some disinformation to halt them in their tracks? If it was thought that such a machine existed, they would have to re-evaluate their strategy, for any attack that involved aircraft dependant on radar guidance. This would be especially damaging to Japanese air attacks that because of their isolation they would be very dependant on long range offensive launched from aircraft carriers. If it was a case of London now controlling the operation, then I was in more danger, for London would not have our interests at heart, we would be expendable. Nonetheless, I remained tight lipped about my reservations and agreed to his plan.

He suggested that tonight would be a good time to introduce the 'Executive' from the company and he filled in the background. The company would be a small electronics firm making parts for both McDonald Douglas in America and for McPherson's in England - the company that makes the Spitfire. They supply the electronic controls for the navigational equipment and for this reason the 'Professor' has turned to them. He had already established a full history for the company and had prepared documentation for both the Colonial Office and for the Port Authorities, to show that the company had existed for some time and had been shipping parts for the last two years. This would be needed in case the collaborators had means of reaching into those areas. Of course, once the scam was exposed these documents would be removed, for the moment they were merely 'Planted'. I asked him would this not mean that if the matter was investigated after the invasion of the Japs they would realise that the Colonial Office and the Port Authorities were involved in the scam. He assured me that there would be no investigation, for if his hunch was right, most of the collaborators would be exposed and taken care of, but not before the 'Fraud' was exposed. We will instigate a police investigation, which will uncover the truth of the matter that the documents, if they ever existed, were false and were obviously planted in case you decided to investigate the company while the deal was being perpetrated. The documents would have been 'Planted' to fool me, it would just be a coincidence that they also served to fool the collaborators. This seemed logical enough. He suggested that I later meet this executive at the office of the company. We would spend maybe 20 minutes in discussions in the office and then emerge to depart, but that we would discuss the matter on the footpath, hopefully Tokyo would eavesdrop. The 'Executive' would know the drill; I was just to follow his instructions.

So I drove alone to the address that James had given me. I met the 'Executive', he explained much of what James had already told me and explained that we were to be phoned when they were ready for us to go outside. Apparently the office, in which we were talking, was visible from the street and there was a good possibility that Tokyo might just approach the window and listen in on our conversation. If he did, we would be phoned and we could carry out the prepared conversation right there. If he did not, then we had the conversation on the street.

When the phone rang my heart jumped, but unfortunately the news was that Tokyo did not approach the window so we had to have our conversation out on the street. When we left the office, the 'Executive' led me towards where Tokyo was hiding in a doorway and with a casual comment, we were suddenly in the prepared conversation. It had to do with the payment for the shipment, I played my part, rather well I thought, and it was all over. We shook hands and parted company.

The next day James again came to my office. He said that everything had gone according to plan and Tokyo had indeed contacted Mister Oyez. They had also identified another collaborator. After Tokyo visited Oyez, they had phoned someone who later showed up. This one was recognised by one of our military intelligence men as a person that they had suspected for sometime and had been watching him. He was working in one of the companies supplying goods to the Garrison. This was a breakthrough, they had the man's background and now they could begin watching him in earnest.

We were to wait a few days before introducing the 'Professor'; he would let me know when.

We had heard from the ship, it was in the South China Sea and on the home leg of its journey.

James contacted me again the following Monday with more news about the collaborators. They had intercepted a communiqué to Jap headquarters. They had checked out the 'Executive' and the company. The files they had planted in the Port Authority had been removed for one night, then returned. The watch had identified yet another collaborator, this one based in the Authority itself. They had photographed the man actually lifting the file. James said that we were now ready for the next stage, setting up Tokyo to raid the office and steal or copy the documentation on the 'Machine'. As the ship was due in port by the weekend, we had to have everything in place for the 'grand finale', so it was time to introduce the 'Professor' and for all three of us to meet and discuss the 'Machine."

On Tuesday I visited the company after work and met the other two actors. We sat in the office examining worthless documents as if they were maps of buried treasures. We got the phone call as anticipated to let us know that Tokyo had made his way to the window, now we had to start talking about the way the machine worked, or rather they had to talk and explain the finer points of it to me. The 'Professor' was then to suggest that the plans should be held by him for safe keeping, but the 'executive' was to insist that they be kept by him in the company safe where they could be examined by his engineers. All this was to appear to convince me that everything was above board, but of course, it was for the benefit of Tokyo to encourage him to break into the office. I was to express some concern about not being allowed to have the plans examined by an independent engineer. They then played their part and convinced me that the matter was so important that the less people that knew of the existence of these plans the better. This would be worth a fortune and the involvement of anyone else in the deal was crucial to maintain secrecy. They speculated on the effect that the 'Machine' would have on the war effort. The 'Professor' calculated that the war in Europe could be over in months once the machine was in mass production. The machine had an effective range of ten miles and a spread of five miles at the ten mile range. Basically what the machine did was to reflect and distract the radar beam sent out by attacking aircraft as they approached their target. And as well as confusing the radar in the aircraft, it also effectively hid defensive aircraft going to attack the incoming ones. As it produced a purely directional beam it only effected radar pointed at it, so aircraft flying away from the beam was unaffected. Therefore attack aircraft were effectively blind while outgoing aircraft had perfect visibility. I must say I was very impressed with the presentation, and had I not known that the whole thing was a fraud, I would be convinced myself. I completed my part by agreeing that I recognised the need for total secrecy and agreed that no one else should be involved.

All the pieces were in place, so all we had to do was put the papers in the safe and leave the office. James called to me the next day, everything had gone according to plan. Oyez had made his expected transmission last night and had relayed the information we had concocted for Tokyo. Now we just had to wait and see if he or his cohorts raided the office of the fake company. He would not be contacting me again until something happened.

I heard no more until Friday. James came to the office with a huge smile on his face, it had worked. Headquarters had authorised Oyez to carry out the raid. This was done last night and there was more, they had tailed Tokyo and he had made contact in the airport with an air traffic controller who, in turn, had passed the documents onto a pilot in charge of a flight to Shanghai. So two more collaborators had been identified, the one in the airport was crucial for he could be of great assistance to the invasion force by directing aircraft with beacons and directions. James said that the prospect of this man being at his post when the attack began was unimaginable. So he would be watched and taken out at the first sign of attack that was if it was decided to leave him in place after the other ones were picked up. I asked him as to the timing of exposing the scam.

He felt that we could afford to give the Japs some time to study the plans before we exposed the fraud, as this might delay whatever plans they had for the attack on the allied bases. On the other hand, as they were co-operating with the Germans they might just let the Germans know about the 'Machine', in which case they would uncover the fraud themselves. So timing would be crucial. They had a 24 hour watch on Oyez and his cohorts and with the interception of his transmissions, we should be able to determine just when they begin to suspect. Then we would have to move fast and expose the fraud to the press to protect me. In the meantime a full scale police investigation is going on into the break-in. We may decide to pick up Tokyo for interrogation, but release him again. We must show a process, that an investigation is ongoing. Then when we are ready, we can expose the fraud committed on me and how I was duped. The Japs will, of course, be kicking their heels that their agents got duped in the process. James also said that it was more than likely that the collaborator at the airport was the one that identified me in the first place. I was angry that this spy had gotten me into all this and vowed that one day I would see his face as he died.

There was much activity that afternoon as the ship was docking the following evening. Chandlers and Wilson were naturally very excited. We had discussed at length and on many occasions the location of the hiding place for the bullion. We had debated whether or not we should just bury it in the back gardens of one or all of our houses, or simply store it in the bank vault. The danger was that if our little fraud scam was exposed by the Japs, then they would search everywhere for the gold and the two mentioned locations would be the first places they would look. It was logical therefore, that we should consider neither. Chandlers had proposed that the gold could be stored in one of their warehouses under an obscure designation. This would be acceptable if we knew for sure that Hong Kong would not be bombed. But we also knew from newsreels from Europe that an invading army does not worry about the amount of damage they inflict. They have no consideration for either lives or buildings. Their priority is to gain control over the land and anything that is destroyed is irrelevant.

There was another alternative, which I was reluctant to suggest and just as reluctant to put down on paper now. However, the reality of the situation is such that while I had hoped that in the period between the ship leaving Durban and its arrival in Hong Kong, we could have produced an acceptable location for the gold. But failing that, I was left with no alternative but to suggest Peepers Passage. My father-in-law, Arthur Aitcheson, was obsessed with internal security, particularly staff loyalty. He had designed the bank in such a way that the manager could use secret passages which led to the front of the bank and there was a slit in the wall through which he could look down on the bank staff and customers below without being detected. He admitted to my uncle Ronald before he died that he never found anyone cheating him, but he was reassured with the knowledge that he had the passage to spy on the staff. I never used it for any purpose, except to store some old safety deposit boxes that were not claimed after the change over to the new system last year. I was only 14 years of age when Ronald told me about it and then one day when he was in a good mood, I asked him to show me. I was thrilled with the idea of this secret passage and when I saw it, I called it, "Peepers Passage". Ronald hit me behind the ear and told me that I should always respect my father-in-law's memory. He threatened me never to reveal its existence to anyone. To that day, I had not told anyone about it. Not even Jeff, he is much too young yet. He's just a child and he would not understand its importance. Maybe in time, perhaps. So that day I had to disclose the existence of Peepers Passage to Chandlers and Wilson after swearing them to secrecy. They were both enthusiastic about the prospect of storing the gold there, for even if the bank was burnt to the ground in an air raid or whatever, it was unlikely that the gold would be uncovered. The only way it would be discovered by the Japs was if they knew of its existence and that would only happen if one of us talked, which meant we were dead anyhow. Or if the bank was the target of a direct hit and all its walls were blown to smithereens, in which case everything was lost. Most of the fighting would take place around the garrison, so it was unlikely that the bank would be singled out for attack.

It was agreed that the gold would be stored there and its entrance closed off. Next came the matter of who would actually move the gold from the shipyard to the bank. Chandlers had already suggested that the captain and a select group of the ship's crew, who already knew what the cargo was, should be used. Both Wilson and I concurred. We had little choice in the matter, it was a fact that by involving any new people, we were further exposing the existence of the gold and thus increasing the risk of betrayal.

I had organised for a jeweller that I trusted to test the gold, to ensure that it was as portrayed so this could be carried out in the captain's quarters on board ship prior to moving the gold. Dulles would be present also and upon approval, we were to conclude our transaction with him. Everything was agreed and we concluded our meeting'

I was very restless that night and slept little and late, being awoken by the housekeeper who had let James in. I tried to eat breakfast but found it difficult; James reassured me that everything was in order. They were still following Tokyo who seemed unaware that he was being followed. I managed to suggest that someone must be using the anti-radar beam on him. He could only see one way. James suggested that the collaborators were totally confident as to their security; they had not for one minute suspected that military intelligence was onto them. I asked him if he planned to be at the dockside tonight. James said he would but that he would be watching Tokyo and planned to arrest him for questioning after he saw the crates being unloaded so that he could not follow us to the eventual location where the gold would be stored. James had said that he did not want to know where the gold would be stored, for the simple reason that if he was ever captured and interrogated by the Japs, he could disclose nothing in connection with the matter. I concurred. I was beginning to wish that I knew nothing myself. I was genuinely concerned about the transactions tonight; I am not normally one to dwell unnecessarily on future events that may or may not happen and the possible outcome. But this was a very big transaction and with the further complication of not only the Japs knowing that something was going on, but that we were selling them an utter deception as well, made the whole thing unpredictable.

I gave little Jeff an extra affectionate hug before I left the house that afternoon. I feared that I would never see him again. I now realise that I have gotten myself into a very dangerous situation, and I have made arrangements to send Jeff to the safest place that I can think of - South Africa - in the event of my demise tonight.

The ship docked at exactly 6 p.m. that Saturday evening. Myself, Chandlers, Wilson, Dulles and my jeweller friend watched as the crew tied her up at pier 9. The customs procedure was then gone through; the pilot that had guided the ship in was on deck with the captain and was apparently going through the ship's manifest. It seemed like ages before the gangway was secured and the pilot disembarked. We were then invited aboard by the captain. Understandably enough, the crew was curious to see the people for whom they had transported this cargo almost half way around the world for. Even though they went about their work, it was notable that they examined each of us in turn as we went below to join the captain in his quarters. Before going below deck, I took one last look about the dockside. I could see no sign of James or his men but I was confident that he was present. A black sedan was parked near the office of one of the shipping agents. Either that was James, or Tokyo.

The captain was a pleasant enough man in his early 50s with almost white sandy hair. He wore a heavy sailor's jacket even though the evening was very warm. Chandlers enquired if he had any difficulty during the voyage. He answered confidently and casually that apart from a polite examination from a distance by a Japanese motor patrol gunboat off the shores of Singapore, they had no problems. He had contact with other vessels, they, too, had sighted the Jap activity, and noted very high activity in the Singapore Strait and the consensus of opinion seemed to be that the invasion was imminent. They had sighted many Jap registered cargo ships off the Chinese coast in the South China Sea. They were apparently putting in to secured ports all along the coast to offload supplies for their ground forces. But he had seen no large gunship at all, no destroyers or frigates. Most reports from other ships suggested that the Japs expected little or no resistance from Allied navy ships in the region. One freighter that they had sighted heading east reported that they had seen a large force of Jap naval ships steaming south of the Philippines, the captain said that, that reassured him that they were safe. The naval force was going in the opposite direction, towards the Pacific out of the South China Sea.

We got to the matter on hand. Chandlers suggested that we examine the cargo. It had been pre-arranged that we would bring two gold ingots from different crates to the captain's quarters and have the jeweller examine them there. No point in letting the jeweller know just how much gold we had. The captain and Chandlers went below to the hold to bring the two ingots. We chatted casually about the coming invasion while we waited, none of us were interested in the conversation, and with every footfall in the passage outside, we turned as one towards the door. It seemed like a long wait but in fact, it was only five minutes. Upon their return, the jeweller was handed the two ingots, he released his breath with shock. I had only told him that we needed gold authenticated; I had not told him that it was in ingot form. He held the gold in his hands for a few moments as he composed himself then he set about his task. He brought a black leather medical case with him which he now opened and proceeded to set out some instruments and vessels containing liquid. First he scraped the surface of the ingots to obtain some filings which he placed separately in two small vessels. He then examined the surface of the ingots where the scrapings had come from; this, he explained, was to establish that the ingots were not merely gold plated. Once satisfied, he proceeded to add a blue coloured liquid to the two vessels with the gold filings in them. The liquid turned yellow, he held one of them up to the light and swirled the contents, satisfied with the result, and he repeated the process with the second one with the same outcome. He confirmed that as far as he was concerned, we had genuine gold of at least 20 carat. There was a collective sigh of relief in the cabin. The jeweller repacked his equipment and with a polite bow he departed the cabin. He had already been paid for his services. I had decided to pay him in advance as I did not want a situation where he might be tempted to negotiate his fees after he had seen the gold.

Now we turned our attention to the matter of Dulles' remuneration. Wilson produced an attaché case which he placed on the tiny desk in one corner of the cabin. Dulles bowed to Wilson and proceeded to count the money. When he had concluded, he closed the case and wishing us well he to left the cabin. We now explained the offloading procedure to the captain and suggested that he chose the crew members that he felt were most trustworthy. He was taken aback a little by the suggestion but held his tongue. Yes he could guarantee the loyalty of any member of his crew, these men that he had hand-picked, were long time acquaintances of his and he would trust any of them with his very life. Chandlers asked him if he could guarantee that they would remain silent about the final location of the gold. He replied that the only complete guarantee was their demise. How could he possibly vouch for men's circumstances in one or two year's time? No one could predict the future. Of course, we had to agree and we gave him the discretion to choose whichever members of the crew he saw fit. We had agreed beforehand that the crates would be stored in the file room of the bank by the crew. From there we would, personally, unpack the crates and deliver the ingots to their final resting place until the end of the occupation.

With all outstanding business being concluded, we proceeded to the dockside to watch the offloading. Two trucks with canvas covering had been brought alongside the ship. The drivers had been dispatched with the explanation that their services would not be required until morning. As the first few crates were lowered onto the first truck by the ship's winch, a commotion broke out behind us. We turned our attention towards the ruckus. The black sedan that I had seen earlier was being surrounded by armed uniformed police. The occupants of the car made an effort to start the engine whereupon a policeman promptly smashed the driver's window and dragged the protesting man from the car in a very unceremonious fashion. The police were shouting commands at the driver and the other two occupants of the car. All three men were spread-legged against the side of the car and searched. Two police cars now came screaming up the docks and skidded to a halt beside the black sedan. All three men were bundled into the back of the cars followed by the rest of the policemen and the two cars sped off. I could only assume that this operation was directed by James, and indeed I was right. Moments later he emerged from the shadows. He merely remarked that it was a fine night for a stroll. We held our gratification until later as we did not want to comment any further while the crew was within earshot.

James later explained to me that they had followed Tokyo and Canton all evening, and they had picked up Oyez and drove down here to observe. He had decided that it was time to bring in Tokyo for questioning and what more an opportune moment? They had been allowed to see just enough for them to report back to headquarters. He went on to say that they had 'discovered' a witness to the break-in at the office of the dummy company who could identify Tokyo and his accomplice as being involved. So they would hold Tokyo and release the other two. The word would go back to HQ that the police had arrested him and this would further confirm the validity of the story that we were selling them. There must be some substance in the story if the police are involved. Of course, once the fraud is uncovered, it will add authenticity to the deception as the police, as well as myself, were duped. James was confident that the Japs would merely see that as one of the hazards of the job, but would be more interested in the eventual result than the loss of one of their operatives. At least this now meant that the collaborators would not know the destination of the gold. There was, however, the matter of the crew. Should the Japs identify any of them they could be interrogated. I mentioned this to Chandlers, he had been thinking along the same lines and suggested that he would order the ship to sail immediately. The crew were back on board to some foreign location, possibly the Americas. There they would be well out of the way. He could arrange work for the ship there and keep it well away from Hong Kong and the Japs.

The trucks were loaded and the eight crew members, whom the captain had chosen, rode with the trucks to the rear entrance of the bank. Once there, they moved the crates into the file room. Chandlers rode back to the docks with them and ordered the captain to set sail immediately after refuelling and the loading of provisions. 'It was near midnight when he returned satisfied that no one had left the ship and that she had sailed, by which time myself and Wilson had made a fair impression on the unpacking and storage. Chandlers told us that the captain was somewhat reluctant but on the promise of higher pay, he conceded and after a full check of the ships compliment he agreed to sail. The work of carefully stacking the gold took us until near dawn. We then had the task of painting the top layers of ingots with a dull grey paint. We mixed the concrete to close the opening to the passage below the file room.

We were totally exhausted by 8 a.m. when all the work was done. There was, however, one other task. Wilson and Chandlers suggested that we meet at the Mandarin for breakfast, we agreed to meet at 9 o'clock. This allowed us time to freshen ourselves up. I need much less time to do that as I needed only to splash my face and wash my hands but I needed the time to update my diary on the happenings of yesterday and last night. I am concluding my entry in this diary now for the detail of what has happened is too dangerous. If for any reason there are no further entries, you, the reader, will know that I am unable to make them for two reasons. Either I am dead, or the invasion has occurred, in which case I will not be able to touch the diary, as at any moment I may be picked up by the Japanese. In any event, the diary will be hidden in a safe place until the end of the occupation."

There was one further entry dated six weeks later.

"I again heard from James on the matter concerning the operation. He had heard from London that a message was intercepted from the German high command to an obscure research program located in Hamburg. The message had enquired about any further updates on the anti-radar research program, as new developments had come to hand from one of the Axis-Allies. This was the Japanese cross-checking with the Germans. London advised that it was time to expose the fraud. He also said that the information had obviously fooled the Japanese as their scientific research had been thrown into disarray by the discovery of the documents. A top team had been assigned to the project and had wasted six weeks on it, effectively distracting them from real work. It could also have delayed the attack on the Allied Bases. He felt that invasion was now inevitable within weeks, perhaps days. So it was time to play out the final act.

'The following day I informed the police that the 'Executive' I had loaned the money to, had absconded after failing to meet the first loan repayment. The police then raided the office and took away some papers amid a flurry of newspaper reporters. The next day the papers ran with the story and then I was interviewed by reporters. I played the part of the offended bank manager who was duped out of $10,000 by an unscrupulous con-man. Fortunately, I assured my customers that I had legal title to the lands on which the false company had its premises. I expressed confidence that I could realise the best part of the loan by the sale of the land. The story was not in the headlines for long as the news of the coming days concerned the impending invasion by the Japanese and the exodus of the local population. All my colleagues in the banking business in Hong Kong had by now agreed that all records of customer's transactions over $1,000 would be concealed. We buried all the relevant bank books for the duration of the occupation.

James came to my office for one last time on the morning of December 6th. He said that all outstanding matters had been cleared up. They had intercepted a message from headquarters asking Oyez to explain how he had been led to believe that the shipment from South Africa was genuine. 'Oyez had taken his own life when military intelligence men had broken into his premises. They had found all the information that they required on his premises to convict him should he have lived. Meanwhile 12 collaborators had been picked up. I asked him about the one from the airport, the one that had identified me. He was still in place and they were going to leave him there until the actual invasion itself. I asked to be notified when this was going to happen as I would like to see the look on his face. James agreed to phone me. James then bade me farewell, as he did not expect to see me again. His work in Hong Kong was done. He expected to be shipped out any hour now, his services would be required elsewhere, the battle for the region was just begun. There were other areas where he could help track down collaborators. I thanked him for his help and shook his hand; I was never to see him again'

My final entry in this diary concerns Foster Dulles. The bombardment of Hong Kong has begun. This morning the first aircraft crosses over the Island and dropped three rounds of bombs on the Garrison. I have heard that although the aircraft were picked up by radar, that there was no effort made to save the personnel at the base. All guns were active and one aircraft was reportedly on fire as it disappeared out to sea. Gunboats too fired on Hong Kong from a safe distance offshore. The garrison guns were fired at the gunboats and they were forced to withdraw. Shelling is coming from the mainland also, but it is thought that this is light artillery and is not having much effect; they are barely able to reach the shanty towns north of Kowloon. Many villagers have moved in from the north fleeing the Jap guns. There are reports that the Jap's are killing all in their path. Locals suspect that this is just hysterical reaction to assure protection here in the Colony.

People are very fearful for the future. We, however, must accept the inevitable. The reality is that we do not have the forces here to withstand the power of the Japs. Our only hope is that the much better fortified Singapore can hold out, at least long enough to allow the reinforcements to arrive, which they surely will, from Britain.

In the midst of this bombardment I received what I consider will be the last phone call. The Japs have targeted the Central Telephone Exchange and it has already been hit.I heard this from a friend of James in the Royal Hong Kong Police. He told me that James had asked him to let him know that Foster Dulles may not be what he reported himself to be. When I asked him to explain, all he would say was that Foster Dulles recently consorted with a family in Aberdeen who were known to be involved in prostitution. It had only very recently come to light that this same family had Japanese immigrants working for them. That was all the contact would say on the matter, but he did assure me that if he found any further evidence he would contact me.

It is late evening now on December 8th, the bombardment has stopped and I do not feel safe to make any further entries in this diary. If, as the police contact said, there is still a danger from collaborators, I shall hide the diary tonight and not open it again until after the occupation which will surely happen one day. I hope I will be alive at that time to place this diary in its rightful place here in the offices of the chairman of Bordes Wanchai Bank."

So that explained the gold, but what of the skeleton in the passage in the bank in Kowloon? There was no explanation. There were two possibilities: one was the remark that his father had made about the collaborator at the airport. He did say that he would like to see his face as he died. The second was did he discover something about Foster Dulles?

CHAPTER TWENTY SEVEN

Maylay rode the elevator up to George's office. It had been a long hour since she left her apartment. At first she had intended to go straight to George's office but on relaxing a little in the taxi, she collected her thoughts. Maylay began thinking about the need for money, all the money that she could lay her hands on. That was when she realised that she did have some at the apartment she owned on the Peak, so she redirected the driver to take her there. Maylay rarely used the apartment now except when she had the occasional affair which she didn't want her children to know about. She collected the $8,000 and packed it in her carry-all and called a taxi to take her to George's office.

Maylay approached the reception desk. Sandra smiled at her momentarily.

"Greetings, Honourable Maylay."

"Greetings Sandra, I wish to see George. Is he in?"

She was a little hesitant in replying. "Ah, I will check. Would you care to sit?"

Maylay knew from experience that there would be no way past this one, so there was nothing for it but to wait. Sandra was on the phone now talking to George. She glanced at Maylay once while speaking in a very low voice. Finally she hung up and turned to Maylay.

"I'm sorry but George is in a meeting. Can you come back in the morning?" Sandra's voice was strained.

"Tell George that I am very sorry too, but I must insist that I see him. It is a matter of extreme importance, a matter of life or death and it is a family matter."

Sandra stared at her in sorrow and reached for the phone again, repeating what Maylay had said to her. George conceded to the meeting and Maylay was shown into the office.

He was sat at his huge desk, no tie, shirt open, this was unlike the George she had grown to know and eventually love. She got the impression that he was making preparation to leave

Hong Kong. There were many filing cabinets left open, loads of files on the floor, floppy disks on the desk like he was copying files from the computer's internal file storage system onto floppies. She guessed that he was then destroying the original files.

"Maylay, I'm sorry about that but I'm really up to my neck. What can I do for you?" He seemed impatient.

"I'm sorry too, George. You know when we first got into this, I thought we would always stick together, be one, a family. Now I'm not so sure."

"Why do you say that? We are a family."

"I have had no support from anyone today, when I needed the support most. Did you call me all day? Did Jason? No, not one phone call to ask how I was. I risked my life to save us all."

"Maylay, you brought the police down on us. Did you know that I have had a visit from the police about that stupid attack on Maxwell?"

"How could they know that you were involved? I've spoken to no one about it, no one knows that you are involved and I only completed your order by killing Maxwell."

"I never gave you any such order, that's complete rubbish!" George screamed at her.

"You did, you told me to finish the job in case Maxwell talks."

"I suggested that you should finish the job, yes, but I never told you to attack him in the first place."

"I beg your pardon, you told me to watch him, make sure that he doesn't cause any more trouble."

"That was in connection with the John Sing dismissal for Christ's sake. You've gutting completely carried away with this. Let me make this clear; I never told you to kill Maxwell. I never told you to finish him off. These are all figments of your imagination. If you picked up on something I said and misread it, then that is your problem. Now I will help you, but don't for one minute assume that I am going to share any blame for Maxwell."

Inside she was raging, she had seen George do this type of thing before. He would deny until the bitter end that he said something, even though he had been heard by others saying it.

"Well do you recall saying that you would pay for Maxwell's death?"

"Are you bugged or something? I never said any such thing! All I said was that if ever money was needed to carry out family business, then I would provide it."

"George, I really don't know how to handle you. You stood in this very office last night at 9 o'clock and told me to finish off the job, right? I said that I would have to hire someone that I couldn't do it myself. I said it could cost $5,000, you said that you would cover it."

"I'm afraid that you did not hear me correctly. You said that you needed to hire someone, yes, but I said that you should have done the job right in the first place. You should never leave a job half finished. As to the money, I said that there was money available from the Golden Fund if it was needed, but that was in a different context altogether. I'm sorry, Maylay, but you took me up wrong."

"After all we've been through together." she muttered, tears coming to her eyes,

"We made such good partners after Jack died. We made a success out of that business, you and I did that, together. Even the nights at the Peak were good, I never loved anyone since you, did you know that?"

"Come on, Maylay, that's the past, that's gone forever. You and I both knew that it could not last, we both agreed at the time that it was just a fling. I felt that you needed comfort after Jack's death and I was there to provide that support. Just like I would support any member of the family. That's all it was, we both knew that for God's sake."

"I loved you then and-"

"Maylay, don't say any more, don't say something you will regret." George stood up now and crossed to the window, looking, but not seeing, the scene across the harbour with its thousands of ships from all parts of the world.

"Jesus, if your sister ever found out, Maylay, she'd kill us both."

"Oh George, let's get away from here, now, today. We can start over again, we'll make it work." She pleaded with him, desperate for the affection that she knew he could provide, she would be good for him, do anything that he asked. She had no problem with him messing about with other women, men need to prove themselves with younger women, to prove that they were still able to attract the "birds", she was Chinese, and she understood that need in men.

"Yes, yes, you go now I'll follow you, grab a flight to Canton. They won't be watching those flights. I'll join you there in a few days-"

"Where? In Canton?" Maylay faked excitement and belief.

"Yes, Canton, I'll travel overland, just in case they are watching me too, in a couple of days. I'll need some time to organise my affairs. I'll have to get my money organised."

"Oh, George, that's terrific! Where will we go from there?"

"Shanghai, and then to Tokyo. And from there? Well who knows?"

"Oh George, I'll make you so happy. You don't have to be faithful, you can have a concubine, a dozen of them if you wish, just as long as you are there for me. I need your affection, that's all."

"How are you for money?"

"Not too good. I've only managed to get $5,000; everything else is tied up in accounts."

"Okay, I'll give you another $5,000, that will keep you going for a few days. Wait here."

Alone now, Maylay glanced about the office, she knew where the safe was, of course, but George kept changing the code because Aggy kept cracking it and helping herself. She didn't care any more, about anything. The family had let her down, and George had turned his back on her. She did not for one moment believe his talk of joining her, that was all bull, typical George. The time had come; Maylay reached into the bag and took out the gun.

She rose and followed him into the other office. He had his back to her when she entered, whether he sensed her presence or heard her would never really matter. George turned, startled.

"I asked you to wait in the outside office"

"I know, George, but I think that there is something you should know."

"What?" He began to close the door of the safe.

"Leave that; step away, no, towards the window." Maylay held out the gun so he could see it, she wanted him in the light where she could see him.

"Jesus Christ, what the hell are you doing with the gun? Maylay, have you lost your senses?"

"I used to love you, George, for quite some time too, but do you remember you used to say to me that you were not sleeping with Aggy while you were making love to me?"

"You're talking about 13 years ago for God's sake, how do you expect me to remember what I said back then?"

"Well I'll tell you, you swore to me that first night that you were desperate, that Aggy was no longer sleeping with you, that you felt inadequate in your performance and you felt that this was why she moved out of the bed. You know, I believed you, you bastard. I kept quiet about the whole thing for months. Then one morning I was talking to Aggy and I mentioned to her how well she looked, how fresh. You know what she told me, that she had just had the best sex ever the night before, a new position that you had tried with her. That was the same night that we had been watching a video and you had tried one of the positions with me, the same position that Aggy was talking about. I asked her had things been bad or something between you and she said, "God no", that these last few months you couldn't get enough of it. All that time you had been bedding both of us. Do you have any idea how that made me feel? Well do you, you bastard?"

"Take it easy, Maylay; you're all wound-up. No, I don't know how you felt. Look, what happened was a long time ago. I was going through a bad patch, the business was a struggle, what with the death of John and Jack, everything fell on me, and I was alone. When you offered to help I appreciated that, you had suffered a loss too, we were both in the same boat. Yes I lied to you about not sleeping with Aggy, but God, I was so desperate for love, I really was not sleeping with her when we first-, did it. But then she came back to my bed, what could I do? I was trapped, I wanted to be with you and I couldn't stop her coming to my bed. I genuinely thought she would go away again. Maylay, I'm sorry, please forgive me." George was trembling.

Good, she wanted him to suffer, make him suffer like she had suffered when she discovered his lie.

"She never left your bed, even though she knew about some of your affairs."

"Come on, so what? Do you mean to tell me that you don't know about her many affairs around the place? She'll fuck anything on two legs and dangly bits."

"Did you ever ask yourself why?"

"I couldn't give a fuck about what she does."

"Well I'll tell you why, she beds around because she hates you."

"Oh fuck off, get out of here." George lost his patience, forgetting the gun. It was his last mistake.

"After you." The report was much louder then she had anticipated, it startled her. But there was another noise, a slow cracking noise, she didn't pay any attention to it, but it was the pane of glass on the window cracking, the bullet had gone straight through him.

George stared at the smoking gun and then glanced down at the blood on his shirt; he hadn't felt anything, well not right away. He was in a state of shock.

She levelled the gun and squeezed the trigger again. This one hit him on the shoulder, he staggered sideways and collapsed against the window, banging his head against it and the glass cracked but did not shatter. Maylay fired another shot, this time hitting him on the forehead. He was propelled backwards against the glass, it shattered and George fell through the opening.

"The fall won't kill you." she commented coldly, but inside her heart was racing, she had finally done it.

For years she had wanted to kill him, ever since the lies about not sleeping with Aggy.

She moved quickly now ignoring the sounds of people screaming on the street far below. Maylay emptied the contents of the safe into the carry-all and left the office. In the outer office she glanced at the floppy disks, was there anything there worth taking? On the one hand she wanted nothing more to do with any of this, but on the other hand, there could be useful information in those floppies. What was he making the copies for? There must be something useful in them. Dulles made a decision; she scooped them up and packed them into her bag. Maylay pulled the tie cord on the top of the carry-all and opened the door. Sandra stared at her from a standing position behind her desk, she made no effort to prevent Maylay leaving.

"What happened? I thought I heard something."

"George will be out for some time, please don't disturb him." Maylay replied as she stepped into the lift.

Down on the street the security guard was returning to the front door in a state of panic. He recognised Maylay, but after glancing at her, he rushed inside to his phone. She hailed a taxi and left.

*

Diver Ho had paid no attention to the second sampan lying about 100 metres off his position until his driver had commented that it was strange that the second sampan had been sitting there and only moved when they set off.

Diver Ho now looked back at the outline of the following boat. He could not make out the occupants as the bow was well up out of the water.

"Did you see who was in other sampan?" he asked.

"I not pay honourable attention but sampan owner is from Kowloon. I see him many times, he works out off Yaumati, but do not know his name. Other man I not know."

"The other man? What do you mean 'the other man'?"

"Just that there was a second guy in the sampan."

"Can you go faster?"

The driver turned the throttle and the pitch of the engine rose as did the bow of the boat.

Within minutes they had begun to pull away and the shape of the following sampan receded.

"Much better engine, Japanese make better product." the driver said proudly. Diver Ho turned his attention back to the approaching Mountain Island looming closer. What was he to do; he had the key, although it was worn miserably with rust. Still the outline of the protrusions could be clearly seen and from that a new key could be made from the outline. He could also clearly see the number imprinted on the handle of the key, '300'. His first instinct was to go back to the bank, the lure of money still attracted him. Bordes-Aitcheson was much less of a threat. He was, after all, an honourable businessman. However, Jason Kim frightened him immensely; he was a crook who used thugs worse then the Tong to carry out his bidding. They showed their ruthlessness this morning in kidnapping Locksmith Ho in broad daylight. They were to be feared. He could leave Hong Kong, of course, but there was the matter of his family, he could not protect them unless the crook Kim could be appeased. The key might be enough to pacify him. It would show him that Diver Ho recognised that he had made a mistake in copying the letter and was making amends by giving Kim the key.

Ho had to make his choice quickly now as they were very close to the Island and Aberdeen was closer then Hong Kong Central. He glanced back at the dot that was the following sampan; they had gained a good five minutes on it, whoever the occupant was.

"Aberdeen Harbour" He said to the driver. The driver moved the long helm pole onto which the engine rudder was attached and the sampan veered to the right towards the mass of boats and ships tied up in the maze that was Aberdeen Harbour. He was confident that once in the maze his followers would lose him.

"I will make quick departure from your honourable 'Walla Walla' and you might continue on towards Hong Kong Central. That might distract the miserable bugger following me."

"I must run the risk of the miserable bugger following me?" The implication of course was not his concern for his safety, more an opening position for the bargaining that would follow.

"I will pay you well, never mind."

"Aiyee, you are most generous, but please to put amount on promise, unable to spend promise."

"How much you charge for trip so far?"

"$200." the driver replied instantly.

"Robbery on the high seas." Ho replied without any malice. "I will not bargain with you, you are a fair man, I will give you the $200 that you request, on the provision that you try you're very best to lead miserable bugger away from Aberdeen."

"You are a decent man, you show much honour. I will comply with your request, upon the grave of my ancestors." The driver watched his passenger as he counted the money carefully. Ho handed over the money just as the sampan approached the first of the flotilla rafts that sampans and other boats could tie up against. He realised that he still had a long way to go to get onto land, but by releasing the sampan early and its continuation out to sea in the direction of Central, might just confuse the follower. It was worth the risk.

He stood ready at the bow as the sampan came alongside, then while it was still moving he jumped onto the raft and began to run towards the cover closer in towards the land. He cast the occasional glance at the departing sampan as it roared away at top speed. Feeling somewhat safer now among the plethora of crafts he paused to look out at sea for any sign of the other sampan. It was approaching the rafts at high speed, in just a few moments he would know if his ploy worked. He continued to move swiftly along the raft avoiding eye contact with those he passed and ignoring the offer of all variety of good and services for sale.

Diver Ho was near the land now, and still he could not be sure that the sampan had passed Aberdeen by as he had lost sight of it. He would not be sure until he gained the advantage of higher ground at the docks. From there he would be able to look out to sea. Ho ran up the final raft and turned to look out at where he would have expected to see the sampan. It was not there. Fear gripped him now and he turned back towards the maze he had just come through. There was a central channel just to his left, but his vision was blocked by the nearest row of boats. He walked towards the channel, carefully watching the visible water. Suddenly there it was, cruising up the main channel towards his position. He stepped back, had they seen him? Ho had got a brief look at the occupant, the face looked familiar.

Quickly now he moved along the dockside, going away from the channel, it would take them less than a minute to reach the shore, he had to find cover. Ho had no idea who the man was who was following him, it must be one of Kim's men, if so, Ho had led him home. He ran across the quayside amid the bustling afternoon traffic and ran into the open door of a teahouse. The teahouse was partially filled, a waiter ushered him towards a table in the rear. He waved his annoyance and motioned towards a table near the entrance where he could see the street. The waiter gestured his compliance and approached.

"The special, and make it quick." Ho snapped, as he sat down. The waiter jotted down his order and departed.

Examining the crowds out in the quayside became mind-boggling; one face ran into the next, each one began to look familiar. He had to shake his head several times to clear his vision as his brain raced trying to place the image he had grabbed in those short few seconds while looking down the channel of the man in the sampan. He was almost positive that it was the same man who followed him from the Golden Moon this morning in the Toyota Crown, but his vision had not been clear then. He had only got glances at him when the car tried to ram him. A few minutes passed and still no sign, the special arrived and the waiter laid it on the table. Relaxing a little bit now he examined the food. Ho realised that he was actually hungry; he had not eaten since morning. He picked up the chop-sticks and began to eat.

"Hmm, this is good." he muttered to no one in particular. He eat the food with the vigour of a starving beggar. He became so engrossed in the food that he failed to see Headboy Kim talking to one of the many street vendors around the quayside. After a brief conversation they both glanced at the doorway to the teahouse.

Ho remembered his duties and looked out at the street, but he was too late, the miserable bugger was at the door. Ho's immediate reaction was to jump to his feet and make a run for it, but feeling suddenly trapped and being caught off-guard, he remained seated. Kim approached the table and sat down opposite.

"You have led me on a merry dance, Diver." Kim said casually.

"I am happy that you enjoyed it. Who are you?" Ho replied, now suddenly confident that he was this man's equal. The pursuer can be perceived as a dark evil force until such time as you meet him face to face, then he becomes a man just like him. And of course he knew him he was one of Kim's men that had kidnapped the old fart Locksmith Ho Chan.

"What was the purpose of your excursion to sea, Diver?"

"Lost my snorkel." Ho replied calmly.

"Your carelessness could be your downfall; I am not in a mood to be toyed with. You sold my Father a document that was not genuine; we wish to have the original document."

"And again I will ask you, who are you?"

"I am son of Kim. Now where is the original?"

"So sorry, but I no longer have the document. Never mind."

"Ah, but I do mind. You see my Father is a very exacting man, he likes things to be right and proper. You sold my father a copy, he takes great insult to this. My father does not take insult too kindly."

"This is the second time that you stated that I sold your father a document. I did not, another did."

"That is irrelevant, you sold the document, the copy, to the locksmith. He in turn, sold it to my father, same thing. You sold a copy and we want the original."

"Then you will have to buy it off the man I sold it to."

"Who is he?"

Ho decided that he may be able to wrangle his way out of this, by just telling the truth.

"Bordes-Aitcheson of the AAB bank."

The Son of Kim looked stunned.

"That was very foolish. You should not have done that, now you will have to wait to see what my father decides to do with you. Come let us go to him" Kim stood and waited for Ho to join him.

Ho stared up at him; he had no intention of going with him without a struggle. He had a close encounter with the dragon; he was not going back into Kim's lair on their terms. He was prepared to go on his own terms.

Diver Ho stood up and in the process, cast a cowardly glance back at the waiter who caught the look and made for the table. Ho joined Kim and made for the door. He heard the waiter's loud shout,

"Hold it!"

Ho continued towards the door, Kim was puzzled by the command to 'hold it' and he turned to look at the person who shouted. The waiter ran up to Ho and grabbed his arm.

"You must pay the bill."

"My friend is paying." Ho explained pointing to Kim and turned to leave. Kim was completely caught off-guard and made to reach for his wallet.

"Just a minute, I am not paying for his meal. He can pay himself."

With Kim distracted, Diver Ho seized the opportunity and made a run for it. As he ran, he could hear the crashing of tables and exchange of blows behind him. He knew that the waiter would not let Kim leave without paying. They would hold him long enough to let Diver Ho escape and gain some distance.

*

Dillon returned to the hotel to shower and freshen up, it had been a long day. There was a message from Stern at the desk, something about an interim report. He ignored it, he had enough of it for one day, and anyhow, Tina was better at doing these types of reports. The thought of her turned him on; he felt that weakness in his stomach, Jesus, he hadn't felt like that for a woman for years. It was quite strange really, Singapore Girl was really attractive, she had that mixture of European strength with dark Asian beauty and the combination resulted in a nice angular jaw feature with sensuous lips and deep compelling eyes. The body too was exceptional, long legs, although she was not overly tall, but it was just the proportions that created this lovely sumptuous shape that made men go weak at the knees and cause a stirring in the groin that can only be truly satisfied by laying down beside her in a winter cabin in front of a glowing log fire, alternatively, on cool satin sheets in a beach hut on a desert island. Tina on the other hand was a typical white American beauty. Perhaps she was more reserved than Singapore Girl, but that could be put down to her Irish Catholic background. But when the moment of acquiescence arrives, then it's like a floodgate opened, she gives her all. His desire for her was greater than for Singapore Girl for one simple reason, he liked her. He had found her interesting to talk to because the last time they had met, they had just got lost in each other, neither of them had any concept of time once they engaged in conversation. That was rare for him, because he was not using any pick-up lines on her. In fact, he had not even thought about picking her up. They were just there doing a job and had some time to spend together. As it turned out, they discovered that they had a lot in common. When he had met her again in Hong Kong he was just anxious to rekindle the kinship. When he discovered that he also desired her it came as a kind of shock to him, he had never really thought of her as a bed partner. Life was a funny old thing; he had always enjoyed sex, but he had never been overly concerned about satisfying the woman. Well, he knew he did most times, but he didn't go out of his way to do that. He never considered himself a stud in the sense that some guys did.

Dillon just enjoyed being with women, not for the sake of the conquest or the achievement, he just preferred women's company, and to find himself holding off to ensure that she enjoyed herself in the mating process, was a new thrill for him. It was weird, that he had to pass 40 to discover that he was more excited to hear her loosing it than his own release. He was getting horny just thinking about her.

After dressing he went down and called Charlie over. He had been waiting in the lobby sitting in one of the large wicker chairs reading the newspaper and feeling important.

"How are you?" Dillon asked when he saw Charlie cringe as he stood up.

"Very sore, Boss. Very sorry I not of more 'herp before, most regrettable." He hung his head in shame.

"Never mind, next time you can go first."

Charlie looked at Dillon but saw from the grin that he was not serious.

"Where to, Boss?"

"The Golden Moon restaurant. I believe that's where Jason Kim hangs out."

Charlie glanced at him again as they got into the car. A look of concern was on the driver's face.

"You go 'settre the beast in the 'berry. If so, many restaurants, good eating houses right here in Hong Kong, no need to go to Aberdeen."

"No, the belly beast is already settled. I'm going to see Jason Kim. I want to find out what his problem is."

"His 'probrem is that he 'rike to 'kirr people."

"He's a bad man then?"

"Very bad, he 'kirr his own son many moons ago. Bad man."

"Killed his own son? Why?"

"He think that son has turned against him, son dating woman cop. Jason not 'rike this, 'kirr son, then woman cop."

"Was he arrested?"

"He own the cops, they afraid of him. He has men working with him that even the Tong is afraid of."

"Good lord!"

"Many better restaurant here in Hong Kong, not 'rose face to change mind."

"I'm not worried about face Charlie, we have a problem at the bank, and Kim is involved so I need to talk to him."

"Better to communicate from distance, by phone."

"I like to look a man in the eye when I ask a question. Don't worry, I can take care of myself."

They carried on in silence. Nothing more was said until reaching the Golden Moon.

"Boss, can I come with you? This man is dangerous."

"Charlie, I don't want to get you into any further trouble, I can take care of it."

Charlie reached into the glove box and took out a revolver and held it out to Dillon.

"Take gun. Maybe not needed, but man must take precaution. Nice to know that persuader is near by."

Dillon was surprised at the presence of the gun; there was no evidence of it earlier in the day when they were in trouble.

"Okay, if that makes you feel better." He took the gun and checked the chamber, six rounds.

"I shouldn't be long." He stepped out of the car pocketing the gun and headed for the front entrance of the restaurant. Charlie started the Merc' and moved up so that the car was in clear sight of the restaurant.

Jason was furious with Maylay, she saw it in his eyes, but she needed his help to get out of Hong Kong, she couldn't attempt to leave by any conventional public transport, the police would be watching the ferries, she needed someone with a motor boat who could take her to Macau.

"You killed him; why in gods name did you do that?" Jason spoke casually not raising his voice.

"He tried to hang the death of Tom Maxwell on me alone, he denied saying that Maxwell should be finished off, and he denied offering money to hire an expert to do the job, that's why I killed him, he refused to pay for the hit" She spoke casually, matter-of-fact, this was Honourable Father she was dealing with, the man that always sorted out the problems.

"Maylay, Maylay, what am I going to do with you. Your thing with Maxwell was personal, I do not know what happened, but it was a foolish move to kill him"

"He had found out about us, he checked the companies' office and found the list of directors, we were all named, it would not have taken long for them to discover Narrow Investments and the true intent of that company. He had to die, it is only logical, I was acting for the family, and I had no time to check with you. He was going to go to Bordes-Aitcheson and expose us. The whole operation that we have steadily built up over the years would have been lost"

"Narrow Investments is irrelevant, the Grand Plan is in tatters, George sold his shares, there was a mix-up at the Stock Exchange, and somehow he managed to sell his shares to Philip Thorn instead of Will King, an unfortunate occurrence. Percy Penderville was selling his shares at the same time and the American bought them. Now we have only the original 7%, plus Maltbie's 3%, once the American entered the market and started buying all loose shares the price went up and the whole thing fell apart. Our only consolation in that matter is that we will have a handsome profit when we sell our shares. We will bide our time and dump them at the appropriate moment"

"George sold his shares?" This was news to her.

"So the Grand Plan is no more, what will we do now?" she inquired, she had suspected as much, at least this would be a relief to her, and now her departure from Hong Kong will not be seen as in any way threatening the Plan.

"Now we must consolidate and consider our position. The most important thing now is to acquire the deed belonging to our Honourable Grandfather and claim what is rightfully ours"

"Will the death of George effect your plans?" It was a foolish question but she felt that if she was going to be blamed for something, she wanted to know in advance. She hated the thought of Jason holding animosity against her.

"Not really, we can get by without him; Aggy has everything organized in such a way that in the event of his death she will control everything that George owned, so now it is back in the family. But as head of the family it was my duty to kill him, and you have denied me that privilege, this is most unworthy of you, you have disappointed me Maylay"

"I apologise Honourable Father-"

"I told you not to call me that, call me Master, no one must know about that, you have offended me again, you must make amends"

"Yes Honourable Master, please forgive me, I will do your bidding"

Jason moved his chair back from the desk and spread his legs apart.

"Come here" He bade her towards him.

She rose and went around the desk, she knew from experience what he wanted, and she laid her bag on the floor beside his chair and got to her knees. Just then there was a knock on the door.

"This is most inconvenient, no, do not move" She was about to get to her feet.

"Move in under the desk" Maylay did as she was told; she pulled the bag in as well.

Jason drew his chair into the desk and she felt his legs against her body.

"Come" She heard him call out.

She could see nothing to the front of desk so she couldn't see you entered but she quickly realised that it was Jason son Headboy Kim.

"What happened you Son?"

"A fight, Honourable Father, but I succeeded in injuring two of my attackers after a vicious struggle"

"This is good Son, but why were you attacked?"

"I was in pursuit of the elusive and mysterious Diver who discovered the document-" Headboy Kim went on to deliver a glowing account of his dangerous pursuit of Diver Ho.

"-Unfortunately, Honourable Father when I was accosted by two of his cohorts in the teahouse I was distracted long enough to allow him to escape. I followed him as best I could after the struggle, but my injuries impeded me such, that I could not maintain a sufficient pace to sustain contact, let alone apprehend him"

"Very well Son, you have done well considering the injuries you sustained. However, I would point out that one of the first lessons of Aikido is to be always on guard for the unexpected. Perhaps you will reflect on your actions of this day and consider what I have said. Now I wish to be alone to consider the events of the day"

Just then the phone rang on Jason's desk and she heard the phone being lifted off its cradle. There was a short pause then Jason said,

"Send him up" The phone was replaced and she heard Jason say.

"Wait Son, there is a Mister Dillon on his way up, take that seat and listen"

"Is that not the American?" Headboy asked.

"Yes it is, I wonder what he wants"

Maylay felt Jason's hand tap her head, like he was patting a dog. She had time to reflect.

Crouched there on the floor beneath the desk, his legs pressing up against her. There was gentle breeze coming through the open veranda door. She felt it on her face now, it helped her stay cool. She thought back to the first time that he had taken her. She remembered the event, but she could not recall how old she was at the time, but she did recall that she still slept with a tiny rag doll and her mother had told her when she was around 15 that she had burned the rag doll in a fit of rage when she was nine. So he must have come to her first sometime before she reached the age of nine years.

She was very afraid of what he had done, she did not know what he was doing, she did not understand the white substance that came from his thing, it tasted revolting, but he was good to her, he would bring her presents and sweets, and only expected this favour of her in return.

Maylay had always been told that he was her uncle, her mother and he were brother and sister. She had always accepted that and she thought no more about it until she was particularly hurt by him when she was about 13 years of age. She was very sore and she complained about the pain to her mother. She was taken to the hospital by her and examined by a doctor in a white uniform. That was when she first heard the word sex being mentioned. The doctor had whispered something to her mother then they asked her what had happened to her. She told them about the cuddles she got from her uncle. Her mother was furious and locked her in her bedroom for several days. She was not allowed to see her uncle for over 18 months after that. She missed the presents and sweets, and after some time she missed the cuddles.

But the time also allowed her to discover reading and books and this in turn lead her to learn about her own body and sex. So when she met him again she knew what he had been doing to her. She was angry with him for abusing her, but part of her wanted that feeling of affection again. Because of her mothers anger though she promised that she would be careful. He enquired as to why she had not visited him, she told him that she had been very sick and could not go out very much. He said that now she was better she could visit again and he would buy her presents. She was 15 then and growing into a young woman and her body was changing. Her mother was more lax now about letting her go out alone and she began to visit him at the restaurant. He offered her a job as a junior in the kitchen and she took it. That was when her mother told her about him. She would not stop her working for him, she couldn't, but she felt that she needed to know that Jason was her father. This information shocked her, not because it effected the way she felt about being with him, but because that meant that her own mother had slept with him. The matter of incest never occurred to her.

She hadn't thought much about it after that; she actually closed it out of her mind.

Thinking back on it now, she had been very angry with him at the time, for two reasons, one he had slept with her mother, his own sister, and then he had slept with her, his own daughter. How had she shut that anger out for all this time? She became quite angry just thinking about it, he was no better then George. She heard the door open and then Dillon's voice.

"My name is Scott Dillon; I want to thank you for seeing me unannounced. The reason I have come to see you has to do with the AAB bank, whom I act for in the matter of deeds which were discovered during a regular examination of the ledger of the bank."

"You assume that I am aware of what you are talking about." Jason seemed evasive.

"Well I apologise, if you are not aware. I would have assumed that George Archibald would have told you of their discovery."

"That is very presumptuous of you, Mister Dillon. Why should Mister Archibald inform me of anything and why would you assume that Mister Archibald even knew of the existence of such deeds or ledgers?" Jason replied angrily.

"Again I must apologise, I had assumed, that your visit to the bank this morning was confirmation that you had been told of the deeds existence and also because another relative of yours Maylay Dulles, was aware of their existence."

"Your assumptions may get you in trouble one day, Mister Dillon." The threat very thinly disguised.

"I've gotten this far in life by making informed assumptions. I do not make assumptions lightly, nor do I fear the eventual outcome of assumptions or their repercussions."

"You impress me, indeed. Now is there any point in continuing this particular aspect of the discussion?"

"Probably not, can we therefore take it, I'm loath to use the word assume, that we will both agree to accept that we are now aware of the existence of such deeds and proceed from there?"

"Well put, Mister Dillon." Jason was beginning to warm to this Gwai-Lo, maybe he would wait for another day to kill him. It might be fun to play with him for a while.

"Very well then. Now the situation that exists is that the deeds are in existence and are legally held by the bank on foot of a loan granted to your ancestor, Jason Kimberley. Except that due to circumstances beyond the control of either the bank

or you grandfather, the first tranche of the loan was not delivered. It was, however, executed. In law this would be accepted
as prima-facie evidence that the first tranche of the loan was
drawn down. This now leaves us with the situation that the
bank are legal owners of the title deeds. The bank, however,
realises that the matter could be contested in court and that is
a position that either the bank or, I presume, yourselves would
neither want or need. What I suggest therefore is a compromise,
a meeting of minds on the matter so that a conclusion that will
satisfy both parties can be reached."

"Do you believe in Joss, Mister Dillon?"

"I believe in the right to justice. Beyond that I have no great
personal beliefs, why do you ask?"

"I believe in Joss and I believe in justice. Justice is something
that sometimes you have to fight for. My grandfather died a hor-
rible death because of these 'circumstances beyond our control'
that you speak of. In reality, the bank failed in its duty to deliver
the first tranche of the loan. Circumstances may have dictated
a result that the bank did not desire. However, they sat on the
deeds, aware that the first tranche obviously did not reach my
grandfather and did nothing about the matter. My grandfather
meanwhile died in poverty and was scorned by all those about
him, except his family. We are a family still and we will exert
our right. Our right to the New Territories and no amount of
talking will change that Mister Dillon."

"Very well, if that is your attitude then I see no reason for
prolonging this conversation." Dillon got to his feet.

"One other thing, Mister Dillon, you can tell your associates
in New York that they will never gain control of the New Territories. They are wasting their time buying that bank. I will
exert the right of this family and win those deeds in court, and
then will they find the price they paid for those shares a little
too high."

"You are misinformed, my bank does not even know of the
existence of the deeds."

"That's a lie, why would they go against the run of the market and buy those shares if they did not think that the prize was the deeds?"

"Either you are misinformed, or your *assumption* is wrong." Dillon said.

There was fury in Kim's eyes, inwardly Dillon took joy in that, but deep down he knew the guy would be trouble in the future.

"Thank you for seeing me. I'll see myself out."

When Dillon had gone, Headboy stared at Jason wondering what to do.

"Please leave me." he said to his son, who quickly left the office.

Now the pressure of his legs was gone he pushed back the chair and he looked at her cowering there. She was crying.

"Why do you cry?"

"I'm sorry Honourable Father, I do not know what to say" Sometimes when you are unsure of the anger that is being directed at you, you are better to say nothing she decided.

"You have disappointed me again; you must repent and satisfy me" He spread his legs again.

When she had done her duty she sat crouched beneath him her head on his lap, waiting for his next command.

When he pushed her away gently her eyes remained closed, she wanted him to think that she too was satisfied. When the blow came it caught her completely unawares and she screamed in fright as much as pain. He had hit her hard on the ear where he knew it would hurt most. Now he stood up and lashed out with his right foot catching her on the side of the head. She heard the jaw bone crack. Maylay screamed.

She felt another blow this time into the ribs, she heard the crack, she yelled in agony. She lay crumpled on the floor, blood flowing from her mouth, the mouth that had just moments ago satisfied him. Why was he doing this to me? She was his own blood.

She felt a kick to her mouth then once more, teeth flew out of her mouth, she coughed blood, she was kicked again this time to the eye, she lost all sight in her right eye. He was going to kill her she realised and she made one last effort to get away from him, her vision was blurred, her head was spinning, darkness swept back and forth like the waves. The waves of the ocean ebbed and flowed.

Her vision became blue like the waters of the ocean, she felt herself drift away with the tide.

She moved with the water, another blow struck her on the back of her head, she tried swimming with the water. She felt something beneath her as her head came up out of the water and she forced air into her lungs, but she had difficulty breathing, her throat was blocked and when she did get some air into her lungs that hurt even more for she knew she had a broken rib she knew she was bleeding internally. She felt that which was beneath her and she knew it was her bag, she reached into it. The blows had stopped and she heard him say.

"Ah, you need a tissue, here have one of mine"

Her hand felt for the butt of the gun, she gripped it and pulled it out of the bag and with all the strength she could muster she rolled over and brought the gun to bear. He was stood over her with a box of tissues in his hand. He had been about to throw the box down on top of her when he felt the dart of pain.

"What have you done?" He gasped. Then as if a sledgehammer hit him he felt the second dart of pain. This time he heard the shot. His eyes rolled up towards heaven, he was dead before he hit the floor.

Alone now she lay there staring at his body, she was unable to move, the pain in her chest was unbelievable. There was pain too in her head and face from the repeated kicks, but nothing like the pain in her chest. She couldn't be sure if she was dead or alive, the pain came in waves, suddenly tremendously agonizing, then as it ebbed it became more tolerable, until she tried to breath, then it started all over again. She tried not to breathe for the air hurt her chest. The peace was complete now, she could hear the ocean, it was beautiful, and the sky was blue, the beach white, and the grass beyond green.

Blue, white, green, her favourite colours, the favourite sound, this was nice.

The image of her daughter cooking at the stove in her apartment came to mind then faded again. Then Tommy walked towards her and held out his hand for her. She tried to explain that she couldn't move, but Tommy reached down anyhow and took her hand, she tried to protest, suddenly she felt totally free of pain and she grasped Tommy's hand and got to her feet and hugged him.

She was free of all the hurt.

*

Diver Ho was in a state of total shock. This had gotten totally out of control and he realised he was in way over his head. This man, Jason Kim was a total lunatic, he had kicked that poor woman senseless.

Ho had been about to knock on the veranda door when he heard Jason's voice greet the woman he called Maylay. He had stopped just short of the open doorway and had intended to wait until the woman left, but then Headboy arrived, then the Gwai Lo that called himself, Scott Dillon. He wondered where the woman had gone because he had not heard her speak or be referred to during the conversations that followed. He couldn't understand it. Then when the Gwai Lo and Headboy left, Ho heard Jason speak to her again. Then there seemed to be a quiet period and he thought all was clear and was about to approach the door when he heard the sound a man makes when he releases the power of the groin.

She must have been playing with his Yin, he figured. But then straight away he heard the woman scream. That was when he let out a gasp of shock. He realised that he might have been heard and began to creep cautiously back down the steps. He heard a noise above and froze. But the noise was that of a sliding door. He heard it slam shut. He stopped, the door was closed. Carefully he crept back up the steps, and that was when he heard the muffled shots, then silence. He had turned to go, but something told him stop. Had Jason shot the woman? If so, then Jason was finished, they would lock him up and throw away the key; he would no longer be a threat to Ho, or his father's cousin Ho Chan. The silence puzzled him. It was total; all he heard were the waves lapping gently onto the beach below.

The tiny voice in his head told him get away but another tiny voice told him that he had to know. While the voices argued among themselves Ho took a step, upwards. He peered cautiously around the door, there was no movement within. He moved his head a little so that he could see the desk. There on the floor was the woman Jason called, Maylay, and beside it the legs of a man. He had to move a little further across the opening to see the rest of the man and then he saw the blood seeping from his chest. Ho looked back to the woman and in her hands he saw a gun.

That was when he knew he had to get the hell away from the Golden Moon.

CHAPTER TWENTY EIGHT

Jeff tried to concentrate on business that afternoon but found it difficult. Everything was going according to plan. The collapse of the OUT shares which made the take-over very attractive, the purchase of the AAB shares by Edward Orrang's organisation thus assuring the continued growth of the AAB as more investment money became available; the discovery of the deeds to the New Territories. Everything was looking good, except for the one fly in the ointment, the bloody skeleton. Maybe nothing would be made about it, but there was always the danger that the identification of the remains could throw a bad light on the bank. The gold was a separate issue altogether. At least that could be explained away, but the nagging at the back of his mind that the skeleton could turn out to be Foster Dulles, annoyed the hell out of him and prevented him from concentrating.

He had phoned his contact down at City Hall who had gone through the record of deaths but could find no reference to the demise of Foster Dulles. It could be that he just left Hong Kong. He could have been killed by the occupation forces and the death never recorded, of course, but this was little consolation to Jeff. He needed to know whose remains they had discovered.

The phone rang, it was Eric.

"Hi buddy, I've got news for you."

"Yeah?" Jeff enquired after a few moments during which Eric left him dangling, he was always doing that.

"I was just talking to Bates from the Colonial Office. I just happened to mention that we had discovered a reference at the bank to deeds signed before the Treaty of 1898 granting the lands of the New Territories to a British subject. Bates went through the roof with hyperactivity. He wanted to know all about it, he's real excited. I'd say you can expect a call from him shortly."

"Jesus Eric, I wish you hadn't done that."

"What's the problem, for God's sake? This is big stuff; those deeds will make your bank a fortune. It could even reshape the future of Hong Kong. That's why Bates is so excited; he feels that if they are genuine, it could effect the talks going on at the moment about the Chinese take-over."

"I appreciate that but I have other problems right now. I don't need the Colonial Office getting all excited. I just can't handle it right now."

"What's happened?"

"Well I suppose you're going to find out eventually. I, or rather Scott Dillon and Tina Bolger, found gold bullion hidden in the bank-"

"Gold bullion?" Eric interrupted. "How much?"

"About $700 million."

"What! Is that Hong Kong or US Dollars?"

"US." Jeff stated flatly.

"Jesus H. Do you realise what this means? Hell do I even realise what this means? My God, that's a king's fortune! But how, who put it there?"

Jeff described what he had uncovered in his father's diary.

"That's how it got there. It's legitimate money and while I have a difficulty in trying to explain it's concealment for all those years, my biggest fear is the skeleton."

"Skeleton?" Eric asked.

Jeff was annoyed with himself that he had mentioned it. He hadn't intended to but he had to explain about that discovery too.

"So who do you think it is? The collaborator? Or Dulles? Jesus, if it was Dulles we could be in big trouble."

"I know that's what I'm concerned about. If it turns out that the body is that of Dulles, there is going to be one hell to pay. I can't establish what happened to Dulles. He just seemed to disappear."

"Oh dear!"

"Exactly. That's what has me bothered. We have to report the matter to the police. They will have to investigate and there's no accounting for what they will find out. It may very well be that my father killed this guy. That would be disastrous for us."

"Why? What difference could it possibly make to anything? Your father is long since dead, he can't be prosecuted posthumously for Christ's sake. Okay, so a crime was committed a long time ago, but so what, if your father did kill him he must have had a reason. I know you, you are your father's son and he would not have killed this guy without a reason. I don't see that you have anything to fear."

"Face is everything in Hong Kong-"

"Ah for God's sake, Jeff, listen to yourself, you're Gwai Lo, and will always be so in the eyes of the Chinese community. No amount of saving face will ever change the way the Chinese view us. It's about time we faced up to that and live our own lives in our ways. Just what percentages of your customers are Chinese?"

"That's not the point and you know that. The community here views what we do with great scepticism at the best of times. Once it did not matter, but now it does, we are very much in a minority, whether we like it or not we will be doing more and more business with the Chinese in the future and we must respect their traditions. Face is important to them, and they judge us by how we behave. If we do not respect face then they will not respect us, and if they do not respect us, they will not do business with us."

"Okay, Okay, fine let's talk about face. You know my feelings on the matter; we've discussed it many times. I believe that if your service is good enough they will use it, regardless of face, but I accede to your beliefs. I think that what you have found out is sufficient to offset any bad publicity you might get for this skeleton. Use the discovery of the gold and the deeds to your best advantage and that will stifle the investigation and any bad press you might get."

"This is what I need to figure out, how we go about it; timing is going to be crucial."

"Exactly, now you're getting the message. Plan a strategy, obviously you will have to inform the police, and you can't delay that for very long. Call the police, tell them you've found what you think is a skeleton, find out from them what they think will be involved. There will be a forensic examination, that will take a few days. Then call a news conference and announce the discovery of the gold bullion and the deeds. We can get one of those media promotion guru's who can plan out a strategy. You need a 'Handler' a 'Spin Doctor', someone that can put a nice shine on this whole thing."

"Okay, now you're talking. Do you know anyone that might fit the bill?"

"No problem, give me until morning. By the way, we're meeting at the Mandarin this evening for a drink, right?"

"Yeah."

"Okay, I might even have some guy by then. There's an Australian guy I know that used to work for Rupert Murdoch, you know the Australian press Baron - an expert in hype building. Let me see if I can get in touch with him. See you after five." Eric was gone, content now that he was involved and had a challenge.

Kay buzzed straight away. It was Bates; he wanted to talk to Jeff urgently.

"Mister Bordes-Aitcheson, we met once some time ago at a seminar-"

"Yes, I recall. Paul, isn't it?"

"That's right, Mister Bordes-Aitcheson. You may have had a call from Eric Ratner?"

"Yeah, I just got off the phone with him, but I must say that he really had no authority to discuss sensitive issues with anyone-"

"I appreciate that Mister Bordes-Aitcheson and may I express the opinion of the Colonial Office in this which is, we appreciate that matters of land ownership are very sensitive, particularly at the present moment. There is a lot of uncertainty concerning the issue of land ownership come '97. However, in our discussions with the Chinese authorities, we are assured that the question of land ownership will not be a major issue. Sovereignty is the main issue. However, and I appreciate the concern that you have about the matter being discussed at all, should it be discover that deeds exist for the New Territories that pre-date the 1898 Treaty, then we should discuss the implications. The situation is delicate; the emergence of pre-Treaty deeds being thrown into the equation could have startling results which no one could predict. We would have to very carefully examine any such deeds to ensure their authenticity. It would be disastrous if it were to emerge that the deeds were fake. The reaction of the Chinese Authorities to such an outcome could be catastrophic."

"I understand what you are saying, and what you have said coincides precisely with my own view. Should the deeds be genuine, I will not be rushing into anything single-handed. I would expect that the AAB and the Colonial Office would work hand-in-hand."

"That is very reassuring, Mister Bordes-Aitcheson."

"Well thank you for your concern. I shall be back in contact with you once I found the deeds and checked them out."

"Oh, I beg your pardon but I had assumed you have already found the deeds, Mister Bordes-Aitcheson?"

"I've found the container in which they are supposed to be stored, but for the moment I am not prepared to open it. I also realise that there are wider implications and wish to take some time to consider the matter before deciding what to do."

"Ah, I see, well I appreciate the time that you have given me, Mister Bordes-Aitcheson and I will await word from you."

"Thank you, Mister Bates." Jeff said and hung up. He recalled Bates all right and he didn't like him, he was a stuffy little jumped-up civil servant with a very high opinion of himself. He wasn't going to rush into anything; this needed to be handled very carefully. He had contacts himself who could reach into the Chinese Delegation who was discussing the future of Hong Kong with the Colonial Office. He planned to get an idea as to the Chinese reaction prior to releasing the information on their existence. The Chinese may ignore the authenticity of the deeds as their philosophy was for common ownership of land. In other words, the state owned the land, but under the circumstances of acquiring the lands back from the British, they may be forced under International law to recognise the deeds as proof of ownership. Bates had indicated as much when he said that sovereignty was the main issue, individual ownership was not. What then could he expect to gain for the deeds? If it was purely a matter of money, the income from rental would be astronomical; there was no way of calculating the revenue. And did he need the money? Not really, it would be worthless from a point of view of making some use out of it. What could he possibly do with what would be in the region of perhaps $1 billion per year? And anyhow, who would pay the rent, tenants, property owners or the Crown? It was likely that the ownership of the title deeds may not be enforceable in practical terms, however, it could be enforced in law but because of the sheer number of legal actions that would have to be taken would make it impractical. Jeff doubted the relative value of the deeds justified the euphoric speculation attached to the discovery of them.

The phone buzzed, Kay said that the gentleman calling himself Diver Ho was in her office seeking a meeting and the matter was urgent. Jeff decided to see him, did he have more information?

Diver Ho was ushered in by Kay; she turned and left them alone.

"Honourable Bordes-Aitcheson, thank you for seeing Honourable Ho at such impolite short notice." he said after bowing politely. Jeff returned the bow.

"What can I do for you?"

"I returned to the site of miserable wreck and retrieved key to safety deposit box. I wish to explain that I also visited descendant of miserable, Jason Kimberley. This man was most ungracious, very disrespectful."

"You visited him before or after you came to me?"

"Before. So sorry, I make a big mistake" Ho hung his head in shame.

"Okay, go on." Jeff was not really annoyed, but he felt that his displeasure might work to his advantage for what was to come.

"I was going to visit this man again to give him a key, but I discover that he has miserable thug follow me. He wanted to 'talk' to me, I do not think so. I get away from thug and then follow him back to the Golden Moon restaurant. You know of it?"

Jeff nodded, he was interested now, this guy was fearless, following one of Jason Kim's thugs.

"I know of place on veranda where I can watch the office where Jason Kim sits. The thug visit him there, then tall Gwai Lo visit. Short talk, then leave followed by thug, then most incredible thing happen. All the time a woman was hiding under his desk. Whatever Gwai Lo said to Kim make him very mad with this woman and he start to kick her. She has a gun and shoots Kim."

"Kim is dead?" Jeff was suddenly excited, this was great news.

"I think so, she shoots him two times in the chest. Here." He pointed at his own heart.

"My God, Jason Kim dead?" Jeff's mind was racing, what did this mean to the deeds? But surely if the evil was in the family, someone else would emerge from the debris to carry on the torch.

"So now you come to me with the key?"

"Yes, Honourable Bordes-Aitcheson, but do not require any form of payment. I wish to rectify Honourable Greedy Beast that take over the mind of Miserable Ho and drive him to make money from treasures in miserable wreck." Ho had remained standing during the conversation, now he drew out the key and handed it across the desk to Bordes-Aitcheson and bowed politely. Jeff starred at the rusted key, its profile reasonable intact.

"You will excuse Miserable Ho and if you feel it in your heart, you might light a Joss Stick for me?"

"Yes Honourable Ho, I will light a Joss Stick for you and thank you."

Ho bowed again and departed. When he was alone again Jeff realised that he felt sorry for Ho. The man had obviously fought with his conscience and realising that he had been overly greedy, sought to compensate for his greed by making a gesture with the key.

Jeff hit the button for Kay's phone and told her to get Charlie to come to his office.

While the key held a lot of importance for him, and would probably open the box without damaging it, his mind kept coming back to considering the matter of the identity of the skeleton. He re-read the last paragraph of his father's diary again.

*

In the street, Diver Ho stopped and leaned against the wall of the bank. He had cleared his conscience now. He had made things right, the letter was back from whence it had come as was the key. He was ashamed of what he had done, his greed had tempted him to do things he should not have. But at least now they were safe, he and Ho Chan and his family. Now he had to decide what to do; leave Hong Kong forever, or stay and help his family out of the depression of poverty?

He had to speak to his father, he had to explain that the greed was gone, and he had done one thing without reward, returning the key. Ho pushed himself away from the wall and joined the flow of pedestrians.

Inside the bank Jeff turned another page and began to read.

"It is late evening now on the December 8th, the bombardment has stopped, and I do not feel safe to make any further entries in this diary. If, as the police contact said, there is still a danger from collaborators, I shall hide the diary tonight and not open it again until after the occupation.

I hope I will be alive at that time to place this diary in its rightful place here in the offices of the chairman of Bordes Wanchai Bank."

He knew that his father died towards the end of the occupation, February 1944 to be exact. So he was not alive to place the diary in its rightful place, so someone else must have done it. If the diary was not touched again by his father, then did he keep another record of events during the war? Jeff went and examined the bookshelves. There were several diaries dated after the war and penned by William Abbott who managed the bank until Jeff was old enough to take over the helm. These were very scattered accounts of the daily happenings and were obviously done under duress, probably due to a commitment to a dying man.

Jeff ignored them after a brief examination and continued along the shelf to examine some older nondescript volumes. These books were quite useless, offering no assistance at all. Then just as he was about to abandon the search altogether, he discovered one thin unlabeled diary with entries made in his father's handwriting. This handwriting was less readable, more rushed and obviously done while he was very much in pain. The date confirmed this.

December 8th 1943.

"While I still have time, the doctor says that I am on borrowed time; I wish to put on record an event which occurred late in '42. The reader of this account will not understand what it is I am referring to unless he has read my early diary explaining the happenings prior to the Japanese occupation.

I do not wish to refer in depth to the occupation or the battle that resulted in the occupation, other than to say that the Japanese lived up to their reputation in so far as they killed many thousands of people here in Hong Kong, as they did in Singapore. The battle lasted 17 days; much of the area around the Garrison was razed to the ground. Much of the commercial area was also badly damaged. Luckily, we have not been damaged. We kept the bank closed after the surrender on Christmas Day '41 and did not open again until May. By then, things had settled down somewhat. Most of the occupation forces were withdrawn leaving just enough troops to maintain order. Business began to move again and some degree of normality returned.

Everything was beginning to look good, apart from a visit from a member of the Japanese High Command, but we had no trouble from them. However, my police contact spoke to me one night in November '42. The police, although most of their powers were reduced by the occupation forces, still kept an eye on goings on. He told me that Foster Dulles was known to be talking to the High Command. In what context they did not know, but the meetings were frequent and usually held at night in various meeting houses around the Island. The police themselves were afraid for their lives, for some officers were tortured and killed by the occupation forces. They were not allowed to carry out investigations of any sort. They were restricted to menial police duties like directing traffic and such like. Although the contact still maintained links with London through Colonial Office staff that had gone into hiding, there was little action that he could take to find out just what Dulles was saying to the Japs. The police were being watched by the occupation forces for any unusual activity that might indicate collusion with the Allies. So he couldn't take any chances of being caught observing Dulles. He told me to be vigilant. I contacted both Chandlers and Wilson and asked to meet them the following night. We had to be very careful because of the curfew so we arranged to meet for dinner in a restaurant in Kowloon near the bank. The restaurant had a rear exit leading to an alley which ran behind the bank. This way, we felt that we could slip into the bank where we knew we would not be observed. No one knew of the meeting, save us three, so I felt totally safe. I had been concerned for some time for the health of Wilson as it had deteriorated slowly during the year. I had not seen him since August and was therefore shocked at his appearance. He had shrunken visibly in stature and his face was a shade of ghostly yellow. His eyes were sad when we joined him, he had obviously been drinking and was in deep depression. He explained that the doctors had only given him a 50-50 chance of survival; he was suffering from ulcers and felt that he wouldn't last.

After dinner we departed singularly via the rear exit and went to the bank. I had fitted night blind's during the battle for

Hong Kong so that we would not show any light on those nights that we had to work late. Nevertheless I only used the desk light so as not to attract the attention of nosy Japanese or indeed the collaborators. In the office, I told them of the fears expressed by my police contact concerning Foster Dulles. I feared for Wilson for his reaction was that of a man having a heart attack. His breathing became rapid and he appeared faint. I gave him a brandy which seemed to liven him up somewhat. Chandlers then informed us that he had a visit from a Mister Yaumati from the High Command to enquire about the movement of our ships. Yaumati had suggested that Chandler's ships were reported to have been used to give assistance to the Allied Forces in Burma. This had no foundation, of course, as he had been very careful to advise the board of directors to be careful about any such involvement. However, Yaumati had insisted in examining the records and the managing director had no choice but to comply. Chandlers had assumed that the event was unrelated to the gold, but upon hearing my doubts about Dulles, he now thought otherwise. I held my fears in check concerning the visit I received from the High Command, for the person that visited me was none other than Yaumati. I thought it best not to mention it considering the state of Wilson's health. We discussed the problem at length and decided that there was basically nothing we could do about it. I thought it best to go along with that but secretly I vowed to take care of the matter after the occupation. We had placed a great deal of faith in Foster Dulles and indeed had paid him well for his service. To discover that he might now be betraying us was intolerable and unforgivable.

The next day I organised for an even further tightening of security at the bank and I purchased a hand gun, I was determined that should I be accosted by Foster Dulles or his cohorts I would not give up lightly.

Two weeks later, the news came of Wilson's death. At first we assumed that it was from his ulcers but later we discovered that he had been picked up by the Japs and died while being interrogated. This frightened both of us to such an extent that I found it difficult to sleep. Chandler decided that it was best for him to leave Hong Kong and he made arrangements to dress as a cargo hand and stowaway on one of his firm's ships. I never saw Chandler again after that and had assumed until recently that he had gotten away safely. However, I since discovered that the Japs picked him up on the docks and took him away. The captain of the ship waited until dawn the following day but he never turned up. The captain had to sail then assuming that either he was imprisoned or had changed his mind. It was only when the ship returned to Hong Kong in the January of '43 that we all realised that Chandlers was dead, for we, those of us who knew of his departure, assumed that he had sailed. That was when I realised that for some reason, Dulles had not given the Japs all the information. It appeared to me that he may very well be giving them bits and pieces of information, perhaps to save his own skin. If only I knew just how much information he had given them, then I would feel more assured as to the course of action I should take.

I decided to take the initiative and wrote to Dulles stating that I had received instructions from Wilson's solicitors that his last will and testimony had left Dulles an amount of money in gratitude for services rendered. I suggested that he should attend a meeting with me and Wilson's solicitor in the bank in Kowloon the following evening which was where Wilson had his account, so I said. I suggested this for I had learnt of his habits and he only received his personal mail in the evening upon returning home from work. This would not give him time to make contact with the Japs and I felt that his greed would prompt him to attend. I was right; he came to the office at 6.30 p.m. as requested. I had arranged with my police contact that he would attend claiming to be Wilson's solicitor. I had drawn up a fake will, which my contact read from. We made up the story that Wilson had left $10,000 to Dulles, which was to be taken out of his account in the bank. Dulles was excited about the unexpected windfall and was quite talkative.

Now I had to lay the trap.

We had a general conversation about the continuing occupation and I suggested that things had settled down quite well, considering. I said that I expected that the Japs were actually going to be good for Hong Kong and that industry was gearing up to supply the Japanese Forces. He seemed surprised with my observation and asked how I had come by this information. I told him that I had recently had a series of meetings with Mister Yaumati of the High Command who was interested in the banking sector and its ability to supply finance for the Government procurement program. I carried on the conversation for some time to convince him that I was on good personal terms with Yaumati. I said that I understood that Yaumati had the authority of the General to carry out negotiations to raise finance. Dulles said that he was on the third level of command and probably had the authority to act on behalf of the General. This was the news that I was seeking.

I had made enquiries through my contacts in the newspapers about Yaumati's position and despite their best efforts, they could not establish what position he held. From this they could only assume that he was in actual fact, a member of the notorious Intelligence Agency.

Satisfied that Dulles knew far more about Yaumati than anyone else, I accused him of being a collaborator and responsible for the death of both Chandlers and Wilson. He was totally taken by surprise and at first denied my allegation, but then we saw the change in him and the arrogance was exposed. He got to his feet and stared at me, called me a liar and a hypocrite. He went on to say that I was finished and that it was only a matter of time before they located the gold. Yes, Wilson and Chandlers had died at the hands of the Japs and so too would I, unless I disclosed the location of the bullion. I pretended to be frightened of him and asked him if we could make a deal, both men were now dead so it was of no concern to me if the gold was given to the Japs. He told me he would save me if I told him. I agreed immediately and told him I would show him the gold there and then provided that he promised to save me. I led him to Peepers Passage and told him to go look at the gold. He went, anxious to see the treasure; I followed carrying the light, my police contact behind me. When he reached the end of Peepers

Passage, he turned to me and said, 'What are you playing at?' I pointed the gun at him which I had concealed in my pocket, 'I'm not playing, I'm doing something that I should have done before now. I'm tidying up the loose ends.' With those words ringing in his ears, I shot him dead. We placed his body in the cupboard at the end of Peepers Passage and closed the door. I remember that my police contact who, for obvious reasons I cannot name, asked me where the gold was. I simply said to him, 'It's not where the collaborator thought it was before he died. The only other people who knew where it is are dead, so the secret dies with them. It might be for the best, men lust for gold, and what can you do with it? Nothing except put it in a hole in the ground, the ground it came from.'

Now as I lay here, probably close to that moment when Christians find out whether it was all worth it, I wonder about what I did that night back in January. I had to protect the gold, which was the responsibility that Chandlers and Wilson gave me; I have done the best I could. When this diary is discovered the reader may be able to discover where the gold is, but I issue a warning; men have died protecting this gold, it is a pariah around the neck of those who know of it. As to who owns it, I have pondered that these last few months. Neither Chandlers nor Wilson have any family to inherit it. I suggest that it be left forever in Peepers Passage. Let Peepers Passage protect it."

Jeff closed the diary and sat starring at its cover, deep in thought. So his father had killed Foster Dulles to protect the gold and in the process, had taking a collaborator out of circulation. So be it, it was a time of war after all.

He stood and absentmindedly replaced the diary where he had found it. It was a time for reflection, he needed to get out of the bank and go for a drink. Yes a drink or two with Eric was just the medicine needed to help settle his mind. Then he remembered the dinner date with Dillon. To hell with it, he'd try and catch him at the Mandarin. He called Steff and said he'd be late and not to worry about dinner. But before he left the office, he had to settle something about the box. He took the box off the floor and placed it in front of him on the desk. He picked up the key and inserted it in the lock and turned it. It moved just a little but then stopped. He was afraid to force it in case the rusty key snapped so he withdrew it and placing the key in his pocket, he placed the box in the reinforced drawer in his desk. It could wait. He would discuss the whole thing with Eric Ratner. Hell he might even get drunk.

CHAPTER TWENTY NINE

Dillon decided that he had enough for one day and had gone back to the hotel for a nap.

It had been one hell of a long day; it seemed like ages ago that he had gone up to Sir Percy's house to do the deal on the shares, for the first time. Then the meeting with Jeff, then the stock market thing. Jesus his heart was pounding just thinking of the excitement of that moment when they realised that the shares they had just bought were not Sir Percy's. The image of the red shirts down on the floor of the Hang Seng was still in his mind vision when he finally fell asleep. Tina came to him in his sleep and got into bed beside him. She began talking about her husband, she had found out that he and Singapore Girl were having an affair and she was planning to poison him. He deserved it. While they made love she plotted out the whole thing, then Dillon saw Singapore Girl standing at the end of the bed. She was wearing a slinky black number that hugged every curve of her body. She began to pull the skirt up slowly. Dillon was transfixed by the sight. Then he heard a scream, it was Tina, she was being attacked by a huge black rat. He told Singapore Girl to hold everything and he ran naked into the passage to kill the rat. But the rat was Jason Kim. Kim turned on Dillon and shouted at him, 'the phone is for you, I assume.' Then Dillon listened and he, too, heard the phone. Jason picked up the receiver and handed it to him.

"Yeah?"

"Scott, this is Jeff. I'm down in the bar and there is a guy here I would like you to meet. Are you busy?"

"No," Dillon replied looking about him. The bedclothes were barely disturbed, he must have slept like a lamb, or had he slept at all?

"Okay, I'll just freshen up and be down in about 15 minutes." He hung up. Christ what time was it? A look at his watch revealed that it 5.30 p.m. He had been asleep for over an hour.

While he felt drowsy and sore from the encounter with Tina's follower in the Mercedes, he was nevertheless refreshed. The shower finally washed away the sleep and he dressed quickly.

Jeff introduced Eric Ratner and an Australian called Jerry Mulligan who, Jeff explained, was a media consultant. Jeff told Dillon about his visit from Diver Ho and the story that he told him.

"Kim dead? Well I suppose that, that settles that." Dillon concluded.

"Makes you think, I only met him a few hours ago and now he's dead, gained and lost a customer in less than five hours."

"They call it 'Joss' around here."

"I guess Kim's Joss ran out." Ratner pointed out.

"We were discussing the method of releasing the information on the deeds and the skeleton. Jerry has some thoughts on it." Jeff brought things back to the matter at hand.

"Could I get a drink first?" Dillon's mouth was parched. The taste of Sir Percy's bloody Port was still lingering. They called a waiter and Dillon ordered a coffee, a cold beer and a Black Russian.

"My caffeine level is extremely low." he explained.

"Okay, this is the way I see the thing. Your problem is the skeleton. Okay, from what Jeff say's we can blow that away in a glow of patriotic propaganda. Your father discovers that the guy was a collaborator, highly dangerous, not just to the bank, but to the Allies as well. It was of vital national importance that the gold didn't fall into the hands of the Japanese. By the way, we never use the word 'Japs', it wouldn't be Fair Dinkum, Okay, these guys are major league. We talk to the cops. Now your father never mentioned the guy's name, so we can't identify the guy. He did mention this James, so we can use him. Shit the guy might still be alive, imagine the impact that would have? Get him over here for a press conference, Okay? What a coup that would be. Retired intelligence officer gives glowing account of how your father saved a major stash of gold bullion from the Japanese Army. We could say that thousands of lives were saved as a result of your father's actions, Okay? Denying the Japanese revenue, that could have built hundreds of fighter planes. Very patriotic, the papers will love it. The cops might just turn a blind eye to the skeleton thing altogether, in which case we say nothing about it and concentrate on the 'saving the bullion from the Japanese' angle, Okay?

Now the deeds thing is something else altogether. Here we are looking for pure glory, no monetary return. We just hand the deeds over to the negotiation team. We don't go for hype of any description, Okay? You may ask why? Yeah. This is the way I read it. We go for the old press conference approach on the bullion, take a very patriotic angle, full publicity, TV, the works. Give me about a week and I'll build up the hype, Okay? Afterwards we then let slip to the newspapers that we also discovered title deeds to the New Territories. We want no hype about it because we recognise that the negotiation are at a delicate stage and don't want to rock any boats. In this we look very good and responsible citizens. Just the sort of image that your ancestors built the bank on, Okay?

Now I come to what you do with the gold bullion. We admit that we are unable to find anyone to inherit. Course you take your fathers portion, Okay. But the rest we then offer to industry and community development groups at rock bottom interest rates. Say three percent below existing inter-bank rates. That will send shock waves through the banking sector, but will sure as hell make you look very good in the rest of the community. The impact we want is for massive development in Hong Kong in both community development and industry thus improving the economy. We call it the Wilson Chandler Development Fund - WCDF for short. Okay it's not the catchiest, but its simplicity will prove that we have the best interests of the Colony at heart. We deliberately keep the AAB out of the title; this is basic modesty that will pay a dividend because we will not be seen to be riding a bandwagon. So how does it sound to you so far?"

"Okay." Dillon replied without even thinking. He had scoffed the coffee and had gulped down the Black Russian and on the lookout for a waiter for another. Jeff glanced at Dillon, a grin on his face, caught his intentions and waved for a waiter.

"Could you just run through that again at normal speed?" Eric asked.

"Okay-" Jerry was ready to start again.

"No hold it, I thing I got the drift of it. I basically like the principle, but the bit about the skeleton bothers me. Dulles' family are still very much around and might take extreme exception-"

"Okay, we keep his name out of it; the cops are not going to have a press conference about it. I'm fairly certain they will understand and realise the implications of releasing the name, that is the effect it would have on his family. Okay, they will go along and keep the name out of the papers. I'm sure that they would agree to stating that they were unable to identify the remains. The Unknown Soldier crap. Lots of people died or went missing during the occupation. I wouldn't worry unduly."

"I hope so; I don't need any more family feuds. So basically what you are saying is that we have one press conference at which we announce what?"

"The discovery of the gold bullion and the way that we intend to use it, the WCDF."

"What if either Wilson or Chandler's relations come forward and claim it?"

"Tough shit. There was no will and if they claim any, most would go to the Crown. Remember, that it was not held on account so would not accrue any interest. You could just write them a cheque for the original value of the gold bullion, $40 million and continue with the rest of the plan. Fuck'em."

Jeff nodded, he hadn't thought of it like that.

"What do you think of that?"

"Sound good to me. Where the fuck is that waiter?" He was dry again. While he was looking around, he saw the magnificent sight of Tina walking into the bar. She was wearing a short black dress slit up the side to near the thigh. Jeff caught his look and looked too.

"Wow." he commented. She had her hair down to just below her shoulders. Tina spotted Dillon and came to the table. Eric,

Jeff and Jerry rose to greet her. Dillon stayed sitting and just admired.

"Hi." She greeted him after the others were introduced by Jeff. She accepted the chair that Jeff pulled up and sat beside Dillon. When she crossed her legs, three pairs of eyes darted a look. Dillon just smiled enjoying this.

"We were talking about the gold." Jeff was uncomfortable; he glanced at Dillon sensing that something was going on.

"Yeah." she replied simply.

"What are you drinking?" Dillon asked.

"What are you on?"

"I'll let you see for yourself." He waved for a waiter and indicated that he wanted two Black Russians and the same again for the other three men.

"I'm going to have to leave you guys shortly. I've got another meeting later," Jerry said.

"Okay, so where do we go from here?"

"Well if you give me the go-ahead, I'll get cracking on setting up the press conference for about a week's time, Okay?"

"I say we go with it." Eric commented.

"Go with it." Jeff agreed. They looked at Dillon.

"Sorry I didn't realise that I had an input to this, but it sounds good to me." He was trying to be nonchalant with Tina. He wasn't going to appear anxious to pay attention to her; well he didn't want to spoil her.

"Any more excitement?" she leaned over and asked. The touch of her arm against his was like electricity darting through his body and converging in his groin.

"Not really, except I met Jason Kim." Right now he didn't want to tell her about his death, that would keep until later. Right now he just wanted to spend time talking to her, he enjoyed the way that people looked at her.

"What sort of guy is he?"

"A nasty piece of work. Let's just say I won't be bringing him home to meet mom. Is that a new dress?"

"You like it?"

"Yeah, and I like what's in it." Dillon decided to not be nonchalant.

"Thank you, I thought you'd like it, I bought it especially for you."

"It'll never fit."

"Get out of it."

"I ain't in it."

"Smartass." she said bringing that particular avenue of conversation to a close.

"So what have you been doing since I saw you last?"

"I decided that I had enough for one day, so I took his credit card and went shopping. I've been in Hong Kong for nearly two weeks and I never even shopped once-"

"Definitely a case for immediate attention could bring on shopping withdrawal symptoms, very serious."

"Okay, Okay, you're one of those male chauvinists that thinks that taking a woman shopping is comparable to a visit to the dentist. Okay, I know where you're at."

"No you got me all wrong. I feel that taking a woman shopping is one of the treasured moments in this short existence of ours that more men should enjoy. I feel that women have been much maligned and ridiculed by men for their shopping habits. I totally disagree with those people who say that men should just give the woman the money and let them off. I think that is creating a dangerous precedent, because in years to come, men will become an endangered species. There is the possibility that shop owners, not being accustomed to the sight of a man in a shop, could shoot some innocent guy making his way into a shop seeking to surprise his new found love."

"Ah shut up, for a minute there-" she punched him on the arm vexed with herself that she had allowed herself to be drawn in.

"What would you like to do tonight?"

"Apart from you?" she replied.

"Behave yourself; I'm not that type of boy." He feigned coyness.

"Ah, lie down." she said as if talking to a dog.

"So what would you like to do, besides me?"

"I don't mind, what would you like to do?"

"Apart from you?" he replied and then erupted in laughter. Embarrassed, he turned to the other three men, who had continued on their conversation ignoring Dillon and Tina. Jeff was beginning to look a little red, he had been drinking brandy since 5 o'clock. It was now past 6.30 p.m. and he had consumed at least six brandies and was well on the way.

"We're just talking over here, never mind." He laughed at himself, he never used Cantonese slang as a rule, but this had been a good and bad day for him and he needed relaxation. A lot had been achieved, and now that Jerry Mulligan was on board with his expertise, he felt pretty good. The next week was going to be a trying time, but as long as there was a strategy clearly defined, he could relax. He felt good about Mulligan being on board. He had heard of him, of course. Mulligan was ex-Rupert Murdoch, and you didn't work for long with that organisation without proving yourself.

Jeff and Eric were deep in conversation about some building or other called the Chan Towers, Dillon was paying them little or no attention as he was more interested in what Tina was talking about.

"Are you serious?" he asked, excited about the prospects for the future.

"Yes. I've been thinking about it for some time now, even before I met you."

"Was it that bad?"

"Oh, if only you knew just how much I've grown to hate him. There's nothing left between us. The only thing that keeps me there is the kid, I was afraid to leave him because of the kid, I didn't want to embroil him in the mess of a divorce. But these last few days since I met you again, I begun to think that there has to be a better way of living one's life. Okay the kid yes, but should I continue on living a lousy life for him? Kids grow up and move on. I've got time to live life yet. I shouldn't be forced to go on living with him just to satisfy other people's wishes, God how much I hate going home to that house every evening. Just to see that big fat slob sat in front of the TV with everything he handles, food, cigarettes, newspapers, remote controls, beer bottles all left in a circle around the chair. He has no interest in the kid, never takes him out, and doesn't even talk to him much. My life is just a mess; I need to straighten it out." She touched Dillon on the arm. "Don't worry, it's not your fault, I was going to move out on him anyhow. It's just that this afternoon showed me what I have been missing. I love sex, Scott, I'm not a nymph or anything like that, I just find pleasure in it. This guy just wants a ride when he feels like it. And I hate the prospect of getting caught in a pregnancy by him. That would tie me down for another few years. I don't want to impose on you, that's not what I'm doing, I'm doing my own thing. I'm moving out and if you want, we can be an item. We're not moving in together or anything like that, I don't want to place any burden on either of us. We will need time to see if we can work."

"Hey, hey, take it easy. I've got a huge apartment, plenty of room, no problem for a kid either. We can share a place, which will take pressure off you for looking for somewhere. No commitment."

"I couldn't impose on you-"

"Shush, it's decided. You move when you are ready. I've got a woman that comes in the afternoons to keep the place clean, so maybe she would extend her time to pick up the kid after school and mind it until you get home."

"Well we can work on that one. How about a walk? I feel like some fresh air."

"Good idea, these guys are in a world of their own."

They bade their farewell and went through the foyer which seemed a little busier than normal.

"That reminds me; I got a message from Stern earlier looking for an interim report."

"Yeah he would, but let's not worry about that till tomorrow. Tonight I just want to spend with you. Let's just talk about us."

"That's good for me."

Out on the street, the heat was still evident although it was now noticeably cooler. The streets were still packed with strollers and window-shoppers. The most noticeable difference though was the noise. It seemed that every conceivable tongue was being spoken loud enough to be audible above the constant din of the trams, buses, taxis, cars and trucks. The general din was similar to New York, but more people were out on the street.

Dillon and Tina turned towards Chinatown further down towards Central. The hustle and bustle on the sidewalk was even worse the midday. At least during the day the streets were full of office workers who were on specific tasks and therefore going from A to B as quickly as possible. But the evening traffic was different insofar as the casual stroller was likely to turn in any direction. Being Gwai Lo helped though as they were a head above those around them so could see incoming darters.

They found themselves down in Chinatown and entered a tiny smoke-filled bar for a beer. The experience was worth the push to get in. When they entered they didn't realise that there were no Gwai Lo in the bar. The patrons were mainly wrinkle faced Cantonese men playing Mah-jong at an electric pace amid noise that could only be compared to a bar in Queens when the Yankees were playing some out-of-towners like the Redskins. The beer was cold and they just had one and then hit the street again, wandering aimlessly among the beer joints and strip-tease bars.

"Care to try your hand?" he asked.

"I don't think that my hand would draw much attention," she replied.

"Well it might depend on what you were doing with it."

"You would have to come up too."

"I'll wait until we get back to the hotel for that experience."

They walked on in silence now for a while, coming to a more seedy area where the Mah-jong players sat at rickety tables on the sidewalk. They turned and started back towards the skyscrapers of Central.

Chapter Thirty

As Dillon approached the Mandarin, he was just a little puzzled at the presence of two police cars parked at the entrance.

"What's going on?" he said as much to himself as to Tina.

"Maybe Jeff got drunk and beat up someone." she suggested.

"Is that not Jeff talking to one of the cops?"

"Yeah I think you're right." He stared into the distance. They were about 100 metres from the entrance now.

The pedestrian traffic had fallen considerably and they moved along the sidewalk quite freely. As they got nearer, Jeff looked towards them. He turned to the cop and pointed at Dillon. The cop called the other cops and they began towards Dillon and Tina.

"What the fuck is going on?" Dillon whispered and grabbed Tina's arm and pulled her towards the edge of the sidewalk. He didn't have a clue as to what was happening, but there was something.

They were near a doorway, nothing made sense, what to do? He moved into the doorway.

One, two, three shots rang out. Dillon felt the blast of concrete particles hit him as bullets hit the wall beside the door.

"What the fuck?" Were the cops shooting at him? He reached for the gun that Charlie had given him outside the Golden Moon. If the cops were going to fire on him, he was not going down alone.

He went to push Tina down out of the line of fire, but she had already done that. He heard more shots, Dillon cowered into the cover of the doorway, but no more shots hit their location.

He chanced a glance at the cops. One cop was laying sprawled on the ground just 20 metres from him. The two other cops were hunched firing at something across the street. A car! The first shots had come from the car; the cops were firing at the vehicle. Dillon still could not understand what was going on but if the cops were shooting at the car across the street that was good enough for him.

Suddenly the gunfire changed. Instead of single shot handguns, there was a deafening burst of machine pistol fire being directed at the two remaining cops. He glanced at the cops. Both died in a sickening eruption of blood and body parts, their bodies slumping to the ground. The gunmen continued firing at the bodies until the clip emptied in their guns. A passing car was caught in the hail of bullets, its windows shattered and the driver died instantly. The car swerved out of control, mounted the pavement and overturned in an explosion of glass. The engine raced momentarily then with a brilliant flash and ear splitting thump, the fuel ignited and with a huge billow of flame the car erupted into a thousand pieces of torn particles. Dillon ducked back into the doorway before the wave of molten fireball hit. He stumbled on Tina, she was still staying down. When the fireball died away leaving only the echo rumbling down the street, he ventured his head out again. The car had exploded just metres from the entrance to the Mandarin.

"Hope to fuck they don't blame me for that and put it on the bill," he muttered over his shoulder to Tina.

Across the road, the car that the gunmen used fired its engine. Dillon still did not know what it was all about and could only surmise that it was some kind of hit on someone at the hotel and some stray shot had come their way.

"They're going." he commented turning back to help Tina to her feet. That was when he saw the blood. "Jesus Christ!" he roared at the top of his voice. Pure animal instinct now took over. Clenching his teeth with sheer anger, he turned back to the street. The car was turning and coming across the street towards him. It was him they were after.

"Fuckers!" he shouted and ran to the edge of the sidewalk to greet them. The car was almost straight on to him and the gunmen had not a clear line to bring their guns to bear. They obviously expected him to remain in the doorway. The attackers hadn't expected Dillon to move so they didn't think to have their guns out the windows, so momentarily they were vulnerable. Dillon trained the gun on them and opened up. He shot the driver first, in the right lower chest. The engine revved but he must have hit the gear stick knocking it into neutral for the car just rolled towards the sidewalk. The passenger clambered to get his weapon out through the window to fire on Dillon but he was on the opposite side of the car.

"Fucker!" Dillon screamed again and fired a shot into the bonnet just below the window. He knew the bullet would bounce and turn and eventually emerge inside in the cockpit taking a lot of metal and plastic parts with it. It did just that, the gunman screamed in horror as a hundred small particles hit him in the chest and face.

"Fucker!" he shouted again as he took aim at the hand holding the gun. He squeezed the trigger. The bullet smashed through the windscreen and blasted a hole in his lower arm. There was satisfaction in the renewed horror of the scream.

"Fucker!" He glanced at the driver, he was alive but immobilised. He starred at Dillon in terror; the thug knew he was as good as dead. The bullet was designed to knock him out of action but not to kill him and he realised that.

Dillon now crossed slowly in front of the car, watching both occupants. The passenger was grappling with his good hand for the gun. Dillon saw the movement, brought his gun up levelled it and fired one more shot. Again the bullet took windscreen particles with it as it passed through the shattered glass and hit him on the left arm. He opened the door and reached in and pulled the passenger by the arm out onto the street. The thug screamed in protest at the agony in his arm. Dillon ignored the scream and propelled him across the bonnet and onto the sidewalk. He grabbed the guns from the floor and seat and checked them for ammo. The Uzis were empty. Dillon discarded them onto the street. He went around the back of car and pulled the terrified driver out onto the ground. The passenger used the interval to try and get to his feet. Dillon aimed at the back of the knee and fired. It's a particularly nasty shot, because the bullet enters meeting a lot of bone, cartilage and tough tissue, it exits slowly taking a lot of debris with it. Those shot in this manner will never take part in a marathon. But the passenger was not going to live long enough to take anything other than a few deep breaths.

"Look fuckers," he shouted pointing at Tina slumped in the doorway. "See what you did? You are brave men. Truly brave. Tell me that is a good day's work?"

They remained silent. Dillon rolled the driver over onto his back and stood on his knees. He screeched in agony.

"Is that what you would call a good day's work?" he repeated.

The driver shook his head.

"Why?"

He shook his head in one last effort of defiance. Dillon lowered his gun pointing it at his groin. The man screamed in anticipation and horror.

"Why?"

"I was told to kill you, woman a mistake."

"You bet ya', who told you?"

"Kim, Headboy Kim." he shouted. Dillon stood off his knees and stepped away. The gunman rolled over but that hurt too and he could do nothing but scream. Dillon levelled the gun and shot him in the side of the head.

"That's better." He walked to where the passenger was waiting his fate. "What about you? What have you got to say for yourself?"

He muttered some obscenity in Cantonese and spat at Dillon. He aimed the gun and smiled at the passenger as he pulled the trigger. It just clicked. The gunman was startled, then hope sprang to his face and he tried to crawl away down the street. Dillon dropped the revolver beside the slain driver and removed the gun from this pocket that he had taken from the car seat. He trained the weapon on the passenger and fired once into the back of his head.

Dillon threw the gun on the ground and ran over to the doorway and sat down beside Tina.

"Oh, shit, life can be such a bitch." His eyes suddenly swelled up with tears.

He was totally unaware of the people coming towards him, or the sound of the sirens as police cars and ambulances rushed towards the scene.

"Why take her? Fuck it, it was me they were after." He wanted to touch her, and yet he couldn't.

He wanted to remember the warm sensuous body, not a piece of dead flesh. He rested his elbows on his knees and began to sob.

Inside the lobby of the Mandarin people were still screaming from the after-effects of the shooting and the deafening explosion. People were running about the place, blood streaming down their faces. The explosion had caused the glass front to implode and rain glass on everyone in the foyer. The initial hail of bullets had been directed at the cops running down the street towards Dillon, but when the remaining cop at the entrance to the Mandarin had opened fire at the car across the street, the gunmen had opened up with the automatic weapons spraying the front of the hotel. People were scurrying for cover when the explosion came.

Jeff was in the action of diving behind a sofa when the explosion sent the shower of glass into the foyer. He had some minor cuts and bruises but was luckier than most. Many people had glass splinters embedded in them. Eric Ratner had been coming into the foyer at the time from the bar and was hit by flying glass in the abdomen and was bleeding profusely. Jeff came to check on him.

"Jesus, don't move. I'll get help." He noticed the concierge coming towards him.

"George, Eric needs help, fast."

"Yes, Mister Bordes-Aitcheson. I'll get the first aid." He rushed off.

"Eric, I've got to go see how Dillon is."

"Yeah, go ahead, I'm fine; all I'm losing is alcohol" He tried to laugh but that hurt. Jeff rose and went through the debris of what was one of the best foyers in the world just a few minutes before.

Out in the street, the bedlam continued. The crashed car was still burning fiercely; someone had brought a fire extinguisher from the hotel and was trying in vain to quench a petrol fire with a water extinguisher. He glanced at the dead policemen as he went down the street. Dillon was sitting on the ground crying.

"What the," he looked into the doorway and saw the shape in the black dress and long legs.

"Oh my god!"

He reached in and felt her pulse pushing past Dillon as he did so.

"Scott, she's alive." he shouted at him. Dillon looked up at him, then at the body.

"What did you say?"

"She's alive."

"Oh thank you, God!" He jumped to his feet.

"Take it easy, don't move her. There's an ambulance on its way." Jeff stood back and looked about for the ambulance. Two police cars arrived followed by the fire brigade.

"Where the fuck is the ambulance?"

Jeff thought that there might be medics with the brigade so he raced over to enquire.

Dillon knelt down beside Tina and spoke softly to her.

"Hold on baby, help is on the way. Just hold on, you're fine." He didn't want to move her, but he just had to find out where she was hit. The blood was coming from around her chest area. But she was laying on her front and the blood was beneath her. He gently turned her and found that the wound was just below the shoulder.

In turning her he noticed that she had another wound, more a cut and bruise rather than a wound. She must have struck her head when she fell. Knowing the nature of the wounds he turned her onto her back and placed his jacket under her head. Jeff arrived back with a medic just as the ambulance pulled up. Dillon stood back and let the professionals take over.

"She'll be fine" Jeff said reassuringly.

"I know that now. Jesus, I got one hell of a fright." He glanced at the two gunmen laying sprawled on the sidewalk. "I killed them in the belief that they had killed her." He said feeling some remorse.

"Do you think that they cared whether or not she was alive?"

"Yeah I know. But I killed them in the cruellest way I could. I could have shot them dead with one bullet each. Instead I used seven shots; I wanted them to suffer before they died."

"I'd have done the same, if I had the guts."

"Guts has nothing to do with it, I was just plain mad."

"Hey, come on, there are four policemen plus that poor bastard in the car that crashed, dead. Plus about ten people injured inside in the Mandarin. These guys didn't give a damn about anyone else."

"Yeah, they didn't deserve to live-"

"Shit-" Jeff cursed looking towards a van that had just pulled up near the Mandarin. A TV crew had arrived on the scene. The reporter was immediately armed with a microphone and the light shone from the top of the camera. They concentrated on the burning car which the fire brigade had not yet got under control. That would make for good footage.

Dillon turned his attention back to the medics hoping that they would get Tina away before the TV people turned their camera on her. The fact that she was American would probably mean that the American channels would pick up on the story and show the footage. Dillon figured that was the last thing that they needed.

The medics had Tina placed on the stretcher and was about to take her away when Dillon stopped them.

"How is she?"

"It's a clean wound, the bullet went straight through and she'll be fine. She lost some blood but apart from that, she's Okay."

"Is she conscious?"

"No, she knocked herself out cold when she hit her head off the ground, but she's fine, don't worry. Her breathing is fine, her pulse is fine"

He stood aside as they took her away to the ambulance. While relived she was going to be Okay, Dillon's inner peace was disturbed by the manner in which he had killed the two gunmen. Their deaths was not the problem, it was the undisciplined way that he allowed himself to execute them that annoyed him. He abhorred unjustified killings, he was in favour of the death penalty, but death, even for the unworthy, should be swift and as painless as possible.

At the moment when he set out to kill these two gunmen, he was concerned only for one thing; that they would suffer before they died. It was a primeval instinct that took over, not for justice, but for revenge.

A senior looking police officer approached him. Dillon hadn't taken a lot of notice of the officials milling about getting statements.

"Mister Dillon, my name is Oliver Smith, I'm aware that this is probably a bad time, but I'd like to have a word with you."

"You didn't understate that."

"I understand that Miss Bolger will be Okay?"

"Yeah, she'll be fine, thanks be to God." Dillon surprised himself; he hadn't used that expression for years.

"I know what happened here. I'm aware of the threat to your life and I accept that you were defending yourself. However, we do have to fill out reports. If you could just give me a short statement, where you were when the shooting started, how you defended Miss Bolger and so on. I understand that you used a revolver belonging to one of the fallen police officers?"

Dillon hadn't been looking at Smith; he had been absent-mindedly looking at the body of the gunman just yards from his feet. Now he looked Smith dead in the eye surprised by the suggestion of the origin of the gun.

"I have no fear of justice; I was carrying a gun-"

"I know that, it just makes our reports more complicated. Justice was done here tonight, not the justice that we would prefer to see, but the reality is that we are dealing with organised crime, ruthless people, who have no value themselves for life. Sometimes we have to cross over the threshold to their brand of values. Hong Kong was well served, perhaps better served then if these men were captured and brought before our brand of justice. I have no sympathy for killers, not this type, but we are answerable to the legal system by which we are supposed to abide. But killers like these abuse the system that we try to uphold and work by. You understand my position? I need to wrap this up without any loose ends, an illegal hand-gun at this location would be a loose end."

"I remember now, when the police officer was shot the gun fell to the ground and slid towards me, I reached down and grabbed it as I feared for my life and the safety of Miss Bolger."

Smith was writing furiously, "Slower please, I cannot write quite that fast." he said casually, as if the previous conversation had not taken place.

Dillon left the hospital around eleven and returned to the Mandarin where the earlier pandemonium had subsided to mere panic. A work crew were busy cleaning the place up and temporary sheeting was being fixed to the shattered windows. Luckily the bar was still functioning and was crowded. He found Jeff and Olli in a booth in the rear and joined them for a drink. He needed beer and a chaser.

"How is she?" Olli asked urgently.

"Sore, but she's fine. It was a clean wound, they're keeping her in just to be sure."

"My god what a day," was all Jeff managed.

"Who was behind all this?" Olli asked.

"Jason Kim. Grandson of Jason Kimberley. He had found out about the deeds by pure chance. Apparently a guy called Diver Ho found a letter addressed to Kimberley going back over ninety years." Dillon went on to tell them the story that the cop Allen Lee had told him at the hospital.

Lee had pieced the whole thing together while interrogating Headboy Kim. They had also picked up the Diver who found the letter and while he had done nothing wrong he was fully cooperative and filled in the missing pieces. Whatever had happened between Maylay and George they weren't sure, but it seemed that Maylay, also known as May Lee, had decided to get out of Hong Kong and needed Jason's help. Obviously something kicked off Jason and he attacked her, but she managed to shoot him dead. There appeared to be some sort of sexual thing going on as when Lee arrived at the Golden Moon Jason's son was caught in the act of closing his father's zipper.

Lee and his partner had been outside the restaurant waiting for a search warrant to raid the building when the call came in about the shooting. So they were in there right away, Headboy was caught unaware and surprised to see them get there so quickly. The cops had noticed two guys leave the building just as the call came in. Lee knew the two guys, they were Joey Chan and Paul Chui. They put two and two together and came up with two bad guys on a mission. Headboy admitted that the two were Kim's cronies and that they had gone after Dillon as they all assumed that it was Dillon that killed both Maylay and Jason as he was that last guy to be in the office where the bodies were found. Diver Ho had been outside the office and he heard the whole thing.

It was apparent to the cops that after Headboy found his father dead, he made a play for power. The two cronies were loyal to Kim and virtually ran his operation on the island. It looked like Headboy sent the guys after Dillon and then called the cops to create an alibi for himself.

That was why the cops were waiting at the Mandarin for Dillon to return.

The cops had found information in Kim's office that detailed his operation in the drug trade, and it turned out that he had cops on his payroll and that was how he had avoided detection, they knew he was a trader but no one ever pinned anything on him. A high ranking officer was also involved.

"Wow, am I glad he didn't open an account with us." Jeff said.

"I think we need another drink." Olli said as he headed towards the bar.

While he was gone, Jeff gestured Dillon closer. Then he glanced around to make sure no one was close by.

"The safety deposit box does contain the deeds." He whispered.

"Really?"

"The diver that found the letter went back down and found the key, he remembered from reading the letter that the boats captain had been given the key to the safety deposit box. He came to me this afternoon with the key. It was all rusted up but you could clearly see the shape of it. I got Charlie to take it to an uncle of his who was in the security business and he got a new key cut, and it worked first time. And there it was. We have the deeds to a massive tract of land in the New Territories."

"But what does it mean, will the Chinese recognise them?" Dillon was intrigued, all Tina's hard work had proved successful. She had done it.

"We'll know soon enough, I've set up a meeting with a guy I know on the Chinese delegation. I'm meeting him on Monday."

"And if they don't recognise them?"

"Then they will cut some kind of deal, they can't completely ignore the existence of the deeds. At the very least it will force them to concede some kind of compromise, and that may well be the changeover period, the British are pushing for 50 years, the Chinese want ten. I think the existence of the deeds will force the issue."

"Wow, that's going to cause some uproar when it hits the fan." Dillon began to work out the implications.

"I don't think it will ever be made public, they will cut some kind of deal behind the scene, if we go public they go into defence mode and dig in their heels."

"So you're keeping this under your hat?"

"When your dealing with the Chinese it's what you keep off the table until the very end that helps you win the game. At the end of the day it's all about face, if they think they have you whipped and you suddenly come up with something that knocks them off equilibrium then they lose face. And it's all about face."

Olli came back with drinks so the conversation ended.

*

Dillon slept sporadically that night. He dreamt of New York rain in August, rain that cooled the pavement and which in turn heated the water and turned it to steam that floated back towards the sky from whence it came.

Tina was one moment alive and beautiful and pressing against his arm as they walked along the sidewalk in that August rain. The next she was lying in the street, her blood flowing in the gutter and evaporating with the heat. The next she was well again walking on a hot beach holding his arm.

He woke in a hot sweat at some stage during the night and heard a distant noise like a constant drumming. He went to the window and opened the door to the balcony. It was raining, pouring sheets of water from the heavens to wash the streets below.

Dillon walked out onto the balcony into the rain feeling it wash away the stickiness of the heat of the night. He stood there in the torrential downpour until he began to feel cold. Returning to the room leaving the door open, he got a towel and dried himself. Sitting on the edge of the bed he thought again of Tina. Why was it that he could not protect her? Twice he had let her down in the one day. The first time when Tommy the thug had attacked her in the car and later then the gunmen had opened up. Why was it that she was the one injured both times? Was God trying to tell him something?

He needed distraction; he turned on the TV and found CNN. The news was full of impending doom on Wall Street, shares were falling at an alarming rate and the forecasters were predicting a crash. Not what he needed. He scanned the channels found something more pleasant and laid back on the bed examining the ceiling. Some hotel ceilings can be quite interesting. The quality of the craftsman, which indicates the quality sought by the hotel builder, can be seen quiet readily. Cracks are a dead giveaway, indicates a rushed job where quality is not a factor at all. But the mark of the trowel is another indicator that the level of craftsmanship leaves something to be desired. Sometimes a swirling pattern can be visible, an overconfident craftsman who's mind is on the money per square metre of plastering he can earn. The dedicated craftsman leaves no watermark at all. He wants the job to be right, he takes pride in that.

He slept again and this time slept until well after dawn. He called the hospital to see how she was, to his surprise he was put through to her room.

"I'm fine, how are you?" she replied to his initial enquiry as to her health.

"I'm great; I just had a good night's sleep and wondered how you were."

"So tell me everything that happened last night?"

Typical woman, looking for news. She was Okay, Dillon thought. He exhaled a sigh of relief and set about telling her about the Kim's demise and all the operations that had been busted.

It was back to normality once again.

CHAPTER THIRTY ONE

Thursday the 24th June dawned like most other Thursdays on Hong Kong.

It was warm; although not as warm as one week earlier when all hell broke lose not only on the streets but also in the Hang Seng stock exchange. Jeff was in his office early that morning, not just because it was the day they were to release the news of the gold bullion, but the day he was going to take over another bank. The plan was simple. The OUT shares had dipped even lower than expected, they were at $9.95 this morning. So he planned to buy all floating shares at 10.30 this morning. That was also the scheduled time for his news conference. The publicity that the impending announcement had generated would attract all media attention, including, he hoped, every banker in Hong Kong. So while he was talking at the event Philip Thorn would be buying OUT shares.

Chances were that no one would notice the binge, until it was too late. He should be able to pick up over 50% of the issued shares for less than $200 million. If everything went to plan, he would offload the Chan Towers for nearly $300 million to the Chinese government. They were on the verge of a decision, in fact he expected an offer today. He glanced down at his notes, it was written with the help of Eric and Jerry Mulligan. It was all positive all good news, he was slightly apprehensive all the same. He was well used to boardroom performances, but addressing public events was something else. He could use a drink, a stiff brandy would help, but should he?

Jerry Mulligan arrived at 9.20 backed up by a photographer and a delicious young blond thing with her hair back in a bow and large rimmed glasses. She wore a tight red dress and her job was to ensure that each and every reporter that attended the press conference got a copy of the chairman's address. She was employed as a magnetic, someone that attracted the male reporters like a moth to flame. Jeff had to admire the way Mulligan organized his people. None of them that he met were hired for general purposes; each one was hired on the basis of not only performing a specific task, but for an appearance that suited the task. Shelly served the specific task criteria very well, and she did look good. Jeff had met her early in the week at Jerry's office and the image presented then was totally different. She wore casual blue jeans, her hair down and no glasses. She was very open and friendly, no airs and graces about her. Today she was different; there was a job to be done so she dressed accordingly. She caught Jeff's look as he checked on something behind the counter and came over to him. She placed her hands on her hips and swayed her hips to one side striking a pose.

"This is a little different to the last time we met"

"Not really, the pegs are still the same, just the camouflage is different"

"I never wear camouflage Jeff, I don't need to conceal anything"

He released a low whistle and shook his head.

"Jess, don't reveal anymore in here, or you'll distract from the gold"

"Careful or you'll distract me, and I've got a mornings work ahead, but then I'm free for lunch"

She smiled at him. She was a tease; he knew that from Jerry, he said that was why he employed her. Men found her irresistible, Jeff could see why. He wanted to talk to her some more but he had things to do, and she wasn't one of them right now.

"Perhaps we can connect later for a drink?" His heart was pounding at the thought of talking dirty with her, she was that type, and she brought out that in men. Could he? Would he? No he couldn't.

Well not right now anyhow.

Balfe arrived at precisely 10 o'clock; he breezed in with his top men in their cleanest uniforms.

"Morning Mister Bordes-Aitcheson, are we all ready?"

Jeff nodded, time was shortening now like there was going to be nothing after the 10.30 press conference. He had nothing else scheduled for after that, he figured that it was best left free in case there were some reactions.

Balfe retreated from the office and Jeff studied his notes again. He was not used to public speaking and he was nervous about the attention he would receive. But the speech had been prepared by Mulligan in consultation with Jeff and was a full disclosure of the discoveries, so he had nothing to worry about. Mulligan was to handle the session and would control the type of questions that he would allow Jeff to respond to.

Kay buzzed him. It was Ching Sun on the phone from Canton. He was the contact that Jeff had inside the Chinese Delegation handling the negotiations. Damn, he hadn't expected a reply from him for some days yet.

"Sing San Bordes-Aitcheson, thank you for taking my call"

"Sing San Ching Sun, thank you for taking the time to call me, your schedule must be heavy"

"Ah so, it rests heavy on my shoulders, but the vital news that you so graciously conveyed to me last week has given me a new reason for concern"

"I realise that this unexpected news would cause concern, and this was why I thought that I should let you know as quickly as possible before rumour leaked out. I wished to prevent upsetting any members of the delegation"

"I took what you told me at face value and spoke to several members of the delegation who I knew to be fairly well disposed to the present regime in Hong Kong and would like to see the continuation of the capitalist system in some form. You should understand that it is not the intention of the People's Republic of China to oppress the very ethos that has made Hong Kong the power house of economic growth that it is. In fact we wish to learn the ethos, and then assist it with the security that the People's Republic has to offer"

"We are of like mind on that issue"

"Good. Now I have to admit that while I was a little concerned that members of the delegation might take an adverse position on the matter we spoke off, in fact, I was pleasantly surprised to discover that they are very willing to discuss the matter of land ownership by individuals with full rights to collect rents and hold title to lands and property. We were concerned that a system such as exists in the People's Republic would apply to Hong Kong whereby individuals and companies would rent the land of the State. However, we realise that land ownership is central to the very being of Hong Kong and are prepared to discuss the matter of land ownership"

"That is very pleasing news indeed. You think therefore that I should consider releasing details on the existence of the deeds?"

"Perhaps you have enough on our plate for this week. It might be best to keep the deeds off the agenda for the moment, and perhaps we can discuss something that the British are anxious to pursue in the negotiations." There was a long silence down the line.

Jeff wondered if that was that or was Ching Sun waiting for him to pursue something, something unpalatable to the Chinese?

"Well one issue the British, and to the business community her in Hong Kong, would be the issue of the length of time allowed for the changeover." Jeff said cautiously.

"Yes we are aware that that issue is causing some concern among the business sector. And we do understand that perhaps a short period of time might effect the prospect of economic development and investment. Perhaps the delegation should consider a longer period to help stimulate investment in Hong Kong. We are aware that investment has been, well shall we say, less than encouraging."

"Investors are nervous, that's true. The problem is uncertainty, what will happen after the changeover? Will Hong Kong prosper or flounder? The ten year changeover period is very short, very few investments, particularly in property, will provide investors with a profitable return in that length of time." Jeff held his breath, but deep down he knew that the Chinese had thought this through, but the problem was face. How to change tack without losing face?

"We appreciate those concerns and it is something that has been brought to our attention. We have noticed the downturn in investment and the fall in property value. You feel that a longer term changeover period would reverse this situation?" Ching Sun asked.

Jeff could barely contain his excitement, this was their way of solving the problem of the changeover period. The matter was stifling investment and property value, so it would be a positive move to help generate growth again.

"I think it would be a very positive initiative, and a bold move by the Chinese government to show that they intended to promote growth and prosperity in Hong Kong."

"Very well Mister Bordes-Aitcheson, I understand the position of the business community in Hong Kong and we do wish to encourage investment. I will take you're suggestions to the Delegation and I feel sure that we can come to some understanding on the issue in the very near future. In the meantime I appreciate that you will keep the deeds safely in you're possession?"

"You can count on that." Jeff replied quickly.

"I understand that you are conducting a press conference shortly, to disclose other matters?"

Jeff was impressed they were keeping up to speed.

"Yes, indeed, I presume that you will be watching TV this evening?"

"Indeed I will. Thank you for your time Sing San Bordes-Aitcheson, I will be back to you in about a week's time and we can discuss the matter further"

Jeff sat back in his chair; they were considering the matter of land ownership? This was terrific news.

Kay buzzed.

"Its 10.25, you late"

"Jess, no time to think now, must talk to my public" He grabbed the typed speech and rushed to the door thinking of the news, if he could release that piece of information on the Chinese reconsidering land ownership and the changeover period, he would be a hero. But hell, who wants to be a hero. Best sit on this for now.

*

Dillon walked into the Criterion Bar and Lounge and went straight to the bar. Maltbie was there himself; he looked down the long mahogany bar and slowly approached Dillon.

"Pint of Guinness," Dillon called as if he was a regular in the bar, sitting himself down on one of the high stools and placing a packet of cigarettes on the bar. He hadn't smoked regularly for about three years, but every so often he broke out. This was one of those occasions.

Paddy ambled up to him and leant on the bar looking him dead in the eyes.

"You got some cheek coming in here after all the trouble you caused," he voice cold and firm.

"I came in for a quiet drink, if you want to cause trouble, live with the consequences. Now is your Guinness imported from Ireland or is it that export shit that doesn't need to settle?" looking him straight back.

Paddy Maltbie was a true green Paddy, Irish through and through. He knew his Guinness; he took pride in serving the best in Hong Kong. He knew well what Dillon was saying about the 'Export' stuff, it was designed to be pulled straight from the tap to the finished pint without the traditional Irish method of filling 80% of the glass then allowed to stand. After a few minutes the head settled and the barman then topped off the pint. The result; a black body and the renowned creamy white head. It was felt that barmen outside of Ireland would never learn the traditional method so they invented a substance that settled in one pour from the tap. Bang goes tradition and the creamy white head.

"You're some bollocks" Maltbie replied, in the best Irish barman tradition of recognizing a fellow bollocks when he sees one.

"The pint?"

"Coming up," Maltbie went to the Guinness tap and earned his first of the day.

The bar was empty of any other patrons. The Criterion opened early to catch the deal makers from the Hang Seng across the road that needed a quiet corner to discuss their contract. They were usually the coffee types but occasionally you got the G & T drinker sneaking in a quick one during the morning.

A Guinness drinker was unusual at this hour of the morning.

Dillon didn't give a shit, he had his job done here, it was mere formality now. He had made a tidy packet on his flutter on the stock market having bought some AAB shares early on Thursday morning and off loaded them again on Friday morning making $1.50 per share. He could have held onto them longer but the news on CNN that morning was not good, Wall Street had indeed crashed that Friday and the following Monday it knocked on to Hong Kong.

All shares had fallen drastically right around the world, and took a few days to settle down. However, AAB was not unduly effected, they fell to around $20, but had recovered slightly and stood at $20.50 this morning. The news that was about to be unleashed though would drive them through the roof shortly. AAB was in the unenviable position of being able to buck the trend because of a series of coincidences, the last of which was going to be unveiled at 10.30. He had picked up just on $US8.000 on his one day transaction, not bad for a little speculation.

Stern had been well pleased with the outcome; the WTB had picked up over 20% of AAB shares and were going to appoint a director to the board. Dillon wished it was him; he kinda liked Hong Kong and wouldn't mind living here. Maybe he would suggest that to Stern when he got back to New York.

But then would Tina move from New York? The thought had occurred to him during the week and he had mentioned it to her. She had said that she would live anywhere with him but they were both high on drink at the time so anything could be said and it would not be a legally binding contract.

She and Olli had finished their report and Olli had flown back to New York on Tuesday with it. Stern had sent him a brief message last night that said-

'Job well done, see you in a week' a man of few words.

Things were going well between him and Tina, the first rush of love had them bedding like rabbits, they just couldn't get enough of one another. The only glitch they encountered was Singapore Girl when she returned last Friday night. He had forgotten her return and was surprised when she called to the Mandarin looking for him.

She looked so good her hair loose a striking white flowing dress, the eyes laughing and challenging at the same time. She wore just a hint of perfume its scent wafting across the foyer as he approached her. She kissed him gently on the cheek; he hugged her, his heart strings being torn between his love to Tina and his desire for Linn's beauty.

She knew from the expression on his face that something was amiss, and not just the temporary arrangements that existed in the remains of the foyer of the Mandarin. He avoided the subject for a while by talking about the events of the night before but she sensed his discomfort and came straight to the point.

"What's wrong Scott, you seem troubled, you're not infected by the lure of some other Golden Gully?" She spoke quietly, concern in her voice.

"Linn, I don't know how to put this but we can't work, I can't fool you. It's not fair-"

"You have found someone else?" There was no anger in her voice, she just stated the fact.

"She's someone that I met a long time ago, someone that I admired then, I liked her but she was not available, she was,- is, -married. We both realised that there was something between us that we ignored at the time. When we met again the spark was still there"

"I knew I could not leave a good looking man like you alone in Hong Kong." Her voice still held no anger, just a little remorse.

"It's not anyone from Hong Kong, we could have met any-where in the world and the same thing would have happened. She's actually American, well Irish American, like me"

"Such a pity, never mind. Does she know about me?"

"Well, I think so, I'm not sure, I know I mentioned you, I couldn't help that you're so beautiful, I was so proud of having a date with you." He smiled at the memory.

"Is she beautiful?" The question genuine.

He released a pent-up sigh of desperation. It would be so simple to just grab her in his arms and take her up to his room and bed her there and then. Then after their release they could sit down and rationalize the best option for them both.

There was no guarantee that he and Tina would work out, there were a lot of tripping stones, a husband, a child, a family, a job, a lot of things to go wrong. They might not work out at a personal level. He knew from experience that the first rush of heady plans confused by love can very quickly come apart in the reality of life when the rush of passion and desire begins to wane.

"Yes she is beautiful," he replied flatly and honestly.

"I'd like to meet her," she said, resolved now to the reality that he was lost to her.

"She'd probably like to meet you so she could see just how much I love her"

"Can we dine together one last time, and break honourable wind like we did before?" He felt helpless, Tina was in her hos-pital bed, she felt good enough to leave but the doctors wanted to keep her for one more day. She had lost a lot of blood and they just wanted to make sure.

He had decided that he would go for one last time with Linn and they had eaten and drunk the night away till the early morn-ing. They walked to the waterfront and there they embraced in what was to be one last hug.

Maltbie brought him back to the future.

"One pint, twenty dollars please"

Dillon threw him a fifty and told him to have one himself.

Maltbie looked at the fifty and watched Dillon take his first careful sip of the Guinness. The first sip brings on an involuntary shudder as the initial taste can seem bitter. But once the taste buds have readjusted themselves they just can't get enough of the black stuff.

Dillon nodded, "It travelled well," and wired into it.

Maltbie filled himself a pint and gave Dillon the change.

"So, you're nearly finished in Hong Kong?"

"Are you ready for another?" Maltbie asked.

"Yeah, why not"

"How about a chaser?"

"Paddy, Powers or Jameson?"

"Let's start with Jameson"

"Jesus I think I'd better cancel the rest of the day," he said with a finality that only comes from a man when he realises that he is going to get drunk.

Maltbie had two big measures of Irish whiskey filled and on the counter.

"Sláinte"

"Slán" Dillon scuttled his; Maltbie did likewise and produced a bottle from under the counter.

"If there's any good in it at all, it's in the lot of it," Maltbie quoted the old Irish excuse for excess.

*

When the two trolleys of Gold Bullion were rolled out the cameras flashed and those gathered gasped in awe. They had listened to Bordes-Aitcheson tell the most incredible story of the discovery of the Bullion about a week ago and how he had researched his father's diaries to uncover the startling events of over 50 years ago. The audience of reporters and officials from the Colonial office as well as other bankers were spellbound by the tale, but seemed sceptical about the existence of the gold. When it was rolled out they were totally amazed.

Jeff finished off his narration by linking the takeover of the OUT bank with the availability of the bullion as security to underwrite the Wilson Chandler Development Fund. As expected some of the bankers present released audible gasps of concern. Jeff set their minds at rest by stating that the fund was being aimed at high risk projects where normal commercial criteria would indicate that the project would not receive backing. He said that he would welcome his fellow banker's involvement in setting up an administration panel to evaluate projects in conjunction with representatives from both the Colonial Office and Trade Unions to administer the fund.

Now that he had suitably impressed them and their minds were distracted by the implications of such a large amount of money being available he took the opportunity to clear the air on the skeleton.

"During our intensive investigation into the explanation for the gold's presence in Peepers Passage we also discovered the remains of a skeleton-" He glanced over at Tina Bolger, she shuddered, he smiled out over his glasses, she nodded acceptance of his acknowledgement.

"-We informed the police of the matter and they removed the remains for an autopsy. They were unable to establish how the person died or his identify. However they were able to establish that he died during the war. We can only surmise therefore that the person was the collaborator who jeopardized the operation by informing the Japanese that Gold Bullion was imported into Hong Kong prior to the war.

The police are keeping an open mind on the matter and will inform us in the event of any new evidence coming to light.

"That, ladies and gentlemen is the end of my statement"

When he had finished Jerry stood up and asked were there any questions, there were.

A reporter asked if his father's diaries were going to be made available.

"Obviously much of the content of my fathers diaries are either of a personal nature or confidential bank business, however, I am aware that historians may wish to peruse the contents, and to this I have no objections. I also recognize that the general public may want to learn more of the events, to facilitate that we have prepared copies of the relevant pages of the diaries. You will appreciate that we have had to conceal certain names and incidents to protect the integrity of both those who have passed on and also those who are still alive"

Another question came in relation to the criteria under which loans would be granted from the Wilson Chandler Development Fund. He saw Mulligan smile when the reporter referred to the fund as WCDF, simplicity works.

Jeff glanced at Tom Maxwell and nodded.

Tom had been well versed in the basics of the fund and he shouldered the question.

Kay took this opportunity to pass Jeff the brief message she had taken from a member of the Chinese Delegation. He read it and smiled clenching his fist beneath the rostrum and punched the air. The Chinese were taking the Chan Towers lock stock and barrel for just short of three hundred million. He muttered an internal 'YES'

*

Tina Bolger stepped outside the bank for some fresh air. It was nearly noon.

It had been some week, a great time; she had met a great man. A tear came to her eye when she thought of the look on his face last Saturday night when he told her of Singapore Girl. The funny thing was, when Dillon first spoke of the beauty of Linn on the day he arrived in Hong Kong, her heart had sank. Not that she had expected anything with him at the time it was just that she liked his company and the thought of him spending time with this beauty he spoke of kinda hurt her.

Then when he and she became a thing she wondered how he would tell Singapore Girl, this beauty of which he had spoken so highly. The thought had occurred to her that if he expressed concern about telling Linn, she was going to say to him, 'Go with her for this one last time to finish it'. She didn't want him to dump her without explanation, that wasn't fair. She was not that positive that she would deny another woman the opportunity of being let down gently.

She knew that Singapore Girl was back on Friday, so when he was so pensive on Saturday she knew he had seen her. She expected him to lie about it. That's what men do if cornered.

She was surprised therefore when he told her that night. She wasn't hurt, yes, but she was also reassured that he was honest.

She looked about the street; this would be a great place to live, away from her family in New York, and boy would they be mad when they learnt that she was leaving the big fat slob.

Cars passing by, people passing by, not unlike New York.

There was a sudden loud report, she ducked.

The traditional noonday cannon was fired.

She straightened up and adjusted her black dress ignoring the strange glances from those passing by that had seen her duck.

"Are you okay?" Jeff said from behind her.

She turned embarrassed.

"I'm fine, just the cannon caught me off guard. I thought you were all tied up with the media?"

"I let Eric and Jerry take over, fancy going for a drink?"

"Yeah, I think Dillon is at the Criterion."

"Okay, come on."

They joined Dillon at the bar. She looked at his drinks, Guinness and whiskey, it was going to be a short day.

"What are you having darling?"

Dillon hugged her as much to get a feel as to tell Maltbie stay clear.

"Looks like you started without me?" She said to Dillon.

Dillon just smiled right back at her and asked Jeff what he was having.

"Let's get wasted"

"I'll drink to that"

Maltbie put two glasses on the bar and poured a generous measure for her.

The three touched glasses and saluted the future.

The End